W9-CRG-442

# THE
# PERPETUAL
# NOW

JEROME J BOURGAULT

The Perpetual Now
Copyright © 2020 by Jerome J Bourgault

All rights reserved. No part of this publication may be
reproduced, distributed, or transmitted in any form or
by any means, including photocopying, recording, or
other electronic or mechanical methods, without the prior
written permission of the author, except in the case of
brief quotations embodied in critical reviews and certain
other non-commercial uses permitted by copyright law.

This is a work of fiction. Names, characters, businesses,
places, events, locales, and incidents are either the
products of the author's imagination or used in a
fictitious manner. Any resemblance to actual persons,
living or dead, or actual events is purely coincidental.

Cover art by the author.

Tellwell Talent
www.tellwell.ca

ISBN
978-0-2288-2283-7 (Hardcover)
978-0-2288-2282-0 (Paperback)
978-0-2288-2284-4 (eBook)

*For Liza*

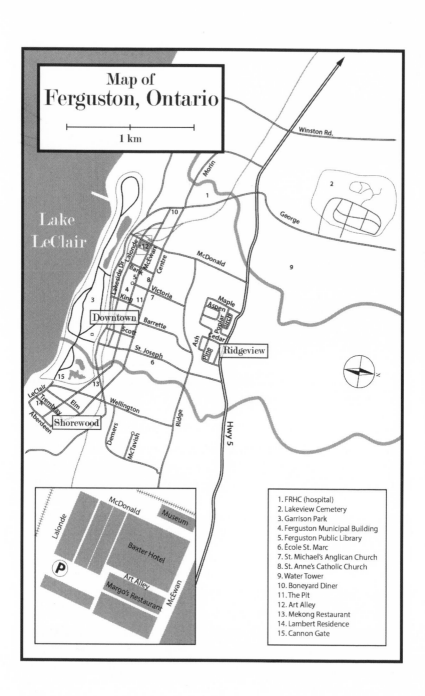

# Map of
# Ferguston, Ontario

|———————|———————|
1 km

Winston Rd.

Morin

1

2

George

Lake
LeClair

10

Lakeside Dr.

Lalonde

12

McEwan

Centre

McDonald

9

Bank

5   8

Victoria

4

King   11   7

Maple

Aspen

Elm

Poplar

**Downtown**

Barrette

Cedar

3

Scott

Ash

Pine

**Ridgeview**

St. Joseph

6

15

13

LeClair

Trembay

Elm

Wellington

14

Aberdeen

**Shorewood**

Demers

McTavish

Ridge

Hwy 5

Lalonde

McDonald

Museum

Baxter Hotel

**P**

Art Alley

Margo's Restaurant

McEwan

1. FRHC (hospital)
2. Lakeview Cemetery
3. Garrison Park
4. Ferguston Municipal Building
5. Ferguston Public Library
6. École St. Marc
7. St. Michael's Anglican Church
8. St. Anne's Catholic Church
9. Water Tower
10. Boneyard Diner
11. The Pit
12. Art Alley
13. Mekong Restaurant
14. Lambert Residence
15. Cannon Gate

# Prologue
### November, 1996

*Great place to dump a body.*

The thought bubbled up to the surface of her consciousness like one of those burps of methane in the shallows of a lake. Martin had christened them "swamp bubbles", random thoughts that came seemingly out of nowhere.

It wasn't the first time she'd had the thought, driving these back roads. She'd just turned onto Baker, one of a small network of side roads—some paved, most not—that meandered their way through the rocky wilderness northwest of town.

She hated these roads at night. In fact, they scared the shit out of her. They were bad enough during the day. It was amazing how you could be so close to a town or village and yet feel so isolated; that's what happened in a region where wilderness, rather than settlement, was the default landscape, where human presence was the exception rather than the rule. These secondary roads, two lanes of cracked and weathered blacktop that snaked their way over ancient rock and through primeval forest, offered few signs of human activity. Unlike the main highway with its road signs promising food, shelter, and fuel for weary travellers, the back roads were marked only by occasional notices of properties for sale, wildlife crossings, or warnings to trespassers to keep out. On either side of the road, which rose and fell and swerved relentlessly, was a wall of impenetrable forest and occasional rock cut. During the day, the feeling she got while driving around here was one of sameness, boredom, and isolation. At night, especially a rainy November night like this, the feeling of isolation was hugely amplified. The near complete darkness was one thing: the knowledge that there was nothing out there but cold and gloom made everything that much worse.

The thought raised its nasty little head half-jokingly, the product of years of watching too many crime shows on late-night TV.

*A great place to dump a body: no one would ever find it out here.*

Obviously, some people lived out here. Doug and Irene, always ahead of the curve, bought a huge lot out this way, and built their dream home on a rocky hill among the pines and cedars. Their home was only a few minutes behind her now and already there was no sign of it. Their long, private driveway led off this road and climbed up and around a hill through thick forest, ultimately ending three kilometres farther on a man-made plateau where the house sat, facing westward. Even if Doug and Irene had every light on in the house, no one on this road could see it. And if there were other homes around here, the same could be said for them.

She forced herself to think happy thoughts. Dinner was lovely: sweet potato and pear soup, locally caught poached whitefish in a mushroom sauce, French green beans and wild rice, blueberry crumble and café au lait for dessert. Doug and Irene's house— with its open concept, vaulted ceiling, exposed beams, and panoramic west-facing windows—was fabulous of course, triggering, as it usually did, a small pang of envy. Conversation was for the most part light and bouncy, talk of food and travel and early plans for the holidays. She did, however, come away a bit dissatisfied after she managed to corner Doug for some serious one-on-one hospital talk while Irene put the dishes away. It wasn't a trivial matter; it was dead serious, and she needed, demanded even, that as chief of medicine he take action on it. But Doug could be so wilfully blind and pigheaded at times. That had put her in a bit of a pissy mood and she left without saying much else; she just wanted to get home to her two guys.

A call from the Campbells' landline a few minutes before leaving had relaxed her a bit. According to Martin, Justin was sleeping peacefully after what had been a nasty little coughing fit earlier in the evening. After some children's aspirin and some flat ginger ale he'd asked for mommy, and fell asleep before his dad could even answer.

She'd spare her husband her frustration when she got home; he had enough on his plate with a sick two-year-old. No use unloading everything on him right now. Not yet anyway. It was lot to take in and it required strategic thinking and informed judgement. He was a smart man, but this would have him way out of his element. He'd want to take action right away, go to the authorities, call his brother for legal advice, and that risked everything coming out too soon. Plus she didn't feel she'd exhausted all avenues yet. The intrigue could simmer a little while longer.

She hated the helplessness of being in no man's land like this, out of cellphone range, for most of the twenty-five or so minutes it would take to get home, but she knew not to push it. The road was dark and wet and the last thing she needed was to find herself stuck in a ditch in the middle of nowhere because her mind wasn't completely on her driving. Stay calm, turn on the stereo—if she could find something other than paranoid right-wing talk radio—or better yet play a CD. In the darkness, under the glow of the dash and the intermittent squeak of her wipers, a smoky voice reflecting on the brilliant flash of young desire, long since extinguished.

Swinging around a curve on a slight incline, she slowed: hazard lights blinking and rear reflectors of a vehicle ahead, pulled over on the side of the road. Shitty time and place for your ride to break down. She approached at a crawl. Her headlights caught movement on the driver's side, then the door opened and a figure stepped out. A man waved his arms above his head, imploring her to stop.

"Shit," she said to herself. "What is he doing here?"

In her heart there was an element of annoyance and some unease, but not fear. Not yet. She couldn't see his eyes as he approached—his hand was raised to shield them from her headlights—but as she lowered her power window, she saw the joyless grin and heard the false cordiality in his voice.

"Fancy meeting you out here, Doctor."

*Someday, and that day may never come, you'll find you're the only person in the room who's right.*

—my dad

# PART 1

# 1

They found Mom's car two weeks after she disappeared.

The police said nothing looked suspicious, beyond the fact that she had abandoned a perfectly functioning Toyota Rav4 with almost a full tank of gas on what amounted to a glorified game trail on a wet November night. The discovery breathed new life into an already sputtering search effort, brief wind in sagging sails that lasted as long as the good weather did.

No further trace of her was ever found. Dad later said it was as if she'd fallen through a seam in the universe that immediately closed itself up. That image always stuck with me somehow, as did the fact that the last CD she'd been listening to in her car was by Billie Holiday. That sounds like Mom.

It took a lot longer for my dad to give up on Mom than it did for the police or the rest of the community. Every chance he got he would drive around the back roads, interrogating strangers, posting his MISSING signs on every community noticeboard and hydro pole within a hundred and fifty kilometres. He took me along, a silent toddler in a car seat. This continued for years: some of my earliest memories are of riding in the car with my dad, a big roll of tape, an industrial stapler, and box of photocopied posters on my lap. The soundtrack to those memories is Billie Holiday.

Eventually, as our forays through the region with the stacks of posters ground to a halt, Dad stopped listening to jazz. He even took down the Billie Holiday poster that Mom kept in her study. Soon after that he stopped listening to music altogether, in the car and in the house, and got me a set of headphones.

After that, Dad changed. As the years went by and the mystery of my mom's disappearance remained just that, he became like one of his once-colourful paisley shirts that had gone through the wash too many times. Dad, the wannabe flower child, the misplaced hippie born half a generation too late, began to seal up his past into boxes: he packed away his vinyl collection, cut his hair short, let the hole in his left earlobe close up, donated all his embroidered denim clothing, and started wearing khakis and tweed. He didn't smile or joke as much, and while it wouldn't be fair to say he ignored me—it's hard to ignore someone who needs so little attention—he would spend long stretches of time in his office, usually with the door shut. Other times he'd zone out completely. We could be in the middle of a conversation and he'd just trail off to nothing, staring off into the distance, his eyes suggesting he was trying to resolve some difficult equation. In a way, I'm sure that's not far from the truth.

For the better part of ten years Dad and I lived in a kind of homeostasis, a waking hibernation where nothing much changed, each passing day, month, year the same as the one that preceded it. That was, until the summer of 2006 when I was twelve. It was the summer of my first and only encounter with what I came to think of as The Big Weird, that fuzzy area between reality as we know it and what current physics are not quite advanced yet to understand. It's when the mystery of what happened to my mom was resolved, at least for the most part—the last piece of that puzzle only fell into place a few days ago. It was, for all intents and purposes, the summer my childhood ended, and as I never had much of an adolescence to speak of, I'm not sure how to describe what came after. It was also the summer when my dad started to come back to me, as close to his real self as he'd been in a decade. And, finally, it was the summer I met the strange little girl who loomed at the fringe of it all, who drew back a curtain no one knew existed and revealed to me—for a brief moment—the unimaginable.

*****

A few notes about my hometown.

Ferguston, Ontario—population 8,078—is a hole. That's not just some gratuitous epithet flung from a distance by a disgruntled former resident: it's an empirical, geographical fact. You can check it out in any atlas. Ferguston languishes like a cold sore on the eastern edge of Lake LeClair in the north-central part of the province, at the bottom of a basin bordered on three sides by a steep ridge. The highest point is Morin Hill at the north end of town—Moron Hill to locals, just because—which is crowned by the Ferguston water tower, one of the old-fashioned types from the 1950s that looks like a gigantic steel jellyfish. When I was a kid, there had long been talk of replacing it, but when push came to shove and the dollars were counted, town council contented itself with a new paint job. It went from a tired industrial green to a gleaming fish-belly white, which somehow made it worse. To this day, it glares down upon Ferguston like a conquering tripod from *The War of the Worlds*.

Ferguston's lowest point, geographically as well as socially, is The Pit, the most notorious bar in town, located downstairs from Shenanigans restaurant. For generations it was the unofficial hub of organized crime in the region, a headquarters for bikers, drug dealers, corrupt public officials, and the rest of Ferguston's most desperate and marginal citizens. It wasn't so much a place to hide as it was a sanctuary you sought if you didn't want to be bothered: the establishment's celebrated bouncers, gentlemen who looked like late cuts from the Pittsburgh Steelers defensive line, saw to that. If nothing else, it was always a good place to find an on-duty cop or a paramedic.

What I came to fully realize, that summer when I was twelve, was that in Ferguston there is something that is just . . . off. If the communities of Northern Ontario were a family, Ferguston would be that one relative you didn't like to talk about: the drunk uncle or crazy cousin, the one who, perhaps as a result of some unfortunate birth defect or long-forgotten childhood trauma, had ended up perpetually angry, paranoid, or not quite right in the head.

My dad was more succinct. He said that Ferguston should replace its current coat of arms—with its moose, beaver, ship, and locomotive—with a far more simplified and representative symbol: an upraised middle finger.

# 2

In addition to The Big Weird to which I alone—to my knowledge, anyway—was privy, the summer of 2006 was notable for a number of smaller episodes of incidental weirdness that were played out in instalments for the whole of Ferguston to enjoy and scratch its collective head over. To the best of my recollection, these began on Friday, May 12. That was the day the weather changed.

*****

*Oh, shit. I'm dead.*

It wasn't widely known, but for about twelve weeks in the spring of 2006, a monster lurked in Ferguston. This was no horror-story monster. It didn't dwell in the sewers, nor stalk the dark woods like the Blair Witch, nor rise from the murky depths of Lake LeClair. No, this monster hid in plain sight. It could be seen on almost any given afternoon, romping merrily across the well-tended grass and sandy shore of Garrison Park. But I knew it for what it was: a ravenous killing machine whose ultimate purpose was to rip me into small pieces and bolt down the bloody scraps.

The beast now stood only a few feet in front of me, head thrust forward, ears up: attack posture, within easy leaping distance of my throat. To this day, I wonder how my bowels didn't let go at that moment.

*I'm so dead. I'm so fucking dead.*

Officially, the creature's name was Cody. Its owner would have had you believe that it was a Rottweiler/Giant Schnauzer mix, but I knew a warg when I saw one. He was an immense black instrument of death, something out of a Tolkien nightmare: in Middle Earth, the orcs of Isengard rode beasts like him into battle. He must have had at least 35 kilos on me, with a coarse black coat, pointed ears, and a Van Dyke that on a human would look dignified but on Cody look satanic. His eyes were brown but opposite his wiry soot-coloured fur they somehow looked red. Possessed.

Now my life expectancy could be counted off in minutes and it was all my fault, as far as I could see. Call it the price for pissing off the dog's owner, who, it should be noted here, had been dating my dad only two weeks earlier.

This requires a bit of context.

\*\*\*\*\*

For all the sex that goes on in Ferguston—for lack of anything else to do—there was very little of it at our house. I was a quiet pre-teen; I'm not sure what my dad's excuse was. The fact was, for about a decade my dad was the most eligible bachelor in town. Obviously, for the first few years after Mom disappeared, Dad didn't think of himself as a bachelor, much less a widower, and the good ladies of Ferguston were respectful enough to give him his space. But as the years went by and it became evident that Mom wasn't coming back, local single women became increasingly bold in their advances, cozying up to Dad at the supermarket or flirting with him at community events. But even this was short-lived: no one really clicked with him and there were only so many women in town. So Dad remained Ferguston's quiet, handsome single father, socially approachable but romantically just out of reach.

Every once in a while, a new person would appear on the social landscape and try her luck, and if Dad was curious enough or lonely enough or desperate enough for adult conversation, she might get a date or two. Such was the case with Karyn, a third-grade replacement teacher who arrived at St. Marc that April to step in for a colleague of Dad's who was going away on maternity leave. Karyn's success with Dad was marginally better than most: they saw each other for a few weeks that spring after which, to the astonishment of Ferguston's men and the poorly veiled satisfaction of its women, she drove back to North Bay at the end of the school year, vexed and bewildered.

That Dad stopped to take notice of Karyn was hardly surprising. Everyone did. She blew into town like a Hollywood A-lister shooting on location, and her impact was immediate. She was blond, pretty, athletic, super-model material if she'd been taller. With her active wear, hand-crafted jewelry, and Chinese characters tattooed just above the crack of her butt, her overall look could be described as artfully dishevelled New Age jock, and it made the men of Ferguston swoon. She was also charismatic and charming. Dad would later say that she reminded him of a politician on the campaign trail: an outsider who knew just what to do to fit in, all smiles and firm handshakes and folksy charm.

Of course, in the beginning I didn't have much of an opinion about Karyn either way: grown-ups are basically a different species when you're twelve. Even as time passed and I began to wonder what, looks aside, Dad saw in her, I was content to shrug it off as another grown-up mystery. Dad was smiling more, and for a while that was enough.

And if Dad was happy and generally more present, I could put up with a lot: I would gladly shrug off Karyn's aggressive cheerfulness, her relentless positivity, and her endless feel-good platitudes. I was prepared to hold my tongue over her frequent outbreaks of foot-in-mouth disease, like the time she brought her grotesque dog Cody to our house and laughingly instructed him to keep his "cotton-picking paws" out of our flower boxes. That she would make a comment like that with me, a clearly biracial kid, standing not two meters away, left me too shocked even to gasp. Dad must have died a bit inside at that one, closing his eyes and giving a sad head shake. He later apologized for her, saying that Karyn probably had no clue that the expression had its roots in American slavery. I didn't much care for the idea of ignorance as an excuse, but I told him I understood and let it go, thinking that if I had to choose a girlfriend for my dad, I, too, would have preferred a complete idiot over a racist.

I was willing to overlook all those trespasses if it meant that Dad was genuinely happy. After a while I wasn't sure he was anymore, but I was prepared to wait it out . . . that is, until our ill-fated walk through Garrison Park.

On the last Friday of April, Dad invited Karyn to have dinner with us after school, and, seeing as it was our traditional takeout night, we ordered pizza. She showed up promptly at 5:00 with Cody, whom she lashed to the railing of our front porch to bark randomly at passers-by, neighbourhood cats, or nothing at all. I was eager to give the adults their space and quickly volunteered to pick up the pizza, and had almost made a clean getaway when I heard Karyn braying from the living room, "Oh, can I come *with?*"

I didn't want her anywhere near me, but Dad misinterpreted the alarm on my face, grinned at Karyn and said, "Don't worry. He was raised by a grammar Nazi." No one EVER finished a sentence with "with" in our house.

The rain had let up temporarily as we set out. Only a couple of hundred metres west of our house, just past where Wellington Drive meets LeClair Street, is the entrance to Garrison Park. It was the scenic route I took to school every day when I wasn't in a rush or getting a lift from Dad, but a winter of almost continual snowfall followed by a spring of near constant rain had left the park muddy and sodden. It was therefore against my better judgement that I agreed to cut through the park so that Karyn could let her dog loose.

We plodded along the soggy path on the easternmost edge of the park, stepping over puddles and dodging the cold drops that fell from overhanging branches. Back when the park was expanded and beautified in the '90s, the developers kept all the old trees and made a few artificial ponds, especially at our end, and it was a huge draw for the local wildlife. Cody was off-leash and ecstatic. He splashed through ponds, chasing after whatever his owner threw for him to fetch, then came galumphing back, shaking mud all over and barking at me for good measure.

Despite the bleak weather, I was beginning to enjoy the quiet of the park, with only the hollow wind and occasional creak of the trees. Karyn, on the other hand, seemed uncomfortable without constant discourse.

"Juss-tin . . ."

There was a singsong quality to it.

"There's something I wanted to share with you," she continued.

*Uh-oh. This can't be good.*

"I saw this amazing film just recently, but I don't feel I can share it with your father. I'm afraid he wouldn't be very open-minded about it. He'd be all: 'It's not very sciency.'"

In all fairness to Karen, Dad is hard core, a ferocious rationalist whose requirements for supporting evidence when faced with an extraordinary claim border on the draconian. Carl Sagan would have loved him. I immediately thought of one of his favourite quotes: "Being open-minded is merely the willingness to consider evidence, not the willingness to accept claims without any." I also doubted my dad would ever use the word "sciency" with a straight face.

"OK," was the best I could manage.

"The film is about the Law of Attraction. Have you heard about it?"

Head shake.

"It's based on a philosophy called New Thought, and I won't bore you with all the history, but basically it says that everything you think and feel can attract events and experiences that are similar. So, negative thoughts will bring negative experiences to you, just as positive ones will bring positive things."

"Really." It didn't quite come out as a question. Karyn noticed.

"Yes, Justin. It is actually very scientific in spite of what you may think; it's based on quantum physics and psychology and neuroscience and stuff. A lot of great thinkers have worked on this, and the powers that be have tried to hide it from the public for a long time."

Dad would have cringed: inane New Age drivel AND a conspiracy theory thrown in for free.

"Uh-huh. How does it work?"

"Well, it's pretty complicated but from what I understand it's a form of energy that all living things have."

*You mean like the Force?*

"This energy—in our thoughts and in our feelings—is sent out into the Universe all the time, and the Universe reflects it back. If that energy is positive, then positivity is sent back to you and good things will happen. If the energy is negative, then negative things happen."

"Right, so if I wish for something positive—"

"No, it's not that simple. It's about sending out positive energy all the time."

"OK, so if I do that the 'Universe' will make good things happen?"

"Well, you have to be committed to it, but yes, in the end good things will come your way."

"How is that different from what religious people say about prayer?"

A laugh.

"No, no, no. It's not the same thing at all! This is *energy*, real energy that exists in your body, that is going out into the Universe."

She kept referring to energy, and I was confused. I didn't know much about physics yet but from what my dad always told me energy was something like heat or magnetism or the force of an object in motion; it was something that was done *to* stuff—I'd later understand it to be a property of matter—not stuff in itself. And the idea that somehow it not only bled out of one's body but did so with enough force that it reached escape velocity, left the atmosphere and dispersed into space, to say nothing about how it was received, read and interpreted by the cosmos which then delivered an individualized and proportional response to the precise original sender, was a bit more than I was willing to accept. And no, it didn't sound very "sciency."

"OK."

"So, for example, if you wish for something—like a job or that special someone—and put enough positive energy into it, it will come your way."

"Well, I'm just twelve years old. I'm not looking for a job or a girlfriend right now."

"All right, obviously neither of those in this case, but you see what I mean. If there's something you really want, I dunno, like a new computer or something—"

"I *have* a new computer."

I wasn't catching on and Karyn was getting frustrated. She sensed that, for some reason, I was completely deaf to this incredible secret she was entrusting me with, and she was clearly annoyed. Evidently, I wasn't as bright as she'd assumed.

"Well . . . I don't know. Think of something you really want, something you feel very strongly about, and if you want it badly enough, it will happen."

I didn't have to say what I said next, but I'd grown tired of listening to Karyn doling out her spiritual Amway. I didn't like her, I didn't like where this was going, and I wanted it to be over.

"I want my mother back. Do you think if I wish hard enough . . ."

It wasn't necessary to finish the sentence.

"It's not . . ." Karyn began.

She ran out of steam almost as soon as she started. She blew out a sigh, glanced away for a second hoping for a way out, then without looking at me, whistled for her dog and moved on.

Within minutes the rain had started again. We picked up the pizza and returned home, with no further conversation. Dad didn't see much more of Karyn after that. I can only guess what she told him about our conversation in the park, possibly hinting that his son was rude and narrow-minded and a bit slow on the uptake, but knowing my dad, he wasn't overly sympathetic. If he hadn't already made up his mind about a future with Karyn, this might have tipped the balance. Within a few days his routine returned to normal, and despite the small size of our town, we didn't run into Karyn much anymore. I still saw her around at school but we never interacted, and Dad never mentioned her. By all accounts, the day after the school year ended in late June, she had blown town.

*****

But that wasn't for at least another month. At this moment, I was staring my imminent demise in the face. For his part, Cody was no doubt eying the soft part of my throat beneath my jawline.

It was a gorgeous afternoon on the second Friday of May. School hadn't let out yet for the day—I had gotten out early for a doctor's appointment in town—and the rain that had been threatening that morning never materialized. On my way home I'd taken the scenic route through Garrison Park as I usually did, and had been enjoying the dappled shadows of the emerging leaves above as they splashed across my face. There were birds singing in the distance, the sounds of young children squealing on the nearby play structure, and waves lazily lapping the shoreline. And in front of me, an immense hyper-carnivore from the Miocene was salivating at its soon-to-be dinner. A good day to die.

"What are you even doing out here?" I whispered at the dog. "And where's your owner? She put you up to this?"

I'd made up my twelve-year-old mind that Karyn had orchestrated the perfect ambush. It all made sense. She owned a four-legged death machine that could probably take down a full-grown moose; she no doubt held me responsible for the humiliating failure of her relationship with my dad and she knew the patterns of my movements well enough, including the route I took to get home from school every Friday. Means, motive and opportunity. Hell hath no fury like the dog of a woman scorned.

The beast had seemingly come out of nowhere. I was on the footpath at the eastern end of the park, and there were plenty of bushes and trees around to provide cover. Karyn was nowhere to be seen, nor were any other humans who might have come to my rescue or at least provided Cody with a choice of entrées.

Flight was out of the question; the chase would be short and bloody. My only option was psychology. Use his name: isn't that what they suggest when placating hostage takers and serial killers?

"Good Cody. Good boy." I never sounded so lame in my life.

His nostrils were flaring in a way that I didn't like and for a moment I wished he'd just get his ghastly work over with. I closed my eyes and waited for the end.

And then things got weird. Just as I was bracing myself for his final lunge, Cody suddenly went squirrelly. The rumbling growl in his throat was cut short and replaced by something that was halfway between a howl and a whine. He lowered himself into a submissive crouch, curling his back end under him; if his tail had been more than a stub, it would have been between his hind legs.

He then started backing up with his belly dragging on the ground; his ears were flat on his head and he was turning his face away as if he didn't want to see what was in front of him.

As weird as all this was, I was clearly no longer the focus of Cody's attention. I risked a glance over my shoulder.

There was a girl standing calmly just a few feet behind me, to my left. I guessed her age at no more than ten, with a lithe build. She was alone and she looked down at the cowering dog with little more than mild bemusement. I've seen chipmunks that looked more threatening.

Meanwhile Cody was getting more upset by the second, and after a few moments of what I could only interpret as confused terror, he decided to bolt. He slipped and stumbled over his muddy paws as he turned around and, without even a last glance backward, took off at full speed up the path.

# 3

"What the hell did you do to that dog?"

The girl didn't answer. In fact, the look she gave me was one of such befuddlement that for a moment I thought she didn't speak English. I was about to repeat it in French when she offered an almost inaudible "Nothing?"

"Well, it wasn't afraid of me. *Something* must have scared it."

She didn't respond aside from a tiny shrug, and just looked off in the direction the dog had fled. I took the moment to give her a closer appraisal.

First off, I didn't know this girl from school and I knew nearly everyone at St. Marc. I'd never seen her around town, either: she wasn't white, so I would have noticed her. She was either new to Ferguston, or she went to the English school across town. Either way, it was a little odd that she got so far ahead of me in the park without my noticing. Also weird for a Friday afternoon: no backpack, no lunch box.

She was well dressed and cute for a kid: bulky purple Aéropostale hoodie, faded Guess jeans rolled up to mid-calf, and immaculate white Reeboks. She was lighter than me but not Caucasian, "olive skinned," with dark brown wavy hair reaching halfway down her back. I noticed a few fresh scrapes on her knuckles, and there was just a trace of pink polish on a couple of her fingernails. Her big eyes were dark and striking: she had strong black eyebrows, long elegant lashes, but with semicircles under her eyes that made her look tired and a little sad. But there was something else.

*Her eyes . . . They're wrong.*

A tormented howl in the distance echoed through the trees. Cody sounded like he was being tortured.

The sound of Cody's anguished wail passed, replaced by Karyn's distant voice hollering her dog's name over and over and imploring him to "*Get-back-here-you-stupid-mutt-what-the-fuck-has-gotten-into-you???*" She sounded like she was getting closer, and if Karyn was able to bolster Cody's courage enough to bring him back this way, I wanted to be as close to this strange little girl as possible.

Meanwhile, I was trying to figure out the least obvious, most nonchalant way of approaching her without looking either scared or pervy, when she made the entire issue moot: she moved up the path and stood next to me, all without taking her eyes off the spot where the dog was last seen. She was utterly calm, as if the menacing presence of Cody and his abrupt and terrified departure had had no effect on her.

"I've never seen you here before," I ventured, cringing a bit inside as I said it. It sounded cheesy, but it was marginally better than "Come here often?" and, in a small town like Ferguston where new faces stand out, it was a legitimate question. I just hoped she'd take it that way. She made the situation easier by ignoring the question entirely, and instead took in the surroundings with her enormous black eyes.

"It's so dark here," she said.

That's when it clicked. Her eyes: they were so dark, black actually, because her pupils were huge.

We just stood there for a bit, not speaking. I didn't mind the silence, and there were things I was noticing about this strange girl as I stood there. She had a faint but pleasant smell about her: spicy, almost but not quite the smell of cinnamon. Also, she gave off heat like a person with a really bad fever.

The idea then came to me: maybe she was *sick*, like *really* sick, like something awful like cancer, something Dad called an *illness*. He used that word when he meant something serious, as opposed to a cold or a bad stomach that might keep you out of school for a day or two. An *illness* was something that some people had to live with, and you had to go to the hospital to have it treated. Maybe that's what it was. It might explain why she was so hot, and why her eyes looked the way they did.

She was also singing softly to herself, so softly that I couldn't make out the words. It was pretty in a spooky kind of way, and vaguely familiar.

"What's your name?" An innocent enough follow-up to my first attempt at conversation.

Her expression didn't change; she just looked around with a very slight crease on her forehead, scanning the landscape. It didn't seem like she was going to answer my question, and again I was right.

"You come here all the time," she responded. It wasn't a question. Weird, because it was true, which meant she'd seen me around. But OK, I'd give her that one. It's a small town. I just nodded.

I stood there a moment, enjoying the stillness at this end of the park, wondering how long I should try to engage this strange girl who didn't seem to understand the basic rules of conversation. A voice then blared out from just a few feet away, shattering our delicate chrysalis of tranquility.

"What the hell did you do to my dog?"

I turned in time to see Karyn straining to drag Cody next to her. But the dog was having none of it: he dug in with his massive hind quarters, pulled his head backward like a scared turtle, folds of skin building up around his studded collar, and then succeeded in slipping free, sprinting back in the direction they'd just come.

"Shit," Karyn hissed. "Goddamn it, Cody, get the fuck back here!"

And just like that, with a final venomous glare levelled our way, Karyn was off again. We saw neither dog nor owner again that day.

A brief moment of silence and the girl spoke up again, as if the whole episode with Karyn and Cody had never happened.

"I can't tell you my real name *here*."

The comment was so unexpected, given the circumstances, that it took me a moment to come back to the here and now, and another to formulate a response.

"Why's that?"

She considered her answer for a moment.

"I'd have to sing it and you don't have enough sounds . . ."

A beat.

". . . *and* it would take days."

*Oooooo-kay.*

I'd learned from a young age to resist the urge to say anything that might be hurtful or rude or even sarcastic no matter how tempting, especially to strangers, so all I said was "So, I guess I'll see you around . . ." and left it at that.

I turned back down the path in the direction of the east exit of the park when I heard her voice from behind. It stopped me in my tracks.

"You can call me Billie. Like the singer."

\*\*\*\*\*

Dad was making dinner when I got home.

"Hands," he said to remind me to wash mine. "I expected you'd be home earlier today," he said as he put plates and utensils on the table. Dad preferred that I kept him abreast of my general comings and goings and didn't care for surprises, given what happened to Mom.

"Sorry, Dad," I said over the running water. "I was at the park."

Like a lot of French Canadians in primarily English-speaking Ontario, we Lamberts—pronounced "lam-BEAR" and not "LAM-bert," if you please—tended to speak English at home. The exception was when we got passionate or frustrated about something. Curse words were *always* in French.

"Yeah, I figured," he said. He pulled dinner—something he wryly called "white-trash tuna casserole," a specialty of the house—out of the oven, and began spooning the bubbling noodles onto our plates. "How was your appointment? You gonna live, or can I start selling your stuff?"

"I'm good," I said as I blew on my food for a few seconds, and waited for Dad to sit down and take off his oven mitts.

"Dad, do you know if there's a new kid in school? A girl, Grade Four or Five?"

He looked at me closely, and his eyes narrowed. "Nnnnno . . ." he said, after a pause. "I don't believe so. I certainly wasn't made aware of it anyway."

"Mm-kay," I said. A pause. More blowing on my food as I stared out the screen door into the backyard. "Would you know if Lakeshore had a PD day today?" Lakeshore Public was the English-language school in town, twice the size of St. Marc.

"Nope, they didn't. And it's not likely there will be any more before the end of the year. Too many snow days to make up for this spring."

Blow. Bite. My gaze returned to our backyard and locked on the lush cedar hedge that obscured the fence behind it. Our back neighbours had a row of young poplars on their side of the fence, and new leaves were just beginning to erupt.

"It's just that there was this strange girl in the park a little while ago, no lunch box or school bag. It was a bit weird to see a kid there at that time."

"Ah. Playing hooky, maybe."

"Yeah, maybe." Another pause. "I think she might have been sick."

"Yeah?"

"She didn't look it but I could feel the heat coming off her, like she had a fever."

He stopped chewing and looked at me for a second. "Really? You must have been close."

I nodded, suddenly aware of how strange that would sound to my dad; I wasn't in the habit of cozying up to strange girls at that age. Dad brushed it off.

"Some people just run hot I guess."

Another pause. Outside, a well-fed robin swung down from one of the poplars behind our fence and alit on another one in our yard off to the right, then immediately took off again, as if realizing it was a bad idea. Odd. I'd never noticed a tree like that on our side of the fence before. Its leaves were bright lizard green and completely unfurled. I pushed on.

"I ran into Karyn and Cody in the park . . . well, Cody first." As Dad's eyes lifted to meet mine, I held a mental debate as to how much to reveal about the encounter, eventually settling on an abbreviated account.

"Anyway, Cody was standing on the path kind of blocking my way, and he didn't seem to want to let me pass. That dog scares me."

Dad suddenly looked serious. "Did he do anything? Am I going to have to have a talk with Karyn?" I knew he'd have preferred sticking white-hot needles in his eyeballs than call his ex-girlfriend about her dog.

"No. See that's what was so weird. This strange girl suddenly showed up, and Cody suddenly went ballistic, like he was facing a charging Tyrannosaurs rex, and took off. Then Karyn dragged him back to find out what happened, as if her dog was gonna say '*It was them! They did this!*' but Cody was still freaked out and he took off again."

"So, in short, nothing happened," Dad concluded.

Given my narrow brush with dismemberment, evisceration and death, I was hoping for more.

"Yeah. I guess."

For a moment I thought he'd say something else, but instead I watched as the muscles around his face relaxed and his focus gradually became detached, floating off like a ball of dandelion fluff in a midsummer meadow. I knew he'd be like that for a while, nearly impossible to reach, so I finished up my dinner, rinsed off my plate and put it in the dishwasher. "Thanks for dinner, Dad."

I threw a final glance my dad's way, watched him for a moment staring blankly out the screen door, then went upstairs to do my homework, my mind drifting back to the pretty little girl in the purple hoodie.

# 4

Summer hit—unofficially at least—the next day, and did so with a vengeance. Ferguston had just gone through its most brutal winter in years, and spring had started off late and wet. There was still snow lingering in shaded areas at the end of April, and with the almost ceaseless rain and endless puddles making just being outdoors a thoroughly depressing prospect, I hadn't taken my bike out. All that came to a decisive end on the second Saturday of May. They were calling for a high that day in the mid to upper twenties Celsius, which, halfway through a spring where the temperature had yet to reach fourteen, seemed nothing short of miraculous. Warm mid-spring sunlight poured into the kitchen, bringing with it the seasonal sounds of songbirds and lawn mowers, sounds that felt like dearly missed friends whose absence isn't fully noticed or appreciated until the moment you see them again.

I improvised a quick breakfast—cereal and coffee, both heavy on sugar and dairy. Then, despite my natural inclinations as a cave dweller, I wrestled my bike from the basement for its inaugural ride of the summer. Dad normally insisted that I get it tuned before taking it out for the first time, but I was compelled to get it on the road and—as they say in Ferguston—just give 'er.

Dad was in the backyard, still sweaty from his morning jog, shaking his head over a curious clump of freshly turned soil about a foot and a half across. "Groundhogs," he muttered when he saw me. It was almost a question. I nodded absently, told him I was heading out, and was halfway to the garage when a stray thought bubbled up in my mind:

*Wasn't there a decent-sized tree in that precise spot just yesterday? A tree I'd never noticed before?*

With tire pressure checked—call that a tune-up for now—water bottle in its holder, and helmet strapped on, I wheeled my bike to the curb. Dad and I lived in a Tudor-style house on Tremblay Street, in an older neighbourhood in the east end of town called Shorewood. Like most of the homes around it, ours was built in the 1920s, which was as close to a golden age as Ferguston ever had. Number twelve Tremblay Street was more house than Dad and I needed, and for as long as I remember living there, we rattled around in it like the last two Smarties in a box. The neighbourhood was still a nice enough area when I was a kid—probably the nicest part of town—with its great big houses, ancient trees and its proximity to the lake, but even then, Shorewood was beginning to show its years, slouching and sagging here and there like an aging grandparent.

A crow cawed nearby, the ubiquitous theme of the Northern Ontario soundtrack. Our elderly neighbour, Mr. Lovato, who lived a couple of doors over, was out in front of his yellow bungalow, inspecting his front yard and taking in the first hints of summer. He was in his mid-seventies but looked ten years older, and like a lot of people in Ferguston, Lovato wasn't about to give anyone the warm and fuzzies. Dad said that Lovato had better reason to be grumpy than most. He was a widower; his wife of over fifty years—and former high school sweetheart—died of cancer ten years earlier, and while as a couple they used to be active in the community—playing golf, hosting bridge games, and volunteering with the Ferguston Players—Dad says Mr. Lovato's temperament took an abrupt turn south when he found himself alone. He never had visitors and whatever family he had kept their distance. He spent most of his time in his living room with his cat, Sketchy, doing Sudokus and watching the Weather Network.

Mr. Lovato did have one passion: his front yard. There was no lawn to speak of; mostly it was a jumble of shrubs, flower boxes, a few big rocks that were meant to be decorative—and some almost were—and dozens and dozens of ornamental figures and animals of all kinds, sizes, and states of disrepair. Dad called it the Lovato Lawn Fauna Rescue Centre, as most if not all of the specimens were either purchased from flea markets, salvaged from the curb on garbage days, or retrieved from properties after the original owners had moved away. Most were typical, garden variety stuff: ceramic turtles, frogs, snails, rabbits, ducks, and salamanders, a doe with two fawns, a family of hedgehogs, and one—and only one—pink flamingo. Others were a bit more exotic: a crouching leopard with fading spots, a very worn elephant-headed figure that was probably the Hindu god Ganesha, a gargoyle, a crumbling Brachiosaurus with half its tail missing, a trio of tiny aliens and a flying saucer fashioned out of a couple of battered hubcaps, a huge chrome elephant, and an odd creature that Lovato himself couldn't identify but that I thought was a poorly executed lemur. No garden gnomes. Not one. "Hate the little fuckers," is how he put it.

Lovato was exactly the kind of cranky old geezer that a kid like me would have been scared shitless of, and most of the local kids were. But in spite of his crustiness I liked him, or at least I didn't run from him, call him names, or throw stuff at his windows. He and Dad had become close over the years, and I sensed Lovato felt protective of me in his way. He was never deliberately hurtful, he never made a big deal of the fact that I didn't talk much, and he appreciated my interest in his collection without boring me to tears about it. Plus, he always called me "Lambert," which I thought sounded cool and grown-up.

"Takin' the bike out for a spin, Lambert?"

He also had an old person's uncanny aptitude for the painfully obvious.

"Yeah," I replied, walking my bike down the driveway.

He stood silently with his hands on his hips, surveying his kingdom from behind his wraparound sunglasses, faintly nodding at nothing in particular. I gave him a moment in case he wanted to say something else, and was about to climb onto my bike and shove off when he suddenly blurted out: "Peculiar weather."

"Yeah," I said.

Then, as much to himself as to me, "Damn peculiar." He glanced up at the sky and around for a moment, shaking his head, then added, "I don't think anyone saw this coming. Everyone has been calling for rain all through next week." A pause, and again "Damn peculiar."

I dutifully looked up and nodded in agreement, and after a few seconds when I was sure Lovato wasn't going to add anything else, I managed a quiet "Anyway . . ."

"Careful out there today, Lambert. That sun'll fry the hide clean offa ya."

"'Kay," I said. I'd never had anything that resembled a sunburn in my life, courtesy of my mom, and I knew Lovato would eventually figure that out for himself, so I let it go. In fact, I was about to head off when he added, almost as an afterthought: "Lot of strangeness around town this morning."

I must have given away a look that said I didn't know what he was talking about because he then added: "You need to get up earlier in the morning, Lambert. The Ferguston rumour mill never sleeps."

I took the bait. "What happened?"

Lovato savoured the moment for a second, in little hurry to get me caught up on the latest. Finally he breathed out a sigh, turned to me, and lifted his head a notch to peer at me from under his dark glasses. "Well," he said, "where to start?"

A quick shrug from me to urge him on.

"Couple of items have got people's lips flapping this morning. The first one is a fish story. Wouldn't normally give it much mind if it weren't for who was doing the telling. You ever heard of J.P. Guertin, or Doug Ingram?"

Head shake.

"No? Really? You've lived here all your life and you've never heard of either? They're as close to celebrities as Ferguston has. Fishermen. Successful ones, too. They've been guiding summer folk on fishing trips around here for . . . well, I dunno how long. Ingram is from Nipissing First Nation; Guertin is a Frenchie, like yourself. Older guys; Guerts is my age, known him since we were kids. Together they must have one hundred years' experience fishing these parts. Anyways, seems they were out on the lake in the wee hours this morning and hooked themselves a monster. Took 'em an hour and a half to haul it in. They managed to get it alongside the boat, but then the beast somehow unhooked itself and disappeared. No photograph, but they did get a good look at it, and they probably would have released it anyway. They say it was a lake sturgeon and, judging by how it compared to the size of their boat, it was close to eight feet long. That would have smashed the record, at least in this province."

"Wow. How much did it weigh?"

"Well, obviously they weren't able to weigh it, but people who know about such things figure it would have come in at three hundred pounds, if it was as long as they say; seventy, maybe eighty years old."

A fish almost twice the size of my dad. My head spun. I was no fish expert, but I did know that sturgeon were something of a living fossil, in that they haven't changed much since the age of the dinosaurs. That something that huge and ancient should be lurking so close to where I lived got my pulse going.

"I didn't know there were sturgeons in Lake LeClair."

A deep, thoughtful nod from Lovato. "Well now you see, that's just the thing. No one did. You might have to ask the *real* old-timers to know for sure, but I did a bit of snooping on the Google this morning and there doesn't seem to be a record of one here. Ever." He paused. "Damn peculiar."

Lovato was silent for a moment, staring off into space. His dark wraparound sunglasses made it impossible to see his eyes, which I found a bit unnerving.

"What was the other thing?"

"Umm?" He grunted, snapping out of his reverie.

"You said there were a couple of items that people were talking about. What was the second thing?"

"Oh, right. The other story is in a different vein altogether. Big sinkhole opened up on Wellington this morning, right behind the McIntyres' house. Haven't checked it out yet, but I hear it's a doozy. Not much history of sinkholes in these parts, but with all the rain we've had, I guess it's not that surprising. Makes you think, though. A bit disquieting."

Sinkholes were a common enough news item in our part of the world, especially in the springtime, though not so much in Ferguston proper. And while a particularly big one opening up right in someone's backyard was interesting, it still didn't have the allure that a giant, ancient, and hitherto unknown lake creature lurking just beyond my front door had for me. Of course I wasn't going to dismiss it in front of Mr. Lovato, so I just nodded.

"Well, I'll be sure to go check it out, but I'm not sure where they live," I offered, knowing full well Lovato would pounce on the opportunity to provide directions.

Fergustonians, like small-town folk elsewhere, have a distinctive approach to giving directions, especially if they've lived in the area long enough. Places located on a person's mental map are identified by their history: who lives there now, who lived there before, and/or what happened on or near the site. Mr. Lovato's directions to the McIntyre house were a perfect example: you head north on Wellington, just past where Demers Street used to continue straight through to Centre Street before the Big Flood washed out the road in '59, and across from where old man Lacroix's barn was blown over during the Big Storm of '73. I had no trouble believing that in years to come people would be referring to the McIntyre house as where the Big Sinkhole happened in '06.

Wellington Street runs parallel to Tremblay one street over, and the McIntyres' house was only a short bike ride away, barely a kilometre, so it was easy to keep my word. It was also easy to spot where all the fuss was going on: two fire engines, two police cruisers, and a few dozen onlookers gathered along the side of the street next to number 211. People had their cameras out, but you couldn't see much from the front of the house and bands of yellow police tape weren't allowing the nosey Parkers any closer. The only indication that anything was amiss was a big poplar at the back of the property that was leaning over uncomfortably toward the house.

"Hmm," I thought. "Bad day for poplars." I listened in on a couple of muted conversations but no one seemed to know any more than Mr. Lovato, and after a while I just left. In fact, I never gave the sinkhole another thought until this article appeared a couple of days later on the first page of Monday's *Clarion*:

## Mysterious monster sinkhole
## devours house in Ferguston

### Jason Bremmer
### The Clarion

[FERGUSTON] A massive sinkhole opened up early Saturday morning on the property of a Ferguston couple, creating thousands of dollars' worth of damage and leaving the residents temporarily homeless.

George and Marjorie McIntyre, of 211 Wellington Street in Ferguston, were woken up suddenly from what they thought was an earthquake. They would later tell the *Clarion* that they heard a sound like an approaching train, followed by a growing rumbling and rattling that came from the dining room.

"There was a groaning and then this huge crash as part of the house was torn off," said Mr. McIntyre. A few hours later, in the bright light of morning, the McIntyres found that an enormous sinkhole had opened up beneath their house, partially consuming their dining room and a section of their kitchen.

"We're so lucky that it wasn't worse," Mrs. McIntyre added. "It happened so fast, and in the middle of the night, we would never have gotten out in time."

Sinkholes are often caused by the creation of cavities in porous rock by successive seasons of heavy rain and winter runoff. When the cavity becomes too large, softer soils above the cavity eventually collapse into it, creating a sinkhole.

Others are created when empty space forms around man-made infrastructure below the surface, such as tunnels, mine shafts, culverts, or water mains. As soil begins to fill in the open space, the situation is exacerbated when water permeates the surrounding soil, weakening it. The cavity expands and eventually the surface caves in.

While they are a common enough occurrence in the region, historically very few sinkholes have been reported within Ferguston.

In fact, the origin of the sinkhole on the McIntyre property has defied explanation by experts called in to look into the phenomenon.

Despite higher than average snow accumulation this past winter, an investigator from the Geological Survey of Canada concluded that the soil beneath the McIntyres' home showed no signs of saturation or advanced erosion.

"And with the absence of any infrastructure," geologist Nick Zukic told the *Clarion*, "we can't for the moment come up with a plausible explanation why a gaping, almost perfectly spherical, 25-foot crater suddenly appeared where it did, or why there was so little water in the bottom."

Meanwhile, George and Marjorie McIntyre are . . .

Suddenly, the random hole in the ground seemed marginally more interesting than the monster fish. I spent some time over the next few days hunting online for further developments on the story, but none came. Sadly, the good people of Ferguston would never get a satisfactory explanation for the mysterious sinkhole, and with the obvious exceptions of George and Marjorie McIntyre, most would forget it before the week was over anyway. Just a minor mystery in a summer that would have more than its accustomed share.

Damn peculiar.

# 5

"Your name is Justin."

"Yeah."

"Your father's name is Martin."

She never turned my way or changed her expression. Her voice was flat. This was neither an interrogation nor an interview. She was simply stating facts.

"That's right." Two for two.

"You don't have a mom. Anymore."

Billie and I were sitting atop a play structure in Garrison Park. It was Monday, and I was on my way home from school when I spied her there, sitting by herself. Figuring there was no harm in being sociable, and having found the conclusion to our first meeting to be unsatisfying, I climbed up and joined her.

The play structure was one of my favourite places to sit and think. It was installed back when they fixed up the whole park and made everything more kid-friendly. The structure was made to look like a pirate ship, with rope netting and three masts, each one with a crow's nest and a zip line that connected them. There were wooden platforms at different levels that replicated the forecastle, the main deck and the quarterdeck, and of course a big steering wheel. Days when it was nice out and I was on my way home from school, I liked to stop for a while, climb up the rigging to the crow's nest of the central mast, and just close my eyes and listen to the lake.

Today, the ship had oddly acquired a noticeable list to starboard.

"Right again," I replied.

Most people in town, many of whom I'd never met, knew the basics of what happened to Mom, but I still felt a momentary twinge of annoyance whenever someone treated it like an open subject, like the published minutes of a town council meeting. I did my best to take it in stride: she was just a kid after all.

"You've been asking around about me?"

"I don't need to do that."

*Whatever.* "That's fine. It's a small town. Everybody knows everybody, and it's not like my story is some big secret." A pause. "And your name is . . . what again? Something really complicated, right?"

"I like Billie. Call me that."

"But Billy is a boy's name."

"Not always."

Another pause. We sat facing the lake, Billie on my right with her forearms on her knees in front of her, turning something around in her hands that I couldn't quite see. She started singing very softly, just above a whisper; again I couldn't make out what the tune was but it was no nursery rhyme or a song from a Disney movie. It sounded grown-up and a little sad. The heat she gave off was palpable, and she smelled like cookies.

"So . . . what happened with that dog the other day? Why was it so afraid of you?"

Billie just shrugged.

"Have you seen it before? Did you do something to scare it?" Maybe she could provide a helpful hint: it might come in handy.

"No. Dogs don't like me. Neither do a lot of things. Most animals just run away. I must smell funny."

I wanted to tell her that I thought she smelled nice, kind of cinnamony, but I stopped myself.

We were quiet again for a moment. Gulls squawked near an overflowing trash bin, and a trio of younger kids chirped and cackled over toy cars in the sand pit. Turning toward Billie I noticed that once again she was without either a backpack or a lunch box.

"I have to ask: have you been sitting here since Saturday?"

I had in fact spotted her two days earlier, Saturday afternoon—the day after the encounter with Cody—in exactly the same spot, sitting in precisely the same position. The only reason I didn't approach her then was because I was with my friend Tommy Chartrand at the time and pointing out a girl that I was even mildly curious about to someone as gross and sleazy as Tommy Chartrand would have been nothing short of disastrous.

I felt like an idiot the moment I asked the question, but she took it at face value.

"No. I can't stay out too long."

"Yeah. My dad's a bit that way with me." I glanced around the crow's nest. "No homework. You're lucky."

"No what?"

"Homework."

"'Home Work' . . ."

"Yeah. Sometimes I catch a break on weekends, but never on Mondays."

She looked confused.

"You're kidding. You mean you *never* get homework??? Oh my god, you're so lucky! What school do you go to?"

"I . . . don't?"

"You don't what? Go to school?" A momentary shock, and then: "Ah, you must be homeschooled."

She didn't look any less baffled but she did offer a response. "I'm always learning. I do a lot of different things and go to a lot of different places." Then she added: "This is a very interesting place."

"Ferguston? You must be new here."

"The water and the atmosphere and the rocks and the plants and . . . everything. There's so much."

"Lemme guess: you're from Sudbury."

She smiled for the first time, and the transformation was breathtaking. It was like the sun breaking through the clouds after weeks of steady rain. Something inside me began to thaw immediately.

"You don't like it here?" she inquired, turning to me. Her face was open and candid.

"Ferguston? It's OK, I guess. I dunno. I've never been anywhere else, not to live anyway. I wouldn't mind living someplace else, but it's not up to me."

"Why not? I can go anywhere. And I do. All the time."

"Well . . . my dad has a job here, and a house, and something called a mortgage. I dunno, we're kind of dug in. I don't even think *he* likes it here, but we stay anyway."

"Why? If neither of you like it here . . ."

I thought for a while. I'd never considered the question too closely before. "I think it might have to do with my mom."

Billie's face gave away nothing. I tried elaborating.

"I think my mom might be the reason my dad stays."

"But she's gone."

"Yes, she's gone."

Who was this kid who kept talking about my mom like she knew anything about her? It should have annoyed me, but somehow it didn't. That smile . . .

"Do you think she'd want you two to stay?"

The fact was I had no idea. Indeed, it occurred to me at that moment how little I knew about my mom, and it was a bit embarrassing to have this stranger—who apparently had either done some snooping about my family or had heard a bit of gossip—ask such precise questions about her that I couldn't answer.

"I don't know."

"Do you think maybe she'll come back, and your dad wants to be here when she does?"

*Wow!*

"You'd have to ask him."

Billie nodded knowingly: "Right. And he doesn't talk," she said.

People who knew my dad in those days knew his public face, the one he wore for his students, their parents, the other teachers, and folks around town. These people knew Dad as gregarious, engaging, sharp as a razor, and quick with a smile, a person who was alert, a superlative listener, and who always, always had something to talk about. His students would often joke to me that his classes often ran late because Dad just wouldn't shut up once he got rolling. That my dad could spend extended periods, sometimes days on end, stringing barely five words together would have shocked a lot of people. That was the Martin Lambert that I—and only I—knew, and no amount of town gossip would have disclosed it. Billie, for whatever source of intel she may have had on me and my family history, had no way of knowing that.

And yet, somehow, she knew—or rather something in the way she'd nodded suggested she understood. The revelation suddenly bubbled up into my mind that maybe here was another person who lived in a similar household to mine, a person with a sometimes non-communicative parent, and that just maybe *she'd* sought *me* out for just that reason.

I began looking forward to seeing her again, keeping a watchful eye whenever I passed through Garrison Park, hoping she was as good at keeping track of my movements as she appeared to be.

# 6

It was a while before I got to speak with Billie again, but I did get a few glimpses of her around town for a few days. These only added to her mystery, not the least because they were completely unexpected and in the most unlikely places. She didn't go to my school, so you can imagine my surprise when I saw her drift past the open door of my geography class one afternoon. I just happened to turn my head for a second and there she was, looking straight at me, and then she was gone. It was all over in less than a second. Of course I immediately asked the teacher to be excused, ostensibly to use the washroom but really so that I could chase after her, but by the time I got to the hallway she was nowhere to be seen. I even went to the second floor so I could do a more thorough search, sneaking glances into other classrooms and even into the girls' washroom, but no luck.

On another occasion, I was on my way to school when I saw her sitting all by herself in a Greyhound bus leaving for Toronto. This big coach was sitting at an intersection right in front of me, and despite the tinted windows I could see her face as plain as day. That in itself was weird enough because you don't expect a little kid like that to be travelling all by themselves to another city, especially one that's over four hours away.

Weirder still was later that same day, after dinner while I was doing my homework and my dad was watching the local news. There was an item about the opening of a brand-new municipal building downtown, and the reporters were covering the ribbon-cutting ceremony from earlier in the day. I just happened to look up at that moment and there, just on the edge of the screen, was Billie looking straight into the camera, holding a green helium balloon. If it wasn't her, she had an exact double because Billie should have been halfway to Toronto when that ceremony was taking place. I must have made some kind of noise because my dad looked at me at that moment. I wanted to blurt something out just then but my mouth couldn't form any words, and before I knew it Billie was gone and someone in the studio was talking about the weather.

I thought a lot about my Billie sightings afterward, at the school, on the Greyhound, on TV, and I asked myself over and over if it had really been her. None of it made any sense, of course, and yet I felt absolutely certain about it. I knew I hadn't made her up; I don't believe in ghosts or apparitions—not then or now—and I couldn't imagine that my eyes were just playing tricks on me or that I suddenly started having hallucinations.

Nor did it help that no one I knew had ever noticed anybody matching her description either at school or at Garrison Park, although my friend Tommy Chartrand said he'd be sure to turn his "chick radar" to maximum if I thought that would help.

"So who's the babe, Lambert?" he asked me once after school. "She *hawwwt*? Totally do-able?"

I was horrified.

"Jesus, Tommy, she's gotta be like ten years old."

Tommy wasn't deterred. I'd once made the mistake of explaining to him that my dad had taken great pains to raise me as a gentleman—something Tommy found hilarious—and ever since he'd delighted in putting on shows of unrestrained depravity, then watching me cringe in revulsion.

"You done the deed yet, Lambert? You get into her pants at least?" he chided.

"Nice," I hissed in disgust. "Congratulations, Chartrand: you're now officially a pervert."

If I'd been living in a book or a movie, this would have been the point where I'd be discovering that Billie was invisible to everyone but me: there'd be a lot of funny looks and shaking of heads, and references to invisible friends and overactive imaginations. I was almost expecting it, getting my mind ready for the teasing and the arguments, but then I caught myself. This wasn't a children's story or a bad sci-fi flick: this was the real world. I just hadn't learned yet that reality is a lot more complicated than most people know.

*****

And then a few days later she showed up. Just like that, with no warning. One moment I'm on my way to pick up Vietnamese food around the corner—it was Takeout Friday—the next she's walking right next to me, as if she'd been there all along. For a fraction of a second I actually felt her presence before I saw or heard her: it was the warmth she gave off, like an oven door opening. That's probably why I didn't scream.

"You never sing. Why is that?"

"What??"

"Sing. You don't sing. Nobody here does."

It took a second for my brain to regain its full functioning. We'd stopped walking for a moment, and I took a moment to look her over. She looked the same: like, exactly the same, as if she'd been copied like a digital file that first day and then pasted into place each day after that.

Billie breezed on.

"I mean, I've stopped singing because people here give me funny looks and pay too much attention to me. Then again, it *is* awfully gloomy here. Maybe that's why."

"You're not from around here, are you? Ferguston isn't exactly a happy place."

That was putting it mildly. Ferguston was decidedly unhappy. According to my uncle Carl and long-time residents like Mr. Lovato, it was as if nastiness and misery had slid down into Ferguston—it's located in a depression, after all—taken root, and festered there over the decades. Crime—especially the violent kind—unemployment, and substance abuse were far above the provincial average. There was also an alarmingly high suicide rate, and a well-documented teen pregnancy problem. Ferguston sometimes felt like a war-torn city where all the buildings were left standing. You could also see it in many of the residents: a heaviness in the way people walked, a clipped impatience in the way they spoke, a cynicism directed at all forms of government and authority, and a deep suspicion of outsiders. Around Ferguston, nice things got trashed and broken things stayed broken.

I continued. "There are worse places, I guess, but if this isn't the armpit of the country, it's in the same area code. No, nobody sings."

The conversation that followed was typical of just about every exchange I would have with Billie, especially in the early going: sometimes confusing, at times fascinating, and, most often, frustrating. For one thing, it was nearly impossible to ask her anything because I could rarely get a word in edgewise. She'd really come out of her shell since our first encounter, and she was bursting with stuff to say. She'd often cut me off with a totally unrelated question, or correct me on something that I'd said, only to go on a tangent of her own.

Case in point. There's a placid little stream that runs beneath Lakeside Drive on its way to Garrison Park and Lake LeClair. As she followed me to pick up our takeout dinner that afternoon,

Billie couldn't resist sliding down to the water's edge and proceeded to leapfrog over the boulders that lined its banks, looking for whatever shiny object or slithering creature that might catch her eye. She beckoned me to follow her, but I declined. "My dad doesn't like me to climb on those rocks," I called to her. "Some of them are covered in algae and they get pretty slippery."

"Your dad won't know," she called back. "C'mon! There's all kinds of neat stuff down here."

"I don't know. He's got kind of a sixth sense about these things."

That did it. "What do you mean, a *sixth* sense?"

I sighed. Another explanation. "It's just an expression. I don't mean he's actually psychic. It means it's *as if* he has a special sense that tells him I'm doing something I shouldn't."

"Well it's a dumb expression!" she shouted back. She hadn't yet moved from the rocks and seemed quite content to yell at me from a distance. "People have a lot more than five or even six senses. I mean, I don't know about you, but I must have a dozen and a half."

I was already getting the feeling that the worst thing I could do was indulge her. I indulged her anyway.

"I thought there were just five: seeing, hearing, touch, smell, and taste."

Billie hissed and then went off on a tirade about how overly simplified that was, that just the sense of touch included five separate senses—hot, cold, pain, pressure, and itch—as did taste, and that your sight involved at least three, and what about others like the sense of balance, of movement, of time, of thirst and hunger and, and, and . . .

Nine-year-old kids weren't supposed to talk like that. Her family must have been real psychos.

She then bombarded me with her own questions, many of which made absolutely no sense. If it weren't for the grown-up way she spoke, you'd have thought she was what some people call "challenged." For example, she seemed to have no sense of what people did with their time or why. The idea of school baffled her, and yet when I told her that there was a law that required kids to go to school, she was mystified. "That's silly. What kind of person has to be told to learn? Doesn't everyone *want* to know as much as possible?" Dad was going love her. She continued, "And how is anyone supposed to learn anything shut away in a classroom? I need to talk to your father." Funny, I was starting to think the same thing.

The whole notion of work and jobs and earning money to live was totally beyond her. I know it can be complicated for some little kids, but Billie was close to my age. She watched transfixed as I paid Mr. Nguyen at the Mekong for the takeout, without saying a word, like she was witnessing some obscure ritual. The moment we stepped out she asked about the whole transaction and I did my best to answer, explaining to her that, as nice as it sounds, you can't pay for food or clothes or gasoline for your car with a song or a story.

The barrage of questions continued as we walked back to my house. They came out of left field, one after another, and were rarely connected. At times it felt like I was being interviewed, not like a celebrity but more like an anthropologist would interview an elder from some remote culture. Everything I said seemed to fascinate her, which was kind of creepy and flattering at the same time. She asked about everything: about me, about Ferguston, about the world. Some of it was really basic stuff, innocent "Why is the sky blue?" kinds of questions. She'd ask about what she'd seen, things she'd witnessed people do or say, simple gestures, the kind of stuff that any nine-year-old with a decent Internet connection and who doesn't live in a bubble would know already.

Some of Billie's inquiries were more philosophical in nature, having to do with humans and their place in the world. One of my favourite was why do people have so much loathing for creatures that are successful in human environments, like cockroaches, pigeons, rats, and racoons. Shouldn't we admire them? "Instead, people call them pests," she said, "and get grossed out when they see them. I even found out," she added in a near whisper, "that there are people whose job it is to get rid of them. Kill them, even!" I answered it as best I could, invoking issues like disease, destruction of crops, and damage to property, but I thought it was a great question and I knew I wanted to spring that one on my dad at some point.

Other times her questions were hard and I had no answer for them, questions that required more advanced knowledge of math, physics, chemistry, and geology than I could be expected to have for another ten years. Those freaked me out a bit because it didn't sound like she was just making them up to impress me, but more like she was educated enough to ask.

I was almost home when I finally got the chance to ask her what I'd been wondering since we met at Garrison Park.

"So, where are you from?"

She paused for a second. When she spoke, it sounded like she was being really careful.

"I . . . I can't tell you."

"Don't worry," I said. "I won't say anything. I mean, I can tell that you're probably from someplace else even though you don't have an accent, and I'm guessing that you must be homeschooled. Where do you come from?"

"Not here." A beat. "Not now." Her voice was quiet and decisive. It didn't invite further questioning.

I was disappointed at first with her avoiding the subject, but I figured she was a bit shy about herself and would eventually open up to me if I was nice to her and kept at it.

What I didn't realize was that she was providing me with the simplest, most honest answer to my question that she, or anyone, was capable of.

*****

Billie observation: "A woman and her kids were having a picnic in the park, and she was complaining about insects. She was saying, 'I tell you, these bugs are going to take over the world someday.' Somebody should tell her they already did . . . a very long time ago."

# 7

"New friend?" my dad asked over a steaming mound of rice and green curry. He had seen Billie and me together through the living room window. There was curiosity in his voice, and something that might have been relief.

Dad got disproportionately satisfied whenever he saw me with someone new. It didn't happen often. Although he knew me better than anyone, even he had trouble sometimes with the distinction between my being an introvert, quiet and happy with my own company, and a shy, socially awkward and misanthropic recluse. I didn't have a lot of friends. When Dad brought it up one time, I told him that I was "socially selective." I'd read that in a book someplace and liked the sound of it.

"'*Socially selective*'?" he'd replied. "Justin, your best friend is Tommy Chartrand, who eats his boogers, has questionable hygiene, and is a few fries short of a Happy Meal." To Dad, Tommy was a *South Park* character with less personality.

What Dad didn't get was that Tommy, like me, was the child of a single parent. His dad—a real Sith Lord by all accounts—left when Tommy was five, and he, his mom and his older sister Tyler were better off for it. Also like me, Tommy wasn't much of a talker. We could spend entire afternoons holed up in my room—me reading, Tommy playing *Blunt Force Trauma* on my X-Box—with barely a word passing between us. Tommy didn't care that my dad was a teacher at St. Marc or that I was biracial, things other kids found awkward. More importantly, whereas everyone in town knew me as the kid whose mom disappeared, making me a subject of community folklore, Tommy almost never brought it up.

I guess Dad was just happy I'd found someone else to talk to.

"Yeah. I met her about a week ago," I told him. "Her name is Billie," although I suspected her real name was a bit more exotic.

"Billie? Hmm." Something flickered in my dad's eyes for a moment then was gone. "She nice?"

"Yeah, she's nice. I don't think she has a lot of friends, though. She's a bit weird."

"How so?"

"Well, for one thing, she asks really bizarre questions. I can't tell if she's really stupid, really smart and a bit of a show-off, or just desperate for attention."

Dad grinned. "What sort of questions?"

"Well, today she asked me 'Are these the only colours you have?' What in the world could she mean by that?"

"Yeah, it's an odd question. Was she talking about your clothes?"

"Ha! That's a laugh. She's worn exactly the same thing each time I've seen her. I think she was speaking more generally." After a moment I added: "I think she's from someplace else."

"Well, maybe she's used to living in a brighter, more colourful place. It is a bit drab around here until all the leaves are out and the flowers are in bloom."

That sounded reasonable. Of course it didn't explain why she found it so dark on a bright sunny afternoon, or what she meant by there not being enough sounds to pronounce her name, but I let those issues pass for now.

"Where did you meet her?"

This was already shaping up to be one of our longest conversations in a while, and I was eager to supply details. I explained that this was the same kid I saw at Garrison Park, that she didn't seem to go to school but that I'd caught a glimpse of her outside my geography class, and that she seemed to just show up out of nowhere. I stopped short of mentioning the Greyhound bus or seeing her on TV.

"What do you know about her?" he asked, but I could tell his interest was fading.

"Nothing. She never talks about her family, or if she even has one, where she lives, where she comes from, nothing."

We sat quietly for a moment, eating and thinking. Dad was drifting again. Soon, he'd be far away, and I'd be pretty much alone for the rest of the evening. I tried a different tack.

"Oh, and she seems to like geology, among a lot of other things."

He bit.

"Geology? Really?"

"Oh, yeah. I don't think there's anything she's not interested in."

"Hm. Bring her over sometime. I'd like to meet her."

Bingo! Perfectly played. I couldn't wait to get these two in a room together. I wasn't sure what to expect, but if nothing else there would be a lot talking, and Dad would be totally present.

*****

On Saturday morning Billie and I were sitting on a bench in front of the main entrance of the new municipal building downtown. This was the same building that was being inaugurated when I saw Billie on the news a few days earlier. She was there when I passed by on my way to the library, as if she was waiting for me. It made sense: if she was looking for me on a Saturday, waiting to intercept me on my way to the library wasn't a bad strategy.

The municipal building was modern-looking compared to the other buildings around it: all glass and concrete and stainless steel. There was a courtyard with an abstract sculpture—which to me looked suspiciously like a bunch of lumpy pieces of concrete and rusted metal—plus some benches and a few newly planted trees. I found Billie in an open area near the front doors: it faced south and was bathed in sunlight, a perfect place for someone who doesn't like the shade. It was also sheltered from the wind—which would have been nice if it weren't so unseasonably warm for May—but sunlight would routinely bounce off the mirrored surface of the building's south face and then reflect off the windows of passing cars. These regular flashes of light got to be irritating after a while and made me wish I'd worn shades.

Billie continued to ask me about everything, while answers to my own questions were few and far between. She would either avoid the question, dismiss it as unimportant, or get distracted by her own thoughts and ask me another one. Even when she did provide an answer, it was often less than satisfactory.

"So, was that you I saw on a bus to Toronto on Monday?"

"Yeah. I was walking past the station and I wanted to know what all these people were lined up for. So I stood close behind this lady and before I knew it, I was on the bus. It was fun."

"Why were you alone?"

"Oh, did you want to come with me?"

"No, no, that's not what I mean . . ."

"I wasn't going to spend much time there."

"OK . . . But then I could swear I saw you on the news that same day. You were right here at the municipal building, at some kind of ribbon-cutting thing."

"Yeah, that's right. There seemed to be something going on and I liked the balloons."

"OK, but how did you get there so fast? From Toronto?"

"Oh, I came right back."

"Yes, but . . ."

She gave me this wicked little smile, like she was sharing an inside joke with me, except I had no idea what it was.

Another car drove past, and another blinding flash of light made me look away. When I turned back, Billie was staring straight ahead. There was a man getting out of a massive neon green pickup truck across the street, heading for the coffee shop next to the library. There was nothing special about either the truck or the man, and I was about to dismiss them both entirely when I suddenly noticed Billie: she was motionless, her gaze fixed straight ahead. Unlike the way my dad gets when he loses himself in his thoughts, she was completely focused, and yet she looked different somehow—paler than usual, unwell.

By the time I turned back the man was gone, but Billie's gaze remained fixed on the truck. It looked pretty new but was freshly splashed with mud. A matching neon green all-terrain vehicle with huge muddy tires sat in the box at the back. If there was anything else, it was covered by a big brown tarp. "Billie . . . What's wrong?" I asked after a moment.

"Do you know . . ." she began softly, then stiffened again. The door to the coffee shop swung open, and the owner of the truck lurched out, balancing a cardboard tray with two large cups and a box of doughnuts in one hand; he held a lit cigarette and a heavy key-chain in the other. Billie was barely breathing.

The man looked like a hundred other men I've seen around town. He was younger than my dad, and much rougher looking. Like a lot of people at this time of year, he was dressed for the outdoors: heavy boots, muddy camo pants, a sweat-stained tank top, and what my uncle Carl calls a Manitoba T-shirt—a quilted down-filled vest—over top of everything. He wore a red baseball cap low over his head so I couldn't see much of his face—he needed a shave—and his hair was long at the back and short on the sides. A thick chain—presumably attached to his wallet—looped out of his back pocket and was connected to his belt. I also noticed that he walked funny: his back seemed to curve backward too much, and he had a pronounced limp.

"What is it?" I asked again. "Is it that man? What about him?"

The man suddenly turned around as if he'd heard something, like someone had called his name, and looked straight at us. My stomach tightened instantly. For some reason I didn't like the look of him and didn't want him looking at me. I could just make out his eyes beneath the visor of his baseball cap, and at that moment I felt reasonably certain that this strange man was going to cross the street and come over to us. Come after us. I never found out if that was his intention because the next thing I heard was the man cursing, stringing together a colourful sequence of *câlisse-d'ostie-d'crisse-de-tabarnak!* from across the street as he spilled hot coffee onto himself, and then cursed some more, adding *maudite-marde-de-saint-sacrament-de-verrat-d'bâtard!* to the mix as he attempted to balance his tray, his cigarette, and his keys to get his door open. Billie watched silently, her body never moving and her expression never changing, as the man climbed into the driver's seat, slammed the door shut, started up the truck, and, throwing a final dirty look our way, pulled away from the curb. There was a squeal of tires as the truck suddenly veered right at a red light before it vanished from our view.

Neither of us spoke for a bit. My heart was still hammering in my chest, my mouth was dry, and it took a moment before I could remember what I'd been doing only two minutes before. Billie, on the other hand, was back to her old self. Her face was relaxed, the tenseness had left her body, and she looked perfectly content bathing in the early afternoon sunshine.

"Who was *that*?" I asked finally.

Billie shrugged, more with her head than her shoulders, but remained quiet. Like on so many other occasions, I was convinced she knew more than she let on. I wanted to probe more deeply because this time I felt it might involve my safety, but at the same time I was suddenly very tired and just wanted to go home. The library could wait. Plus I didn't like being subjected to the blinding flashes of light from passing cars.

"Look, I'm going to skip the library today. I'll see you around, OK?"

She looked at me and offered me the tiniest smile in response.

"OK, bye," I said getting up off the bench. Billie raised her hand out of her lap and gave me a little wave, but still said nothing. As she smiled that little smile and looked at me with those huge black eyes and her long pretty lashes, it began to occur to me that Billie was quite beautiful for a little kid, if no less strange.

I began to head back in the direction of home. Only a few steps away from the bench I could already feel the breeze from which I'd been shielded until just now. I thought of the strange man in the neon green pickup truck, how Billie reacted to him, and how quickly she recovered once he left. It was an odd moment, one that left me feeling a bit unnerved. She was a unique kid, frustrating at times but fascinating in so many ways, and there was a definite comfort in her presence.

From the corner of my eye I saw another flash of light. I stopped and turned back, thinking of asking her if she wanted to hang out someplace else, suddenly feeling good that I was going to spend more time with her, and then the sinking feeling upon seeing the suddenly empty bench behind me.

# 8

There used to be a big coffee-table book at the Ferguston Public Library called *Mimics*. It got pretty worn out over the years; personally, I must have borrowed it at least a dozen times, to say nothing of all the times I just leafed through it in the stacks. It was all about organisms whose bodies have evolved so well to blend in with their environment that they've become almost impossible to spot. All classes of animals have them: mammals, birds, reptiles, fish, insects, cephalopods. The book had page after page of full-colour photos where you tried to pick out the creature from its surroundings. Some were harder than others: the octopus on an outcrop of coral, the stick insect on a twig, the sea dragon—a kind of seahorse—swimming amongst the weeds in the Sargasso Sea, and my favourite—not the least for its name, *Uroplatus phantasticus*—the Satanic Leaf Gecko. Looking at these images, you knew the creatures were there, but they were so perfectly camouflaged you couldn't make out their shape. If you were patient enough, you might eventually spot a landmark of some kind, usually an eyeball, that would give the creature away but a quick glance would tell you almost nothing. Of course a picture in a book, where you can study it indefinitely, is one thing; out it the real world they must be close to invisible. For the longest time I felt Billie was like that: most of the time I saw only an average cute if slightly odd nine or ten-year-old girl. But there were times every so often when I couldn't help suspecting I was looking at something else entirely, that there was something I was missing that was hiding in plain sight right in front of me, camouflaged.

\*\*\*\*\*

As a kid I didn't know anything about military history, local or otherwise, so when Billie suddenly turned up at Garrison Park later that afternoon and asked me about the ceremonial cannons at the east entrance, I had to read the plaque. I explained to her that apparently there had been an Armed Forces base in Ferguston between 1919 and 1972, hence the name of the park. It was abandoned and all the buildings were taken down when the government decided it didn't need as many army bases anymore, and a park was built over where the base had been. The cannons— which I later learned were brought in from the United States and had never been used—were placed at the entrance of the park so people would remember that the base had been here, as well as to remember the soldiers from the area who fought in the wars during that time.

"But, what *for?*" she demanded.

"The cannons?" I asked. "They're weapons."

Nothing. A blank stare. I tried again, with a bit more detail.

"A long time ago, they were used in wars. You pointed them at your enemy and you put a cannonball—a big metal ball, I dunno, about this big—into it and using gunpowder you made an explosion that sent the cannonball toward your enemy."

"I know what wars are, and I know what a cannon is, Justin. I'm not an idiot."

"Oh." A beat. "Then . . . What's your question?"

"What are they for? Canons, weapons, wars."

*Really?*

"Uhhh . . . You mean why people fight? Is that what you're asking?"

"Yeah?"

"Well . . . I dunno. A lot of reasons, I guess."

A look. *Such as???* Then, rather than wait for an answer she plowed on. "You people fight all the time. Sometimes it's just two people, using just your hands and feet and stuff you pick up off the ground. Other times, it's whole big bunches of people shooting stuff at each other. They hurt each other and often the people around them and they don't care. Why?"

"Maybe someone does something the others don't like, or has something the others want," I suggested.

"That's crazy."

"Oh, I agree. But that's the way it goes, the way it's always gone. People go to war. People all over the world have fought for all kinds of reasons for thousands of years, and millions of people have died, and—"

She looked away from me, toward the lake. "I know, I know," she said. "I've seen . . ." and then stopped herself.

She was quiet for a while. I'd gotten used to talking to her like she'd lived in a cocoon somewhere and had never heard of lots of the things that I knew and took for granted. But until that moment I had treated it like a game: I was playing teacher, like my dad, except that I had only one student and I taught her every subject in the book. Until that moment, I had at least half believed that she was playing along as well. Looking at her now, I knew I'd been wrong. She wasn't playing. She was totally bewildered, and I felt horrible that I'd been the one to explain such a terrible thing to her. As an afterthought, I would have to remind myself to ask her what exactly she'd seen and who she meant by "you people."

"I'm sorry," I finally said. "It's just that I'm used to hearing about wars at school and on TV. They're terrible but they're common. Just this spring, a lot of soldiers from Canada—and at least one from right here in Ferguston—have been sent away to a place called Kandahar to fight a group of people called the Taliban. Some of these soldiers will never come home. Wars happen all the time, and there's not much anybody can do, or wants to do, to stop them."

"See? I don't get that."

Billie looked upset and completely baffled, but didn't insist on an explanation. Instead she wandered off, arms crossed, head down, in the direction of the lake. There wasn't much of a beach at this end, just a lot of coarse gravel that eventually gave way to larger rounded stones—cannonball-sized, I couldn't help noticing—and eventually a rocky shore that stretched out eastward for some miles. She walked as far as the bike path that followed the shoreline, and stood staring at the lake. I followed, wanting to be close to her, but not wanting to crowd her and forcing her away further.

The gentlest breath of wind was coming off the water. Gulls wheeled and screeched overhead, and a raft of mallards were paddling over to see what the shallows were offering in the way of food. There were a few other people around, and no small number of dogs, but for the most part they kept to the sandier areas of the beach or near the picnic tables toward the middle of the park.

At this end of the beach everything was still. I would have been satisfied to stand there next to Billie for a long time, just watching the birds, listening to the waves wash over the pebbles, and enjoying her warmth, not speaking. At the same time I was feeling bad that I'd caused her to walk away, and would have been just as happy if she'd start up with the questions again so we could resume our teacher/student routine. More than anything I wanted to undo our previous conversation, talk about anything else. In this place, she didn't need to hear about wars, or weapons, or the terrible things people do to one another.

"Is that what you think happened to your mom? That someone did something terrible to her?"

I didn't often think about my mom in those days. I never really knew her; most of my memories of her came from my dad. Every once in a while, she'd come up in a conversation: something would trigger a memory of her and he'd tell me a story of their time together before I was born, or when they were new parents, or some such thing. But these tended to get repetitive, the same story told the same way over and over, and they never succeeded in filling up the blank spaces in my mind about who she was. Also, talking about Mom was the surest way to make my dad drift off into la-la land, where I couldn't hope to reach him without having a tantrum. It's sad to say, but my mom was not a subject I spent a lot of time on.

That said, I have no doubt that thoughts of my mom were very near the surface at that moment. Though I don't remember Dad ever mentioning it out loud, there had always been more than a hint of something sinister in Mom's disappearance. There were newspaper clippings where the term "wrongdoing" and "person of interest" had been mentioned, although these were never fully fleshed out and nothing came of them. And now, with talk of war and weapons and the incomprehensible things that people do to others, thoughts of Mom couldn't have been far behind. Billie didn't read my mind so much as follow my thoughts through to their logical conclusion. Sadly, I didn't have enough information to provide a proper answer.

"I don't know," I said finally. "Again, you'd have to talk to my dad."

Billie nodded thoughtfully, then went silent, moving closer to the water. Even though there were benches nearby, she found a smooth enough spot on some boulders near the water's edge, and sat peacefully staring out at the lake, running her hands on the stony surface beside her.

"You were two when your mom disappeared."

"Yup."

"So you don't remember her very much, I guess."

"Nope."

"What do you remember?"

The words weren't near at hand and I had to think a bit. Billie didn't seem to care; she sat quietly, like she had all the time in the world.

"Well, you see," I began, "it's complicated. I'm not even sure my memories are my own. I've been told so many things by my dad and my mom's family, and I've got all these photos and videos on my computer. I can't be sure if what I remember are my memories at all."

"OK," Billie continued, not missing a beat. "What do other people say about her?"

From everything I'd heard—from my dad, my mom's family, her colleagues, her friends—my mom was the perfect ... everything: wife, mother, friend, daughter, sister, colleague, physician. She was brilliantly smart, kind, funny, compassionate, patient, wise, witty, dedicated and tireless at work, quirky in just the right way, and gorgeous to boot, with bright laughing eyes, a radiant smile, and what Dad called a very cute figure. She saw the positive in just about every situation, forgave without reservation, never lost her cool or complained or criticized unduly, and yet never took any shit. She was also reportedly a great cook, a talented musician, and could even have made a career—rumour has it—as a seamstress if medicine hadn't worked out.

In short, my mom was a quasi-divine figure with the benefit of having left behind tangible evidence of her existence. She was better than Jesus.

"Oh, you know, the usual: practically perfect in every way."

Billie smiled and nodded. I continued.

"I have this dream about her, every so often. I've been having it probably since I was six. I don't know what brought it on, originally—maybe a movie I saw or something I learned in school. Anyway, I've never told anybody about it, not even my dad. I'm not sure I would have even told a therapist if I'd had one."

Which makes what happened next so hard to explain. It all came pouring out, as natural as breathing, this dream of . . .

*. . . my mom on the beach at Garrison Park, the mom of my fantasies, her smiling face full of love and mischief, suddenly becoming this immense and beautiful living monument, like the Colossus of Rhodes or the Argonath in Middle Earth, while all the other kids in town are staring up at her in awe and rapt admiration. A fog bank suddenly sweeps in from the lake, obliterating everything, and I'm wandering alone, cold and afraid, calling for her, hearing voices of other kids and some are laughing, mocking—"Poor Justin can't find his mommy!"—until the fog begins to lift and the Wonder of the World that was my mom, there only minutes before and just beyond my reach, is gone, and the voices of the other kids and their parents are drifting away with the tattered remnants of the fog, saying how sad it all is, how terribly, terribly sad.*

\*\*\*\*\*

Billie was what you'd call "tactile." She would run her hands through and over just about everything: beach sand, tree bark, pine cones, surfaces that were smooth, or rough, or wet, or greasy, dried leaves, flower petals, steel benches, stone walls, water, mud, concrete, rubber, desiccated insects, discarded feathers, and every kind of fabric imaginable. It got so it became normal, just another weird thing she did. In fact, I didn't even mind when she started touching my clothes and even my hair. She was extremely gentle, and there was something about the heat she generated that I found comforting.

She resumed her stroll, scanning the gravel for objects of interest, which for her could be anything: an oddly shaped piece of driftwood, a bottle cap, the shell from a tiny snail, a random scrap of bone. She picked up a small black fragment of rock and brought it close to her face to inspect it. "Meteorite," she said. "Iron."

I stopped in my tracks. "What? *Really???*" Whatever leftover dark thoughts that may have been lingering in my mind evaporated instantly. That Billie had actually found a chunk of something that fell from space was huge. That she acted so casually about it was incomprehensible. "That's amazing!"

"Not really. There must be lots of it around. Something really big hit nearby a long, long time ago. This is just a tiny piece. Here." She placed the black stone in my hands. It was small, maybe an inch wide, charcoal grey, and looked like hardened putty.

"Wait, how can you be sure?" I asked. It occurred to me, if only briefly, that I was taking the word of a kid—a kid even younger than me who couldn't even grasp the basic concept of homework—for something I bet not one grown-up in a hundred would get right. Of course, given how badly I wanted it to be true, I wasn't going to take much convincing.

Instead of answering, Billie just gave a small one-shouldered shrug and continued scouring the beach. It was a shrug I recognized, one I'd learned not to question: it was exactly the shrug my dad used when he meant to say "Isn't it obvious?"

It didn't matter. I had a piece of a meteorite! I was holding something in my hand that was unspeakably old and had travelled unspeakably far. This was better than if I'd found a gold nugget. Dad was going to freak!

# 9

Convincing Billie to come to my house proved to be a lot tougher than I'd expected. As soon as I mentioned that maybe she'd like to come over for a bit, meet my dad, and possibly have some lunch, she stiffened. I was so certain she'd agree right away that I had to grapple for an argument to persuade her when she hesitated.

"Umm . . . I don't think I should," she said.

"Why not? My dad's really nice; he knows all kinds of stuff and he loves to talk. You'll like him." Then I added, "He's like me, only a lot smarter."

"No, you don't understand. I'm not really supposed to stay out too long."

"Yeah, you've said that before. What do you mean? In the park? With me? What?"

I could tell she was getting uncomfortable with the subject, and I considered dropping the whole thing, but it all seemed too weird.

"Are you afraid of strangers?" I continued. Then I remembered the episode in front of the municipal building: the man in the neon green pickup truck. "Not everybody is mean or dangerous, you know. Not even in Ferguston. What about other kids?"

Something in her body softened, just a bit. I pressed forward: "You hang with me, don't you? Well, it will just be me and my dad. And he's a teacher—he's really good with people, especially kids. He's kind of a big kid himself, actually. Plus we don't have to hang around with him much. I just want him to meet you. He'll like you, I promise."

I could feel her relenting. I knew I had her: she was a nerd, and the one thing that no nerd can resist is being in the presence of older, smarter nerds. I just didn't want to scare her off.

"You don't have to stay long. And we live close by."

"Good," she said finally. "Your way of getting around is not very efficient."

My mind didn't stay on that last comment very long. It certainly wasn't the strangest thing she'd ever said, and while I didn't know many kids her age who would ever use the word "efficient" in a conversation, I'd already reached the conclusion that Billie wasn't exactly ordinary. Plus, as we approached my house, my attention turned to the little blue MGB in the driveway.

"Cool!" I said. "My uncle Carl is here!"

*****

The car was old. In fact, it was already old when my uncle bought it years before. It was well taken care of for the most part, but you could see spots of rust here and there, and there was a crack in the windshield. Its black convertible roof was down and, as usual, Carl had left a mess inside: endless bits of paper, gum wrappers, coffee cups, a tangle of bungee cables, and the odd article of clothing. On the rear bumper there was a chrome plaque next to the licence plate, one of those Jesus fish but with feet sticking out the bottom and the word "Evolve" in the middle.

Billie didn't care about, or even notice, the car. She just stood in the driveway, staring up at the house with her big black eyes. "It's OK," I said. "Carl is great. He's like my dad only he manages to be cool and a nerd at the same time. He kind of looks like a wizard." Billie remained silent but offered no resistance when I touched her arm to gently urge her forward, and we moved up the driveway to the front door.

It always felt like a holiday whenever Uncle Carl came over to visit. He was the oldest of four, and even though he never married nor had any children, he made more than enough noise on his own to compensate. In the old days, you'd have called him a *bon vivant*, a lover of life: he loved to discuss, argue, and tell stories, especially when there was a lot of food and drink. He was a natural musician—he could play almost anything—and unlike my dad, he could sing. Whenever he came over, there was always music playing, coffee brewing, and voices engaged in lively discussion. In his later years he'd taken to smoking a pipe, and on those occasions when he'd visit us from Sudbury, the fragrant wafts of blue smoke were as sure a marker of his presence as his MGB in the driveway or his biker boots in the front entrance.

Unlike my dad, Carl was an authentic flower child from the '60s, and he still looked the part. He'd protested against the Vietnam War, demonstrated for civil rights, defended Indigenous people, the poor, the falsely accused, and the environment. Carl had degrees in both Criminology and Psychology and was near the top of his class in law school. Over his career he worked as both a prosecutor and public defender and—according to my dad—made friends and enemies in equal measure on both sides of the aisle.

Dad said that, no matter what his job was, Carl usually had better qualifications than anybody he worked for. No one knew the system better and he was about the best-connected person around.

Billie and I came in through the front door, stepping over Carl's huge black boots and his weathered violin case. Walking down the hall toward the kitchen I could hear voices speaking softly but, in typical Lambert fashion, fast and passionately. There were sounds of clinking glass and creaking of chairs on the hardwood floor, and the smell of something rich and meaty bubbling on the stove.

"Dude," Carl said when he saw me. We're not much for ceremony in our family, but I could tell he was really happy to see me. His long, angular form was leaning back in his chair, clad in a blue work shirt and faded jeans with the knees stitched over by hand. Gandalf in denim. Behind the whiskers was one of the best smiles in the world, and though I never saw him without the beard, it's the smile that made him look the most like my dad; that and the very Lambert way he used his hands when he talked.

"And you must be Billie," I heard my dad saying. I felt Billie getting closer to me; the warmth was unmistakable. I assumed she felt intimidated, but for just the briefest second something warm flashed in her eyes. It was there, then it was gone, and she fell into shy mode. Dad stood up and welcomed her as if she were a new student in his class: he was relaxed and friendly and completely charming, in a slightly goofy-dad kind of way. His public face.

"I'm Martin, Justin's dad, and this is my big brother Carl," he said while indicating the two empty chairs at the table. "You can join us if you like. We made some chilli." He then reached into the cupboard for two more bowls, plucked some spoons out of the drying rack, left them next to the stove, and seamlessly resumed his conversation with Carl.

I sat down on the chair nearest to Carl and watched as Billie took her cue from me, mimicking me almost exactly. As I listened to the grown-ups have their conversation, I stole an occasional glance in Billie's direction, watching as she wordlessly took everything in. This was going to be the first time I'd see her in any kind of social situation and I looked at it as a kind of experiment.

I leaned over to her and asked her if she wanted to try some chilli, and when she just stared at me in wide-eyed silence, I got

up, ladled a heap of chilli into a single bowl and brought it back
to the table with two spoons.

"I don't think I can eat that," she said in a near whisper.

"You want to try it and see?" I offered.

Billie gave me a vigorous head shake, and the first part of my
experiment was over.

I tried something different. "Billie found something really
cool on the beach today," I announced. Billie was staring down at
the table in front of her, the same thing I always did when a teacher
asked a question I didn't know the answer to, and I felt a pang of
guilt for drawing attention to her. "Oh yeah?" my dad asked her.
"What did you find?" Billie reluctantly looked up at him, then
quickly over to me for help.

"A piece of a meteorite," I said, trying to steer Dad's attention
away from Billie. I got up from my chair to squeeze my hands into
my front pockets, pulled the stone out of my pocket—along with
a generous helping of sand and lint—and triumphantly handed
it to my dad. I felt like a knight presenting his king with nothing
less than the Holy Grail. Dad turned it over in his hands, his
eyes level, and a tiny crease appearing on his forehead. I expected
arched eyebrows, even a faint whistle to indicate how impressed
he was, but he just turned it over between his fingers and handed
it off to Carl.

"What makes you think it's a meteorite?" my dad asked
finally. I was momentarily stung that Dad reacted to my finding
with skepticism rather than supporting my excitement with a
"Hey, that's really cool!" I knew deep down that he was just doing
what any good scientist does; it was something he talked about
all the time, but I wasn't prepared to have my bubble burst quite
yet. I looked over at Billie whose expression hadn't changed since
she arrived, and it occurred to me that I hadn't once doubted her
conclusion about the stone. She had pronounced it as something
extraterrestrial in a way that was matter-of-fact, like it was perfectly

obvious and not in the least unusual. Why couldn't she be wrong about this? She was just a little kid after all.

"It's metal," Carl said suddenly. "I bet if you were to smash it with a hammer it would only flatten."

Instant vindication! Thank you, Uncle Carl. "Metal! That's just what Billie said. Apparently, it came from a huge impact that happened near here a long, long time ago. Right Billie?"

Billie said nothing, but offered the weakest little nod as she turned her gaze to my father.

"Well, I don't know about that," Dad continued. "There's no impact crater around here. In fact, the closest big one I know of is about a thousand miles away, in Québec. Lake Manicouagan. You can see it on any map."

I could understand my dad's continued skepticism: Billie was just a strange little girl. On the other hand, I couldn't explain my own loyalty to her, except that she accepted my answers to her own questions without hesitation. I was holding my breath, hoping she had a rebuttal answer for my dad, when Carl finally settled the issue.

"You need to brush up on your region's geology, Martin. The entire Sudbury Basin was formed by an impact, even though you can't see it from the surface. It's the second biggest impact crater in the world and one of the oldest: two billion years or so. All the minerals that this region is famous for came up to the surface as a result of being struck by a huge meteor." He handed the stone back to me. "Now, as to whether this actually came from the meteor itself or if it came from everything that was blasted out of the crater during impact . . ." He left the thought unfinished, but whatever doubt it left wasn't enough to dent my conviction.

"Either way," Carl finished, "you've got a good eye, Billie."

*****

Eventually the conversation between my dad and my uncle had shifted to the local scene, then to the latest news in regional crime, misfortune, and random stupidity. Even though he lived an hour and a half away, Carl was a living encyclopedia of Ferguston's dark and seedy side. He liked to save the more colourful stories for when I was around, and—to my delight as a kid—he usually didn't censor them.

"So there's this guy, works in town pouring concrete. Big strong guy. Played Junior A hockey for a while and, as enforcers go, he showed some promise. Shredded both knees in separate dirt bike accidents and had to quit hockey, but he parlayed his modest notoriety into a job as a semi-celebrity bouncer. Got laid off because of anger issues—at The Pit, if you can believe that: tells you something about his temperament. Anyway, thanks to a connection he managed to find part-time work at McEachern Concrete; they're resurfacing some of the sidewalks downtown. The other day some drunken idiot former client of mine comes stumbling down Lalonde Street, sees the freshly poured cement, and can't resist the appeal of immortalizing his footprints in the sidewalk, with all the workmen standing right there. Somehow, he sneaks through them and gets three good tracks in before our wannabe Bob Probert crosschecks him with a rake. Guy literally flies out of his shoes straight into the path of Bunny Gingras's oncoming Silverado. Killed him instantly. Now our guy with the rake is charged with manslaughter. He's looking at the very real possibility of spending the next twenty years in prison, and all he can talk about is how this asshole had it coming to him for fuc—sorry, Billie, messing up his work, and what an awesome hit he put on him." Carl heaved an immense sigh that left him oddly shrunken for a moment. "This town."

There was an interlude of quiet shaking of heads, while no one spoke or looked at each other. Billie, meanwhile, looked perfectly relaxed and comfortable now that she was no longer the focus of attention. It therefore came as a bit of a shock when Carl, in an effort to lighten the mood, blurted out, "So, Billie, tell us about yourself. Where are you from?"

I could sense Billie immediately go into shy mode: her body tightened up, her eyes got big and her mouth got small. I felt terrible that my uncle had ambushed her like this, and I was about to protest or answer for her when she squeezed out her first words since we arrived.

"Where am I from?" Her voice was barely a whisper. Her eyes turned to me, as if looking for instructions.

"Yes, do you live nearby, hon?" my dad offered. Overall it seemed like a simpler question, so I didn't intervene.

Billie looked at me again before turning back to my dad. "Yeah. I guess. Sort of."

"Are you going to need a drive home?" my dad asked.

She shook her head. That's when I had a brainwave: "Can she stay over? Do you want to stay over?" Of course, what a brilliant idea! Why not? It was the May long weekend, there was no school on Monday, I'd done all my homework, and Billie was clearly homeschooled anyway, so what harm could it do?

"Doesn't bother me," my dad said. My heart soared. I couldn't remember the last time I had a friend stay over. "What do you say, Billie?" my dad continued. "Would you like to?"

Billie looked back and forth between me and my dad, and shook her head. "I really shouldn't."

"You could call your parents," I suggested. "Ask permission. I'm sure they wouldn't mind. Everyone knows who my dad is."

"It wouldn't be advisable," she said after pause.

*Advisable?* How many pre-teens said "advisable"? I saw my dad and Carl exchange grins at that one.

Then she added: "I can't stay out too long. It's not good for me."

"Are you sick?"

"No, I'm not sick. But—"

"Do you have a weak immune system, Billie? Are you afraid of catching something?" Carl asked.

She looked at Carl for a moment shaking her head, then looked down again to answer.

"It just isn't healthy for me to stay out in the world for very long."

"Did your parents tell you this?"

"I don't have parents," she said.

Wow. I didn't see that coming, but it seemed to explain a lot. I backpedalled as fast as I could. "Oh, man. I'm so sorry." My dad would have told me to leave it at that, but Billie had left a kind of window open just a crack, and the temptation to push through it was too much. "Who do you live with then? Relatives? Another family?"

"It's hard to explain," she said. "It's more like a whole collective."

# 10

I felt helpless watching Billie on the receiving end of a bombardment of questions from two grown adults, one of them an experienced lawyer. At first, I thought it was odd that Dad and Carl should show so much interest in what sounded to me like the ramblings of a young kid with an overactive imagination, but it became clear soon enough that something else was going on. Carl was probing for something.

To their credit, both Dad and Carl were very gentle, and tried their best not to make it a flat-out interrogation. They changed the subject from time to time, talked about their own experiences, cracked a few jokes, and involved me in the discussion. Eventually Billie began to loosen up, but still didn't make the process easy for anybody. Many of her answers were limited to "Sort of," "I guess," and "I dunno," and that didn't include the times when she just shook her head, shrugged, or said nothing at all. She'd have been a disaster on the witness stand.

I was initially so shocked when Billie said that she had no family that I didn't pick up on the significance of her following answer, that she lived with a "collective," even though Carl and my dad looked quickly at each other when she said it. When Billie was sounding more relaxed, Carl asked her where she lived precisely, to which she replied: "Oh, pretty much all over the place." The rest of the conversation was mostly between Carl and Billie, and continued along these lines:

"But when you go home, where do you go?"

"You wouldn't understand."

"OK. Can you tell me a little about where you live? What's it like?"

A pause. "It's not like here. It's so dark and cold here. Where I'm from it's always warm and bright and beautiful. There's no sadness or anger, no disease or hunger or war, there's no want for anything."

A beat.

"Wow. It sounds beautiful."

"It is."

"And you say it's nearby?"

"Yes."

"Can you show me? Can you take me there?"

"No."

"'No' you can't, or 'No' you won't."

"Neither. And I really should go soon. I'm not supposed to stay out for too long."

"We'll get you home soon, Billie. I just want to know about where you come from, your 'collective' as you call it. Who is in charge? Is there someone who takes care of you, who protects you?"

"No one is in charge." A pause. Then, "Protects from what?"

"I dunno. Outsiders, for instance. Other people, from outside of . . . wherever it is you live."

"You mean like you people?"

"Sure. Like us. We're outsiders, right?"

"I came here because I wanted to. I'm not afraid of you." At this Billie looked at me and offered a small smile for the first time.

"But who is in charge? Who makes the rules?"

Billie must have been feeling a lot more comfortable because she actually laughed at that. "There are no rules."

"But you said you're 'not supposed to stay out for long.' That sounds like a rule."

"That's not the same. It's for my own safety."

A pause. Dad spoke up this time. "How old did you say you are, hon?"

"Nine?"

"Do you have other friends your age?"

A head shake from Billie.

"Any friends at all?"

Another head shake. "Not really." My heart broke a bit at that.

Carl redirected his questioning to its original line, very lawyer-like. "So, coming here is risky for you?"

"Only if I stay too long."

"Are you afraid of getting sick if you do?"

"Something like that."

"And yet you came anyway."

She nodded.

"Why did you come, then?"

She looked at me, then back at Carl.

"I came for Justin."

\*\*\*\*\*

A few hours later, I was sitting in my room, listening in on the conversation Carl and my dad were having beneath my window. It was a warm evening and still pretty bright out. My dad and his brother were sitting on the patio finishing their beer. Billie had gone home a short time earlier—she declined the offer of a ride, insisting she lived nearby—and Carl had taken his fiddle and beer outside to enjoy the weather and unwind.

I loved the lonely sound of Carl's fiddle, even more than his guitar. There was something about it that sounded like history, like people and places long gone, times remembered in sepia photographs and antique shops and dusty old leather-bound books. To this day, whenever my dad speaks about history, the soundtrack that goes on in my head behind his voice is Uncle Carl's fiddle.

The screen door to the patio banged open as my dad stepped out, and Carl's fiddle fell silent. There was a pause as someone sipped a beer. A mourning dove picked up where Carl's fiddle had left off, then it too went silent.

"She's . . . interesting, don't you think?" Dad said.

"Yeah." A chuckle from Carl. "Cute, too. Sweet. And she's obviously very fond of Justin."

"You know who she reminds me of, in a way? Élise. The way she used to get when she was dead certain she was right about something."

"Funny, I was going to say she reminds me of you. She has some of your mannerisms down pat."

A pause.

"So, what do you think?" my dad resumed. "You think there's another fringe religious group in town? It's been a long time since the last one."

"It's the first thing I thought of: no family, more like a 'collective'? I dunno. They'd have to be pretty low profile. I'll ask around."

Another pause, and the clink of a beer bottle against a patio stone. Carl spoke up again.

"Whoever it is, they've done a pretty thorough selling job on her. She really believes she's living in heaven on earth."

"Do you think we should alert someone?"

"Like who? The police? Children's Aid? There's no evidence that the kid is being abused or neglected. I'm a little concerned with her high temperature, and especially her eyes: dilated pupils like that are often a red flag for drug abuse, but she doesn't show any other symptoms. In fact, aside from looking . . . I dunno . . .

a bit tired, she seems physically and emotionally in good health. She's a bright kid, too. A bit sheltered maybe but sharp as a razor."

"It's odd," Dad said. "She says that she doesn't have any friends, and is worried about getting sick if she hangs out too long, but at the same time she seems to have free rein to come and go as she pleases. Unsupervised. Plus, don't you think it's a bit strange for people who are obviously successful at staying away from the mainstream to live so close by?"

"My sense is that we're dealing with a very small group, maybe even a single household, hiding in plain sight. That would explain their apparent proximity. They must be few in number, otherwise people would have noticed."

"Well, whoever they are, Billie seems awfully protective of them. She's not about to lead us to them."

"Not if she can help it."

"Another thing, something Justin mentioned before. When they first met, she seemed to know a lot about him already. Makes me think she's been interacting with more people than she's letting on."

"Yeah, I thought about that. But then, I hate to say it but you and Justin are kind of celebrities around here. She wouldn't have to go far to get info on you. Probably the adults who are caring for her have filled her in. If they're locals, and there's every reason to believe they are, they'd know all about your history. You afraid Billie is going to try to recruit him? Attempt to 'save' him, or something?"

"I dunno. But one way or another I'm going to have to talk with him, make sure he keeps his eyes open."

# 11

The next day was Sunday so I slept in until 9:30. I was awakened by the smell of breakfast cooking and the sound of Carl's fiddle. Stumbling into the kitchen I saw a stack of pancakes next to the stove and my dad laying out strips of glistening bacon onto a plate. The smell of fresh coffee was intoxicating.

"Good timing, dude," my dad said. "You can set the table."

Still barely half awake, I gestured in Carl's direction. "Wha . . . ?" I croaked in weak protest. My uncle sat with his fiddle, grinning on the opposite counter from Dad.

"Sorry," my uncle said. "I'm providing the entertainment."

There are certain fundamental truths involving breakfast that my dad and I lived by. One is that the best breakfasts involve syrup; that morning's was no exception. Another is that bacon is, unequivocally, finger food. Third, giving coffee to a twelve-year-old is perfectly acceptable, provided it's tempered with enough cream and sugar.

I was halfway through my pancakes when Dad brought me into the previous evening's conversation with Carl.

"Has Billie ever talked to you about religion, or shared some, I dunno, unconventional views about the world?"

"No. She doesn't really 'get' religion." That was putting it mildly. Then, after a second I added, "You think she's part of a cult, don't you?"

"Well, it's crossed my mind. You have to admit, it would explain a lot."

In fact, it explained almost everything. It explained how she seemed so smart about some things on one hand and yet so ignorant about the workings of the real world on the other. It explained the way she talked about the rest of society, as if she weren't really a part of it. It explained the secrecy around her home life, and why when she did talk about it, she described it like some kind of paradise. Of course it didn't explain a few odd things, like her strange eyes, or her high temperature, or the way she seemed to just show up out of nowhere, but neither did those things exclude the possibility that she lived with a cult.

We sat quietly for a while. The wall clock in the kitchen was ticking way too loud for my liking, so I was happy when Carl picked up his fiddle again. He plucked it once or twice then let it go silent.

Dad finally spoke up. "All the same, I'd still like to know: have you ever seen anyone hanging around Billie, or lingering nearby when you were together . . . someone who looked a bit, shall we say 'sketchy'?"

"No," I said. Then I reconsidered. "Wait a minute. Yeah, I did actually. Yesterday. I met up with Billie downtown near the library. We were sitting in front of the new municipal building, just hanging out, and there was this man. I think he really scared her, because all of a sudden she got all weird—didn't move or say anything."

"Can you describe this man?" Carl asked.

I thought a moment, trying to visualize what was really just a mere moment the day before. "Well," I began, "he was younger than either of you; I'm not sure how old. He was wearing a baseball cap so I couldn't really see his face too well. He had that funny haircut that you talk about: short in the front and long in the back. You call it Hockey Hair."

Carl almost did a spit take. "A mullet. Also called the WWF cut. Gee, really? In Ferguston? What are the odds?"

"Yeah, *that* really narrows it down, doesn't it?" Dad was grinning. "What else?"

It was good to hear them laugh again. I perked up. "I dunno, he looked pretty average. He was coming out of a coffee shop. It looked like he'd just been off-road. He had a bright neon green pickup and a matching green ATV in the back. It was all muddy."

I sensed the mood change immediately, as if the temperature had dropped ten degrees. Neither my dad nor Carl was smiling anymore. "What colour was the pickup, J?" Carl asked.

"Green," I replied. "Neon green."

They looked at each other for a moment, then back to me.

"Did you notice anything peculiar about this man?"

I thought for a second. "Uh-huh. He walked funny. Bad limp, and his back was . . . I dunno . . . arched backward."

Something seemed to have settled onto the two men, a confirmation of sorts.

"Justin," my dad said. He was speaking slowly, carefully. It was a tone I almost never heard from him; it was almost like when I get into trouble, except his eyes were gentle. "Did the man do or say anything to you?"

"N-No. He didn't do anything, really. He just stared at us, and I thought for a second he was going to come over and talk to us, and that scared me a bit, but then he spilled his coffee on himself. Then he just swore a lot, got into his truck and drove away."

Carl picked up the questioning. "Have you ever seen this man before? Did he seem in any way familiar? Think about it. Take your time."

I didn't need to. "No. I mean he looked like a lot of people around town, you know?" Carl nodded, so I continued. "But there was nothing about him that seemed familiar." I was thinking back to the day before. Then I added: "You should ask Billie. By the way she reacted, it was like she knew who he was. And she was scared."

Dad and Carl looked at each other again. "We'll have to talk to Billie," Carl said. The fact that my uncle was so interested in this man was really creeping me out. He was a public defender and had worked for a while as a Crown prosecutor: he knew a lot of bad people. "Did she say anything at all to indicate how she knew him?"

I thought back again. "No. She started to ask me something, but then was quiet. I really got the feeling that she was afraid of him. I would never have noticed him at all, but Billie looked like she'd seen a ghost."

Dad and Carl were quiet.

I was almost afraid to ask. "Who is he? Is he a cult leader or something?"

Dad and Carl looked at each one last time, and Carl gave a shallow nod, took a deep breath, and began.

"No. His name is David Raymond and he's been bouncing around the region all his life. He's never had a full-time job since I've known him, or any kind of formal schooling beyond the seventh grade. Mostly he lives off the money he inherited from his father. His dad—Luc Raymond, a real piece of work in his own right—was hurt on the job at the lumber mill years ago and then sued his employer. Some people say he actually injured himself deliberately, and I wouldn't have put it past him. Anyway, they settled out of court and old man Raymond went home with a multi-million-dollar settlement. He didn't live long enough after that to blow it all; David grabbed what was left and he seems intent on spending his way into an early grave."

"No such luck yet," my dad muttered.

"What do you mean?" I asked.

"Well, it seems David likes toys that go fast. In the past twenty years he's bought, and trashed, pickup trucks, dirt bikes, ATVs, speedboats, personal watercraft, and snowmobiles. He crashes them, rolls them, sinks them, and drives them up trees and over cliffs, and somehow lives to tell the tale. He must have a list of injuries a mile long, almost as long as his rap sheet. You said he walked funny?"

I nodded.

"Multiple back and limb injuries, and a cracked hip, plus god knows how many concussions. It's like he's trying to kill himself but the boy just can't seem to get it right, and the province keeps footing the bill to put him back together."

Dad made a hissing noise and shook his head. "Asshole."

Carl continued. "Yep, it seems the only place David Raymond has visited more than the hospital emergency room is jail, which probably explains why he hasn't killed himself by now. He's about thirty-two years old, give or take, and he's spent almost half his life in and out of jail. He started off with petty theft, B&Es, drug charges; moved on to drunk and disorderly, common assault, larceny, and some drug trafficking. From there he went on to weapons charges, aggravated assault, and extortion, not to mention suspicion of aggravated sexual assault and manslaughter, but those last two were never proven. And I'm probably forgetting a bunch of stuff."

Carl sipped his coffee, and spoke up again. "He also has known connections with white supremacist groups and motorcycle gangs. He makes for an obviously attractive recruit: a non-existent moral compass and access to lots of cash."

"How come you know so much about him?" I asked. It seemed strange, even for Uncle Carl, to have so much info on some random guy, even if he wasn't exactly a model citizen.

"I've worked in the system for years. I'm supposed to know these things. And this guy has had a bad reputation for a long time. We've been keeping track of him since he was a teenager."

My dad chimed in. "Justin, you have to promise me that if you ever see this man again, whether he sees you or not, you'll tell me right away. And if he ever comes near you and attempts to talk to you, you'll get out of there. Promise me."

"Sure, Dad," I said. "Of course. But what would he want with me?"

Dad took a deep breath, and actually moved his chair so he could get closer to me. I felt I knew what was coming, and it scared me so bad I thought I'd be sick. Carl jumped in before Dad could say anything.

"Ten years ago, he was picked up and questioned by police on a missing person's case. At the time the cops referred to him merely as a 'person of interest,' but we all knew they suspected foul play and that he was the prime suspect. Problem was that there was not enough evidence and the cops had to let him go. The accusation has hung around him like a bad smell ever since and he's pissed about it."

"But what does that have to do with me?" I pleaded. I was almost in tears. "I don't even know who he is!"

"He knows who you are, Justin," my dad said. "We suspect he's responsible for the disappearance of your mother ten years ago."

# 12

I suppose it wasn't a conversation my dad would have chosen to have with me so soon: he has a talent for procrastinating, and I was only twelve at the time. Still, looking back I guess he found enough of the story had come out already that he couldn't wait any longer to fill in the gaps; plus he had Carl on hand to provide details, and together they must have figured that I was mature enough to handle it. There was a lot to take in.

What I'd known up to that point about what happened to my mom was the basics, what almost everyone in town knew. On a November evening nine and a half years earlier, Mom went to a dinner party at the home of some friends of hers. Her hosts were Doug and Irene Campbell; Doug was my mom's boss at the local hospital—the Ferguston Regional Health Centre—and he and Irene had become really good friends with my mom and dad. In fact, the Campbells were instrumental in bringing my parents to Ferguston and starting a life there: they helped them get a deal on their house, helped my dad find a job at St. Marc, opened up all kinds of useful connections around town, even loaned them money when they were getting started. Dad still kept in contact with Irene as much as possible, but after my mom disappeared Doug began to pull away; being one of the last people to see my mom, it seemed Doug somehow felt responsible for what happened to her and couldn't let go of his guilt. It was really very sad.

My dad didn't go to the dinner that evening, although he had planned to right up to the last minute. The babysitter my parents had booked for the occasion, Francine Gauthier, had to cancel because she got hurt at hockey practice and she had to go to the Emergency—which is where Mom worked, ironically enough—to have her ankle X-rayed. I was unwell that evening too; Dad said I was running a high fever, and that night I was too sick even to cry. Mom almost cancelled her evening out and there had even been talk of driving me to the ER, but Dad talked her out of it and encouraged her to take the evening off. After checking on me one last time between 6:30 and 6:45, she left the house.

By all accounts she had a lovely time at Doug and Irene's. She had a delicious dinner of whitefish and wild rice, skipped the wine when offered and drank sparkling water instead. At around 9:30, she called my dad from the Campbells' home phone to tell him she'd be leaving in less than ten minutes, which, according to Irene Campbell, she did. Her last words to him were "See you soon."

When she still hadn't come home forty-five minutes later, Dad started getting inklings that something was wrong. The first thought was that Mom had had car trouble in a remote area. The Campbells lived in a beautiful home about twenty-five minutes northwest of town, on a side road that leads into a wooded area; their closest neighbour at the time was more than a kilometre away. Back then, it was a virtual dead zone for cell service. A quick call to Irene confirmed that mom had left some time earlier, at which point Doug went out in his own vehicle and combed the local roads for over an hour. Then, just before 11:00, something happened that would haunt my dad for ten years: he received a very brief call from my mom's cellphone. The call lasted only a few seconds and was mostly just interference, which was common in those days. He told police later that there was nothing to indicate that she was panicked or frightened, but that it was hard to determine anything because of the poor quality of the connection.

My dad describes the next forty-eight hours as the worst of his life, worse than anything any person should have to endure. He spent the rest of that night on the phone with the police, the Campbells, the hospital, anybody he could think of. He would have put me in the car and driven all over the region looking for Mom if the cops hadn't talked him out of it. Even then, Doug had to come over and give him a sedative because Dad was nearly hysterical. I spent most of that time with Irene, who took a couple of days off work to take care of me. When the fever broke, apparently the first thing I said was "Where's Mommy?"

The next days, weeks and months were a mess for Dad. The school granted him as much time as he needed to deal with everything, which consisted of endless interviews with the local press, desperate pleas on TV and radio to everyone within 150 kilometres, and lots and lots of driving around. The community got involved in the early going, and big search parties were organized with people fanning out in all directions—using the Campbells' home as the starting point—looking for any trace that might lead to Mom. Of course so much of the area around town, particularly toward the north and west, is dense woodland that is difficult to search in the best of conditions: in the cold and wet of mid-November, it must have been dismal.

Thrown into the mix were relatives from both sides of the family who came to help in the search effort, to lend Dad a hand, and get some answers. Mostly they kept my dad sane, and in this respect, they proved to be indispensable. They ran errands, made phone calls, organized searches, cooked meals, looked after me, and basically helped Dad keep it together. For the most part they stayed at our place: in spare rooms, on couches, wherever we could fit them.

Those early days were genuinely hellish for everyone. In particular, I think about my mom's dad, Grandpapa François, who arrived a week after Mom's disappearance. Although he was as discreet and soft-spoken as always, Dad says there was a resolve in his manner that left no doubt of his intention: he was not leaving Ferguston without his daughter, dead or alive. He ended up staying for over a month, eventually heading back to Montreal just before Christmas, weary and demoralized. Dad called him regularly with updates after that, and while we continued to visit my grandparents a few times every year, Grandpapa didn't return to Ferguston for a decade.

The discovery of Mom's Rav4 two weeks after her disappearance was the one and only break in the case. It was found by a pair of hunters on a remote forest road some forty kilometres northeast of town, far beyond the established searched radius. The road itself was completely overgrown, almost invisible, and wound its way through a huge wooded property belonging to an investor from Toronto named Collins who hadn't been there in years and who had to be reminded by police that he even owned it.

Sadly, the initial excitement surrounding Mom's car was short-lived. A new sweep was carried out from the spot where it was found, but despite a renewed interest in the case and the added urgency of the coming winter, few volunteers could be coaxed into scouring the forest, brush and high grass in the chill drizzle of the late Northern Ontario fall. A brief and half-hearted hunt was undertaken and no new evidence was turned up. The police carefully explained to my dad that given the remoteness of the location, they now had to consider that the vehicle was dumped there deliberately in an effort to hide it. This was the first direct suggestion my dad heard of that the police were considering foul play. Of course, he would eventually learn that not only had the cops been thinking for some time that a crime had been committed, they even had a prime suspect.

In the early days of the investigation, the police interviewed pretty much everyone my mom knew, which naturally included most of the staff at the hospital, especially the Emergency Department. It came out in due course that a few days before she disappeared, there had been a bit of an incident at the ER in which Mom was implicated. She hadn't told my dad about it, presumably because that kind of thing happened all the time. It involved a well-known troublemaker and drug-seeker who came in one evening complaining about his back and demanding painkillers. When he was turned away by the nurses at the ER, he began to kick up a fuss, demanding to see a doctor. My mom came over and repeated exactly what the nurses had just told him: that the Emergency Department wasn't a Shoppers Drug Mart, that they'd all had it up to there with his repeated pleas for meds, and to leave the ER so they could take care of people who genuinely needed help. The man made a bit of a scene, hurled a few racial slurs and vague threats my mom's way, and left before hospital security guards could close in. No formal complaint against the man was ever made, as he was well known to everyone and generally considered harmless. He could be counted on to make an appearance every few weeks, either with some fresh injury to be treated or demanding drugs. He was known to police as well, and while he had yet to earn the notoriety he would get in the years to come, David Raymond quickly became the first and only suspect in the case of my mom's disappearance.

*****

It seems David Raymond had been a really bad kid before he became a really bad man. Dad says that's hardly surprising considering his pedigree. Luc Raymond, David's father, was by all accounts a paranoid, violent buzz saw of a human being prone to bouts of drunken rage, who would express his anger on his wife and only son with his fists or whatever household object was handy. After four years of physical, verbal and psychological abuse, Shelley-Anne Séguin had decided that enough was quite enough, thank you very much, and had the good sense to hightail it out of Ferguston, leaving her pit bull of a husband, their already troublesome three-year-old son, and the name of Raymond far behind.

As Luc had about as much aptitude for parenting as a goldfish has for calculus, David spent the next thirteen years of his life splitting time between various foster homes and juvenile detention facilities, periodically turning up at his father's house for short intervals when he got desperate enough for food and shelter. After a while, Luc shipped him off to live with the child's grandmother up north, a move that likely did little except shorten Grandmaman Raymond's life expectancy by a decade. In spite of Eugène Raymond's best efforts, the eighteen months David spent in New Liskeard, Ontario, were far too little and woefully too late to convince him that attending school had any benefit, that there were other ways of getting what you wanted in life besides stealing it, and that there were alternatives to deception, intimidation, and brutality when dealing with other people.

David returned to his father's house for good when he was sixteen, after old man Raymond received an out-of-court settlement—rumoured to be in the millions—from his employer following a horrific workplace accident. There were persistent rumours that whatever happened at the sawmill that day was only an accident because Luc's attempt at tampering with company equipment—so that he could later sue the owners—went disastrously awry. Of course the sabotage couldn't be proven conclusively and the gruesome nature of the accident drew so much unwanted publicity that, in the end, Luc got what he wanted. And although it did cost him most of his right leg and a sizeable chunk of his right hand, he did get the unexpected bonus of never having to go back to work. Meanwhile, he benefited from the return of his son who could run errands for him in brand-new vehicles Luc couldn't drive himself. With Luc's mobility severely impaired, the only abuse David had to endure from his father now was the verbal kind.

Luc, meanwhile, was spiralling deeper into batshit craziness. Despite his considerable resources he spurned all forms of rehabilitation, choosing instead to sequester himself in the squalor of his home, chasing away any social workers, public health nurses, former work associates—he didn't have friends—or other unfortunate do-gooders sent to check in on him—they were few—and spending his time making paranoid and abusive phone calls to his former employer, the media, city council, his lawyer, anyone he could think of. Every so often the walls would close in on him enough to drive him out of doors, and Carl laughed at the memory of Luc Raymond cruising the back roads in his wheelchair, sticking out his mangled thumb to passing vehicles for a ride, then raising his intact middle finger and cursing like a drunken sailor with Tourette's at everyone who had better sense than to stop.

Old man Raymond would eventually drown in a shallow pond behind his home, apparently after getting thoroughly shitfaced and wandering off too far in his wheelchair, which then got stuck in the mud and upended in three feet of water. His son found his half-frozen body on a cold and wet April morning over a week later, and mourned the old man's passing by throwing a huge party and buying a new pickup truck and two snowmobiles.

By the time he was in his early twenties, David Raymond had taken to calling himself D-Ray and was running with a crew of a half dozen or so fellow knuckle-draggers who called themselves the Vipers. They would have liked to be a metal band if only one of them had talent, so instead they limited their activities to drugs, booze, and vandalism. Police regarded them as one gangbanger wannabe and his band of blunt instruments: a general pain in the ass, but not really dangerous.

Continuing with his band analogy, Carl says that eventually the Vipers split up, mostly over "creative differences." Some members tried unsuccessful solo projects and ended up in jail. Others tried to reform the gang under a different name, but if you can imagine that D-Ray was the smart one in the Vipers, it's not hard to figure out how inept the rest of them were by themselves. D-Ray, meanwhile, had fallen into a pattern of buying whatever fast-moving, gas-guzzling vehicle tickled his fancy, trashing it because he couldn't be bothered to read the owner's manual and learn to drive the thing, and eventually ending up in hospital with a variety of broken bones. His doctor would prescribe him painkillers, which D-Ray must have either popped like Skittles or sold to his buddies for quick cash, because he got to be an all-too-frequent visitor to the hospital Emergency Department, complaining of terrible pain and in need of pharmaceutical relief.

This is what he was doing when he confronted my mom a couple of days before she disappeared, and which he suddenly stopped doing immediately after.

# 13

I went to bed early that evening, and spent the next few hours alone in my room struggling to process everything my dad and uncle told me about my mom. I now had to consider the very real possibility that not only was her disappearance the result of a crime, but a crime committed by someone who was known around town, someone whom I'd seen.

I wasn't sure how to feel: angry that somebody could ruin the lives of so many people so easily and get away with it; excited that, with a suspect known to police, just one break in the case could result in the guilty person being apprehended; scared that this terrible and dangerous person actually knew who I was; injured because such an awful thing had been done to me and my dad on purpose; sad because the new details of the story somehow made my mom closer, more real; betrayed that the system that I had intuitively trusted—where grown-ups in positions of authority made sure people followed the rules and punished those who broke them—a system that my own father, as a teacher and especially my uncle as a lawyer, were a part of—failed so completely; and, finally, helpless, because if the police couldn't do anything to put this man away for what he did, what could I do? I was just a kid who spent his days with his books and his computer, reading about past times and faraway places. I wanted to cry, to explode in a fit of anger, and I couldn't do either because everything—my energy, my anger, my fear, my sadness—had been drained away, drawn out in a single, prolonged blow. I felt like a deflated soccer ball.

Eventually I drifted off to sleep to the sound of a police siren, an all-too familiar part of our small town's nightly soundtrack.

*****

Monday was Victoria Day, so I slept in. Typically, on the morning of a holiday I liked to set my alarm to go off at the usual time, about 7:00 a.m., just so that I could savour the satisfaction of turning it off and going back to sleep for another three hours.

That morning was no different. Eventually I snapped awake just before 10:00 and simply stared at the ceiling, replaying the conversation from the day before for what seemed like hours before finally getting up. As much as I didn't know what to do with myself, I did know that I couldn't sit still in my room. I needed to do something, to go somewhere, to make sense of things. I got dressed right away—normally unthinkable at this hour on a holiday—grabbed an apple instead of sitting down to a bowl of cereal, and left the house as quickly and as quietly as I could.

I didn't want to talk to anybody, and even telling my dad that I was going outside would have involved some degree of conversation: "Where are you going?" "I don't know." "When are you coming back?" "I'm not sure." "Will you be back for lunch?" "Maybe." "Are you OK?" It's that last one that I wanted to avoid the most. The last thing I wanted to do was talk about my feelings. I just wanted to feel them in quiet, and explaining that to my dad would have been complicated. I was only twelve and didn't have the language for it, and Dad wouldn't have been satisfied with "I don't really want to talk about it." He would have sat me down.

Dad wasn't always the most effusive person at home, but I was all he had in the world. He loved me and worried about me, and would gladly become more talkative if he knew I was troubled by something. He couldn't have helped it: he was a Lambert, a fixer.

It was a bright cloudless morning and promised to be another brilliant day. I had a jacket on to ward off the morning chill, but I knew I'd soon be tying it around my waist: it was unseasonably warm for the third week of May. Hard to believe that only six weeks earlier we were getting pelted with thirty centimetres of snow, eighty-kilometre-per-hour gusts, and a wind chill of minus are-you-fucking-kidding-me. That morning I left my bike in the garage: my mind required that I walk, somehow. I couldn't remember deciding on my eventual destination; my feet had taken over and the rest of me was just along for the ride.

I passed through the cannon gate at Garrison Park walking west, holding to the bike path as it wound its way under the trees, with the lake to my left. The park was deserted except for a single jogger and his dog, and they would soon be out of sight. I was in no hurry, but my pace never slackened. I felt like I was being driven somewhere, and I was as powerless to change my speed and direction as I would have been as a passenger on a bus.

I half-expected to see her there, up on the play structure where I'd seen her before, staring out at the lake from the crow's nest in her purple hoodie. Maybe more than half-expected. Billie was the only person that I cared to talk to at that moment, if only because she'd be such a distraction. I wouldn't have to talk about what I was feeling: I'd be too busy fielding her endless random questions. I knew that the key to getting your mind off something wasn't to do something mindless, like mowing the lawn or shovelling snow or even taking a walk by yourself: you need to do something mind*ful*, and replace what's currently on your mind with something else that will keep it just as busy. The one thing you could say about Billie is she kept your mind occupied.

As I approached the play structure from the southeast end of the park, I could see she wasn't there. There was, instead, a huge flock of starlings mulling around in the sandpit. It had been a long time since I'd seen such a large gathering of starlings. There had to have been well over a hundred, maybe several hundred, covering the sand, lining the crossbeam of the swings, and roosting in the young birch trees that had been planted only a few years before.

There was also something faint but distinctive in the air: sweet, pleasant, like a bakery. Her smell.

"I must have just missed you," I thought aloud.

Oddly, there was not a single bird on the ship, a fact that I found both comforting and disquieting. They showed no signs of alarm as I got nearer to the sandpit: either they hadn't noticed me or they simply didn't care. The fact that they weren't flying off got creepier and creepier as I approached, and I decided to take the long way around the sandpit to get to the play structure rather than walk straight through the flock. Somehow, I was convinced that if I'd continued on, I would have waded right into them, ankle-deep in twitching, pecking starlings rustling around by the hundreds in all directions, unperturbed by my presence. That would have been just too much for my already reeling mind to handle.

I climbed up the rope ladder of the center mast all the way to the crow's nest, and settled down into my usual spot . . . our spot, now. It was going to be a warm day again despite some clouds that were moving in, and on this holiday Monday the park would be starting to get busy within the next couple of hours. I was happy to claim this place while I could. I had a lot of thinking to do.

I closed my eyes and listened to the lake in front of me. There was a comfort in its permanence, its consistency, the regular lapping of its waves, like the breathing of some giant sleeping organism. Its rhythms were regular and utterly predictable: freezing and thawing, fed over the millennia by creeks and streams and rain and melt water, and countless generations of fish and insects and birds that hatched and lived and mated and died, to be consumed again and reprocessed by its waters and sediments. This was a process that was governed by simple physics and chemistry. I could get my head around those.

Ferguston, on the other hand, confounded and angered me. I sat in the crow's nest with my back to the town, not wanting to acknowledge its existence. I resented Ferguston. I resented its streets, its buildings, its parking lots, and its power lines. I hated it for creating a person like David Raymond. I hated it for betraying my mom, who had come to work at a hospital, to help people who were sick and hurt and distressed, and was disappeared for her trouble. I was beginning to learn that there was a whole underside to this place that I'd never suspected, and had it not been for a strange girl who was clearly from someplace else I would never have known about it. I didn't have a clue where she was from or whether or not she lived with a cult, but from the few things Billie had told me about her home I began to think it was a much better place.

For all of Billie's strangeness, I was also starting to realize that we had a lot of things in common: our understanding—or maybe our lack of understanding—of the darker nature of the world was one.

I thought about my dad and why he persisted in living in a town that took away his wife. Why didn't he leave, start over somewhere else, someplace better? Surely it wasn't for work: he was an excellent teacher, as bilingual as they get, and would have no trouble finding a job anywhere in the province. I doubted it was for me: I didn't have many friends so there wasn't much attaching me to the place, and because my marks were good, I could be dropped into pretty much any other school without difficulty. As far as family was concerned, there was only Carl who lived nearby, if an hour and a half's drive can be considered nearby. Dad's sister Suzanne lived in Ottawa with my grandparents, Jeannine was in Toronto, and all of Mom's family was in Montreal. The last thing

I wanted was for him to become one of these sad, bitter people who just got used to wearing Ferguston's misery on their bodies. We could go to any one of those big shiny cities to the south and east and begin again, forget about this godforsaken place with its mosquitos and brutal winters and desperate angry people tearing around in their pickup trucks.

But the more I thought about it, the more I knew this was impossible. Maybe it was something he could have done if Mom was still around, start a new chapter in a new city, maybe even have another kid. But Dad was Dad, and this place and its history had its hooks in him deep. As long as the question of Mom's disappearance remained unresolved, and as long as the person—or persons—responsible were still cruising around town unpunished, he wasn't going anywhere. Whatever the outcome and no matter how long it took, he had to see this through to its conclusion. This was his purpose and I knew it, even if he didn't. And that morning, staring at the lake from the crow's nest of a fake pirate ship in Garrison Park, it became my purpose as well. No matter what it took, we'd figure it out together, once and for all, and get the hell out of Dodge.

As if to put an exclamation mark on my inner rant, the huge flock of starlings that had been silently going about their business all this time suddenly burst into flight. There were no chirps or squawks or any other song to mark their departure, just a huge muffled "*Wftftftftftftftftftftft*" as they took to the air. There seemed to be even more birds than I'd thought; maybe more had arrived quietly while I'd had my back turned. They were everywhere. They rose out of the sandpit, out of the trees, off the other play structures, in a continuous thrumming cloud of grey-brown bodies. It was unreal, hundreds and hundreds of them, rising in a wave that, when it reached a certain point in the air, suddenly became a single living entity, as if guided by one mind. It looked like an organism, a living cloud that rose, dipped down suddenly, swirled and stretched, then gathered itself in and rose again. It swirled above me for a few moments, hovering as if gaining strength, then finally lifted and moved off to the west under a now overcast sky, disappearing over a stand of pines.

What was likely no more than a few seconds had seemed so much longer, and it wasn't until the starlings were gone that I realized that I'd been holding my breath the whole time. I finally exhaled and, still a bit shaky, descended the rope ladder and left the park.

# 14

I've often thought of what caused me to stray from my usual circuit that day and zigzag the long way around to get to the library. Rather than take Lakeside Drive to King Street and downtown, I took St. Joseph north, then took Lalonde west, and finally turned north again on Barrette. There isn't much there to interest a kid; it's an older residential neighbourhood with great big trees and a lot of turn-of-the-century homes with businesses that operate out of the ground floor—law firms, clinical psychologists, accountants and the like. In any event, had I decided to continue to King Street I would have noticed that most of the downtown businesses were closed for the holiday, which in turn would have reminded me that the library would be closed as well. It's impossible to know for sure, but it's likely that I would have turned around at that point. I don't know where I would have headed from there, but I almost certainly would not have found myself on the corner of Barrette and Centre Street when I did.

There's a gentle incline as Barrette Street heads north, in the opposite direction of the lake. It's not a busy street, so there's only one traffic light, at the intersection with Centre. When I was about thirty metres from the intersection, I stepped off the right-hand sidewalk with the intention of crossing Barrette and heading up to the intersection, where I would then turn west on Centre. As I did, a quick honk from a car coming up from behind dissuaded me, and I stepped back onto the sidewalk. The car was moving pretty fast, too fast anyway for Barrette Street—where the posted speed limit is 40 km/h—no doubt trying to catch the green light. I looked back at the oncoming vehicle, a blue Honda CRV, and saw a brilliant flash reflected off the car's windshield that caused me to turn away. It lasted only the smallest fraction of a second, but its reflection was so bright and so intense that I saw spots in front of my eyes for some time after. It must have been unbearable for the driver who was looking straight into it. A second or so later, I heard a loud screech as the driver hit the brakes and swerved violently to the left.

I'm not sure whether I actually remember all the details that followed or if my mind filled them in afterward, but I seem to recall the blue smoke and smell of burning rubber from the squealing tires, even the black marks on the faded asphalt. All this came to a sudden and horrible stop as a cement truck coming southbound on Barrette Street slammed into the CRV's passenger side at full speed. There was the briefest blaring of its horn before it struck the car with a sickening crunch barely twenty metres from where I was standing.

The impact was unbelievable. I felt a shock wave move through my clothes, my hair and my body. The CRV seemed to take on the properties of simple cardboard: it was folded, lifted off the ground, and carried along effortlessly. The truck was moving with so much force that it continued to plough ahead a good distance with the CRV wrapped around its front end before bumping over the far curb and coming to a full stop on someone's front lawn, leaving a trail of shredded metal, churned soil and turf, and bits of broken glass behind it. The cement mixer's engine rattled for a few moments longer, then coughed to a stop as a cloud of smoke and steam poured out from its crumpled hood. The driver's side door then swung open, and as the truck driver began to clamber out of the cab, he looked back up the street. Still rooted to the ground I followed his gaze, and there, in the middle of the northbound lane of Barrette Street, just a few metres ahead of me, stood Billie.

*****

As clear and detailed as every moment was up to that point, the events in the minutes that followed all seemed to blend together. I do remember immediately moving in Billie's direction, which I suppose indicated to the truck driver that he could focus on the poor occupant of the car he'd just crumpled. I have no recollection of what the driver did or much of anything that happened on that side of the street in those early moments. Instead I rushed over to Billie: even though the immediate danger had passed, I thought it somehow essential to get her out of the road. That she'd appeared to have come out of nowhere moments earlier hadn't completely escaped me, but the fact I'd had my back turned at the time, combined with everything else that was going on, was enough to keep my conscious mind from dealing with that for now.

She came with me readily enough, and it struck me then just how calm she was. Here she was standing just a few feet from a horrifically violent accident—for all I knew she might have been hit by flying debris—and yet she didn't appear the least bit disturbed. I took her by the arm—as warm as ever—and led her to the sidewalk on the right-hand side of Barrette, on the opposite side from the wreckage. I found us a spot under one of the huge elms that line the street, and sat down in a heap against it. Billie, for her part, was quite content to stand, watching the growing activity down the street with utter fascination. I knew it was important to stick around: the police and the paramedics would arrive soon and they'd want to talk to any eyewitnesses, which by the looks of things was just the two of us. Plus I was still too scared and shaken to go anywhere.

But what to do with Billie? She appeared calm for the moment, but who knew what would happen later on? She might be traumatized, she might freak out, go into hysterics; she might even have sustained an injury without knowing it. I didn't yet know what role if any she had in all this, except that she had been right in the midst of the accident: from where she'd been standing, she would have seen everything. Even at the best of times, Billie wasn't the most skilled person at social interaction, and I was sure she'd be at the center of a lot of attention soon enough. If she was too freaked out to talk, I would have to speak for her, and I didn't know so much as her last name.

Already a crowd was gathering across the street: people were swooping toward the scene of the accident like buzzards, others stood and watched from their driveways and lawns. Cars from both directions had stopped and pulled over. I saw the cement truck driver gesticulating wildly, one moment focusing on the wrecked CRV—and presumably the driver who, by all evidence, was still inside—the next pointing in the direction of the impact site. I watched as his searching eyes scanned the debris field, darted to the far side of Barrette Street, and eventually lighted on Billie and me, at which point he got visibly more excited and pointed in our direction. My stomach tightened as some of the onlookers looked our way, but their attention quickly turned back to the CRV. Nearly everybody had a cellphone out and was—

My cellphone! Dad! I'd been so preoccupied that I'd totally forgotten about him. The last thing I wanted was for him to find out about this by seeing me on TV. I called his cell and our landline, leaving messages along these lines: "Hi Dad, I'm with Billie at the corner of Centre and Barrette, there's been a huge accident, it just happened a few minutes ago, Billie and I are witnesses, we're both OK, just fine, no worries, but the police will be here any minute and they'll probably want to talk to us. Call me."

As I put my phone away, I found that I was OK enough to draw a deep breath and take stock. For the first time since the collision I looked myself over to make sure that I hadn't been hit by flying glass without noticing. I'd read that happens. Everything seemed fine, not so much as a scratch, so I looked up at Billie who was still standing next to me, taking in the action from across the street. She had the strangest look on her face. I expected to see something like fear or horror but instead all I saw was confusion. She hadn't uttered a word since I saw her in the street, and I'd figured she was in shock, despite her apparent calmness. Now I realized that wasn't it at all. She was completely perplexed, as if she was watching a movie intended for grown-ups and didn't understand the plot.

"Billie?"

No answer right away. I tried again.

"You OK?"

She nodded absently, her expression never changing.

"What were you doing in the middle of the street? Where did you come from?"

She answered as if the question was completely irrelevant. "Oh, I was just . . ." trailing off. "The driver of that blue car," she continued, pointing across the street. "He saw me and then just turned away. Then that big truck came along and hit the blue car. Why did he do that?"

"He obviously couldn't stop in time. And he didn't expect the blue car to turn in the first place. So he . . . T-boned the Honda." I regretted my choice of words immediately.

"*Tee-boned?*"

"Sorry. T, as in shaped like the letter T. Meaning he hit the car broadside." There was no way I was going to try to explain the steak reference. "In other words, the cement mixer hit the blue car at a right angle."

Billie nodded, seemingly satisfied for the moment. But just for the moment.

"'Cement mixer' . . ." She had a way of inquiring about things without really asking a question.

"Yeah. The truck is a cement mixer. Used to bring cement to construction sites."

She gave me a funny squint indicating she needed further explanation. I sighed. Dad does the exact same thing.

"Cement, you know? They use it when building houses and stuff, especially the foundation? They pour it into a shape and it hardens. It's like liquid rock."

"Liquid rock??? You mean like magma? That's ridiculous. There's no way that truck is carrying magma."

"No, of course not. You're right. It's not magma. It's not hot, that's why they have to keep it turning so that it doesn't harden."

"But . . ." I could tell she was getting flustered. She was now frowning a bit, as if the entire process was just silly. "Why go through so much trouble? It's so inefficient. Why don't they just—"

That was enough. Time to bring the conversation back to the here and now. "Anyway, that was a really bad collision. I can't believe it actually happened in front of me. I'm still all shaky. Are you sure y—"

"She's dead."

I stopped cold. "What? Who?"

"The woman in the car."

"The driver? I thought—" I'd thought the driver was a man, but it had all happened so fast and there had been so much light reflected off the windshield that I hadn't been able to make out who'd been behind the wheel.

Billie's voice was completely flat, expressionless. "No, he's still alive. The woman next to him: she's dead." I hadn't even noticed a passenger.

A quick look at the remains of the CRV crushed up against the grille of the cement truck left little doubt. It was hard to even recognize it as a car. If there had been someone in the passenger seat, she wouldn't have stood a chance. Nor would the driver for that matter; what would make Billie think he'd survived was beyond me.

Billie sat down next to me against the tree, and wordlessly we watched the spectacle across the street and listened to the first wails of approaching sirens.

# 15

Within minutes everyone was there: the consequence of living in a small town. Police cruisers and fire trucks arrived pretty much together, with ambulances a few minutes behind. A van from News12 reached the accident site moments after the ambulances, and with the paramedics and firefighters focusing on the wreckage, the cops were left to keep the nosy press people at bay, outside of the area they were establishing as a perimeter. There was lots of yellow tape.

Access to Barrette Street was immediately cut off in both directions, so people were streaming in on foot to see what was going on and craning their necks to gawk at the wreckage. There was a bit of a commotion when a silver Jetta stopped near the intersection with Centre Street, and a woman came running out toward the roadblock. She didn't even close her car door. She slipped under the perimeter tape and ran toward the accident scene calling for someone named Cathy. I could hear her from across the street; her voice was loud and firm, demanding answers but not hysterical. She was immediately intercepted by a police officer.

She identified herself as the sister of one of the occupants of the car, and she'd been informed that there had been an accident. Because of the angle that she approached from it's not likely she would have seen much—the cement truck blocked her view of the CRV—which was probably a good thing. I lost sight of her as a cop gently manoeuvred her away from the wreckage to a place behind an ambulance.

For his part, the driver of the cement mixer was now sitting on the ground next to the curb, being tended by paramedics. He looked awful. He was red-faced and agitated and seemed to be trying to get to his feet, but was gently urged to sit down again and at one point was made to breathe from an oxygen mask. On a few occasions he made vague gestures across the street toward Billie and me, and I knew it was just a matter of time before someone in uniform came our way.

Meanwhile, most of the attention was focused on the crumpled Honda. From our vantage point it looked as if the passenger side was still pressed against the front end of the truck, and all the firefighters were busying themselves around the driver's side. A number of contraptions were brought out from one of the fire trucks, each connected to the truck by a yellow hose. Some were hard to make out but one in particular, though I'd never actually seen it before, could only be what people call the Jaws of Life, a device designed to pry open twisted and crumpled metal. The men went to work, cutting here, spreading there, deliberately and methodically. At one point the driver's side door was removed, and the large white bladder-like form of an air bag popped out like the guts of a giant butchered fish.

I hadn't noticed how quiet everything had become until that moment when suddenly there was a shriek and, for a brief instant, I caught a glimpse of a ghostly white hand and forearm protruding a bit from the wreckage. Within seconds a firefighter stepped in front of it and blocked it from my view, but the screaming went on for a while. There was more commotion, and I could see people trying to restrain somebody: it was the woman from the Jetta. She flailed for a bit, seemingly trying to reach the remains of the CRV, and then suddenly just crumpled to the ground.

For what seemed an eternity the whole world was filled with the woman's excruciating wails. It was hard to listen to and all I wanted to do was get away, to be anywhere but on that street. Billie seemed just as fascinated as ever. She was still watching a movie that she didn't understand, but the wonder of it all outweighed the confusion. Eventually, the wails exhausted themselves and became hitching sobs, and then finally, mercifully, a series of long, tired moans.

"She sounds really upset," Billie said. I didn't respond, and she remained very quiet and still for a good while after that.

*****

The cop looked young, a lot younger than my dad. He was also bigger, at least as tall as Uncle Carl, and a lot thicker. Of course, all the equipment he had on made him look that way, especially the bulletproof vest, but he was obviously someone who worked out a lot. His arms were as big around as my legs, and he had almost no neck. His head, with its short ginger hair and small green eyes, looked like a small cube atop his vast shoulders. It made him a bit funny-looking, but for all that he seemed gentle enough and he spoke with a very soft, young voice. He came up to us, apparently in no particular hurry, smiled and waved and offered a friendly "Hey, guys . . ." as he approached.

Billie, for her part, wasn't sold. Sitting next to her, I sensed her going into what I'd come to think of as "frightened-mouse mode" from the moment the cop began crossing the street: big eyes, tight mouth, arms wrapped around herself, and absolutely still.

"How are you guys doing?" the policeman asked, stopping on the sidewalk in front of us. His name tag read "Franklin."

I watched his little eyes carefully for a second to determine if he had an interest in one of us in particular. The moment his eyes fell on Billie, I spoke up: "We're fine."

His eyes turned back to me, and he smiled. "Good. Good to hear." On closer inspection, he seemed to have a strange sheen about him. Maybe he was just sweating under his black uniform, but his face had a shiny, oily quality that became unpleasant to look at after a while.

He looked around for a bit as if taking in the scenery then continued. "My name is Dale. I'm just talking to people to find out if anyone might have seen what happened. The driver of that cement truck said he saw you at the time of the crash."

I couldn't tell if "you" meant me, Billie, or both of us. He continued. "Whatever you guys saw, whatever you can tell me, would be super helpful." He tilted his head sideways and looked at Billie quizzically, then smiled. It was a goofy, guy-next-door grin. Yup, he was good.

He turned his attention back to me. "What's your name, guy?"

*Guy?* I wasn't sure I liked that. Sure, my dad and my uncle called me "bud" and "dude" all the time, but this was different. This cop was an authority figure on official business. He wasn't family and he wasn't a friend. A certain formality was to be expected; even at twelve years of age I knew that.

"Justin. Justin Lambert. I think my dad will be here soon."

He nodded. Then, looking at Billie he asked, "And what's your name, hon?"

Billie's huge stare shifted from the policeman to me. I figured the likelihood of her answering a perfect stranger's question, let alone such an imposing figure, was about the same as the prospect of it suddenly raining frogs. I jumped in. "Her name is Billie. She's my friend." Then, as if it explained everything, "She's really shy."

Constable Dale Franklin smiled again. "OK, fair enough. Guy, can you describe to me where you were and what you saw?"

I was liking this cop less by the minute. First off, he may have been friendly in a used car salesman/game show host kind of way, but he was condescending and disrespectful: I had already told him my name and it wasn't "guy." Second, I didn't like the way he just assumed I was going to answer his questions. Weren't they supposed to say something like "I'd like to ask you some questions *if you don't mind, if that's OK, would it be all right if...*"? I still hadn't heard from my dad yet, and I was beginning to feel uncomfortable with this big sweaty cop staring down at us, even if he was just doing his job. Plus, he didn't even ask if we were OK: a *"Howzitgoin?"* delivered from ten metres away didn't cut it.

"Umm . . . I'd rather wait 'til my father gets here," I stammered. "If that's OK." I figured "father" sounded more formal and grown-up than "dad."

His thin lips tightened. I knew annoyance when I saw it: a crack in his otherwise perfectly smooth veneer.

"Sure, no problem. We can wait for your daddy to come along."

*My "daddy"? Ouch!*

He continued. "But we like to get witness testimony as quickly as we can, while memories are still fresh. I'm sure you understand that, right, guy?"

I was furious. "My name is *Justin*." He just laughed. It was both smarmy and dismissive at the same time. The veneer was melting away like wax.

"Sorry, 'Justin.' Look, you guys are witnesses to a serious accident, and I need to know what you saw. It's that simple. Now we can have us a nice easy chat right here, or else—"

"Or else what, Constable Franklin?"

A voice I knew, a voice I loved, but not my dad's. Under the circumstances, the best surprise imaginable.

"Surely, Constable Franklin, you're not about to question a pair of minors without a parent or legal guardian present, are you?" The relief at seeing my uncle Carl was like stepping out of a cold swimming pool and being wrapped into a warm beach towel. He came striding up Barrette Street, his big grey ponytail bouncing on his back, and that wicked grin under his beard.

As Franklin slowly began to deflate, he looked at me, then back at Carl, then back at me. "Lambert," he muttered. "Justin *Lambert.*"

# 16

I'm sure Carl could have given the police permission to interview me as soon as he got there if he'd felt like it, but instead he made Constable Franklin sweat it out a bit until my dad arrived. He wasn't going to make things easy for him, and he seemed to be getting some enjoyment out of it as well. I later learned that there was a bit of history between the two: Carl told me that Franklin wasn't so much a bad cop as one who liked to cut corners, and that he had a talent for charming people into getting what he wanted, both on and off duty.

Billie and I were both a lot more relaxed by the time my dad showed up, sweaty and out of breath in his faded Jimi Hendrix T-shirt. With Dad propped against a tree catching his breath, Carl supervised Constable Franklin's questioning. He began with me, because even Carl was uncertain about what to do about Billie.

I recounted everything I could think of. I talked about heading north up Barrette Street, about stepping into the street to cross, and then being prompted back onto the sidewalk when the CRV honked its horn behind me; about turning to look at the car, about how it was moving faster than it should have been, and—after a few seconds' consideration—about the bright flash I saw reflected in the CRV's windshield. Franklin frowned just a bit at that last detail, making a quick but very deliberate glance at the sky that had been overcast since mid-morning. I then told him how the car suddenly hit the brakes and veered left into the middle of Barrette, where it was T-boned by the cement truck, then pushed back down the street, coming to a stop on a front lawn five or six houses down.

"A flash of light? From what do you think, Justin?" There was no missing the skepticism in his voice.

"I don't know. I wasn't looking at it. I had my head turned around. I was looking over my shoulder at the oncoming car. I saw the flash reflected in its windshield. It was over in less than a second. And then the car drove past me."

"OK . . ."

"Then there was a screech and the horn blared and the car suddenly turned and hit the brakes at the same time, really violently. Then the truck came in right away and—"

"Wait a second, Justin. Go back. You said after the flash that the car kept going?"

"Yes."

"I just want to understand. You heard the honk, you turned to look at the car, you saw a flash of light reflected in the windshield, and then it drove past. Is that right?"

"Uh-huh."

"And only once it passed you did it suddenly veer into the left-hand lane?"

"Yes. It wasn't very long, a second or so, but it wasn't . . . you know . . ." I paused, looking for the right word. "Instantaneous."

"So it wasn't the flash that made the driver hit the brakes and turn . . ."

"I . . . I don't think so. I can't really say." I was beginning to feel heat coming out from under my shirt. We were about to wade into territory that for about a thousand reasons I didn't want to explore.

"So what do you think made the car swerve?"

There was a pitched battle going on in my head: my eyes desperately wanted to turn in Billie's direction, and my brain fought them with everything it had, hauling back as hard as it could to keep them fixed on Constable Franklin. Somehow, my brain won out. "I don't know. I was looking at the car, not ahead of it. I didn't see beyond."

The cop fixed me with his gaze for what must have been only a second, but felt like hours. His face was marble. There was no sound for a hundred miles.

"OK," he finally said, as reasonably as anything. "And Billie, is it? Where were you during all this?"

She looked at me, and though her expression didn't seem any different, I sensed the onset of panic. This wasn't lost on Constable Franklin. Carl jumped in.

"Careful, Dale. This girl doesn't have a parent or legal guardian present. She's just a friend of my nephew; neither my brother nor I qualify."

Franklin backpedalled. "I just want to assess her condition, Mr. Lambert. She might have been physically injured or traumatized." He turned back to Billie. "Are you OK, sweetheart? You look a little pale. You feeling all right?"

A quick, nervous nod. I could see she was breathing through her nose, and her eyes were locked on the big policeman. She remained silent.

"I just want to know if you saw anything, and to make sure you're all right. Where were you when all this was going on?"

Without shifting her gaze from Franklin, she slowly lifted her right arm and pointed toward the street. You couldn't tell exactly, but she seemed to be indicating an area less than eight metres from the impact site. There was shattered glass and wreckage everywhere. I could see pieces of twisted blue metal, what might have been a windshield wiper, and a squarish object with rounded corners that turned out to be the CRV's passenger-side rear-view mirror. If Billie had actually been standing where she was pointing, she would have been pelted with debris.

The expression on Franklin's face suddenly changed to one I recognized immediately: the look of the concerned grown-up. "Are you sure you're all right, Billie? Has anyone looked at you to make sure you're OK?"

Billie shook her head.

"Do your parents know you're here?"

No answer.

Franklin produced a cellphone. "Do you want to call them, tell them to come here?"

It was time to intervene. "Billie is spending the weekend at our place. My dad and I are going to take her home this evening." Then, in a desperate grasp for credibility, I added: "Right, Dad?"

Franklin gave me a quick side glance then focused again on Billie. "Is that right, Billie? Do you want Justin's dad to take you home?"

Billie nodded vigorously, without looking at me. That sold it.

"All right, but I want to make sure you're OK." He reached for a walkie-talkie that was clipped to his left shoulder. "Two-one."

A fuzzy response: "*Two-one, go ahead.*"

"I've got a female, approximately ten years of age. No signs of external injury, but request a paramedic for a possible 10-46."

"*Two-one, 10-4.*"

Franklin turned to Billie. "Billie, I've asked for someone to come over and check you out just to make sure you're OK. You good with that?"

Billie's head whipped around this time, looking at me with eyes that were scared and pleading. She was shaking her head. I scrambled to intervene on her behalf, for what it was worth. "She said she's fine. We've been sitting here for a while, no problems. She's OK." I turned to my dad and uncle for help, but they remained motionless and completely quiet. No help was coming from them. Finally, Carl spoke up.

"Actually, Justin, Constable Franklin is right. Someone has to make sure that Billie is OK. It's basic procedure and there's no getting around it. Everything will be fine."

Billie's voice came up for the first time, tiny and frail. "I'm not hurt."

"Yes, I'm sure you're fine, honey, but I have to make sure. We can't take any chances. You could have been hit by something, and just not noticed yet. It happens all the time."

Billie was shaking her head furiously, and she had her fists balled up. She turned to me for help, her big eyes imploring me to put a stop to this, but all I could do was shrug. She was shaking like a leaf and looked like she was about to cry.

Franklin again: "Don't worry. It will only take a minute. And I'd still like to hear what you saw earlier. Would that be OK?"

Her response was so faint that, at first, I wasn't sure she'd even spoken; then I felt her warm grip around my forearm. "I want Justin to be with me."

*****

Things only got more complicated from there. A paramedic, a pretty bi-racial woman who introduced herself as Debbie, came over from across the street where she'd been working on the grief-stricken woman who'd collapsed earlier. She said the examination she wanted to give Billie would be fairly thorough, and because it would involve having Billie remove parts of her clothing, she suggested she conduct the exam within the confines of an ambulance to preserve Billie's modesty. Billie started to freak, or at least it was the closest thing to freaking I'd seen from her yet. Nor did things improve when it was explained to Billie that I couldn't be in the ambulance with her. Billie began shaking her head again, hissing in my ear, "I can't take these off, Justin. I can't do it. You have to tell her. *I can't!*"

"Why? Is it, like, against your religion or something? What's wrong?"

Billie shook her head and rolled her eyes skyward in a gesture she reserved for comments of monumental stupidity.

"No. No, no, no. That's not it at all—"

"You're shy? Is that it?"

"It's OK," Debbie's gentle voice broke in. "If it's that important we don't have to do that here."

Debbie agreed to keep the examination at a superficial level, saying that anything requiring privacy could be conducted later. Billie remained silent; she neither assented nor objected but generally regained her composure, and with everyone else in agreement we all followed Debbie to the ambulance, Billie and me together, my dad and Uncle Carl behind us, and Constable Franklin bringing up the rear.

Debbie completed Billie's examination within minutes, but it took less than ten seconds for her to figure out there was something distinctly odd with Billie. Not surprisingly, it began with her eyes.

"Billie," she began, "have you been putting any kind of drops in your eyes?"

Head shake.

"Have you been taking any medication? Pills? Injections?"

Another head shake.

Debbie gave a weak shrug with her eyebrows and continued her exam.

Despite the big pupils, a quick test concluded that there was nothing wrong with Billie's vision. Debbie then very carefully placed her fingertips on Billie's neck and moved them around, and looked up suddenly. There was no mistaking the alarm on her face.

"You're really *very* warm, Billie," Debbie said, almost in a whisper. "I can feel the heat coming off you." There was a definite unease in her voice. "Are you feeling OK?" She waited for a response, and Billie dutifully nodded her head. "Do you have pain anywhere?" Another quick head shake; she wasn't exactly relaxed yet, but I could tell she knew she was in good hands.

Feeling the need to normalize things, and knowing full well that Billie was unlikely to respond to anything that wasn't a direct, closed-ended question, I added: "She's always been like that." I didn't feel it necessary to specify that, as far as I was concerned, "always been" amounted to a little more than a week.

"Is that right, Billie?" Debbie asked. "Are you always warm like this?"

"I guess," she replied. "Yeah."

Debbie produced a thermometer. It was one of those digital ones, white with the little display window and an on/off button. Debbie continued: "I'd like to take your temperature now, Billie. Would that be OK?" Billie nodded. I was certain that Carl and I were thinking the same thing at that moment: *Watch carefully, Constable Franklin. This is how it's done.*

"Just open your mouth, and I'll place this under your tongue. We'll keep it there for just a moment."

Within less than a minute, it beeped three times. Debbie removed it gently from Billie's mouth and looked at the display. Her expression didn't change, but she looked directly at Billie when she spoke: "Billie, you have a very high fever. A person's body temperature should normally be around thirty-seven degrees Celsius; yours is almost forty-one. We usually bring people to the hospital when their temperature is that high. Are you sure you're OK?"

She was apparently feeling more and more comfortable with Debbie, because she spoke clearly above a whisper for the first time. "Yeah," she said. "I'm fine."

Debbie for her part was less convinced. She was placing her hands on Billie's neck, her shoulders, her arms. "I dunno. It's not just your temperature: you feel . . . strange."

Her look moved to the rest of us. Confused shrugs all around.

"Well, I still would like to bring you to the Emergency at the hospital so they can run a couple of tests. It'll be done in no time and then you can go home. Justin can come with us if you like. Is that OK?"

Billie looked at me, then looked back at Debbie and nodded.

"Good. Thank you, Billie. Now, is there any way of reaching your parents? This is important."

Billie shook her head.

"Are they here in town?"

"No."

"Don't they have cellphones?"

"Cellphones don't work where they are." A perfectly reasonable and believable answer, especially in our part of the world. Debbie didn't contest it, but I saw Dad and Carl exchange glances at that one. Did Billie have parents or didn't she? Or did she feel that explaining her home life would be too complicated under the circumstances?

Turning to the grown-ups, Debbie added, "All righty then, but somebody is going to have to find this child's parents as soon as possible. Otherwise, we'll need to get Children's Aid involved."

Satisfied that Billie was in our—meaning me and my dad's—care for the time being, Debbie told the others that she'd be taking her to the Emergency Department in the ambulance, and that I was going to ride along at Billie's request. Dad and Carl would follow in Carl's MGB, while Constable Franklin remained at the scene—apparently, he had a few more witnesses to question, and one way or another it looked like he wouldn't be getting much out of Billie.

"See?" I said cheerfully. "Everything is going to be fine."

With that, the rear doors of the ambulance snapped shut, and we were on our way.

*****

Debbie's full name turned out to be Deborah Williams, and watching her chatting and laughing with the driver in the front of the ambulance, she seemed even prettier than when I'd seen her earlier. When she was talking with us on the street, or conducting Billie's exam, she'd been all business, and as gentle as she was, there was a seriousness about her that somehow must have blunted her features. Now she was more relaxed and, in the company of her co-worker, her features had loosened up. Her hair was done up in cornrows and her long braids were tied back in a ponytail. She was short, her skin was just a bit darker than mine, as were her eyes, which were more brown to my hazel. She, too, was a person who worked out a lot: her overall build was stout, her shoulders and arms were muscular, and her rolled-up sleeves revealed a barbwire tattoo around her toned left bicep that gave her a bit of unexpected bad-ass flair. Her smile, which was now coming more readily, was dazzling.

I also picked up from bits of conversation that she must have been much older than I'd originally figured. She made reference to her many years on the job, and, more importantly, to a son who had just been accepted into graduate studies at Lakehead. That would have made her at least as old as my dad. While my dad's face had lines—around his eyes, especially—Debbie's seemed to defy time. She was pretty, she had spirit, she was obviously really smart, and she was gentle with kids: the perfect match for Dad.

"I knew your mom, Justin."

I was used to people knowing who I was without my having to introduce myself; that happened all the time. But no stranger had ever told me flat out of the blue that they'd actually known my mom, in any context. This was definitely a first. It got my attention like a bell going off, and even Billie seemed to notice.

"Really?"

"Oh, yeah. I used to see her all the time at the Emerg. I can't say we were all that close—Élise had a kind of polite formality about her—but she was always friendly."

Élise. Aside from my dad and my uncle Carl, I couldn't remember a single person who'd ever referred to my mom by her first name, at least not around me. She was always "your mom."

"She was a hard worker, our Élise. Always went that extra mile, and she *never* lost her cool no matter what kind of shit we brought in. I'n't that right, Steve?"

The driver grunted his approval and nodded deeply. I couldn't help but smile. Debbie had used a four-letter word—albeit a pretty mild one—unselfconsciously, free of malice or irony, in front of two pre-teens and didn't apologize for it. I loved that. Add "genuine" to her growing list of qualities.

"She talked a lot about you, Justin. You were just a young thing of course, not much more than a baby, but she was so proud of you. She'd come in and talk about you non-stop, about something you'd said or some milestone you'd reached. With anyone else it might have gotten tiring, but the way she lit up when she talked about you . . . you couldn't help getting caught up."

A lump suddenly formed in my throat. It came out of nowhere: a huge ball of emotion was rising up from my stomach like a big tree branch you hook into when you're fishing. It rises from the murk, and when you first see it you don't even know what it is. Debbie was looking straight ahead out the windshield so she didn't notice right away, but Billie did.

"She loved you so much, Justin. She'd be really proud to see what a fine young man you've become, you know tha—" She cut herself off as she turned to look at me. "Oh, shit, now look what I've done. I'm sorry, honey. I didn't mean to upset you."

"I'm OK," I mumbled. I wasn't in the habit of crying in the presence of strangers, and I felt like an idiot blubbering in front of such an attractive woman. "Fine young men" shouldn't be brought to tears so easily, but I was completely caught off guard. It was Billie who, inadvertently, brought me out of it.

"What's wrong with you?" she whispered, looking alarmed.

"Nothing," I said, managing a weak smile. "I'm fine."

"Are you sure? Because your face is leaking."

# 17

The ride to the hospital was short so there wasn't time for a lot of reminiscing, but Debbie Williams had left the door to the vault about my mom open just a crack, and the prospect of getting info from a different source than my dad was irresistible. She was reluctant at first, but in the moments before arriving at the hospital, she confided a few historical tidbits to me: that she was present in the hospital emergency room on that evening a few nights before my mom disappeared and witnessed first-hand David Raymond's tirade as he demanded medication for his pain and directed threats, mostly against my mom, when the meds were denied to him; and, unknown or forgotten by almost everyone else, that Raymond hadn't been alone, that he'd had a companion with him at the time. There seemed to be little if any agreement as to the identity of D-Ray's buddy, but whoever this mystery person was, he either died, left town entirely, or had been keeping an extremely low profile ever since. What was remembered, at least by Debbie, is that this person was desperately trying to keep David Raymond quiet during the entire scene and was largely responsible for successfully getting him out of the ER waiting room before security arrived. I would have pressed Debbie for more, but by then we'd pulled up at the Emergency entrance.

"Justin," she said, beckoning me through the parting doors of the ER. "Come here for a sec. I don't have much time." My dad and my uncle were just arriving behind us, and Debbie began herding Billie and me into the ER waiting room ahead of them, dropping her voice to a hurried whisper. "I don't know how much you know, or how much your dad thinks you need to know, about what happened to your mom all those years ago. Your dad loves you and wants to protect you; I can't blame him for that. But I also think you deserve to know all the facts, at least as far as anyone can say for certain. Nobody has answers to all the questions, especially not the big ones, but people talk, you know? Bits and pieces of the puzzle get put together over time. If ever you want to talk some more, you just call me. I don't know everything, but I've learned a few things. Like I said, people talk. Everybody here knows me, and if you ask them, they can tell you how to reach me. In fact, there isn't anybody in this department who wouldn't drop everything to help you. They all loved Élise very much." With that, she turned away and went up to the ER reception desk where she began making arrangements for Billie's examination.

*****

Billie had become agitated again immediately after leaving the safety of the ambulance and Debbie's calming presence. She was fidgety as we waited for someone to take her to an examination room, gawking at every passer-by, be they hospital staff, patients, paramedics, or security. She looked out windows, down hallways, and around corners whenever she could, as if she was scoping the place out in case she needed to make a quick exit. At one point, a woman in blue scrubs came over to tell us that someone would be over soon to take Billie to the examination room. She made the mistake of thinking that I was "Billy" while the real Billie sat quietly making no effort to correct the error. When the nurse left, Billie became increasingly alarmed.

"This is taking a long time," she hissed. "Too long. I'm going to have to go soon."

"You mean go to the bathroom? There's one around the corner."

"No. NO! I mean leave. I told you: I can't stay out for very long."

"Do you want to use my cellphone to call your . . . your family . . . or whatever . . . tell them where you are?"

She looked pained at my ignorance. "No, Justin. I just have to leave soon. I've been out for too long already."

I knew there was no way anyone was going to let her leave, so I tried to make light of it in the hope of calming her down.

"What, is it a religious thing? You have to be home before sundown?"

Billie looked annoyed with me, and clearly didn't care for my second reference to a religious prohibition within the past hour. I tried something else.

"Or are you like a reverse vampire, and can't be out in the moonlight?" I smiled, pleased with my cleverness. Billie just rolled her eyes. She looked so much like Dad when she did that.

"Plus, that person said they want samples from me," she hissed. "What do I do?"

"Oh, don't worry. Didn't Debbie mention that to you already? It's no big deal."

"But I can't. I don't have anything to give them."

I usually took Billie's moods seriously, because wherever she was from there were a lot of everyday things that she didn't know and she scared easily. This time, however, I couldn't help but chuckle.

"The only thing you have to give them is a urine sample."

She frowned, confused and skeptical.

"You just have to pee into a small cup. They'll give you a plastic cup, you'll go to the washroom, and . . . well . . . pee a bit into it."

She looked horrified. "I . . . I can't go to the bathroom . . . I . . ." she stammered. She seemed really bothered by this process, as if she were being asked to improvise a speech in class on something she knew nothing about. I tried my best to appease her.

"You shouldn't worry, Billie. I've done it before. They don't need much."

"But . . . but . . . And then they said they wanted *blood!* What does that mean? I can't give them blood. What am I supposed to do?" By now she was genuinely upset, and her voice had risen enough to get my dad's attention. He remained quiet, but I could tell he was listening in while keeping his eyes focused on the open *National Geographic* on his lap.

"Billie, it's OK. You won't have to do anything. They'll take the blood *from* you. They'll put a small needle in your arm, right about here"—I indicated the inner part of my elbow joint—"and draw a small amount of blood from you. It's really not a big deal. You'll barely feel anything."

Something changed in Billie at that moment. It wasn't like when we saw David Raymond that time in front of the municipal building, or even earlier in the afternoon at the accident site when Constable Franklin questioned her. She was less like a scared kid, and more like a frustrated adult. It was her voice: it was older, and more serious than I'd ever heard. She wasn't yelling or pleading or whining. She just spoke very clearly, as if explaining something urgent to a small child. "You don't understand, Justin. I can't give them blood. I can't give them anything. I'm not like you."

"Billie, they only—"

"Justin, listen to me: It. Won't. Work."

I wasn't sure whom I was dealing with anymore, but this was no longer a small, frightened child. This was more like a cornered animal. It was her voice, this new voice, flat and cold, that scared me the most. By then even my dad had noticed the difference, but he was as much at a loss as I was. I was half expecting her to bolt out of the ER waiting room at any moment when another nurse, a male one this time, came along.

"Billie? Come this way please."

Billie's response was quiet but definitive. "Justin is coming with me." It wasn't meant as a request, but the nurse, who had barely even glanced her way, took it as one. "That should be fine, but he'll have to wait outside the examination room."

Her hot hand reached out and took my arm. The look on her face was one of quiet resolve, something else I'd never seen in her before. I made a quick gesture to my dad to indicate, "It's OK. I've got this," and allowed Billie to lead me along. We followed the big male nurse through the ER lobby, past the main reception desk, and proceeded down a hallway with a number of thick coloured bands running along the floor. Whatever Billie was planning in order to get herself out of this situation—for whatever reason—I was just going to have to play my part when the time came.

The nurse led us into a small, overly bright room with an examination table, a small desk and two chairs, and a cabinet from which he produced a pale-yellow hospital gown, placing it on the table. "The doctor will be here in a moment, Billie. Meanwhile, you'll need to put this on." He then left without another word, leaving the door ajar. Billie stood sullenly facing the door, making no movement toward the examination table or the gown the doctor would be expecting to find her in. Minutes ticked by.

"Do you want me to step out while you put that on?" I asked eventually.

Her voice and her face remained expressionless. "I'm not putting that on."

"Oh. What if—"

The doctor breezed in at that moment, smiling and giving us a quietly cheerful "Hey, guys," as she placed a folder on the desk and sat on a swivel stool. Whether or not she noticed the still-folded gown on the examination table, she made no indication. Instead she looked us over for a moment and said, "I'm Linda. You're Justin, right?" I nodded. "I understand Billie asked for you to be around for her exam. That's fine, but at one point I'll have to ask you to—"

"I have to pee." Billie's voice was small again, and she stared at the floor as she spoke. The scared little girl was back, where the desperate, cornered animal had gone, and whether it had vanished altogether or was just hiding, I had no idea.

"Oh," said the doctor. "That's OK. There's a washroom just down the hall on the right. Can you take this with you when you go?" she asked, holding out a plastic specimen jar. "You just need to fill it up to this line." The doctor's manner was gentle and matter-of-fact. "When you come back you can put this gown on, and then I'll ask Justin to wait outside. We'll be done in no time."

Billie took the cup without a word and, as she stepped out of the room, she beckoned me with her free hand. "Justin?" I looked at the doctor, unsure of what to do, but when she just smiled and nodded at me, I stepped out quickly, joining Billie in the hallway.

"What—" I began to ask, but Billie had already begun moving toward the washroom.

It was windowless and very small, just a toilet, a sink, a soap and a paper towel dispenser, and a wastebasket. She hesitated before going in, then turned to me, said "See ya," stepped inside, and closed the door behind her.

What happened next probably took all of a second, maybe less. I can remember three things: the hollow *clop!* of the empty plastic cup hitting the floor; the brilliant flash of light that appeared as a blinding outline around the bathroom door; and the gentle thump as the door was momentarily drawn inward against its frame. Then nothing: utter stillness except for the hollow sound of an empty specimen jar rolling back and forth on the tile floor.

I didn't need to open the door, let alone call for Billie. I didn't have to do either of those things because I knew that Billie wouldn't answer. It's not every day that your entire concept of reality is turned on its head, but somehow on that Victoria Day afternoon when I was twelve years old I just accepted it. I stood there outside the washroom, not knowing what to do next, and I began to cry for the first time since the horrible accident on Barrette Street; really weep, not like the two or three stray tears that fell in the ambulance when Debbie Williams talked about my mom. The entire sequence of events suddenly washed over me like a big wave. I cried for the poor victims in the blue Honda CRV who'd been pulverized by the oncoming cement truck; I cried for the truck driver himself whose life would never be the same as a result of the accident; and I even cried for the victims' friend who'd gone into hysterics and had collapsed in a devastated heap before my very eyes. That woman had cried for something she understood but couldn't accept; I was now crying for something that I couldn't understand but accepted anyway. My only friend, this strange little girl who called herself Billie but of whom I knew nothing else, had, in a brilliant flash of light, literally vanished into thin air.

# 18

It only took a few minutes before I realized that, crazy as this situation was, things were going to get a lot more complicated very soon unless I acted quickly. As her only contact and the last person to see her, I was going to have to explain how this strange little girl with the high temperature and strangely dilated pupils had managed to slip out of a windowless washroom and exit the hospital totally unseen, thus dodging an important examination and potentially endangering herself. Beyond that, I was eventually going to have to deal with what had happened to Billie and where she'd gone, but that was far too big a question for my mind to handle at the moment. For now, I was more concerned about the grilling I was in for, not only from the hospital staff but from my dad as well and, for all I knew, the police.

I got up off the floor where I'd allowed myself those few moments of wallowing, opened the door and stepped into the washroom. Although I was pretty confident of what I would find, I needed to confirm that the washroom was in fact empty. It's what any good scientist would do. The inspection was quick: the room was basically an empty cube with only the barest of necessities. I looked upward and behind the door, and satisfied with my inspection and, having gotten my shakes and tears under control, I went back to the examination room where the doctor would be waiting. There she was, still seated in her swivel chair talking on a cellphone. She smiled at me as I stepped in and just as she ended her conversation I went on the offensive before she could even breathe.

"Where's Billie?" I asked.

She looked blankly at me, at a momentary loss for words.

"I was going to ask you the same question."

I stuck my head back out the door, looking up and down the hallway. *This is the best performance of my life*, I thought to myself. *They'd better remember me at Oscar time.*

"I thought she'd be here by now. The washroom is empty."

A brief pause.

"I thought she was with you," the doctor said.

"She was," I jumped in, "but then I had to go too, so I went to the men's room down the hall. You mean you haven't seen her?" The best defence is a good offence.

The doctor stood up, her expression of confusion now changed to something that was a combination of annoyance and concern. "For heaven's sake . . ." she muttered and walked back toward the nurses' station. She was wearing dressy black shoes with heels, and her brisk pace made a clacking sound down the hall that rang with authority. As she inquired at the nurses' station, I continued to the waiting room where Dad and Carl were still seated. "Billie's gone," I said, which prompted another round of "Did-you-see-her-No-I-thought-she-was-with-you," with Dad looking exasperated but not entirely surprised. "Well, she did look awfully stressed by the whole thing," he said. "She probably decided to bail and went looking for another exit. I bet they find her in a broom closet someplace."

When a thorough search of the Emergency wing turned up nothing, it was concluded that Billie must have found her way to the main entrance of the hospital, and had simply strolled out the front door before anyone could be alerted to her absence. And while the prospect of a mysterious nine-year-old with no known home or family wandering out of the hospital on her own was worrisome, the general feeling among the hospital staff was one of resignation rather than panic. Police would be notified and asked to keep an eye open, but the issue wouldn't get their highest priority. Personally, I figured it was unlikely that Billie would be found if she'd decided she didn't want to be. She was in the wind.

Still, Dad and I were asked to go to the police station to make an official statement, which basically amounted to us telling them everything we knew about Billie; in other words, almost nothing. By the time we got home it was well past dinner time, and any plans we'd had for our annual Victoria Day Long Weekend Inaugural Summer BBQ had long since been nixed. We settled for pizza and lemonade. Carl stuck around for an extra night rather than head back to Sudbury, and he and Dad spent the rest of the evening in hushed conversation over beers in the kitchen. There was no fiddle music this time, and I didn't catch any of what they said. Instead, I stared up at the ceiling in my room, replaying the events of the day, and trying to come to terms with what I knew I could never ask another human being to explain.

*****

I owe my uncompromising skepticism to my dad. Critical thinking runs deep in my family—it's in the Lambert DNA—and even at twelve years of age I was still very much my father's son. And despite what happened to me during that summer of '06, or maybe because of it, those feelings never changed. After what I experienced—which I can still barely describe let alone attempt to interpret—claims of UFOs, ghosts, Bigfoot, astrology, psychics, telekinesis, demonic possession, crop circles, and all brands of conspiracy theories, pseudoscience, and quackery today seem depressingly unimaginative.

While Dad taught me to remain outwardly diplomatic, inside I was sighing and doing eye-rolls whenever I heard claims that others described as paranormal or supernatural. I learned that once you've eliminated all the usual human failings—faulty perception, unethical reporting, fear, gullibility, greed, or just wishful thinking—you're usually not left with much beyond somebody's say-so or a picture that could have been Photoshopped. I was labelled early on at school as the skeptic, the debunker, which would have been socially catastrophic if not for the fact that I was so quiet to begin with.

At the same time, I was still young enough that part of me *wanted* some of these things to be true, if for no other reason because it would be really cool. I knew deep down that how badly you wanted something to be real was irrelevant, and that no amount of wishful thinking could make something true. But on another level, I was still at an age where I would have loved just once to experience something genuinely otherworldly. And so there I was, faced with just that situation: I'd experienced something I couldn't explain, I didn't know enough to make sense of it, and my twelve-year-old imagination just wanted to take flight. The implications were huge, terrifying, and irresistible.

I knew I had to be smart about it and approach the problem like a scientist and not like my classmates, who were all too prepared to accept the wildest work of Hollywood screenwriters as a plausible version of reality. I began by taking stock of what I knew, and then I listed the possible explanations in order of likelihood, saving the least plausible for the end.

My first explanation was that Billie hadn't disappeared at all, and she'd been either hiding in the washroom or had found another way out, a possibility that I had eliminated the moment I stepped in. There were no places to hide, nor could she have escaped through the ceiling as they so often do in movies: there were no panels on the ceiling, and Billie was far too short to reach the ceiling if there had been, even if she'd stood on the sink.

Second, Billie hadn't vanished but had gone out through the washroom door without my noticing. Also not possible. Contrary to what I told the doctor, I didn't leave to use the men's room but had been present and fully conscious the entire time.

With those two explanations eliminated, I was left with some possibilities that left me both creeped out and excited. The first of these was too awful to contemplate, but happily wasn't supported by any evidence either: the flash had been an explosion and Billie had been instantly vaporized. The problem there of course was that there had been no noise of an explosion or a shockwave. In fact, there'd been the opposite of a shockwave—the door had been drawn inward, not outward, and very gently at that. Plus, when I'd looked in, the washroom was intact; it wasn't messy and it didn't even smell bad. Nothing explosive had happened . . . at least not while Billie had been there.

What was left? This is where my young scientific mind ran out of sane possibilities and all the science fiction I'd ever read or watched started to kick in: ideas involving a secret government/ scientific/military agency using some kind of teleportation technology; time travel; or that Billie was an alien from another world. I felt silly entertaining any one of these, however briefly, and dismissed them instantly. Why not an angel or a ghost or some test tube mutant for that matter?

I stared up at the walls of my bedroom, at the images of dinosaurs, of great whales, of planets and nebulae and galaxies, a star chart, and a periodic table of elements. On the shelves were rock and fossil samples—some real, some replicas—dinosaur figures, and my cherished books. Jostling for space on my desk next to my iMac were my plasma ball, a plastic brachiosaurus skeleton, and a telescope that used to belong to my dad. With the exception of a big map of Middle Earth and a few posters of jazz musicians, I had surrounded myself with science. As full of beauty and wonder and awe as all these things were, I could get my mind around them; I knew they could be understood, their place in the cosmos explained. Even if I wasn't yet fully fluent in the language and concepts, I knew there were other people who were and who could put these phenomena into context, people exactly like me but with a bit—OK, a lot—more education. Everything fit, everything had its place, no matter how big or ancient or complex. What happened to Billie *had* to fit into the big cosmic picture in some rational way and if I couldn't figure it out someone else could, if not now then eventually.

I drifted off into an uneasy sleep, and dreamed I was swimming beneath the surface of a vast and brilliant lake, as clear and bright as the sky, where I could breathe the water and where tiny fish in brilliant blues and purples and greens, smaller than grains of rice, swam all around me in untold multitudes, covering me, speaking to me, asking my name.

*****

I spent the next few days half expecting my entire world to implode. Even though everyday life seemed, on the surface at least, to have returned to normal, I found it impossible to concentrate on anything. I was convinced that at any moment I was going to be called to the principal's office or summoned to our front door, where I was going to be asked some very difficult questions that I was completely unqualified to answer. My stomach would clench whenever I heard my name.

What worried me the most was that whatever had happened on Monday was just too big for me to be the only person to know about it. And the more I thought about it, Billie's disappearance at the municipal building and the blinding flash of light that caused the accident on Barrette Street suggested that Billie had been doing it for some time. Someone else might have seen something. People would be talking. There would be whispers about Justin

Lambert's strange new friend. Already a number of people had interacted with her that I was aware of. There was no reason to think there wouldn't be more. They probably didn't know much, but they'd be able to describe her, and they'd know that she was connected to me in some way.

I tried to convince myself that my business with the police and the paramedics was all nicely tied up, that as far as they were concerned the issue of the strange girl who called herself Billie was closed, and that I'd done nothing wrong to begin with. But I couldn't escape the feeling that there was so much more going on, and that I was right in the middle of it. All I could do was keep my head down, not draw attention to myself, and hope everything would blow over.

And for almost a week I thought it just might. By Thursday I had pretty much put it out of my mind, mostly because I had a huge history presentation to prepare for on Friday and by then my brain couldn't contain much that didn't have to do with the Acadian Deportation. By the time the weekend arrived I was just so relieved that I'd survived the presentation that the events of the previous weekend had pretty much faded to nothing.

That was until Saturday. I didn't always accompany my dad on his weekend errands, but it was bright and warm and I felt like getting out. It didn't matter that he'd planned to make stops at the pharmacy and hardware store—*bo-ring!*—I was restless and needed to move around in the world. Plus, my unspoken reward for such selflessness was a lunch out: burgers, nachos, or better yet poutine at Joey's Curbside Diner on McEwan. I'd even made a point of not having breakfast that morning in anticipation of an extra-large lunch with Dad, so by the time we stepped outside of Gingras Hardware my stomach was sending out warning signals.

Dad was making a joke about it when he suddenly stopped cold. I actually continued for a few steps before I noticed he was rooted to the sidewalk in front of a hair salon. He stood perfectly still, his eyes fixed on a hydro pole that had grown a thick skin of rusted staples from decades' worth of flyers. His face was blank, his mouth very slightly open. I was used to his occasional departures from the here and now, but these didn't happen much in public, and only when he was sitting still. "Dad?" I called to him. A hint of a nod after a second or two indicated that he'd heard me but he remained frozen in place. Still not breathing a word, his hands hanging limply at his sides, he beckoned me over with the slightest twitching of the fingers of his left hand.

When I arrived at his side and followed his gaze, I got a weird chill, and my stomach started to clench all over again. It was Billie. She was staring out at us from a colour photo on a laminated sheet of City of Ferguston and District stationery. Just above the photo were the words "Have you seen this girl?" along with a blurb suggesting that she might need medical attention, and if anybody had information on her to contact the Ferguston detachment of the Ontario Provincial Police, followed by a 1-800 number.

But mostly it was the photo that had me transfixed. It looked to have been taken on Barrette Street the day of the accident. There had been a lot of media people after a little while; some of them must have been taking pictures of everything in and around the accident scene, and Billie happened to be in the background of one of them. Someone—the police, Constable Franklin, maybe?—had recognized her, zoomed in, and cropped the photo around her head and shoulders. She wasn't in perfect focus, and although it was quite plainly Billie, you couldn't make out too much detail: her eyes, for example, looked dark but you couldn't tell that there was anything strange about them. Not exactly a school portrait, but good enough for a reliable ID.

"Remind you of someone?" Dad asked, so softly I thought for a second he was talking to himself.

How could it not? The only other flyer I'd ever seen like that—at least that wasn't about someone's lost family pet—was the one Dad kept in his office at home, a copy of the one he made ten years earlier when he was scouring Northern Ontario for some trace of Mom. I had very vague memories of those desperate drives, of my dad pleading with the locals for information, of posting his signs all over the region hoping for even an echo, a breath of a rumour. He'd used a photo of mom he'd taken a few months earlier, at an agricultural fair we'd all gone to during a weekend trip to the Eastern Townships of Québec. It had been one week before the end of summer vacation, and—as it turned out—it was our last holiday together as a family.

I've seen many photos and video clips of my mom, but the most enduring image of her, the one that lives with me every day of my life, is that photo taken at the Brome Fair in Québec when I was two. And now, in a weird way, I was looking at it again. More than seeing my friend's face on what amounted to a wanted poster, that's what sent the chill through me: I wasn't sure if it was the angle of the photo, the quality of the light, or her expression, but Billie's resemblance to my mom was startling. I couldn't begin to imagine how it made my dad feel.

When I finally tore my gaze away from the hydro pole and looked up at my dad, I thought for a second that he'd lapsed again into Neverland. I was wondering how long I'd have to stand next to this living statue, in public this time, before people started to take notice, when he did something unexpected. Without shifting his eyes or changing his expression, he reached up and calmly removed the flyer from the pole. He was very deliberate, gently pulling each corner over the staples that held it in place, making absolutely sure as not to tear the page more than necessary. He wasn't getting rid of the flyer, tearing it down so that no one would see it: this was something he intended to keep.

We moved on. Now that I was sensitized to them, I saw Billie's wanted poster everywhere: on lamp posts, in store windows, on a community billboard. There was even one in the entrance at Joey's where we stopped for lunch. As excited as I'd been earlier, somehow the prospect of sitting in a diner full of people with my friend's photo posted in the entrance for everyone to see had curbed my appetite. I was convinced that I was being watched.

Dad kept the flyer close to him as we took a seat in a booth toward the back of the diner. He made sure the table's surface was clean and dry before he placed the flyer, face down and unfolded, next to his place setting. He even moved it farther away when the waiter brought over my poutine for fear of gravy spatter.

We sat in near silence for a while until Dad finally got Carl on the phone. It was mostly a one-sided conversation, and I tried as best I could to piece together what they were talking about between my dad's "uh-huhs," "yeahs," "Oks," and "reallys?" He barely touched his lunch. During one stretch of intense listening he picked up the flyer and looked it over as if trying to decipher some code. He hung up suddenly with a barely audible "'k", and sat for a second staring at his club sandwich before looking up at me. "Well . . . that was interesting." He took a sip of water, held it in his mouth for a moment, thinking, then added: "We need to find Billie."

*****

Leave it to Carl for the latest news. According to my uncle, the driver of the ill-fated Honda CRV on Barrette Street had regained consciousness late Wednesday and while he had yet to speak to the media, by Thursday he was coherent enough to provide police with his version of the accident. As a result of his testimony, Billie had surfaced as a subject of some interest to the authorities, and it had nothing to do with skipping out on an examination at the hospital Emergency ward.

The man's name was Paul Worthington, and at about 11:00 a.m. on Victoria Day he and his wife Cathy were headed downtown for a holiday brunch. He told police that they were driving north on Barrette and were startled by a sudden flash of light as they approached the intersection with Centre Street. He remarked that this was odd because the sky had become overcast by then. His first thought, for a fraction of a second, was that there'd been an explosion, except that there'd been no bang or shock wave. He remembered his wife saying "Jesus" as it happened; she was surprised and a bit annoyed, but not alarmed. Then, about a second later she yelled "Paul! Look out!" and that's when he saw the little girl standing in the middle of their lane exactly where the flash had been. He'd already taken his foot off the gas when he'd seen the flash but was still moving at a good clip, so he swerved as hard as he could into the left lane to avoid hitting her. He didn't remember anything after that.

Once he regained consciousness, he was able to give a description of the girl he saw, and when police returned a day later with a sample of photos taken at the scene, he quickly identified Billie as the girl from Monday. He also identified me as having been present moments before—he had had to honk at me to keep me from crossing the street in front of him—but he said that I was alone and never connected me with Billie. He was also pretty insistent that, in his mind, the flash of light and the girl were linked somehow, and that as far as he was concerned the kid in the road was ultimately responsible for the crash and the death of his wife.

That Billie was identified as having been present at the moment of the accident was nothing new: the truck driver had claimed as much within minutes of the police arriving at the scene. Efforts to get any details about Billie had been a dismal failure, but there had been no reason to suspect anything beyond her just being at the wrong place at the wrong time. Kids were always doing that kind of thing, weren't they, playing in the street, heedless of traffic? Drivers always had to be on the lookout. Nor had the truck driver ever mentioned anything about a flash of light. But according to Carl, Mr. Worthington's testimony must have been convincing enough for police not to dismiss it as the babblings of someone looking for a scapegoat, mysterious flash of light or not. No longer just some kid playing in the street at the wrong moment, the cops were apparently now looking at Billie as the possible perpetrator of some act that led to a woman's death. Things had now taken a very different turn, a very serious one, and the look on my dad's face and the flatness of his voice left no doubt.

# 19

**Unexplained flashes of light perplexing Fergustonians**

**Jason Bremmer**
**The Clarion**

[FERGUSTON] In what is either an unsettling case of mass hallucination or some mysterious paranormal phenomenon, residents of Ferguston have been reporting strange and intense flashes of light over the past few weeks.

Beginning in mid-May, there have been a growing number of reports of extremely intense light flares around the region. To date, half a dozen such accounts have been made public.

"It was just the strangest thing," said Ferguston resident Ronald Kelly, who saw one of the flashes last Wednesday while driving along Ridge Road. "Suddenly there's this blinding flash just off to my left. It was there and gone in less than a second, but it was so bright it left spots on my eyes."

There seem to be no discernible pattern to the flashes, aside from their intensity and short duration. They appear to have occurred at all times of day, and in every part of the greater Ferguston area. According to witnesses, the flares are not associated with any noise or disturbances, and tend to be close to the ground.

"It definitely wasn't lightning or an explosion," said another witness who asked not to be identified. "I only caught a quick glimpse, but it didn't come out of the sky and it was totally quiet. It was all over before I knew it."

"I don't want to say it's aliens or something supernatural, necessarily," said another anonymous witness, "but I wouldn't rule out anything. It's just as likely as anything else."

Other more prosaic ideas have been offered as possible explanations for the phenomena. Some have suggested a mysterious atmospheric electrical event known as ball lightning, while others claim that the flashes are merely reflections of sunlight coming off shiny reflective surfaces, like glass and chrome. This has certainly been the case on Lalonde Street in the downtown, where the new Ferguston municipal building, with its south-facing all-glass façade, has generated numerous complaints from drivers and pedestrians alike.

A spokesperson for the OPP agreed, warning against what she called "tall tales" and "urban legends."

"People need to calm down and not jump to outlandish conclusions," said OPP communications officer Sharon McNeil. "We've seen this kind of thing before: somebody sees something they don't understand, and before you know it we're being invaded by extra-terrestrials or the government is conducting secret military experiments."

With the bright sunny weather Ferguston has enjoyed . . .

I remember feeling a bubble of panic rise from my stomach as Dad read the cover story on the Saturday edition of the Ferguston *Clarion*. The paper had been sitting on the bench next to him in the booth at Joey's, and after skimming the cover story Dad looked up and down the front page, then quickly leafed through the rest of the paper.

"Odd," he said. "Carl said that Worthington had described a sudden flash of light on Barrette Street right before the accident, but it's not mentioned here. Bremmer obviously wasn't made aware of it, or it would be all over the place."

Jason Bremmer operated the Ferguston *Clarion*, our local and fully independent newspaper. The *Clarion* came out three times a week in those days, and Bremmer was its editor in chief, primary reporter and columnist, photo editor, and layout artist. He ran virtually the entire operation from his basement, except for the printing, circulation and advertising, which were handled by a small staff at the *Clarion*'s office downtown. Everyone in town knew Bremmer, though few had ever met him in person. Dad said that was because he weighed close to four hundred pounds and never left his house. He hired interns to do his legwork and sourced out things like photography, but it was still no small miracle that he could do all the reporting he did without ever leaving his cellar. He was known to be a tireless worker, relentlessly dedicated to his paper, and completely devoted to the community. Dad said he was about sixty, a bachelor, born and raised in Ferguston, and had been running the *Clarion* since high school. He knew the town and its inhabitants inside out, an impressive feat for someone who was essentially a shut-in. Nothing got by him, and if something didn't make it into the paper it was only because Bremmer didn't think it significant.

Dad generally liked Jason Bremmer: he'd been unfailingly supportive at the time of my mom's disappearance and always provided coverage whenever St. Marc launched community outreach activities like roadside clean-ups and stuff. On the other hand, he could be a handful. Bremmer was a notorious conspiracy theorist, and was not known for his bedside manner; he could be gruff, impatient, a bit rude, and would shamelessly misquote and take words out of context. He also fancied himself a journalist of the highest order, and would become livid when his integrity was questioned.

Dad was still working things over in his head when he spotted an item on the last page. His expression changed, softened, and he turned the paper over to me so that I could see what had caught his eye. It was the obituaries section, and at the top was a photo of an attractive woman, probably in her late thirties, smiling for the camera. The photo was cropped, but I could tell it had been taken at an outdoor café in a foreign city. The hairstyle suggested that the photo was a bit dated, but the woman looked happy: the image was probably taken during a memorable holiday. Of course I recognized the photo. I'd seen it only a few days earlier on the front page of Thursday's *Clarion*, in Jason Bremmer's coverage of the accident on Barrette Street. Immediately below it was an obituary for Cathy Worthington.

*****

A death in a town like Ferguston is a little weird. It's not that the town is so small that everybody necessarily knows the deceased personally, but almost everybody shows up at the funeral anyway. And it's not so much a matter of showing support for the bereaved, although I'm sure in many cases that's part of it. But people in this town will notice who is at the funeral and who isn't. And they remember.

The bells from St. Michael's Anglican were tolling as Dad and I stepped out of the diner. We'd been so wrapped up in Billie-business that we'd completely forgotten that Cathy Worthington's funeral was that day. We'd discussed it briefly earlier in the week, but hadn't revisited the subject since. Dad thought it was important for us to go the funeral on Saturday; part of it was the simple fact that I was present on Barrette Street at the moment she died and it was likely by then that everyone in town knew it. I would be expected. But Dad also felt that he and I should make a point of being present at important events in town, like attending fundraisers for the hospital or the library, or joining in whenever the town organized a beach clean-up day, or volunteering for my school's open house, or other gestures of good citizenship. Dad saw it as a way of giving back to the town, particularly for the support that people in Ferguston gave to us in the days, weeks and months after Mom disappeared.

I didn't mind doing my civic duty, but I wasn't as convinced as my dad that I owed Ferguston anything. I was too young to remember the search efforts for my mom so I don't really know how much of the town was involved. The way my dad tells it, everybody and their dog—literally—were out combing the landscape in all directions, turning over every leaf in an effort to find my mother. But from what I'd been able to put together, they gave up pretty quickly, as soon as the weather turned nasty. And they didn't find a single thing: it was a couple of out-of-towners who found her car. For as long as I can remember, all that Ferguston had left for me were the pity-filled looks and the unwanted local notoriety as "the kid who lost his mom." Well, excuse me, I thought, but I didn't lose my mom: she was taken from me, forever, and someone in this town did it.

*****

My dad and I never had much use for churches, and there were no fewer than nine of them of various denominations in Ferguston. When asked, Dad referred to us Lamberts as "Paper Catholics," meaning that on paper, at least, we were Catholic. Mom had been marginally more devout than Dad and largely to please her church-going parents she had me baptized. After Mom disappeared Dad kept up with the rituals for a little while, going as far as having me take my first communion when I was in Grade Two, mostly as a public relations gesture. After that we stopped altogether: no confirmation for me no matter how it looked. We may have made it to Christmas Eve midnight mass for a couple of years, but beyond that the only reasons we ever had to find ourselves in a church were weddings and funerals.

Not surprising then that we both felt a pang of relief when we realized we'd missed Mrs. Worthington's church service. We could still make it to the cemetery. There would be a short service at the gravesite and a lot of people would be hovering around the periphery: close enough to hear what was going on and far enough ostensibly to give the bereaved their space, but mostly not feel too uncomfortable. We could easily dissolve into the crowd, do our neighbourly duty, and slip away after an appropriate amount of time if we found the service was running a little long. Dad was a bit anxious—no doubt he still had Billie on his mind—and even though the lot at Lakeview Cemetery wasn't yet full, he parked on the side of the secondary lane that lead onto the grounds, anticipating an early exit.

It was bright and sunny again that day so you could expect the local do-gooders to be out in full force at Lakeview, and they didn't disappoint. Dad later suggested, only half-jokingly, that had the funeral been held on a weekday instead of a Saturday the turnout would have been even better: there was nothing like a funeral to provide a guilt-free reason to get out of work for a few hours.

From a distance we could see the family of the deceased clustered around a coffin, forming a black knot of people maybe a dozen and a half in number. They stood motionless, trance-like, their blank eyes staring downward at nothing in particular. The coffin, adorned with a huge arrangement of white roses, sat gleaming silver like a brand-new car on a strip of artificial turf. Closest to the coffin was a very frail-looking figure in a wheelchair whom I guessed was Paul Worthington, fresh out of hospital. The rest of the crowd, and it did qualify as a crowd, formed a loose, less formally attired semicircle some distance behind and around the immediate family.

We soon found that the light breeze that had kicked up off the lake had made it all but impossible to hear the graveside service from where we stood. Dad moved in a bit closer, but when he asked me to come with him, I declined; like most of the onlookers, the need to hear what was going on was overpowered by my desire to keep a safe distance from all that sadness and death. Instead I hung back with the others, vaguely listening in on the half-whispered chitchat passing back and forth around me. Two gentlemen to my right were engaged in office talk; it sounded to me like they may have been colleagues of Mrs. Worthington, although her name never actually came up in the conversation. To my left were a woman and a man, youngish-looking, she in jogging gear, he in jeans and a hoodie. Again, neither was talking about the proceedings or the recently departed: some stuff about the delivery of furniture and something that had to be jettisoned from the house to make room for it. I slipped back a few steps and drifted to the right, making my way behind the onlookers toward a line of trees, all the while keeping an ear open for potentially useful gossip. It didn't take long.

"—scary. Do you really think there's a terrorist cell in Ferguston? C'mon!"

"I'm just telling you what [*unintelligible*] said. He heard [*something-something*] bomb went off that made the car swerve."

"A bomb??? Is that what he said?"

"[*Blah blah*] something to cause that. And supposably [*blah blah blah*] was right nearby at the time. That's why the police are looking for her."

Holy crap. I froze for a moment, then inched my way over a few feet behind someone else not involved in the conversation, a tall man in a dark grey suit. I wanted to get as close as possible to listen in, but stay far enough behind to not be seen. They weren't exactly intellectual giants—Carl would have had a riot with them: he would have called them Tweedle Dee and Tweedle Dumb—but I had to hear them out.

The first speaker—whom I came to think of as Tweedle Dee—continued.

"—thought that was because she might have been hurt . . . you know, from being too close to the accident."

"Well *of course* that's what they're *saying*!" Tweedle Dumb responded. He was the heavier and taller of the two. He wore a baseball cap backward with a Metallica patch above the visor, and a faded denim jacket over a red-and-black lumberjack shirt. He held a beer can in his left hand, his plump pink fingers looking like stale cocktail shrimp. "What else would they say? But just think about it for a second. If she *was* injured, what's more likely: hurt from the accident or from an explosion that *she* caused? Now, if you ask me, *that's* a reason to split from the hospital." He let it sink in a bit and then added, "And how do you think she was able to get out of the hospital by herself?"

"What, you think she had help? You think it's like . . . an inside job?" I couldn't quite tell if Tweedle Dee was asking seriously or just finding this funny. I sure wasn't.

"Maybe. That would explain a few things. But mostly I'm thinking the cops want her for questioning. She's what they call a 'person of interest.'" He paused. "And, I mean, you saw the picture: she's *obviously* a Mooslim! And you know . . . *those people* start their kids really young . . ."

My face was suddenly hot and my hands were shaking. I had never wanted to hit someone so badly in my life, but I wasn't raised that way, and making a scene wasn't in my best interest at the moment. I considered storming off, finding my dad and telling him everything, but again I held back. As maddening as this racist jerk was, he was proving to be useful. I would wait it out. Breathing as quietly as I could, I pushed my fists into my pockets, looked down at my feet and bit down on my lip to keep from screaming.

Tweedle Dee was continuing.

"A sleeper cell? In Ferguston???"

"Why not? Where do you think they train their new people? They start them off real young and in small, out-of-the-way places that don't draw much attention."

The first guy chewed on this for a bit. "Yeah . . . I dunno. Maybe. Seems like you might be reaching on this one, Bill. I'm not saying it's impossible, just . . . it might not be the most likely thing. You know? I mean, we're talking about Ferguston here."

Tweedle Dumb seemed lost for a bit, then, unfortunately, found his way again. "Maybe the kid's part of some kind of doomsday cult or something."

A snort came from the man standing directly in front of me. Apparently, I wasn't the only one listening in, but I for one didn't find the exchange very amusing. I froze for a second as Tweedle Dumb gave the man a quick glare; he then turned back to his buddy who was ruminating on this latest theory.

"Yeah. See, *that* I'd believe. For sure."

Tweedle Dumb pounced. "Absolutely! These cults are everywhere, Ted—"

Of course. It had to be "Bill" and "Ted."

"—Hell, there are some right around here. They pass themselves off as simple farmers, but they're into all kinds of weird shit, and you'd never know it."

"Oh, yeah?"

"*Hell*, yeah! Sure as shit, you can bet all the kids have the same dad, and this one has probably been pegged for some kind of sacrifice."

The man in front of me snorted again, only louder and followed by a wet hiss. He was shaking his head. He was taller and better dressed than the other two and a lot older.

"Do you hear yourself, man?"

Tweedle Dumb—Bill—assumed a defensive posture, without looking directly at the man in front of me. "Jus' sayin' . . ."

A laugh. "No seriously. What are you basing any of this on?"

"Hey, man, I'm just putting two and two together—"

"—and coming up with twelve, apparently. What do you know, really? Police are looking for some kid who may have witnessed an accident, and they haven't yet figured out who she is. In other words, you know precisely nothing."

"Fuck you, pal. I know what I know." Bill was pissed about being shown up by this older man, especially in front of his buddy, but despite all his bluster he was visibly intimidated. He gave a departing glare, snorted a "Whatever, dude . . ." and stalked off with his buddy in tow.

The man in the grey suit watched them off, then, noticing me for the first time gave me a tired grin. "Makes you wonder how many villages out there are looking for their idiot. God knows we have more than our share in Ferguston."

I liked this man. I wanted so badly to believe that he was more representative of the prevailing mindset of Ferguston than those two knuckleheads. Either way, I was satisfied for now with what people were saying, and what they knew or thought they knew about Billie, which was a lot more than I expected. If Billie ever showed up again—and I was somehow convinced she would—she was going to have to be warned.

# 20

A line of trees separated the modern section of Lakeview Cemetery from its older one. There was a lot of tangled undergrowth, and here and there some spindly young maples trying to eke out a living, but for the most part this dividing swath of vegetation was dominated by a dozen or so gigantic white pines. Their towering bare trunks suggested they'd spent most of their very long lives in what had been a crowded forest, and now they stood out from their low-lying surroundings like skyscrapers. They were among the last survivors of the old growth forest that my dad said had existed here for eons. It was like something out of Tolkien, like Fangorn or the Old Forest on the outskirts of the Shire: the last giants of the Ancient World that remained standing, left to watch helplessly while the rest of their kind were cut down and dragged away. It made me incredibly sad. I'd never know how many were lost, probably hundreds in this patch alone, all of them centuries old, all just to make space to bury dead people.

Away to my right, a gravel driveway cut a narrow gash through the brush, leading into Lakeview's old section. There, the drive split in two: on the left it encircled the weathered tomb stones of

Lakeview's earliest occupants along with a single large mausoleum at the very center, while on the right it culminated at a work shed at the back end of the graveyard. Behind the shed, a low stone wall marked the western edge of Lakeview Cemetery, beyond which was Winston Road, some fenced-off pasture lands, and finally the beginnings of the intermittent woodlands to the west and north of town.

I found myself drifting away from the crowd of onlookers; whether they were sincere or just morbidly curious, I felt the urgent need to distance myself from them and I was suddenly grateful that Dad had never held a memorial service for Mom.

There was a bit of a slope that led into the older graveyard and from my vantage point I could see it almost in its entirety. The grounds were completely deserted, and while well-tended, unlike the newer section there were no flowers on any of the graves: all was green grass and grey stone.

I reached the gravel driveway and as I headed down the slope, I noticed a young deer picking its way between the weathered gravestones up to the left near the mausoleum at the center of the grounds. It was small, probably just a year old, too young to sport antlers yet if it was male, but old enough to have lost its white baby spots. The animal's golden tan colour and bright white underside were in marked contrast with the intense green and sombre grey of its surroundings, and made me wonder why I hadn't noticed it a moment earlier.

"Where did you come from, you little sneak?" I whispered, vaguely smiling as I approached. "You remind me of somebody I know."

I turned around for a moment, looking back toward the funeral service to see if the crowd had begun dispersing; if so, my dad would soon be looking for me and I knew how much he hated losing track of me, even for a few minutes. There didn't seem to be any change: there was still a large loose semicircle around the bereaved, so I continued onward.

The ground levelled off where the gravel drive crossed over a muddy stream, the giant pines towering above either side. I stepped into the old section of the cemetery, now climbing a gentle slope, and followed the drive as it split off to the left. The difference between the old section and the new was glaring. The plots were smaller, as were the monuments, and although the lawns were equally well tended it was pretty clear that aside from a regular trim this side didn't receive the attention that the newer one did. The shrubs around the periphery looked neglected, the fencing was in disrepair, and a number of gravestones were leaning over.

I moved up amongst graves and gave the inscriptions on the monuments a closer look.

> *Hélène Maryse Chaput*
> *Née le 15 mars, 1921*
> *Décédée le 26 décembre, 1952*
> *Nous ne t'oublierons jamais*

> *In memory of Gordon P. Phillips*
> *Beloved husband of Agnes*
> *Born June 28, 1855*
> *Died October 31, 1923*

> *In loving memory of our beloved son*
> *Bradley James Ellis*
> *Born July 22, 1900*
> *Died February 12, 1903*

The stones were noticeably older and more weathered than those of the newer section. In the oldest of them, the engraved text was barely legible, like old wounds long healed. There was also a sameness to these earlier markers, tending to be smallish and seemingly cut from the same stone. The most recent gravestone that I could see on my quick inspection was from 1961, with the majority of those that were still legible dating between the early to mid-1920s to the late 1950s. A few were much older still, with the earliest that I could actually decipher dating to the late 1880s. I also noticed a preponderance of French and Irish surnames. Interesting.

I continued my survey, brushing away dirt from some of the stones that lay flush to the ground.

> *Irene A. Murphy*
> *Born August 25, 1919*
> *Died April 3, 1920*

> *Catherine G. Murphy*
> *Born January 18, 1921*
> *Died March 7, 1921*

> *Bébé Dompierre*
> *Née et décédée le 21 février, 1900*

> *Frances Carpentier*
> *Daughter of Gilles and Lucy*
> *Died November 11, 1903*
> *Aged 4 years*

> *McConnell*
> *In Memory of Patrick*
> *Son of John and Kathleen*
> *Died August 12, 1919*
> *Aged 2 months*

A disturbing pattern was emerging: a disproportionate number of children never made it to their sixth year. There were also a surprising number of women in their late teens and twenties. At first, I thought I was in an area designated for young people, but a more thorough inspection indicated otherwise. I conducted a quick count, did some conservative mental math, and from what I could tell at least one in four burials was for a child under five years of age.

I was stunned. I tried to imagine the parents and siblings of these little kids, and the shock they must have felt from losing someone so young. Or was it more commonplace in those days, with young women dying from complications during childbirth, and children succumbing to diseases like TB, polio, and the flu, not to mention accidents? I tried to imagine living at a time when young deaths were so common, and wondered whether this commonness made it hurt any less.

As I looked up again to take stock of where I'd wandered to, I was startled by the presence of the young deer I'd seen earlier, now barely two metres away. It was weird that I hadn't noticed it at all since I'd approached this side of the cemetery; and yet there it was all of a sudden, big as life. The deer seemed oblivious of me, casually nibbling at the longer shoots of grass right next to the mausoleum where the tractor-mower couldn't reach.

I'd never been so close to a wild animal like this in my life, not including birds or squirrels or raccoons I might have chased out of the garbage. It was the sweetest thing I'd ever seen. I was close enough to see its little pink tongue as it chewed, and the subtle flick of its enormous ears to ward off a mosquito. I couldn't be sure if it even knew I was there, and I didn't dare move a muscle for fear of scaring it off, until it took another step more or less in my direction and calmly looked straight at me. It was fixing me with its huge eyes, looking in no way alarmed or even surprised I was there. Its eyes were like shiny black marbles, with a dot of white fur above each one and long pretty lashes. It took another step and now I could make out the slightly pebbly texture on the underside of its black nose and hear the soft smacking of its mouth as it chewed. It had a patch of white fur on the upper part of its throat, about the size of my hand, that looked irresistibly soft, and with one more step I'd be able to reach out and touch it. As if reading my thoughts, it took another step toward me, its gaze never wavering from mine. The little pink tongue came out and licked its muzzle, and I was now close enough to catch a whiff of the fresh grass it was eating. It was so close I could have seized its head between my hands if I'd wanted to. I could make out every detail of its face, the texture of its fur, even hear its breathing through its glistening nose, and as I stared into its black featureless eyes, I could feel heat emanating from its body, and detect a smell that was something like, but not quite, cinnamon.

For the briefest flicker of an instant I had started to form the thought, *I should have known*, which may have been accompanied by the beginnings of a smile. The feeling, as fleeting as it was, reminded me of when you finally see the hidden image in a stereogram. But the thought vanished before it had really gained any footing, as I suddenly found that I was staring at Billie. The transformation was instantaneous: there was no gradual morphing from deer to girl, no shifting from animal to human features. One moment I was looking at this bold young wild creature, the next Billie was occupying the very same space.

I must have looked terrified because Billie's expression was a lot softer than usual. Instead of the curious-yet-mildly-annoyed face she wore a lot of the time, she looked genuinely concerned for me. "Hey," she offered in a soft voice, extending her hand. "It's OK. Really."

But for the moment at least it really wasn't OK. Uh-uh. No sir, not at all. Until just now, even in my craziest imaginings, Billie was girl from the future who had been popping in and out of the present, part of some time travel/teleportation project. The sudden appearances and disappearances may have been more than a bit freaky, but that didn't change who Billie was. Until now, Billie had just been a little girl. But I had just witnessed her transform instantaneously from a deer to a human. No tricks or diversions

153

or optical illusions. Little girls didn't do that. Billie was officially something else.

I began to back away. If this is what the truly extraordinary was all about, my instinct told me that I wanted no part of it. Earlier that week I was upset at her disappearance from a totally enclosed space. Although I had to deal with the implications of that, which were enormous, I didn't even see it happen. And still I cried like a baby. This transformation before my very eyes was too damn much, and if I didn't want to turn into a blubbering moron and lose any hold I still had on reality, I had to remove myself from the situation. Right frigging now.

"Justin, don't be afraid," she said. She didn't move toward me but kept her hand out, beckoning me back with her fingers. "Sit down, and we'll talk."

I was shaking my head. No, I didn't want her talking to me. I didn't want her looking at me. I didn't want whatever she was to have anything to do with me. It was as if all the world's leaders suddenly took an interest in me and wanted to chat, only a billion times worse. I was small and unimportant and wanted to stay that way. If she wanted to sit down for a polite little *tête-à-tête*, she should be doing it in front of the UN General Assembly, or a room full of Nobel Prize winners, or Stephen frigging Hawking, somebody brilliant or important. Not some nerdy pre-teenage kid from Ferguston, Ontario.

I wanted to turn and run, but my feet were slabs of lead. With my eyes still locked on Billie, I willed myself backward a few steps, dragging my feet over the ground, first crunching over gravel, then sliding over grass. Three steps back, then four, each step a bit easier than the one before it. Billie stayed where she was, her expression passive, no longer imploring. It looked to me like she'd resigned to let me go. She let her hand fall back to her side and was saying "Justin, you're going . . ." when I backed into a small grave marker that caught me just below my knees. I fell backward in a heap, landing square on my butt, my jaw slamming shut in the process.

Billie, for her part, squealed like it was the funniest thing she'd ever seen. "OMIGOD! You're such a klutz!" she howled, holding her stomach. "That was *SO* funny! Do that again, *pleeeeeeease!*"

Whatever Billie was, her sense of humour was still very much that of a nine-year-old girl.

*****

"What . . . are you?"

My composure and dignity were at least partially restored, which wasn't a bad feat all things considered. My breathing was shallow and I still had tears in my eyes—a combination of having had reality brutally turned on its head and of having my spine jarred by falling on my ass—but I'd at least gotten myself under control. My voice was still a bit shaky, and I spoke in a near whisper for fear of crying again.

Billie was now sitting next to me, her back against another tombstone. For the moment at least I didn't want to look directly at her; Billie seemed to understand this and didn't press it.

"That's a little complicated, actually." I didn't realize it then, but that was maybe the biggest understatement in human history. In fact, trying to explain what she was would be like trying to explain string theory to a blindfolded six-year-old using half the alphabet and no number larger than three.

"I'm told I'm really smart." I managed to summon up just enough courage to be sarcastic. "Try me."

She looked up toward the Worthington funeral. "Well, it's going to take a while to explain, and you don't have much time. Your dad is going to be looking for you very soon."

She was right. Even from a distance I could see people fidgeting, putting on jackets, picking up things they'd set down. The burial proceedings were coming to a close, and I suddenly realized how exposed we were talking out there in the open. Given enough time someone was going to see us, and things could get awkward.

"People are looking for you, too," I said. "I guess you're not too worried about that."

Billie gave me a little smile and half shrug but didn't reply. I pushed a bit further.

"So . . . I'm guessing you're not really a little girl . . . any more than you're a deer."

". . . or a poplar or a sturgeon or a flock of starlings for that matter," she said. "Those are just shapes to make things easier. Shapes for something that has no shape."

"All that was you? Why . . ."

"Just experiencing the world in ways that I couldn't as a nine-year-old girl."

"When did you start talking like a grown-up?" She smiled again, clearly pleased, then continued while I attempted to digest everything.

"It's just that you don't have a word that really describes what . . ." She left the thought unfinished, reflected for a moment and tried again. "See, I don't even know whether to use *I* or *we* or even *it*. I guess . . . I'm part of a continuum."

"Well, I remember you said you were part of a collective," I recalled, "to my dad and my uncle. We'd pretty much decided you were part of a cult by then." A pause. "What do you mean by 'continuum'?"

"A single, conscious . . . being. A pretty big one, I guess, by the way you people measure things." She smiled. "It's going to take too long to explain, really. I'll try again when we have more time. Let's just say for now that I'm not something you've ever experienced."

That wasn't saying much. I wasn't even thirteen years old. I wasn't about to say it out loud, but sex wasn't something I'd ever experienced either, although I could certainly get my head around it.

"I have to go. Come." She beckoned me over to the west wall of the mausoleum. It was the side that wasn't visible from the main part of the cemetery. We were completely hidden from view, and for a fleeting instant I thought she was going to try to kiss me. I hesitated for just a second; looking at this skinny little girl it was so easy to forget that I wasn't dealing with an actual person, or even anything that fit my definition of life. It was still too soon; my brain was in no hurry to give up its sense of what was real. "Quickly!" she said. I moved closer.

"Umm," she began very gently, as if she was speaking to a toddler. She was choosing her words carefully; I appreciated that. "You see . . . space and time, at least the way you understand them, don't really apply to me. I'm kind of . . . outside all of that. I'll do my best to explain everything later. The good news is that you don't ever have to worry about me. Yes, people are looking for me, and you're right: I'm not too worried about that. But that doesn't mean I don't have to be careful. I don't want things to get complicated for you." She gave a quick glance around and continued. "Actually, this isn't a bad place to meet. It's pretty well blocked from view on most sides, and besides the groundskeeper, not many people ever come here." She took my hand in hers, and she looked into me in a way I'd never known was possible. It was almost tactile, like walking through smoke. "I do have to be careful, Justin, but I can find you at any time. If ever you want to talk to me, just come here."

Billie then let go of my hand, and with that warmth suddenly gone I realized that the only thing that mattered to me at that moment was to hold on to it.

"I'll see you soon," she said and smiled as if she'd just made a joke. She then stepped away a couple of paces, said "Cover your eyes," and put her left hand out as if she were about to give someone a handshake. At that moment an intense white light appeared, beginning at her fingertips and stretching vertically in both directions. It was so brilliant it was hard to look at, but I couldn't make myself turn away. The entire process lasted barely a second, otherwise I might have suffered permanent eye damage; as it happened, I'd have the afterimage tattooed to my retinas for the rest of the day. Meanwhile, Billie's hand seemed to be inserted into this brilliant seam of light, which then divided into an untold number of lines that looked like the pages of an enormous book. She stepped forward between these pages, oblivious to the blinding light, and vanished into thin air, her form seeming to dissolve as she stepped through the threshold. As the pages of light closed over her, the seam disappeared with a *thhp!* as if a vacuum had drawn it shut from the inside.

I stayed where I was for what seemed like ages, staring at the spot where, as far as I could determine, Billie had stepped out of reality. For a moment the air had been disturbed, motes of dust and pollen that had been floating past swirled about in odd patterns, only to be recaptured by the prevailing breeze. I sat idly, as still as the monuments around me, for how long I had no idea. Finally, after a time that was impossible to guess, I stood up, my legs cramped and shaky, and made my way back to the cemetery driveway to find my dad.

# 21

I felt bad about keeping my dad in the dark about my meeting with Billie in the graveyard, not the least because he was genuinely worried about her and even said we needed to find her for her safety. Of course, I now knew full well that her safety had never been in doubt, but explaining to Dad how I knew that wasn't going to be easy, so I decided to keep everything to myself, at least for the time being.

With the comfort of knowing that Billie was going to be fine and, more importantly, that I was going to get to see her again and have my questions answered, my life could go more or less back to normal. I still had an enormous secret, bigger than ever it turned out, but now I was excited about it rather than stressed out. I knew I was going to have to work out a plausible excuse for regular excursions to the cemetery, but with summer vacation just around the corner that was going to be less of a problem.

As the days became weeks and May became June, I started noticing something else. It began as an awareness of an absence. Any seventh grader anywhere will tell you that the final month of school is far and away the most stressful and emotionally charged time of the year. Normally I would have felt a gradual but definite tightening of my stomach, stretched—no pun intended—over three weeks, culminating with four or five days of panic-stricken, caffeine-fuelled adrenalin rushes to finish up year-end assignments and cram for final exams—such as they are in the seventh grade— my insides gradually liquefying as due dates crept closer.

That year, my usual descent into panic simply didn't happen. It was as if I'd developed a cushion, a protective emotional layer against anxiety. I was calm, I was focused, and I could think with a lot more clarity than before, kind of the way I imagine people feel when they give up caffeine or drugs or alcohol. It was weird. I mean, I had always been a pretty decent student, but I'd usually found it all too easy to be distracted. Not that spring. Even my dad noticed. After dinner I'd head up to my room, burrow myself into my textbooks and class notes, and study until I couldn't keep my eyes open. Dad would check in every night, sometimes more than once, just to see if I was still alive, sometimes bearing food and drink—study fuel, he called it. I'd recite my presentations to him or have him read my assignments, but that was just to have another ear for last-minute editing and there was almost never any tweaking to be done. Dad would just sit there with his eyebrows arched, give me a perplexed shrug and stammer out some tepid suggestion: add a comma here, take the "The" out of the title, make this into two sentences rather than one. He was usually very careful with praise, so his response to my work that spring stood out. He'd say stuff like "Wow!" or "That's great, Juss . . . I don't know what to say," and after reading my final history essay, he said: "I'd give that an A-plus." Evidently my history teacher agreed.

In the end, all the deadlines came and went, I breezed through my final weeks with more ease and less stress than I ever had before, and, as I headed home after that final Friday, I found myself looking forward to the coming weeks, catching up with

Billie again and finally getting some answers to questions I barely knew how to ask.

*****

Being the only child of a middle school teacher has its perks, especially during the summer. It's like a long weekend that lasts two months. Add to that the fact that both Dad and I like the same things, and that at twelve years of age I was still a year or two away from a real summer job, and you start to get giddy at the possibilities. On Saturday morning, the day after school ended, over a celebratory breakfast of waffles and sausage, Dad and I were plotting strategy as to where we would go and what we would do with all that time. Of course there were the no-brainers: trips to Toronto, Ottawa, and Montreal to visit the relatives, and our yearly wilderness canoe excursion. Those were pretty automatic and represented maybe a week and a half over the entire summer.

In addition to the yearly visits and camping, my dad suggested that this might be the summer he would finally take me out west. He'd already started looking at the possibility of flying us somewhere, maybe Alberta or, more tantalizing still, Arizona or Nevada, then renting a car and spending a week driving around, seeing the sights. My mouth fell open. For a paleo-nerd like me this was the equivalent of a football fan going to the Super Bowl. Half a world away my dad was saying something along the lines that it wasn't a done deal, that he was still working on it, blah blah blah, but I was long gone. In my mind I was already prospecting for dinosaur fossils in the badlands east of Calgary, or riding a horse down into the Grand Canyon, or standing on the lip of Meteor Crater in Arizona. For most kids my age the dream holiday would have involved a theme park somewhere, roller coasters and deep-fried junk food and movies on giant screens, or maybe a week on a beach. It certainly wouldn't have included wandering a windswept and dusty wasteland, eyes in the dirt, looking for bones, projectile points and ancient pieces of pottery. My dad just sat and watched amused as I jumped up and down like a four-year-old, going "Yes, yes, yes, oh please, yes!" before finally stepping in and becoming a parent again.

"Gee, I'm glad you're not too disappointed, Juss. But that would still be more than a month away, and until then I'd like you to use your time productively." I knew what he was getting at. He was encouraging me to do some kind of volunteer work somewhere in town to get me out of the house and hopefully contribute to society a bit. By that point I was so excited that I would have gladly agreed to cleaning the toilets at The Pit downtown, on a Sunday morning, for free.

Earlier in the spring we'd talked about where I would work, but since my last encounter with Billie all I could think of was finding a way to volunteer mowing the lawn and doing grounds maintenance at Lakeview Cemetery. My dad was a bit surprised at first and while it seemed on the surface to be a tad morbid, he had to agree that it was a sensible enough idea: outdoor work, lots of fresh air, and the solitude would naturally appeal to an introvert like me. It was a long shot of course: they might not need any volunteers and it might not be an everyday thing even if they did, but he figured I could complement it with a few days a week at the library or clothing depot. Anyway, he said he'd make a call or two for me, but I would have to look into the library myself.

Deal!

\*\*\*\*\*

We spent the rest of that Saturday morning poring over my dad's atlas—old school—looking at every conceivable destination of interest in the American Southwest and Western Canada. Already, the excitement normally reserved for our annual camping trip had faded into the background, and all I could think of was getting out and telling Billie all about our looming adventure in the land of the setting sun. Plus, I figured I'd swing by the library on my way to the cemetery to ask about volunteering, feeling somehow that the sooner I got that started the sooner our departure would arrive. Certainly Dad was impressed with my initiative, so he didn't ask questions as I grabbed a water bottle and took off on my still oversized twelve-speed bike toward the west end of town.

It was going to be another scorcher of a day: the wind I felt on my face as I was speeding across town was a bit like that waft of air you get when you open a dishwasher that has just finished its cycle. It couldn't have been more appropriate for the first day of holidays. It's what you wait for all year when you live in Ferguston, and it fuelled me as much as my sweet and sticky breakfast had. I took the bike path through Garrison Park, zipped over the footbridge past the marsh at the eastern edge, and watched as a great blue heron heaved itself into the air sensing my approach. Picking up speed, I swung to the right where the path divided, uphill past the sandpit, past the swings and play structure, exiting the park and crossing a still tranquil Lakeside Drive at near full throttle. Appropriate that I should be heading west, I thought.

Approaching the intersection of Scott Street, the pedestrian signal began flashing the red hand, so I crouched low onto the handlebars and bore down, my legs pumping in a smooth, confident rhythm. I made the green light at Scott with time to spare, and the next one at King Street as well. I was soaring. On any day other than this unofficial first day of summer I probably would have missed both those lights. On another day I would have been slower, more careful, more mindful, and I would have almost certainly noticed the neon green pickup truck keeping pace with me two blocks behind.

# 22

I found Billie right where she was supposed to be, almost: in the older section of Lakeview Cemetery, sitting with her back against the south wall of the mausoleum. We'd originally agreed that the west wall was less visible, but there was no one else around and I figured she knew best how to take care of herself anyway so I let it go. Besides, she was clearly enjoying the sun.

We didn't say much at first, just wandered from one gravesite to the next, absently reading the grave markers, gradually making our way uphill into the newer section. In typical fashion she had one hand out, her fingers grazing the surfaces of the stones, feeling the contrast of textures, the smooth polished faces and more roughly chiselled contours. To my mixed alarm and amusement, at one point, Billie stopped in front of a grave, stooped and pulled a purple chrysanthemum out of a stale bouquet drying out in front of a stone of pinkish granite. Leave it to Billie.

"No one leaves flowers on the other side," she said, pointing back beyond the stand of trees behind us. "Why not?"

"Well, those graves are really, really old. The children and even the grandchildren of those people would be elderly by now. There may not be anyone left to leave any flowers behind."

"That's so sad."

"Yeah, it is. Uhhh, Billie . . . You know, I don't think you're supposed to be picking flowers from the bouquets that people leave at the gravesites."

"Why?" You really had to spell everything out for that kid.

"Because they're not for you. You can't take things that don't belong to you, Billie."

"I know that!"

"Those flowers are for the deceased." I regretted saying that the moment it left my lips.

"But those people are *dead*." She held up the mum. "The person whose grave this came from died in 1978; her body has been decomposing for over twenty-five years."

Already this was turning into a conversation I didn't want have with her. Like Dad always says: pick your battles. "No . . . Yes, you're right. I don't think that person minds. Sorry."

Billie gave a deep nod of vindication. She could be so cute.

I tried to provide some context. "It's just a gesture. People often feel at a loss when someone close to them dies. One moment they're there, the next they're gone. They miss them and it hurts. So they go to where their body was buried and they leave something for them, just a token, something that had some meaning. Could be anything."

"Yeah, I noticed. A lot of pictures. Someone back there left money."

"Really? I've never seen that before, but sure, I guess. It probably has something to do with leaving coins with the dead to pay the ferryman." Billie gave me a look of bewilderment that made me, once again, regret setting off on this path, but this time I figured it was worth a full explanation. And besides, I actually knew the answer to this one.

"A long time ago people used to believe that the spirits of the dead had to cross a river on a ferry to get to their final resting place, and that the man who operated the ferry had to be paid, otherwise you couldn't go across. So people started leaving coins either on the eyes or in the mouths of the dead before they were buried, so that they could pay the ferryman."

"But if they're dead . . ."

"I know what you're going to say. It was just a belief that was popular a long time ago. I think people do it now just because it's tradition."

Something in the look on Billie's face suggested I'd wasted my time. Instead, she stuck a hand in her front pocket and pulled it out triumphantly, producing a fistful of weathered coins. "Look: almost four dollars!"

"*BILLIE!!!*"

\*\*\*\*\*

I have no doubt that Billie had never intended to keep the $3.85 she found on the grave of Sgt. Arthur R. Smithson—deceased Oct. 30th, 1917—that she only wanted to show it to me because she thought I'd find the coins themselves interesting, but I wasn't going to get off her case until she returned them to their rightful resting place, which she did eventually. I figured she could keep the flower.

I shook my head as I watched her. This wasn't going as I expected. I'd been anticipating this meeting for a few weeks, playing it over in my head, and in every scenario, I was either nervous or excited or even terrified. This was, after all, a person whom I had not only seen transform herself instantaneously from a deer to a human, but also vanish into thin air by opening a seam into the very fabric of reality. Before my own eyes! She had demonstrated, quite effectively, that she wasn't of this world. By all rights, I should have been reduced to a drooling idiot around her.

And yet she was behaving in a way that was exactly what you'd expect from an—albeit precocious—nine-year-old kid, and here I was as annoyed and amused by her as I'd always been.

But I had questions, and as far as I was concerned, Billie and I had made a deal.

"So . . . What are you?"

"I'm sorry. What?"

"Are you, like, an alien?"

"HA!"

"I didn't really think so. A time-traveller from the future?"

"No."

"Please don't tell me you're an angel. I don't want to have to start going to church and begging for forgiveness."

This time she actually squealed. "*Omigod!* An 'angel': that's hilarious! I don't even know what to say about that."

"But seriously, if I were some really religious person—and most people in Ferguston are—you could hardly blame me for thinking I was talking to God . . . or at least a stand-in."

"Well, you'd be disappointed. I don't make stuff, I don't perform miracles, or listen to prayers, or do things to reward or punish people, or even know what people are thinking." She paused a bit, the half grin on her face fading, subtly shaking her head.

She continued. "In a way, I'm like you. In the same way that you're part of this universe, made of the same stuff as everything else in it, I'm also a small part of something else . . . part of a much bigger whole."

It wasn't much to go on, and as a basis for comparison it was pretty, well, basic. "Yeah," I tried, "but are you part of a civilization? Are there a lot of you?"

"Umm . . . No, that's not it. You see, that's the main difference between us. I'm part of a single, continuous . . . thing . . . an entity." She tilted her head to the side, seeing if I was catching on, then added: "Each one of you is a single individual being with its own mind, its own identity, right? Well I'm part of one consciousness. There's really no proper word for it. I guess you can call it 'a continuum.'"

"Where are you from?"

"Well, again, there's no simple answer to that. In relation to you, I'm from everywhere and nowhere at the same time."

I paused for a second, retrieving a memory from earlier. "When I asked you that the first time, you said 'Not here. Not now.' You weren't avoiding the question, were you? You were actually answering it. You're not from here, and you're not from now."

Billie nodded.

"OK, but where do you go when you . . . step out of here?"

"I suppose you can call it another dimension, if you like, where space and time as you know them don't . . . apply." Sensing my frustration she added, "I'm sorry, Justin. It's hard to explain."

"I know: it's 'outside of my experience.' OK, what about what you said about colours, and sounds . . . and your name?"

"Oh, that's just about light and sound that are outside your range of perception. And as for my name, the name of the continuum, there is no real name in the way you're called 'Justin.' You don't need a name if there's nobody else around to use it. If I had a name it would be more like a description of ideas that have no translation, and would take . . . well, a lot more than a few days to describe."

I was becoming aware of just what a contradiction Billie was. On the one hand, as in the instance with the grave offerings, she had the innocence of a child even younger than she appeared to be. But on the other hand, like at that moment, she was like a grown-up, wise and mature, patiently explaining difficult concepts to a much younger mind.

A stray idea suddenly bubbled its way into my mind.

"If you can come and go in and out of reality whenever you like, why were you so freaked out at the hospital?"

Billie pondered that one for a bit. "Well," she began, "first of all, I can't spend too much time here at a stretch. I'm not made of the same stuff as you are, and if I'm here too long . . . let's just say unpleasant things happen."

"Like what, for example?"

"Well, in the same way there are certain things you wouldn't want to leave in water for too long . . ."

"You'd dissolve?"

"Dissolve, break apart, disintegrate, yeah."

"That's awful!"

"Not really. There's . . . a lot of me. It would be like a single drop in a billion, billion oceans. Even less. No big deal. But anyone seeing it would freak. And I didn't like where things were going, all the questions and the idea of tests and everything. I was worried I wouldn't be able to get away without causing a major commotion. Plus, I can't help reacting to things like a nine-year-old kid."

"Why not just give them what they wanted?"

"What? My name? My address? Who my parents are? You're funny."

"OK, but what about—"

"A blood sample? A pee sample? I told you that already: I don't have anything to give them."

"You mean you can't . . . ?"

She shook her head. "Also, I knew things would get complicated as soon as someone touched me. You saw how Debbie reacted."

"Because you're so hot?"

"Not just that." She extended an arm. "Squeeze. As hard as you can."

I gripped her left forearm with my right hand and squeezed, then suddenly stopped and stared at her.

I expected the warmth. What I didn't expect was the feeling in my hand: her arm felt like a steel bar wrapped in a layer of stiff foam rubber, like you get on the handles of exercise machines.

"You can squeeze a lot harder than that. I'm like that all over. Where you have soft parts and harder parts, I'm like this everywhere. Plus, the clothes are part of me. I can't so much as roll up my sleeves or take off my shoes. A doctor trying to examine me might find it weird."

Understatement of the year.

"But you have scratches on your legs, and that looks like a scab."

"They're not real; they're decorations, details. I'm not a real little girl. I'm a copy. A pretty good one, but still a copy."

"Not that good. You had those when I first met you. They should have healed by now."

She examined herself thoughtfully. "Yeah, it's not perfect but it's getting better. I had to learn a lot at the beginning. Like about density; I'm not made of the same stuff as a real little girl and I guess I miscalculated. You might not have noticed the first couple of times we met, but I weighed over two hundred kilos. I was afraid I was going to break your pirate ship."

We were both silent for a moment. A "copy." So many questions were clamouring to get out, and I didn't know how to triage them. *A copy of . . . ?*

"Why were you so afraid of D-Ray that day I met you near the library? You didn't have anything to worry about."

She paused, looking at me, choosing her words carefully. "I was afraid for you."

"But the way you reacted—"

"Like I said, I'm a copy of a real person. A real person with real emotions. I feel what Billie feels."

"So 'Billie' is a real person?"

"Yes, just not from here."

My mind was swimming. I went back to my original line of questioning. "What if someone at the hospital had stuck a needle in your arm: what would have happened?"

"Not much. There's no blood to draw out. The needle wouldn't get very far, and then it would either bend or break. I told you: I'm not made of the same stuff as you are. This"—she said, indicating her body—"is just a shell."

"So you could be anything you want to be? A little girl, or a baby deer, or a tree, or a flock of birds, like you said?"

". . . or the grass you walk on or even the air you breathe."

The beginnings of a cold tickle started to inch up my spine.

"So why a little girl? Seems to me if I could be anything I wanted I'd—"

"'Cause I couldn't talk with you if I was a tree, could I?"

Fair enough. "But you could be anything? Or anybody?"

"Well, yeah, in theory, and I take all kinds of shapes when it's helpful, but would you be talking to me if I were some old lady, or some man in a suit? This way at least you wouldn't be afraid of me and I wouldn't draw too much attention to myself. It's a small town and I don't want to be too conspicuous."

"So, no fire-breathing dragons, I'm guessing."

"Ha, ha. I can only *copy* things; I can't make them up. Fire-breathing dragons have never existed. It has to be something or someone that exists or has existed, here or . . . elsewhere."

My mouth fell open and my eyes nearly rolled out of their sockets. The immediate implications weren't lost on my twelve-year-old imagination.

"Oh. My. God. That means, you could appear as . . . *a dinosaur??*"

"Don't even go there! The answer is NO!"

"I wouldn't tell anyone! I wouldn't take any pictures, I swear. Please! PLEASE! Just once. Just for a few seconds . . ."

"Justin, stop it! It's out of the question. Can you just imagine what would happen if anybody else saw a dinosaur? Here?"

"Actually, knowing Ferguston, probably not much."

"It doesn't matter. Dinosaurs don't belong here. Their place is in the past. It would be *so* wrong! I'm trying to blend in here, and that would be really messing things up."

Something in that last statement nagged at me a bit. I was going to have to bring it up again: there was way too much to deal with right now. "OK," I continued. "So . . . you can go backward in time?

"Yeah. Backward, forward, sideways."

"I'm sorry: sideways?"

"Uh-huh." Billie paused for a second, piecing thoughts together in a way that would be coherent to me and that the nine-year-old avatar she'd created for herself—precocious as she was—could express. "You see, time is just like another place for me." The look on my face couldn't have helped much, so she tried again. "OK. Have you ever seen an ant farm? Maybe at a science fair or something? You take two sheets of glass, stand them on their sides and fill the space in between with sand—"

"Right," I said. "And then you put ants into it and they dig out a colony and you can see them inside moving around in their tunnels."

"Exactly. Now imagine if you were to do that but you made the space in between the sheets of glass so narrow that the ants couldn't move sideways. At all. They wouldn't be able to walk next to each other, or even turn around; they could only go over top of one another or underneath. Eventually you'd have generations of ants living out their lives in this place who would only know a world of two dimensions: up/down and back/front. They would have no idea, no concept, of side to side. Even if they were a lot smarter than typical ants, they'd have no way of even imagining it."

"OK. Except—"

Billie smiled. "I know what you're going to say: the ants themselves have width, and so do their tunnels. You're right. It's not a perfect comparison. Better would be if you had creatures shaped like ball bearings rolling through a tube: there's just enough space around them that they could roll forward or backward. Of course, maybe after a long time the really smart ones would be able to imagine a width greater than their own bodies, but it would be almost impossible to demonstrate. You get the idea?"

"Yeah." She was a lot like Dad. When she got going, she was hard to slow down.

"OK. Now you, Justin, from your position outside the ant farm or whatever, have a point of view that they could never imagine. First of all, you're a lot bigger. Also, you can see them from the side, from the top and from underneath, right? Well, I'm in that kind of position in time—well, space too; they end up being pretty much the same thing. At this moment, here right now, I'm just like another ant standing in front of you, in one of the tunnels in your colony." She pointed toward the mausoleum beyond the line of trees, in Lakeview's older section. "What you saw that time last month would be like watching another ant suddenly punch a hole into the side of the tunnel, and then seeing that hole disappear."

"OK . . ."

"Moving through time is as easy for me as walking around in any direction is for you. Backwards, forwards . . . and sideways, 'sideways' meaning I can exist for as long as I want in what is for you a single moment. For you everything else would be frozen. Right now I happen to be moving in the same direction as you in time; it's like we're walking together in the same direction on a sidewalk, or like the ants moving forward through their tunnels. But if I wanted to, I could turn right or left or walk backward, or even run far ahead of you."

"What would that be like? What would I see?"

"Well, that would depend on me, I guess. You wouldn't necessarily notice anything, as long as I came right back to the exact same spot. Otherwise it would just look like I disappeared. You've seen that before."

"Those bright flashes of light."

She nodded.

We were both quiet for a moment. The heat of the late morning was becoming a physical weight, and the breeze still too feeble to keep it at bay. It had a presence like a teacher walking between the rows of a classroom during dictation, smothering any noise. Silence through oppression, Dad called it. If not for the intermittent whirr of a small engine somewhere to the east—a chainsaw maybe?—there would be almost no sound at all: just the occasional chickadee from the big pines down the hill, or a mosquito whining near my ear. Billie seemed to be enjoying the stillness, the heat, the light, and it seemed rude to interrupt it, but there was something that was nagging at me.

"Billie, when you pop over from . . . wherever it is you go, do you know exactly where you're going to appear?"

She seemed a bit surprised at the question. "Yeah," she answered. "Pretty much."

"'Pretty much?'" I asked. "Sorry, it's just . . . You've mentioned you don't want to be conspicuous, so obviously you need to be careful about where you suddenly appear. Right? Because of the flash of light and all . . ."

A bit of a frown now, a very subtle stiffening in her neck and shoulders. "Yeah . . . What? Why?"

"Sorry, it's nothing . . . just . . . Remember the accident on Barrette Street? The traffic accident? I didn't actually see you so I don't know for sure, but didn't you just kind of appear in the middle of the road?"

Billie's expression dissolved into something like confusion, as if I'd just asked her a question she'd never had to ponder before.

"Really? Maybe . . . I don't remember." I stared into her face for a moment, looking for something that I probably wouldn't recognize if I saw it. Those black eyes weren't giving anything away.

How could she not remember? She'd been within a few feet of a horrific collision involving a cement truck. I'd felt the shock wave myself. Based on where I first saw her on the street, she must have been showered with bits of glass and chunks of flying metal. That she'd come out of it without so much as a scratch was a whole other issue—apparently, she didn't bruise or bleed—but how could she not remember where she was? I wanted to push the issue, but she'd already opened so many other doors, I barely knew where to begin. It would have to keep.

I decided instead to pick up where we'd left off. "So cool that you can go back in time," I said in the most wistful voice I could muster. "I don't suppose you could take me with you . . ."

"Sorry, but your past has already happened for you. You can't go back. It's done."

"Oh." Disappointment cushioned by low expectations.

"As I said, you're in a dimension where time flows only in one direction: forward."

"So what about the future?"

"No. You belong here and now, Justin. It would be really . . . awkward. Besides, even if it was possible, you'd be stuck. As I said, *you* can't go back in time."

So "no," but not an absolute "no." I'd have to file this one away for possible future use. Onward: "What about—"

My cell chirped. A text message. Dad: *Sudbury this aft? Dinner with Carl? LMK ASAP.* He was getting better with texting abbreviations.

"Gotta go, Billie. See you here again? Soon?"

"Sure." Then, as an afterthought: "Something you should know, Justin. Remember that awful man, the one with the funny hair and the limp?"

A cold vice instantly gripped my stomach.

"The one your dad called D-Ray? He followed you in his truck this morning. You lost him by taking a shortcut he couldn't follow, but he could have figured out that you were coming here."

I suddenly needed a washroom.

"You have to be more careful," she continued.

She really was a master of understatement.

I was especially wary on the way back home, looking in every possible direction as I sped through town, scanning for any telltale flash of neon green. I considered telling my dad, but had dismissed the idea by the time I rode up the driveway. I didn't want to freak him out over what might be nothing. On the other hand, I had decided on the purchase of a rear-view mirror for my bike as soon as possible.

# 23

*Tabarnak!*

No. Bigger.

*Crisse de tabarnak!*

No, bigger still. Bilingual even.

*Shit de crisse de tabarnak!*

My guts felt like they'd just been plunged into a vat of liquid nitrogen. For the second time in as many months my terror gauge had buried the needle. This was bad.

I suppose it could have been worse. I might not even have caught sight of the truck at all had it not been that god-awful colour, somewhere between piss-yellow and puke-green. It wasn't my newly acquired rear-view mirror that did it, either. Rather, it was a random sideways glance to my left as I pedalled away from the library on Lalonde Street that gave it away: there, reflected in the mirrored façade of the municipal building, keeping pace with me about twenty or so metres behind, was David Raymond's pickup.

Coincidence? Maybe.

Maybe, I thought, he's had a habit of stopping at the Timmies near the library and I'm only noticing now because I've been sensitized to his presence. Entirely possible. Yeah, chill. Don't assume that just because D-Ray is on the same street that he's stalking you. It's a small town.

I'd find out soon enough. I decided to make an impromptu turn right on King Street in a few moments. If he followed me, I was probably in trouble.

I slowed to a near crawl, allowing D-Ray's enormous wheeled tree frog to close the distance, and began to ride straight into the intersection. At the last possible moment, I made a sudden right turn, accelerating as I did. D-Ray had to make a last-second adjustment and his massive tires screeched as he swerved behind me, cutting off another vehicle in the process.

*Yup, I'm in trouble.*

There was a tremendous blast from the truck behind D-Ray, which I absently noticed in my mirror was none other than Bunny Gingras's pickup, identifiable by the Gingras Hardware logo on the door and the dent from Carl's dearly-departed former client on the grill.

*"Mon ostie d'enfant d'chienne!!!"*

"That's one pissed off Bunny," I thought, smothering the urge to break into hysterical laughter. Then, reaching the intersection with Lakeside I made what I hoped was another unexpected move and turned right again, the opposite direction from home. It worked, which was both good news and bad news.

*He expected me to turn left. He knows I live that way.*

Another sickening squeal of tortured rubber behind me as D-Ray stopped to avoid hitting another vehicle. More cursing, in English this time. I was now moving west on Lakeside Drive where the posted limit was 60 km/h, which meant most drivers did at least eighty. What little leg up I had on D-Ray would evaporate in moments. I made another sudden turn . . .

*If I survive this, Dad will kill me!*

. . . this time darting diagonally across Lakeside and getting a well-deserved horn blast from an oncoming pickup truck in the process.

*Jeez! Doesn't anybody in this town drive a car anymore?*

A moment later, I was in Garrison Park. With its gates and concrete bollards preventing access to anything larger than a mountain bike, D-Ray wouldn't be following me. I was safe for now, but then what?

I wasn't going to be able to hang out in the park indefinitely. What I wanted more than anything was to get home behind a securely locked door, even if my dad wasn't home from his errands yet. D-Ray was probably right now swinging back eastward down Lakeside Drive and if he knew where I lived—and, somehow, I had little doubt that he did—he would be circling Shorewood like a hungry shark long before I got there. There was only one exit from the park at its east end, but it was also the quickest route home, not two hundred metres to my front door. Any alternative route, while unexpected, would leave me vulnerable for too long.

A few minutes later I was steps away from the cannon gate at the eastern edge of Garrison Park, peering out between some thick cedars for any signs of D-Ray's vomit comet. He could have circled a few times already, so I figured I'd give him plenty of time to come around again. This time I had the upper hand: positioned as I was, I'd see him coming before he'd ever see me.

A stray thought bubbled up as I waited. Why now? I had so completely metabolized the notion of David Raymond as enemy of the Lamberts that I had never stopped to ask myself why he should be so interested in me all of a sudden. It didn't make sense. I'd always been around; and, Ferguston being Ferguston, I wasn't hard to find. If he wanted to stalk me, why did he wait until now? In fact, I'd never even heard of him until the conversation with my dad and uncle back in May, and it's not like either of them would have—

The hulking green form of D-Ray's pickup swung with ponderous grace around the corner of Aberdeen onto LeClair Street about two hundred meters away. It was heading straight for me, its headlights almost perfectly aligned with the cannon gate. Somewhere behind the dark tinted windshield David Raymond might be looking directly into my eyes and I'd have no way of knowing.

*Shit!*

Certainly he'd have to know that that's where I'd be emerging from eventually. I thought of ducking lower against the cedars but reconsidered: if he could see me already no amount of ducking would help, and if he couldn't I didn't want any sudden movement to give me away. The truck came within less than thirty metres, then, without reducing speed, turned north up Wellington. As he drove past, I saw that his driver's side window was open and for a moment I got a clear look at him. His eyes were focused on the path over to my right, only a few metres from where I was concealed by the dense cedars, and for only the tiniest fraction of a second I was certain that his gaze locked with mine. My breath caught, and he was gone.

I had to move quickly, not knowing if he might swing by for another pass. I launched my bike out from the path and dashed at my best approximation of warp speed in the direction of Tremblay Street. If D-Ray decided to come down my street this time and not Aberdeen—one block farther east—as he had done the last time, I was sunk. I rounded the corner and looked up Tremblay, half expecting to see the neon green pickup bearing down on me. Nothing. With the exception of Mr. Lovato puttering around in front of his house, the street was totally still.

"Afternoon, Lambert," Lovato called to me, beckoning me with a small ceramic toadstool he gripped in his right hand. "You expecting a visitor today?"

"Ummm . . . No. Why?"

"Some hideous green truck has been circling the neighbourhood just now. Stopped a couple of times in front of your house, then drove off."

*SHIT!*

I gave a vague head shake and casual shrug as if it were nothing, the vehicular equivalent of a wrong number, but my insides were in turmoil. My eyes darted up the street again, then to Lovato's front door. The animals of his menagerie were eyeing me suspiciously, and I wanted nothing more than to get indoors.

"Do you think I could I get a glass of water, Mr. Lovato? I'm parched."

"Water's not running at your house, Lambert? All right. Come on in."

I was glad he didn't question my request any further. Telling Lovato it was a lot safer to spy for D-Ray from his living room window than from my own would have been complicated. He placed the toadstool daintily next to a family of terra cotta snails, and led me to the door. With a final glance over my shoulder toward the street, I stepped into the protective gloom of Lovato's bungalow.

*****

"Here's your water."

Lovato handed me some tepid water in a small plastic cup like the dentist gives you after a cleaning. I finished it in one gulp. Lovato stared glumly at the empty cup, then brought it back to the kitchen. He didn't offer me another.

The house was warm but dim despite the brilliant sun outside. With the drapes drawn, the main source of light came from a TV off to the left in the family room. It faced away from me so I couldn't see what was on, and the volume was set to a low murmur. That and the soft hum of an electric fan were the only sounds.

"Coffee cake?" Lovato called from the kitchen. He hadn't exactly invited me into his home, so I was left standing kind of stupidly in the entrance. Mostly, I was looking for an excuse to move to the living room and peer out through the curtains in the bay window.

"Sure," I called back. "Love some."

In fact, there was something about the place that made any offer of food a bit unappealing. There was a yellowy stillness in the house, and a stale smell of unwashed dishes, overflowing wastebaskets, and urine—whether animal or human I couldn't tell.

"Well, don't just stand there like a dead stump. C'mon over. This isn't the *Caf-fay dez arteests*."

I penetrated deeper into the gloom, stealing a quick glance over my shoulder toward the living room window. The wheat-coloured drapes were drawn shut, but they were just sheer enough to provide a hazy picture of the world beyond. Nothing moved. Inside, Lovato's home was a scatter of newspapers and magazines, plastic grocery bags, unopened mail, and discarded articles of clothing, everything coated in a thin layer of cat hair.

"Agnes Thompson's young one . . . I forget her name . . . she brought this over a couple of days ago." Lovato had cut out a tiny cube of brown cake from a baking dish. It hadn't been covered and the exposed sides were dry and crumbly. "Sweet little thing. Can't bake worth a damn."

I thanked him and popped the entire thing in my mouth. It wasn't hard to do. "It'th good," I lied as I chewed, secretly hoping he wouldn't offer me a second piece. He didn't.

Lovato shuffled over to the family room, deposited himself into a well-worn armchair, lifted the remote control with a shaky liver-spotted hand, and raised the volume. A perky voice was reporting on a stubborn high-pressure system that seemed intent on lingering over Ferguston. Lovato responded with a discouraged hiss and killed the volume. He paused for a moment, seemingly lost in thought, then spoke up. His voice was low but surprisingly clear.

"So, Lambert: David Raymond's got you looking over your shoulder, does he?"

I was taken too flat-footed to answer. I guess the look on my face did it for me.

"Don't look so surprised. I'm old but I'm not senile. The paranoid glances, Raymond's ridiculous truck circling the neighbourhood, not to mention the well-known family history. You think I'm an idiot?"

"N-no. No, of course not. I didn't think—"

"Relax, son. Can't say I blame you. Kid's a regular nuisance, he is. Kind of wish he'd take up another dangerous hobby, like ice fishing in April." He slurped something from a cup that had been sitting for god knew how long on the small table next to his armchair. "So, you say something to piss him off?"

"Me? No. Not at all. In fact, I can't figure out why he's suddenly so interested in me."

"In you or your whole family? It doesn't matter. You see him in your rear-view before this?"

I saw no reason to lie. "Yeah, couple of times."

"Tell anyone?"

"Yeah, my dad and my uncle, but only after the first time. They wouldn't—"

He waved me off. "Someone must have said something to him, a cop maybe, telling him to back off. It wouldn't take much. If he's anything like his old man, the cheese slid off that boy's cracker a long time ago."

"You knew his father?"

A snort.

"Luc? Ha. There was a case for the books. Knew him all his life. He got worse over the years, but even when he was a kid, he was crazier than a two-peckered billy goat. Ran in the family. He had five brothers and four sisters, each one nuttier than the next, with maybe one exception. Never really knew his wife Shelley-Anne; she was a dozen or so years younger than Luc. By all accounts she was perfectly normal—smart enough to get away from Luc anyway—but it'd be surprising if young David didn't inherit at least some of the crazy from the Raymond clan."

"You said there was one exception in the family."

"Y'uh. That'd be Steven—sorry, Stéphane—Luc's oldest brother. He's the one I knew best. He was a few years older than me. Bright guy. Him and one of the sisters were the only ones of the Raymond family to finish high school, far as I know. Worked like a bastard to get as far as possible from Ferguston and his nutcase family. I think he ended up in the insurance business in Montreal."

"And the rest?"

Lovato's eyes widened and he heaved a big sigh.

"Well, there's a tale long in the telling. Let's just say that there must have been something in the water at the Raymond house. That or their poor mom was conceiving over a radioactive dump. Had herself a whole litter of nutbars: a regular Oh Henry! factory, she was."

He had another slurp from his mystery cup. By then an immense black-and-brown angora cat had slunk into the room and took up residence on Lovato's lap. Lovato continued as if he hadn't noticed.

"The first couple of kids were OK, by and large, but each child after that got closer and closer to the edge, you know? They also got progressively nastier and there was a stretch during the '50s and early '60s that the Raymond boys were Ferguston's answer to the Dalton gang. God help you if you ended up in their crosshairs.

"'Course, eventually the boys all ended up dead or locked away, either in prison or the booby hatch. Luc was the family's crowning achievement. He was the youngest. By the time he was ten, you knew. You could see in his eyes that he'd already taken the express train to Loonytown. And he was spooky. Brutally violent, even as a kid. You'd never know what would set him off; he'd lose it over nothing and he'd *remember*. Whatever slight he held you responsible for, real or imagined, he'd harbour it. He'd go about his business, nursing his anger, and weeks or months later he'd set your car on fire. I remember when he was seventeen, always plotting the most extravagant schemes of revenge. Against everybody."

For a moment I'd forgotten he was talking about D-Ray's father. It all sounded so familiar.

"Luc never amounted to much; his greatest accomplishment was staying out of jail. Like a lot of young folks at the time he got work at the copper mine northwest of here, which was good while it lasted. Then the bottom fell out, the mine closed, and Luc was adrift again. 'Course he had no schooling or skills to speak of, nothing to fall back on; couldn't be bothered. He just figured he could outsmart everyone, make some big score without having to work at it. Even after he managed to find a decent job at the sawmill thanks to some connection, he couldn't leave well enough alone. With him it was always: 'I wonder what I can take these suckers for?'

"He was reckless, too. Rash. Never thought anything through. Not the best schemer—I mean, witness what happened to him at the sawmill, dumb bastard. When you think of it, it's amazing he lived as long as he did.

"When he was between jobs, which was often, he was worse. Luc always had some tale of woe about how he was wronged by the company—whichever one had just fired him—by the authorities, society at large. There was never a shortage of people to blame: native people, Jews, blacks, immigrants, you name it. Everyone owed him, and by god he'd make them pay. From there, it's easy to see how he got linked up with the swastika crowd."

Lovato grimaced and shook his head with a bit of a hiss. He stroked his cat absently, staring off into space.

This was an area that Dad never liked to talk about, and so I was only vaguely acquainted with the general concept of white supremacy groups and what they were all about. What little I knew came mostly through overheard conversations between my dad and his brother; Carl knew a lot of bad people. I knew they were around, that they hated pretty much everyone who wasn't white, and that in later years they tried to pass themselves off— and this always confounded me—as Christian organizations. You'd catch them on the news from time to time, demonstrating, in a perpetual state of pissed-off-ness: invariably male, with shaved heads or military buzz cuts, covered in tattoos, and lots of camo. They never struck me as devout churchgoers.

"A course," Lovato continued, "you gotta figure a place like Ferguston is the perfect breeding ground for that kind of thing. Always has been, since I was a tyke. Lousy economy, almost no prospects for growth, a pretty uniform population in terms of race and culture. Those few who manage to get an education hightail it out of here as soon as they can. Thems who are left behind are badly educated, broke, angry, and of course white. Kind of describes the Raymond clan in a nutshell—pardon the pun. These yoyos are nothing new; not that they paraded around in bed sheets or wore those stupid pointy hats in the old days, but you'd hear about them every so often, catch bits of conversation in bars and coffee shops. Nowadays they're calling themselves 'white nationalists,' and in the last fifteen years or so they've become more organized, entering candidates in local elections and such. Ol' Luc really missed his chance—he was dead by the time they'd gained much of a foothold in Ferguston—but they were drawn to young David like flies to shit."

Lovato was quiet for a moment; his breathing had become a slow, raspy wheeze. Then he gently shoved the cat from his lap and leaned in toward me, looking me directly in the eyes for the first time since I'd stepped into his home. He cleared his throat and when he spoke his voice sounded tired and much older.

"Lambert, you've got to understand something about David and his whole fucked-up family: they don't like non-white people and there's nothing short of a group-rate full lobotomy that will change that. Nor would they want to change. They like themselves the way they are: angry and full of hate. Old Luc thought he was on some kind of holy mission; now it's up to young David, as the last of the line, to keep the legacy going. Did you know Luc and his brothers were solely responsible for running a number of immigrant families out of town? Tormented them to the point where life in Ferguston became unliveable. I'll bet your parents were on David's radar the minute they moved in. And he'll never be satisfied. Don't think just because your mother is gone that David Raymond is done harassing you. Sorry to be the one to tell you, but you'd better get used to the sight of him in your rear-view mirror."

I was shocked almost senseless: that D-Ray's hatred for my family ran so deep, and that Lovato could be so forward in telling that to a twelve-year-old. For a moment I didn't know whether I wanted to yell, cry, or vomit.

"I have to go," I somehow managed without my voice breaking, and moved to the door.

Lovato stared blankly at the TV for a second. If he was aware of the fact that I was shaking and close to tears, he didn't show it. When he spoke again, it was almost to himself.

"Of course, given Raymond's social circle, someone's bound to make him disappear sooner or later. That would save us all a lot of trouble."

# 24

D ad and I eventually decided that our trip out west would take place in August, beginning on or around the 14th. We'd fly to Las Vegas and rent a car, and would spend seven or eight days exploring the sites in western California, Nevada, and Arizona, whatever we had time for. Highlights were to include, naturally, the Grand Canyon and Meteor Crater in Arizona, but Dad was also curious about a number of other places, like Death Valley and Sequoia National Park in California, whereas I wanted to visit some of the dinosaur fossil sites in Utah. We decided on a couple of must-sees, and figured the rest we'd play by ear. With the countdown officially started, I needed to find something—preferably productive—to occupy my time and keep me from going crazy. I could barely sit still as it was.

As good an idea as it seemed at the time, my original plan to do volunteer maintenance work at Lakeview Cemetery became a lot less appealing the minute Billie informed me that David Raymond had followed me part of the way there, and was abandoned wholesale after he stalked me around my neighbourhood a few days later. The distance between my house and the cemetery was several kilometres, a lot of them on roads that saw precious little traffic, and seeing as I'd be using my bike to get there, I would be extremely vulnerable should Mr. Raymond decide to follow me again. Add to that the remoteness of the cemetery itself and the fact that there would be very little—if any—supervision, and I'd be a sitting duck should D-Ray ever find out that I could be found there on a regular basis.

Dad actually came up with the creative idea that I should volunteer with the *Clarion*, chasing down leads for stories, taking photos, running errands, and whatnot. He'd even contacted Jason Bremmer directly and explained my situation, but Bremmer turned him down flatly when he learned I was only twelve.

"I'm sure he's a really bright kid, Mr. Lambert. But I'm running a newspaper here, you understand? A *newspaper*. Not a daycare. Send him over when he's eighteen." * Click *

Billie and I continued to meet at our regular rendezvous spot, only not as regularly as I'd originally hoped, and I did the best I could to scatter those meetings as randomly as I could over the next days and weeks of July. It was during one of these early meetings with Billie that I explained my plans for the summer, the trip to the US in August, and my dilemma about where to volunteer for the next five weeks. While she couldn't help smirking at my enthusiasm for a trip that she no doubt viewed as slow and ponderous travel through space and time, she somehow managed to keep from interrupting me with a million and one annoying questions, and was even helpful in the end.

"You're right," she said. "It would be risky to come here every day. And I don't need you to come here at all; we could meet some other place. I just like it because it's quiet and it's nice here in the sun. Plus, I find all these graves interesting." She sat on this last point for a moment, giving the grounds a slow, sweeping gaze. "Anyway," she continued, "like I said, I can always find you."

"Thanks, but what can I do in the meantime? I'm apparently too young to volunteer at the *Clarion*. The library was the only other place I thought about but they don't need help this summer. Apparently, someone else beat me to it."

Billie was quiet for a moment then asked, "What about the hospital? Maybe you can do some volunteer stuff there? Everyone there loved your mother, and I'm sure they'd be more than happy to help you."

I was less than thrilled about that prospect initially. Not surprisingly, what little I knew about hospitals came from my dad. By all accounts, Mom loved her job at Ferguston Regional Health Centre and had a lot of affection for her co-workers there. By extension, and given all the support he received after my mom's disappearance, it's also not surprising that Dad held the hospital staff in high esteem as well. That said, Dad made no secret of the fact that he regarded hospitals as places that any sane person would want to avoid unless absolutely necessary. In his words, they were places of "shit and piss and blood and vomit," places of debilitating disease and traumatic insult to the human body, places of fear, sadness, anger, and desperation. How would I tell Dad that I wanted to volunteer there? That any person, let alone a twelve-year-old kid on summer vacation, would choose to work in such an environment for free was going to be a tough sell.

"I'm not sure it's what I or my dad have in mind," I offered.

"Well, I'm sure they need help with a lot of things besides all the yucky stuff. You know, like in offices."

"You mean like *filing*?" I started to laugh for the sheer absurdity of it: a being from another reality, whose knowledge for all I knew spanned the known universe, was recommending that I spend my summer filing. At the very least, it sounded funny coming from somebody who didn't even believe in classrooms. I would have thought she'd want me to be outdoors surrounded by nature, or at least in a library surrounded by books.

"I think it would be helpful." That voice again: patient, mature, knowing, like it was coming from someplace else. I stopped laughing.

"Yeah . . . maybe . . . I'll ask my dad."

Later that afternoon, at my request, my dad placed a call to family friend Irene Campbell, wife of the chief of medicine and who worked for the FRHC administration. The next day she called back, spoke to me for five minutes, and the following Monday morning at 9:00 I arrived for my first day of volunteering at the Ferguston Regional Health Centre records office. And Billie was right: it would prove to be most helpful.

*****

Given that I've never been the most social of creatures, working in a records office wasn't the worst option. What they had me do hardly qualified as brain surgery—they didn't do that at FRHC anyway—so I had minimal supervision. I was tucked away in a back room in the hospital's administration wing where I couldn't do much damage, far from the Emergency Department and reasonably close to the cafeteria, so I couldn't have picked a better location. Because I wasn't being paid, they couldn't really ask me to dress in any particular way, and aside from a temporary ID card I wore around my neck there was nothing to identify me as staff. That relative anonymity, along with the fact that I was still just some random twelve-year-old kid, ensured that visitors left me alone on those occasions when I wandered out of my cave, as I came to call it.

The person I was going to be helping out in the records office was named Sandra, and whether she knew who I was or not, she gave no indication. She was, however, extremely grateful to have me there, repeating over and over that she was totally swamped, that she'd been begging for help for months, and that if it were up to her they would be hiring me full-time for the summer. I don't think she knew how young I was, and there was no way I was going to tell her. She was really cute.

My duties were simple enough. Twice a day I would make the rounds of the various departments in the hospital with what amounted to a shallow shopping cart, collecting files that were no longer needed, and return them to the records office where I would check their number off a list, and then file them away. Like I said: not exactly brain surgery. When I wasn't doing that, I was helping Sandra on a much longer-term project: preparing a huge backlog of documents for digitization. Sandra taught me how to use her desktop scanner, a process that took five minutes to learn and another thirty to become utterly bored with.

Aside from that, I was pretty much on my own. I wasn't being paid so I could start and end my day when I wanted, and I could have lunch whenever I pleased. Sandra had only two rules: do my best to stay out of people's way in the event of a crisis, and don't discuss the contents of the files with anyone. ANYONE. Ideally, I shouldn't be reading them at all, but because this was going to be almost impossible to avoid completely, I was to keep in mind that these files and documents contained a lot of personal information and thus were to be regarded as strictly confidential. That evening I mentioned it to my dad, who just shrugged and wondered just how seriously the hospital took its confidentiality policy if they were willing to allow their records to be handled by a twelve-year-old kid who couldn't be made to sign a confidentiality agreement. I pretty much put the issue out of my mind at that point, but there would be major implications later on.

\*\*\*\*\*

There's something called the Law of Truly Large Numbers that basically says that with a nearly infinite number of things going on at any one time, at some point events will inevitably converge and pretty much anything can and will happen over the long term. If it transpires in a way that is relevant to us, and we happen to notice it, we go "Wow! Amazing coincidence!" Most of the time, though, we don't notice or we don't care. Some people don't "*believe* in coincidence," which I always found to be an interesting choice of words. They would prefer to think that there is something otherworldly about such phenomena, that there is something going on beyond the understanding of mere humans that is leaving its supernatural or divine fingerprint behind in these events. I guess they find the idea that coincidences are the simple and inevitable result of ongoing interactions between endless numbers of variables—people, things, events—occurring simultaneously to be overwhelming and scary or otherwise unsatisfying. Coincidences are a lot less impressive when you look at the big picture; it's just that the big picture is REALLY big.

I bring this up because of the two coincidences I experienced on a drizzly Tuesday afternoon, a week after I started volunteering at the hospital. The first occurred after running into Debbie Williams in the hospital cafeteria and a conversation we had at a diner nearby; I didn't piece that one together for a long time, but it explained a lot of what happened shortly afterward. The second happened when I got back to the records office after my lunch break, and it felt like a bomb going off in my brain.

What wasn't a coincidence was bumping into Debbie at the cafeteria: it's a small hospital in a small town, she's a paramedic who finds herself there on a daily basis, and the day would eventually come when I'd decide not to brown bag my lunch and we'd cross paths at the cafeteria. As it turned out, she saw me before I saw her and came right over—as much as I'd like to flatter myself, I can't honestly say she came running—all smiles and speaking low in a voice like brown sugar: "Master Lambert, fancy meeting you here."

I stammered a clumsy "Hi . . ." trailing off awkwardly like I should have more to say but hadn't actually planned on anything. I hoped I didn't look like as much of a dork as I felt, but seeing Debbie brought out a lot of strong feelings, some of which were at odds with one another. Obviously, she was strong and smart and pretty which jump-started my metabolism and gave me a pleasant tingle. But because I'd only met her that one time, I also associated her with a bunch of things that were not much fun to think about, not the least of which was the spectre of some sinister backstory about my mom that I hadn't yet learned, which left a dead weight in the pit of my stomach. She rescued the situation gracefully by asking what I was doing there and, after I'd stumbled through a garbled explanation about volunteering in the records office, asked if I'd prefer to join her for lunch outside of the hospital.

"I admire your courage and all, but there are better places for lunch than this, even in Ferguston. I'll get you back in time, plus I know Sandra so you won't get in trouble. Promise." Of course I was going to say yes as soon as she asked, but before I could say anything, she'd already sweetened the deal. "My treat."

The rain—the first anyone had seen in weeks—was little more than a soft mist and the early afternoon was warm and still enough that the shower was actually pleasant. I did a bit of a double take when we reached her vehicle in the hospital parking lot. I would never have imagined Debbie Williams in a full-sized Ford SUV, especially not such a fancy one. I was never an expert on cars but I knew expensive when I saw it. It was clearly brand new, and Debbie had a glint of pride when she saw my reaction. "My new baby . . . because all my other babies are gone."

It was an all-too-short drive to where we would have lunch, an unassuming little dive I must have passed a thousand times without ever noticing. Given where I'd been spending a lot of my time recently, the name of the place took on a personal meaning: The Boneyard Diner. "This humble little spot has a bit of notoriety. It was, to my knowledge, the last eating establishment in the province to go smoke-free. Believe me, management here fought the smoking ban tooth and nail. Gotta give 'em one thing: they know their customers." Debbie snorted a laugh and shook her head. "There's no atmosphere, the clientele is a bit sketchy, and your feet might stick to the floor, but they make the best burgers between here and Orillia."

A bell jingled as Debbie swung the door open, and we were greeted by the irregular flickering gleam of the overhead fluorescents, muted country-western music, and the combined waft of meat on the grill, boiling fries, and freshly brewed coffee that made my stomach rumble. On a TV above the bar, monster trucks were blasting flames out of their back ends as they clambered over the shattered corpses of lesser vehicles; presumably there were no UFC highlights on at that hour.

"And they know me here," Debbie added, a fact that went a long way to putting me at ease. There were no kids in the place, no families. Most of the customers were men my dad's age or older, and many wore outdoorsy work clothes or coveralls, baseball caps and tired, dissatisfied looks on their faces. Although the place was busy, I didn't see a lot of food being consumed; a few random people picked at fries on their plates or nibbled on toast, but mostly people were just sipping coffee.

We found a booth next to a window at the far end of the diner, and a red-faced woman with intense scarlet lipstick and breasts like twin zeppelins immediately swung by with menus, her expression brightening as soon as she saw my dining companion.

"Hey, Debs! Good to see ya, hon! Who's your handsome date?" The waitress winked at me and Debbie gave me a crooked grin. I wanted to drop through the floor.

"This is Justin. He's a friend of mine and he's volunteering at the hospital this summer. Justin, this is my old friend Iris. We went to high school together."

"Haven't seen you here before, Justin. I thought I knew all the cute guys in town. Where have they been keeping you, gorgeous?"

I was only just learning at that age that there are some questions for which there are simply no intelligent answers. My eyes wandered back and forth for a second searching for any safe place to land, when Debbie came to the rescue. "Two cheeseburgers with fries and gravy, Iris. I'll have water and Justin will have . . . a Coke?"

"Please," I said, managing a smile. I knew I had to be blushing, so I redirected my gaze for a moment just to compose myself, focusing on the back of some man's head in the booth behind Debbie.

"Anyway," Debbie resumed after Iris had darted off, "I've been coming here for years—and, don't get me wrong, the staff here are wonderful people—but I'll bet a week's salary that this is the first time two black people have ever eaten here at the same time." She lifted her water glass.

"To history making in Ferguston," she said and winked.

# 25

I spent the first few minutes of chitchat volleying Debbie's questions about the end of the school year, my plans for the summer, and how my dad was doing. From the tone of her voice and the focus of her eyes, she appeared to have a genuine concern for me and my family. She asked how my dad and I were getting along, and if I ever felt lonely. When I told her I didn't have very many close friends her brow knitted up a bit, an expression I guessed came with her profession. On the other hand she nodded with approval when I told her about our upcoming visits to the relatives, and she looked positively elated when I told her about our trip to the American Southwest in August.

"That sounds awesome, Justin! Really! I'm so happy for you. Those are going to be memories you'll cherish, believe me." She was quiet for a moment and then, becoming self-conscious of her own earnestness, took a deep bite of her burger and let out a small "mmmhh" of satisfaction. I was fully expecting her next question, but was grateful all the same that it came out the way it did.

"So, have you seen your friend Billie at all this summer?"

A simple yes or no question. It made me feel a bit better that I didn't need to make up some elaborate lie; a simple one-word lie would suffice.

"Nope."

Debbie chewed on that one a bit then added, "I think about her a lot, and whatever became of her. What a strange child she was. She was a friend of your family, right?"

She was fishing, looking for a nibble, an angle. Billie was an unsolved mystery and, like a lot of intelligent adults, Debbie was uncomfortable with loose ends. I was going to have to be careful.

"I didn't know her family. I just saw her around a couple of times and we got to talking. I think she was from out of town."

Debbie wasn't buying the casual-acquaintance story. "I think she was important to you, Justin. And I *know* you were important to her. I'm not sure of her ethnicity, but there aren't many other non-white children in Ferguston; it's not surprising she'd gravitate to you. You sure you haven't heard from her? A call, a text, an email?"

"Nope. No calls or texts or emails." Technically not a lie. "I don't even know if she has Internet access." Absolutely true: what Billie had access to was *way* beyond Internet.

She ended her inquiry there, but I knew she could see through me like a storefront window. Her gaze was palpable, like sitting in front of a space heater. There was a bubble of discomfort rising up through my insides, and I turned my glance away again, locking it once more on the man sitting behind Debbie. He was facing away from me, not much to see: faded blue baseball cap, short-cropped hair, skinny sunburned neck with a black hairy mole on the left side, obscure snake-like tattoo poking upward from the collar of a grimy white T-shirt. Meet Mr. Everyman, Ferguston edition.

I eventually broke what was becoming an awkward silence by going on offence.

"So . . . where are you from?" Debbie almost did a spit-take and I immediately felt stupid for the question. It was exactly the kind of thing I got from locals who didn't know me, who looked at my brown skin and just assumed I had to be from elsewhere.

"Believe it or not, I was born in Sudbury. Yes, Justin, there are black people in Sudbury." And then, in a feigned conspiratorial whisper she leaned forward and added, "We're *everywhere!*"

The laugh that burst from her then was like a gloriously refreshing fountain on a hot day, and I felt we'd gotten around a troublesome corner. She got to talking about herself and her family—turns out her dad was from Barbados, her mom second generation Italian—about growing up in Northern Ontario as a visible minority, and about living in a community like Ferguston that glossed over its real nature with a thin veneer of what passed for tolerance. "The thing that amazes me to this day is how some people can look me straight in the eye, convinced that they're not racist, behave as if discrimination and hatred are things that only happen elsewhere in the world, and then without batting an eye will say the most awful things about Indigenous people, Asians, immigrants from India or Pakistan or the Middle East, you name it. I see it every day. I dunno. It's . . . troubling."

"Well," I offered, "I haven't experienced that much racism here. I find the people in Ferguston to be pretty tolerant."

A muffled snort from Debbie. "'*Tolerant*'. Don't much care for that word anymore, to tell you the truth. I'm not sure I'm satisfied with being merely tolerated. '*The people here really tolerate me.*' Gee, thanks a lot folks. How progressive of you."

She stopped herself and dialled it back a bit. "Sorry, Justin, but I'm not about to break my hand patting these people on the back for not burning crosses on their front lawns. It's like getting all excited that your date doesn't have a criminal record. Woo-hoo. Child, please. There's plenty of racism here. You're lucky. You may have been sheltered from it, being the only son of a white man who is also bilingual and a popular member of the community. I'm sure people *are* really nice to you. Why wouldn't they be? Most probably don't even think of you as a person of colour—and all credit to your dad and everything, who's doing the best he can under difficult circumstances, but I doubt it's ever occurred to him that he's raising you as a white person. Anyway, most people around here wouldn't consciously say anything overtly racist to you. But the comments pop up all the time, consciously or not. I'm sure you've noticed."

I had: Karyn's—Dad's would-be girlfriend's—"cotton-picking" comment immediately sprang to mind, as did Tweedle Dumb's line about "Mooslims," but there were others.

"You wanna see just how tolerant people are in Ferguston?" Debbie continued. "Why don't we ask Iris to change the music in here from country to rap or hip-hop and watch people completely lose their shit; or see how they'd react if they'd ever had to face a group of black teenagers coming down their side of the street; or listen in when they hear about a protest in the US somewhere over a white cop who has shot some unarmed black kid. Your impressions might change."

We were both quiet for a moment.

"I'm sorry," Debbie continued, her rant spent. "You're fortunate to be the son of two very beloved people in this town. You could probably live out the rest of your life here and not have any problems."

*The rest of my life in Ferguston? Bite your tongue.*

After a few moments to allow the air to clear, the conversation picked up again, eventually turning to my own family, particularly my mother's side whom I only saw a couple of times a year. I talked about my grandparents and my countless aunts and uncles and cousins in Montreal, and about their unshakeable optimism that my mom would someday be found "alive and well just you wait and see," and how my grandpa repeated this without fail each time I visited, his conviction based on an iron-clad faith in God and confirmed by vivid dreams of Mom's return. I told Debbie about how I was showered with affection and gifts and food whenever I visited and how I promised my relatives that I'd do more to learn about Haitian culture and history as I got older, and how unlikely that was as long as I lived in Ferguston, Ontario. Which brought the conversation around to why my dad was still here. Which brought it finally to my mom.

"I was fond of your mother, Justin. We all were. I remember when I first met her. It was her first day on the job at the hospital Emergency Department. She didn't know anybody and was just getting the hang of things, and I was thrilled that the new emerge doc was not only a woman, but a *sister*, and close to my own age too. We just kind of hit it off."

"Did you know her well? Were you two, like, close?" At that time I'd never met anyone who claimed to be a close friend of Mom; Doug and Irene Campbell, while friendly, didn't quite qualify. As far as I knew, Mom didn't have any besties in Ferguston.

"Weeeeeell, I'm not going to say we were that close. Élise was pretty reserved and didn't open up much to people. She kept a professional distance most of the time."

That, I was expecting.

"But, I will say that she and I had some fun together. I did manage to get her to unwind a few times." Debbie sat back and smiled, her eyes drifting upward as she summoned a happy memory. "Get a few beers into her and she'd let her hair down. Not exactly a wild woman, but she'd surprise you."

"Wha . . . What do you mean? What did she do?" Indeed, what could my mom possibly have done?

"Well, for one thing, you know she could sing, right?"

"Ummm . . . no. I didn't know that."

"Well, me and some friends took her out a few times—Girls' Night Out, you know—and a couple of those times were Karaoke Night at Shenanigans. Your mom sang 'Waiting in Vain,' by Bob Marley. She was awesome!"

That, I wasn't expecting.

"Really??? You're serious? My mom actually sang? Like, in public?"

Debbie laughed: a big, heartfelt laugh. I immediately sank into my seat, convinced that our little booth was suddenly the focus of attention in the diner, but the atmosphere in The Boneyard remained detached and sombre.

"Yes, Justin. She was completely unselfconscious, and wonderful. A huge hit. You would have been proud of her."

I didn't know what to think. To a twelve-year-old, just the idea of a parent singing in public—or doing anything to attract attention for that matter—was cringeworthy, but I hadn't been there to witness it and it's not like she was dancing on the tables. Funny that Dad had never breathed a word of it before, but whatever. I decided I was going to be OK with it.

"What else?" You could never be too careful.

"Oh, that was about as crazy as she ever got. We're still talking about Élise Lambert, here." Debbie grinned again when she saw my relief and continued. "We went out a few other times—no male strippers, I promise—but we'd do things like visit psychics, have our palms read, that kind of thing. No big deal."

*What???*

No! Oh no, sorry, beg to differ, Ma'am. On the contrary, that was quite a big deal. A HUGE deal. That was a far bigger deal, in fact, than if she'd gone to a male strip club, as far as I was concerned.

This felt like betrayal.

You see, having been raised in the Lambert household, there were certain intellectual principles that I lived by. One that I embraced fully and enthusiastically was my dad's deep-rooted distaste for all forms of superstition and hocus-pocus. If anything, at twelve years of age, I was even more dogmatic than he was. To his credit, Dad was nuanced about it. He recognized that there was a spectrum: daily horoscopes on one extreme, fundamentalist religions on the other. And while he could concede that some forms were worse than others, his basic view was pretty clear: superstition was never benign. At its best, it was intellectual junk food, tasty, fatty, sugar-coated and deep fried, artery-clogging crap that people consumed as entertainment but that served no other purpose than to keep humanity stupid and afraid, an impediment to intellectual and social progress for thousands of years. That was the best-case scenario. At its worst, it got people killed. Yeah, Dad was hard core.

This was a fundamental Lambert family value, and the fact that my mom, my dad's wife, his one true love and life partner, could actually go to—and pay for!—a psychic on more than one occasion was inconceivable. Worse yet, my mom was a physician, a practitioner of science-based medicine, who according to my dad had little patience for New Age quackery and so-called alternative wellness practices, and was openly suspicious of any health professional who's occupation had a name that ended in "-path." How could she go to a psychic? Was it just a lark, an evening's entertainment, or was it something bigger, an essential philosophical blind spot, a cultural holdover from her family's heritage that she never outgrew or bothered to part ways with?

Was I making too big a deal of this? Of course I was. I knew that as a twelve-year-old. I mean, it's not like she was burning witches at the stake or leading a crusade to wipe out the infidel. But this was behaviour that was not only unexpected, but completely antithetical to the image I'd fashioned of my mom all those years. It left me shocked and feeling slightly untethered.

If Debbie sensed a change in my mood, she didn't show it. Certainly she had no way of guessing the impact her little revelation had on me, and it wasn't a topic she had much interest in lingering on anyway. She had bigger fish to fry.

She paused for a moment, looking square at me, carefully putting together what she would say next. "Is it safe to say you know all about David Raymond?"

The heaviness in my stomach again. "Yeah," I replied. "My dad and my uncle Carl told me the story. How he was the only suspect—or what did they call him?—'person of interest' in the case. Police couldn't find any solid evidence on him and he was never charged."

"That's right. At least, that's the official line."

"Official line? What, do you think he didn't do it?"

"Ha! Don't make me laugh. I know everyone is presumed innocent until proven guilty, but you'd have to be an idiot to think he's not responsible. And it doesn't help that he has a well-known dislike for non-white folks." She paused, her eyes narrow and fixed on mine, her gravelly voice low and steady. "Is that all your dad and uncle told you?"

"Pretty much."

"Do you want to know more?"

# 26

"Did your dad ever mention that D-Ray might have had an accomplice, or at least that somebody else knew something?"

"No. I only know what you told me: that there was someone else with him on that night at the Emergency Department when he argued with my mom."

"That's right. He held back just far enough the whole time that he didn't appear, or barely appeared, on the security video. There certainly wasn't a good shot of his face, and Raymond was making such a fuss that no one paid any attention to this other guy, or at least not enough to give police a useful description."

"So? I mean, that doesn't make this person an accomplice, does it?

"You're right. On its own it doesn't. But there's more. A few nights after Élise disappeared a colleague of mine, Steve—you met him, by the way, he was with me in the ambulance when we brought you and Billie to the hospital—was called to attend to someone who had got into a fight outside of The Pit. According to witnesses—and there weren't many—this person was having an intense disagreement with our friend Mr. David Raymond.

No one got the gist of the argument, but it was pretty clear that it was D-Ray who went all Jean Claude Van Damme on the poor guy, and proceeded to rearrange his face with the blunt end of a Scotch bottle. Steve says that there was a lot of bruising but that the lacerations were mostly superficial and he cleaned and dressed the wounds on the spot. When the cops asked him if he wanted to press charges against Raymond he refused; the guy then took off into the night and the whole incident was dropped. A bartender at The Pit said he'd seen the guy hanging around with D-Ray before but didn't know his name. If the cops ever knew who he was, they've since forgotten. Bar fights in Ferguston aren't considered a high priority. Remember, this was only a few days after your mom disappeared; there was no reason at the time to connect D-Ray to anything, and he definitely didn't have the spotlight on him that he would have later. According to Steve, our mystery person had a genuine fear of Raymond—not surprising, the guy's a brutal fucker, pardon my French—and he just wanted to get away from the situation as fast as possible. No one reported ever seeing him again."

It was a compelling story and it made sense on the surface, but I was still Martin Lambert's son, and my dad had taught me to be skeptical.

"So you think this is the same guy from the Emergency, and that he knew something about my mom's disappearance. So he either took off or D-Ray killed him. Is that what you're saying?"

Debbie could read my doubt, and it was obvious she didn't want to be taken for a conspiracy theorist, no matter how much she hated David Raymond.

"Well, I'm not sure even I'm ready to label D-Ray as a double-murderer."

There was a sudden clink of metal against porcelain as the man directly behind Debbie stirred a bit, the vinyl upholstery in the booth squeaking under his shifting weight. Realizing for the first time that there was a person in the next booth, Debbie dropped her voice, startled and embarrassed.

"Shit . . . I should be more careful." She gathered herself and taking a quick sip of water, she resumed. "No, I think this mystery guy left town a long time ago, but yeah I think he knew something. And there's another thing, something that has gotten under my skin since all this happened. That night at the Emergency, he was *scared*."

"Well, you said D-Ray was a brutal fu—sorry, a dangerous person."

"No, that's who I'm talking about. D-Ray was terrified. The way he went on when your mother turned him away, he seemed, I dunno . . . desperate; more scared than in pain, anyway. Élise was talking to him from across the Emergency Department reception desk, telling him not to come back. How did she phrase it? Something to the effect that his line was cut off. Odd, isn't it? I mean it's not like she, or anyone else at the hospital, would have ever indulged him in the first place. What was he expecting? And then he went nuts, started throwing around racial epithets, threatening her, telling her she didn't know what she was doing, what she was getting herself into. It never sat well with me, like there was something else, something a lot bigger just under the surface. Mystery man or no mystery man, my gut tells me there's more to this whole case than most people think."

Debbie paused, sat in stillness regaining her composure. I don't know whether she was drained from her story or feeling self-conscious for having engaged a twelve-year-old in such a disturbing conversation, but she kept silent for a good minute or two. From my position, with my back to the far end of the diner, I could see almost the entire place, and I did my best to refocus my attention away from the awkward silence in our booth. It was already past 1:00; I'd been away from the hospital for over an hour, but I'd been told by Sandra at the records office not to sweat my lunch breaks seeing as I wasn't being paid anyway.

The lunch crowd at The Boneyard was beginning to thin out. Iris was making small talk with an elderly couple at the counter, saw me watching her and winked at me, then resumed her conversation. The man in the next booth slid out of his seat and plodded toward the cash in running shoes still soggy from the wet weather. Iris broke off her chat with the old couple to ring the man out, giving him his change and a quick half hug with her free arm.

"Good to see you again, Craig. Don't be such a stranger, you hear?" she chirped. There was some history there; it looked like a casual enough friendship, I guessed fairly old but not terribly close. The man mumbled something out of earshot and, without looking back, stepped out into the soft summer rain.

"I should get you back to the hospital," said Debbie, her voice suddenly sounding tired and craggy. As we clambered out of our booth and headed toward the cash, she linked her arm around mine, like an old person would do with someone much younger. I was too startled and shy to say or do anything about it, so we just strode to the cash like some May-December couple on their wedding day.

Debbie settled the bill, said a quick "See you soon" to Iris, and with a beaming smile from our waitress we left the diner. Debbie didn't speak again until we got into her SUV: she slipped the keys into the ignition, but stopped short of starting it up.

"I'm sorry if I said too much back there, Justin," she said. She had somehow aged twenty years in the past three minutes. "That might have been too much information, too soon . . . and not all of it very appropriate. I apologize, really." Her brown eyes were heavy and she had trouble holding her gaze on me. I tried to sound unaffected and tell her that it was no big deal, but she held up her hand to hold me off. "I hope I didn't say anything to scare you or upset you. I just didn't think you should be kept in the dark, and I guess I tend to overestimate how old you are; you don't carry yourself like a twelve-year-old. You're a fine young man, Justin. Your mom would be very proud of you." She sniffed back what might have been a small sob and shook her head with a laugh. "Look at me, will ya? I'll probably scare you away. . . you'll never want to talk to me again." It stung to see such a strong person look so vulnerable. And that such an attractive—and, I thought, sexy—grown-up woman should worry about a kid like me not wanting to talk to her again was inconceivable. I wanted to be comforting, to say something more than "No it's OK, really, no problem" but this was all so big, so adult, so outside of my experience that I just sat there, useless, once again cursing the limitations of my age.

We rode in silence back to the hospital. When we got to the main entrance, she left the car running, and I figured I'd be jumping out with a quick "Thanks for lunch" and that would be it. Despite the awkwardness I didn't want to leave her company, I wanted to talk some more, about all kinds of things, and I was sad to think I might not see her again socially. I was therefore surprised and delighted, as I began to open my door, when Debbie said, "One second, Justin," pulled a pen and a business card from the car's center console and proceeded to scribble something down. She handed me the card and said, "My cell number. Call me, any time. About anything." She then gave me a quick but fervent hug, which surprised me with its strength and intensity. I returned it as best I could, and just as suddenly I was released. Without another word, Debbie shifted the vehicle out of park, giving me just a moment to step out and make my way toward the sliding doors of the hospital's main entrance as the big SUV lumbered off into the grey afternoon.

\*\*\*\*\*

I was still buzzing from my eventful lunch break when I slunk back to the records office, almost half an hour late. My thoughts were rolling and tumbling like socks in a dryer, my mind reliving every detail of my lunch with Debbie Williams in random order.

I was tingling, still smelling her scent from when she hugged me a moment ago, still feeling the firmness of her body and the strength of her embrace, still seeing the details of her face, her dark eyes, her crooked smile. I imagined a version of her ten years younger, talking and laughing with my mom—"Élise" to her—across the emergency admission desk or over coffee in the cafeteria. I would have been a toddler then . . . and Debbie was older than my mom.

And my mom, about whom a completely unexpected side was suddenly revealed through an otherwise innocuous anecdote. I started to wonder just how many more revelations had yet to be made, how many I wouldn't like, and ultimately, how little did I really know her. She'd been gone for ten years and yet she was full of surprises.

*****

"Mmmm . . . someone's been to The Boneyard!" Sandra sang out from her desk, the smell of the grill announcing my presence from a full ten feet away. I offered a sheepish "Sorry, Sandra . . ." but she was quick to head me off. "Don't worry about it, Justin. Debbie just called me to let me know she'd held you up." She stopped what she was doing to look at me with a grin that looked a lot like Debbie's.

"How was your *daaaaaaaaaaaate*?" Oh, she was enjoying herself.

"It was nice." Trying to sound like something resembling casual. "I think I ate too much."

Sandra wasn't going to be diverted. "She *likes* you! She thinks you're quite the gentleman."

"She's old enough to be my mother."

"And then some. She's old enough to be your mother with three or four siblings ahead of you. But you know"—Sandra's voice was a playful singsong—"May–November . . . happens all the time."

"Having fun, aren't you?"

"Oh, yeah!" she giggled. "Lots! That's OK. You should do your afternoon file run now. I can torment you some more when you get back."

I made sure to take my time with my afternoon rounds, saying "hello" to everyone at the various departments, making polite chit-chat, asking open-ended questions about what everybody did, and doing my best to sound utterly fascinated. I was also beginning to get to know people's names, and they in turn were learning who I was. Not everyone had known my mom, but even those who'd been hired in the years since she disappeared had all pretty much heard the stories; and given my appearance it was easy enough for most to make an educated guess of who I was—although I was a bit irritated when one person guessed I was the son of one Deborah Williams.

By the time I got back to the records office, Sandra had apparently come to the conclusion that my delicate twelve-year-old male ego had been bruised—no doubt because I'd taken so long on my rounds—and toned down the razzing accordingly. She pointed to a daunting stack of files on my workspace in the back of the office and said sweetly, "The Great Wall of Charts over there is all for scanning, Justin. There's no big rush, but feel free to get started on it any time. I'm going away on holiday the day after tomorrow and I'll be gone for a week and a half, so try to do as much damage to the stack as you can while I'm away."

"What if I finish it all before you get back?"

This was a possibility she obviously hadn't considered. "Umm . . . well . . ." she trailed off. "Promotion? Double your salary? Fast-track to sainthood?" She got me with the last one, and I gave a good-natured snort that brought her smile back.

Shaking my head and laughing under my breath, I began to stack the low piles of folders into taller piles, and the Great Wall began to look more like the Two Towers. I hefted the first one that came to hand. It must have been almost two inches thick:

somebody with a history. I sighed. There were quite a few like this, and eyeing the sheer volume of files, I figured I'd be lucky to get half of it all done before school started in September. Ah well, no time like the present. I reached for the staple remover, flipped open the folder, and stopped breathing.

On a sheet stapled to the inside of the folder, just below the file number and above some much edited general information, was the patient's name: David Luc Joseph Raymond.

# 27

I must have groped for a chair and sat down, though I have no memory of doing so. I do remember my mouth being really dry. The rest of the office began to recede, with Sandra slipping off into the distance with it. There was no sound, no voices, no more Muzak in the background. The only light I was aware of came from directly overhead. My eyes went up and down the first page, not even knowing what I was looking at. It was a copy of a hospital form: a lot of boxes and lines filled in with somebody's undecipherable cursive, a larger space with something more lengthy scrawled in it, other boxes checked, numbers hastily printed, a stamp, one area circled in red.

I shook my head and looked again, determined to be more discerning, more scientific. Start at the beginning: Record of Admission. OK, clear enough. Check the date: April 13th, 1990. Do the math: sixteen years ago. According to D-Ray's date of birth on the inside cover of the file, he would have been sixteen years old. Admitted for . . . fracture of the right ulna, in addition to lacerations on his right hand that required suturing.

I had to stop reading. I was feeling giddy, light-headed and sick to my stomach. I started to thumb through the file. It was a mishmash of documents, lots of official hospital forms, admission records, an alarming number of X-rays, surgical records, copies of letters and reports on hospital letterhead, photocopies of prescriptions, photocopies of handwritten notes, sticky notes, photocopies of sticky notes, it went on and on. I thought it was overwhelming until I glanced at the tab at the top of the folder and saw the file number plus a small red 1, followed by a slash and then a small red 3. Another quick glance at the stack of files next to me confirmed my suspicion: there were two more folders with the same file number, one of which was at least as thick as the first. Three folders: I was looking at D-Ray's entire, detailed medical history.

"You good over there, sir? You seem awfully quiet." Sandra voice suddenly sounded as if she was a foot behind me, looking over my shoulder. Shit!

"Yeah, I'm good. Got a thick file here, and I'm having trouble pulling the staple out. Don't worry, I'll get it." Another effortless lie: I was becoming uncomfortable with how good I was getting at this.

"Ah. Well, don't damage your nails, sweetie. Not sure you can afford a manicure on your salary, and you don't qualify for workman's comp." Ha, ha.

I was glad to see she hadn't moved from her desk and couldn't see what I was actually up to, but I was going to have to be careful. Sandra was a close friend of Debbie, and Debbie had some very strong opinions about David Raymond; if she shared those opinions with me, she wouldn't have hesitated to talk about them at length with her friend. I slid the three D-Ray folders to the side and moved on to some less suspicious ones. As long as Sandra was still in the office I was going to have to stick to my actual job. I wasn't yet sure what, if anything, I was going to do with this incredible find, but I knew that decision would have to wait at least until my supervisor was away on holiday.

*\*\*\*\*\**

In fact, by the time I got home that afternoon my curiosity was already getting the better of me and I was beginning to change my mind about waiting. I made the final decision that evening while watching a rerun of *CSI* with my dad. Beginning the next day I was going to be the absolute model volunteer: I was going to come to work bright and early every day and work that scanner like a demon. I was going to do my best to totally demolish as much of that mountain of patient files as possible, every page of as many folders as I could finish, all nicely scanned and saved as PDFs in their proper directory on the records office computer's C drive. Oh, and while I was at it, I'd quietly and harmlessly make an extra copy of each and every document in D-Ray's file, and save it to a CD I'd burn using the office's disk writer. Piece of proverbial cake. I had no earthly idea what I was going to do with it all, or what precious and elusive nugget of information I thought I was going to uncover, but I figured I'd worry about that *after* I'd compiled everything.

Given the thickness of the folders, combined with all the other stuff I had to do during a typical day, I figured I'd need at least one full day to scan the entire contents of D-Ray's medical records, probably a bit more. I also figured I'd need to get it out of the way as quickly as I could and then scan as many others as possible so it wouldn't stand out should anyone do some detailed checking. Discretion was vital. I was only doing my job, but if it got out that the son of the woman who disappeared was—by coincidence or not—scanning the confidential medical records of the only person suspected in her disappearance, it might draw a few second glances.

The biggest issue that I could think of regarding my new summer project was whether or not I should tell my dad about it. On the one hand it was pretty clear to me that what I was planning was ethically, and probably legally, problematic to say the least. Although at the time I couldn't have expressed it in terms of violating D-Ray's right to privacy, I knew enough that what I was planning amounted to something like theft. Dad would freak.

On the other hand, we were talking about David Raymond here, not some random, innocent, law-abiding Fergustonian. Although he'd never spoken of him to me until that spring, it was pretty clear how Dad felt about D-Ray: to say Dad outright hated him wouldn't have been a stretch. In fact his bitterness at D-Ray's ten-year evasion from justice was slowly and steadily gnawing away at him, and although he'd kept it well hidden from me all those years, once revealed I could see it for what it was. It was an illness, a cancer, and it was as plain and visible to me as his gradually greying hair. Sitting on the couch with my dad that evening watching a *CSI* rerun, I thought I might be able to offer him some hope. Maybe, if there was something that had been missed in their previous investigation, some detail from a doctor's note, some statement made by somebody who'd either seen him or examined him, or some seemingly random remark made by D-Ray himself, anything that could implicate him in something, it might be enough to convince the police to give D-Ray another look and reopen the investigation into my mom's disappearance. At the very least, I hoped it might be enough for Dad to overlook my less-than-ethical actions in getting a hold of it.

As it turned out, Mom herself had taken care of that a long time ago.

*****

In the end, the entire process of scanning, saving and copying the contents of D-Ray's hospital file took a day and a half. I'm sure

I could have cut it down to one day, except Sandra was still in the office on Wednesday so I had to be careful, and after she'd left, I kept stopping to read the documents.

It was difficult reading at first. The files were a jumble of paper, much of it hard to decipher, from a whole range of sources going back many years. They told a story that was at once fascinating, confusing, and sometimes hilariously gruesome. How a single human being could sustain that much abuse to their body over such a long period and continue to function was, if nothing else, a tribute to the durability of our species . . . that, and a testament to one man's epic life-long stupidity. I started to compile a list of D-Ray's injuries over the years. From the age of sixteen, he had suffered wounds worthy of medical attention to his nose, left cheekbone, orbits of both eyes, jawbone, upper incisors, clavicle, both shoulders, left bicep and pectoral muscle, right ulna, right hand, fingers of both hands, ribs, lower thoracic vertebrae, both knees, and left tibia, not to mention reconstructive surgery to his pelvis, repair to severe tissue damage on the left side of his abdomen—apparently he'd been perforated by a tree branch during a snowmobile accident—a handful of knife wounds, at least one gunshot wound, multiple concussions, overdoses, one instance of alcohol poisoning, and more abrasions, lacerations, and contusions than I could count. What remained of D-Ray was stitched up, pinned together, and rebuilt over the years thanks to the dedicated efforts of the Ferguston Regional Health Centre surgical staff and paid for by the Ontario taxpayer. Dad would have a fit.

By Thursday afternoon I had copied the last of the files to my CD and after putting the original folders on what was to become my Finished pile, I spent the rest of the day poring over the documents, or at least those that I could understand. That was when the sheer magnitude of my enterprise started to sink in. Not only was I going to need grown-up help in figuring this stuff out, I didn't even have any idea of what I was looking for. TV shows made everything so simple: all the characters were fully versed in just about every discipline you could think of, so nothing was mysterious for very long, and they had seemingly endless abilities and resources that they could draw from even when the clock was ticking.

I pushed out a huge sigh and glanced at the clock. It was already past 5:00 and my stomach was grumbling messages to me that it was time to head home. Dropping my CD and water bottle into my backpack, I passed a quick glance around the office, switched off the lights, and headed out.

*****

In retrospect, it didn't take long to figure out where D-Ray got his intel on me, my probable whereabouts, and to whom and about whom I'd been speaking recently. D-Ray seemed to have a decent network, which made his otherwise excellently executed ambush a bit less impressive.

There were two sets of bike racks at the hospital. I'd left my twelve-speed on the smaller one at the rear of the building. It was more convenient because it was closer to the records office, but the rear of the building saw a lot less foot traffic and was thus more vulnerable. Until that afternoon, I'd never thought of it as a problem.

I was picking up speed as I swung my bike down and around the southeast corner of the hospital, when I had to brake suddenly to avoid running headlong into a poorly parked vehicle in the side lot. The vehicle, a huge, mud-spattered neon green pickup truck, was parked on an angle with its tail end sticking out into the driveway. If I'd been driving a car and not a bike, I might have taken the rear bumper clean off. As it was, I screeched to a stop, my forward momentum carrying me out of the saddle and leaving me pitched forward over the handlebars. I had just the time to gasp a breath of relief for avoiding what could have been an ugly collision, when David Raymond lurched gracelessly around the back of the pickup, blocking my only escape.

"Well, well . . . Lookie here!" D-Ray was grinning as he propped himself against the box of his pickup, but there was no humour in that grin . . . or many teeth for that matter. It was the first time I'd ever seen him up close, and the first thing that came to mind was how come someone who had come into so much money had never bothered to get a set of dentures. The next thing that struck me was how could this man possibly be ten years younger than my dad. The lack of teeth didn't help, but the years hadn't been kind to D-Ray overall; I'd just gone over his entire medical history, so I could attest to that first-hand. Now as I looked at him, this lifetime of violence was laid out for me like a roadmap, the scars and distorted features like dramatic landmarks on an otherwise bleak landscape. His lopsided face alone spoke of his brutal past, with its one sunken cheekbone and distinctly twisted nose. His grey-green eyes were deeply lined all around, with heavy dark sags underneath. There were at least a couple of notable old scars, one that cut through his left eyebrow and another that ran over the bridge of his nose: fight trophies.

There was still room to imagine he might have been handsome as a young man, but nearly two decades of drugs and violence along with a scraggly growth of beard—that was not without its fair share of grey—covered that up pretty decisively. Like so many of the guys in town he wore a baseball cap which I suspected covered up a prematurely receding hairline; whatever hair was left cascaded in a dirty-blond mullet out the back of his cap.

From what I could see, D-Ray hadn't changed his clothes since the last time I'd seen him. He was wearing what my dad says was once called a muscle shirt but was now referred to as a wife beater; the low neck and the lack of sleeves revealed several more scars, including a tracheotomy scar at the base of his throat, a wicked scar across this right clavicle that looked like a giant centipede, and the tip of what must have been an impressive scar near his left armpit. I could only guess how many more scars were covered up by the numerous tattoos that adorned both of his arms. On the subject of tattoos, an impressive bluish black serpent coiled all the way around his shoulders and just under this throat. His baggy camo pants were splotched with paint and mud and were held up with a thick black leather belt, the centrepiece of which was a gaudy silver western buckle. On his feet he wore work boots that looked like they'd been soaked in acid, then dragged over a gravel road for a thousand miles. I made a mental note that he'd left them untied, a detail that might come in handy.

D-Ray had closed his distance from me to only a few feet, making a quick escape almost impossible. As he moved, I noticed that the stance he'd assumed to lean against the truck had more to do with his distorted posture than it had with displaying a comfortable swagger. Watching him move this close showed just how crooked and hobbled he really was. And while he was also very lean and his arms were ropey with muscle, making him no doubt a tough customer to tangle with in close quarters—like a cornered rat, I imagined—I figured that in open space he could be outdistanced in short order by either one of my grandmothers.

"Hey there, guy," he said. "Thought we'd have us a little chat." His voice was scratchy but surprisingly high-pitched, and the absence of his four top incisors, combined with the vestige of a French-Canadian accent, corrupted his *th*s into *d*s and *t*s.

"I've gotta get home. My dad's expecting me." I straightened my posture and tried to sound as confident as possible, praying my pubescent voice wouldn't betray me with an ill-timed squeak. "He knows I work here."

"Oh, I won't keep you long," D-Ray continued, his voice taking on a sing-song quality, as if this was just some light and friendly social banter. "You'll be home soon enough. I just thought I'd introduce myself officially, seeing as you seem to think you know all about me already." It came out as "I juss t'aught I'd innerdooce m'self" and "you seem to t'ink you know all aboot me . . ."

"I don't think—"

"You can save it, bud. I know who you been talking to, and I know what she's been saying about me. It's nothing new. I been hearing that same shit for ten years."

"I don't know who you're talking about," I said. Of course I knew exactly who he was talking about, and was already starting to figure out how D-Ray had heard about our conversation: the silent figure who sat behind Debbie at the Boneyard Diner, Mr. Soggy Shoes, whose face I never saw. Didn't the waitress use his name as he was leaving? Anyway, I thought I should keep D-Ray talking and maybe extend the odds of someone coming out of the clinic, seeing what was going on, and bailing me out.

"Oh, I think you know, kid. I'm talking about your coloured friend, your homie." D-Ray made an awkward gesture with his right hand as he said "homie," no doubt intended as a mock gang sign. It was painful to watch. "You know? Your 'sista.'" Another hand sign. "That fucking nigga bitch medic you hang with," he finished.

"Coloured h'riend," "h'ucking": evidently, he had trouble with *f*s as well.

The grin had left his lips by then, and he kept his eyes fixed on me, watching my every move, trying to assess if I was about to make a run for it. Meanwhile, my gaze was darting around, eventually landing on the entrance to the clinical wing. By this hour it was unlikely that there'd be many people still working there, but I was hoping I might fake him out. At the same time, I found myself pulling my backpack tightly around my shoulders, suddenly conscious of its precious and incriminating cargo.

"No one's coming for you, you little shit, so just relax. Look, I don't care what you heard from your fucking medic friend or the cops or your dad or even that crazy hippie uncle of yours: I never did your old lady, you hear? Yeah, she had her nose in a lot of other people's business instead of minding her own, and maybe she just pissed off the wrong folks, or she had an accident, or maybe she ran off with some dude. See, I really don't give a fuck. I said it then an' I'll say it now: *it wasn't ME!!!*"

As I stood silently in front of him, listening to his tirade and looking at his complexion redden and the veins in his neck begin to bulge, I felt some of my fear begin to soften, to morph into something else. At the same time there was something in his tone that was also changing; there was an urgency, a desperation that I didn't expect and that suddenly turned my stomach.

I glared at him, now full of anger and disgust, wishing for the umpteenth time that I were ten years older. I wouldn't care if he was considered extremely dangerous, or if there was a good chance that he was carrying a concealed weapon at that moment. At that instant I felt confident that, if I were just a bit bigger and stronger and more experienced, hell, if I weren't at that moment straddling my bike, I would have turned him into a broken, bleeding, oozing pile of crap. I knew every one of his weak spots: his reconstructed hip, the pins that held his knees together, the limited reach of his left arm, everything. Like that ignorant racist douchebag at the cemetery, the one who had called Billie a "Mooslim" and suggested she was a terrorist, I knew I could take this piece of shit down with one well-placed kick.

I don't know if D-Ray noticed any change in my demeanour—I certainly felt it—but when I tuned in again, he seemed to be making a last-ditch attempt at sounding threatening. ". . . so you'd better hope I don't come around for you again," he was saying. "This is a small town and I know everyone here, and I can find anyone at any time, so don't think I couldn't find you again in a minute if I wanted to."

A sudden loud squeal made us both turn in time to see a large black Buick coming to an abrupt stop only a few feet behind me. The driver was a huge woman in a grey business suit whose incensed bawling could be heard before she even swung her door open. She was already in full voice as she hoisted her frame out of the driver's seat, and it was immediately obvious that her target was the crooked dude in the wife beater leaning on the snot-green pickup.

"What the sweet holy fuck do you think you're doing, sonny???" she bellowed. She wasn't just big: she was gigantic. It might have been the fact that she and her car were stopped on a bit of an incline looking down on us, but she seemed to loom like some monstrous creature from the Cretaceous. She had to be at least my uncle Carl's height, and much, much heavier. And she had a voice to match, like a trumpet on steroids. Her black hair was pulled back tight behind her head, and her vast face was turning a bright scarlet as she took a step away from the car to assess the roadblock before her. Her eyes had D-Ray pinned like an insect against the rear fender of his truck, and he half turned in her direction to mutter some feeble retort, only to be mowed under immediately.

"You got fucking shit for brains, you asshat? Where'd you learn to fucking park? I'd come down there and smack you silly if I thought you had half a brain to knock into place. Now get that vomitous piece of shit out of my way, you fucktard, before I get security over here to drag it away."

As stunned as I was—I'd never, ever heard an adult use that kind language, not even in Ferguston, let alone a woman, let alone a woman in a business suit—D-Ray was completely unmanned. His jaw hung open and he clearly had no idea what to do with his hands. I doubt a woman had ever spoken to him that way in his life, and for an instant I caught a glimpse of what David Raymond might have looked like as a three-year-old.

With D-Ray temporarily immobilized and turned to face this new threat, I saw my window and jumped. I stood on my bike pedals, dug in as hard as I could and, with a quick motion, swerved around D-Ray and his truck. As I zipped past, I offered D-Ray a parting shot which surprised me as much as it did him:

a well-placed elbow which connected squarely with the side of his head. It was remarkably violent, a lot more than I expected, although I honestly had no idea I was going to do it until it was done. As I sped out of the lot toward George Street, the last thing I heard was the big woman calling out, "Good job, kid!" and then to D-Ray, "Now move your fucking truck, dickwad!"

# 28

Every kid in the world knows that you NEVER, EVER snitch on a bully, no matter what they do or threaten to do. It's a no-brainer. No matter what a bully has done or has threatened to do to you, it's nothing compared to what he will do if he is forced to have a sit-down with a parent or a teacher or a principal. You see, up until then, whatever he's done was done with some—albeit perverted—sense of fun, at least for him: they're usually not angry at the time. If you squeal on him not only will you *not* prevent him from bullying you again, you'll piss him off. You can then add anger and revenge to the toxic mix of sadism, intimidation and insecurity that is already messing up this unfortunate individual, and you'll spend the rest of your school year—at the very least—looking over your shoulder. And that's just a school bully. D-Ray was "a whole other critter," as Carl would say. He was a grown-up, had a wider territory, and was a lot more dangerous than anyone I've ever known in school. Plus it's one thing to be told off by a teacher, another—I could only guess—to be visited by law-enforcement. If I told anyone about my encounter with him in the hospital parking lot, the repercussions would be huge.

On the other hand, if I played it right, I might be able to turn it to my advantage.

I don't remember much about the ride home, except that I must have gone extremely fast for fear of D-Ray following me. By then, I had no doubt that he knew where I lived, but I wasn't going to make it easy for him. Dad wasn't home when I got in, so I made my way up to my room, making sure to lock the front door and my bedroom door behind me. Dad would find it weird, but at this point I didn't care.

I immediately sat down at my computer, determined more than ever to dig up something of substance out of the countless documents that I'd scanned over the past couple of days. Even if I didn't find anything—or recognize anything at the moment, which I hoped was more likely—at least it would give me something to do with myself. I was still shaky, scared, and pissed off as I fumbled with the CD and slipped it into my iMac. Had I been a grown-up I would have had a drink to steady my nerves; the only thing I had in the fridge was Mountain Dew, and that would have had me climbing the walls.

I had arranged the PDF files in folders labelled by year; and everything within each folder was also labelled chronologically. I double-clicked on the first folder—1990—and then on a file icon at random, just to have something to look at. It turned out to be a psychological assessment from when D-Ray was sixteen. Probably not incriminating by itself but it did provide some context. I jumped straight to the summary:

> In sum, David Raymond is a 16-year-old adolescent male who presents with a severe history of persistent disobedience to authority, as well as of engaging in serious acts of aggression and violence. David meets the diagnostic criteria for Conduct Disorder according to DSM-III-R.

David Raymond's behaviour is characterized by a lack of empathy for those whom he has hurt, and an absence of remorse for his social and moral wrongdoings. His pattern of extreme manipulation to get his way, his unashamed violation of the rights of others, and his criminal behaviour indicate a strong predisposition for the later development of Antisocial Personality Disorder in adulthood.

There was a lot in that which I didn't understand, but I could get a general idea that, according to this psychologist, a Dr. R. Lichtman, D-Ray at sixteen seemed to have all the markings of a fledgling sociopath, short of setting fire to puppies. I clicked on a bunch of other files in quick succession: a dozen, fifteen, twenty, until my screen was filled. I let out a long sigh and glanced quickly over each one: admission record, admission record, X-ray, admission record, X-ray, surgical record, more X-rays, blood work, more admission records, urine analysis and toxicology report, still more X-rays, consent forms . . . it was overwhelming.

It then occurred to me that I could at least narrow my search: no sense in wasting my time with records dated prior to the year my mom began working at the hospital. I closed all the files I'd opened from 1990, and I went directly to the folder marked 1996—the year my mom disappeared—double-clicked it, and began opening everything.

Although I had personally scanned most of it just the day before, I felt like I was only now looking at the contents of this folder for the first time. It was mostly a lot of forms of different kinds, plus some letters, some short notes dashed off on official-looking stationery, and a few sticky notes, some on their own, some attached to larger documents. Many had hand-scribbled notes on the margins done in marker, lines highlighted in yellow, and, in a few cases, arrows pointed out words or numbers that were circled in red. As I started to read the documents, I was reminded once again that I wasn't going to get anywhere without the help of an adult. I would have to share my plans with a grown-up, which meant taking a huge risk, but I couldn't see another way around it.

I was just reflecting how '96 seemed to have been a better year for D-Ray—no X-rays that I could see—when I heard a sudden rattling of the deadbolt on the front door signalling my dad was home. Locking the door when someone is home, especially in the middle of the day, is considered a bit odd in small-town Ontario, even in a place with a less than idyllic history like Ferguston. The moment he saw my shoes in the entrance he called to me, and the weirdness of the situation could be heard right away in his voice. "Juss??? You home?"

I launched my web browser, its window covering the entire screen, concealing what I'd been doing. Then I stood up, took a deep breath, unlocked my door, and stepped into the hall. Dad was standing at the base of the stairs, looking up at me with an expression that I watched turn from uncertainty to mild relief to renewed concern.

"What's wrong, Justin?" It came out as more of a command than a question.

"Dad," I said in something just above a whisper, "I need to talk to you."

\*\*\*\*\*

I told him everything. I started with my encounter with D-Ray, his ambush in the clinic parking lot, his pathetic plea of innocence followed up immediately by his threats against me, the timely arrival of the giant she-orc in the black Buick and her verbal evisceration of D-Ray, and my climactic escape, including clocking D-Ray on the side of the head with my left elbow— although I made it sound like a happy accident. I even told him about my lunch with Debbie Williams, and everything she said about the incident in the ER with D-Ray and his mystery friend. The whole time, my dad remained impassive and while he did tense up visibly as soon as I mentioned D-Ray and how scared I'd been, and grinned a little at the story of the big woman, all in all he listened quietly and very attentively. But if I thought I was good at reading my dad, there was nothing I could do to crack his poker face during the second half of my narrative.

"There's something else," I continued. I saw it as the second half of a bad news/good news scenario, but my dad might see as bad news/bad news, and I had no way of knowing until I spilled it. I took another deep breath and plunged. "I've told you about what I do at the hospital, right, about how they're digitizing all the patient records? Basically I open a folder, and scan each and every document in the folder—forms or X-rays or whatever—and save everything as PDFs onto their hard drive. It's not exciting, but it's easy."

So far, my dad had remained completely inscrutable, but then I hadn't said anything particularly revealing or problematic. That was about to change.

"Anyway, yesterday I opened a new patient file and was about to start scanning the first document when I realized . . ." I half turned in my swivel chair and closed the browser on my computer, revealing the screen full of PDFs. My dad, sitting on my bed opposite me, squinted the tiniest bit, but his face showed no emotion. Of course, he had no idea what he was looking at.

". . . it belonged to David Raymond."

No reaction from Dad, or at least no change in his expression; he just sat immobile on the edge of my bed. I pushed on.

"His file contains three folders: hundreds of documents, going back sixteen years."

Still nothing, but his eyes were now clearly focusing on my monitor.

"I finished scanning everything today, like any other patient file . . . except . . ."

Dad's face was stone.

". . . I kept a copy."

I waited for the reaction. It was going to be a long, slow burn. Dad has never been one for total detonation, even when he's at his most angry; Lambert men aren't known for being demonstrative. Usually he brings his hands to his face, pinches the bridge of his nose or, when he's deeply upset, begins working the balls of his hands into his eye sockets. That is usually followed by running one or both hands through his hair, turning his face away slightly, and—if he's epically pissed—standing up fully straight and assuming a teacher pose. I knew what would be coming then. He'd begin by telling me that I had violated a trust, that what I'd done amounted to stealing, that no matter who David Raymond was or what he'd done in the past, he was entitled to privacy, and that I had no business even reading his files, let alone making a copy of them. He'd talk about issues of confidentiality, of personal privacy, and—this would be typical Dad—if I showed no appreciation of those ideas as a young person, I'd find them easier to ignore as an adult, and that was how people and ultimately societies became corrupt. He might then say how surprised and disappointed he was, and how he was amazed that I didn't know better. On the other hand, if he thought that I genuinely didn't know how important these things were he'd begin to ease up, and start taking it on himself. Either way it would end with him saying that he hoped I'd learned from this and, mostly, understood the importance of everything he was saying. He'd then confiscate my CD, ensure that I hadn't copied everything onto my hard drive, and my investigation would be over before it had begun.

I waited. Dad's grey eyes were deadly serious, still riveted to my monitor. His mouth was a thin line, his body motionless except for the rhythm of his breathing. As long as he remained silent, I felt I still had a window.

"I figured if I . . . if *we* . . . could find something, anything, in all these documents that . . . I dunno, showed that he did something, or that he was involved in something, against the law . . . that maybe we could report it to the police . . . or . . ."

Without any response from my dad, what little momentum I had built up to that point simply evaporated. He remained silent, his gaze still fixed to the computer screen. If nothing else, at least I knew he hadn't mentally floated off someplace: his stare was focused, just like when . . .

"Dad?"

It was a look I'd seen not long ago, when he'd first laid eyes on Billie's "wanted" poster downtown.

I turned to the screen, trying to see what had captivated him. "What is it?"

He stood up, and stepped closer to the computer, pointing to a file on the screen that was partially covered by a number of others. It seemed to be one of many short documents I'd come across, created on some professional-looking stationery. Along the left-side margin were handwritten notes in red ink.

"That," he said finally, "is your mother's handwriting."

# 29

That's pretty much all it took. There was no meltdown, no lecture, no quiet but stern reprimand, not even an apparent wrenching inner conflict about the ethical implications of what the next move should be. I'd been hoping that D-Ray's threats would be enough to tip the balance of Dad's feelings in my favour; I never imagined that luck would offer up something as immediate and real and compelling as notes from my mom's own hand.

It took hold of him completely. I gave up my chair and for about twenty minutes he sat in front of my computer, poring over the documents on the screen and opening other folders seemingly at random, muttering to himself. I began to explain how everything was organized, then just trailed off. Dad then suddenly stood up and, still staring at the monitor said, "I'd like a copy of everything, please." He then left the room to make dinner, and I sat there wondering what I'd just gotten us into.

For the rest of that week and all of the next, we talked of little else. Dad seemed to have completely forgotten about the whole episode in the hospital parking lot, which in retrospect was a bit disquieting; normally he would have called the police, or insisted that I immediately stop volunteering at the records office, or at the very least have a serious sit-down with me about safety. Instead, D-Ray's file had become my dad's white whale, and if I worried about having created a monster, at least I could draw comfort from the fact that he hadn't taken my project away from me or even ignored my potential contributions to it.

Of course there were downsides, namely he'd become so engrossed in the D-Ray Project, as I came to think of it, that he forgot about other stuff that we'd planned, or had planned to plan. For instance he totally forgot that we'd intended to leave on our annual summer visit to the relatives that Friday. When I mentioned it, he just gave me a momentarily embarrassed "oops" look, and promised to reschedule it to the next week, but that I would have to remind him. I told him I would, for that and for our southwest trip: there was no way I was going to allow that to slip past, no matter how obsessed he became.

At the center of all the excitement were close to two dozen documents in D-Ray's file—all dated from 1994 to 1996—that featured my mom's handwriting. More than half of them were copies of documents from a doctor named Geoffrey Coleman, and from their size and contents my dad concluded they came from a prescription pad. Dad joked that Dr. Coleman's penmanship was exceptionally good for a physician, even though I could barely make out a thing. He said that the prescriptions that seem to have interested my mom were for Percocet, which my dad described as an industrial-strength painkiller. There were other prescriptions as well, for a variety of drugs, and apparently my mom had looked at those as well—you could tell by the red scribbles she left behind. Most important were the numbers that Mom had circled, often with one or a series of question marks next to them; in at least one case she'd written *WTF???* which provoked a spit-take from my dad and a muffled smirk from me.

"She was concerned about dosages by the looks of things," Dad said. "I need to talk to somebody who knows something about this."

The other thing that seemed of interest to my mom was D-Ray's toxicology reports. I'd already followed sports long enough to know what urine tests were all about: analysis of a patient's urine for traces of various—usually banned—substances. Dad figured that D-Ray's tox screens should have lit up like a Christmas tree with all the drugs—legal and otherwise—he must have had in his system. And sure enough they did—testing positive for THC, cocaine, oxycodone, and methamphetamine— but Mom's comment on the margin of one report in particular added an interesting wrinkle to the story:

*Pos. for opiates, but where's the Perc?*

She'd also circled the date of the report. There had been a prescription for Percocet barely a week before.

"What does that mean?" I asked.

"Well, it's interesting," Dad said. "I think it means that if Raymond was taking Percocet, it should have showed up in his urine screen. Certainly his doctor was prescribing them pretty regularly. I could be wrong, and I need to check with another doctor to be sure, but it *looks* like your mom suspected that D-Ray wasn't taking his meds. And if he wasn't, where was all the Percocet going? He might have been dealing . . . and possibly with his doctor's help."

I stared at him blankly.

"Time to make some phone calls."

\*\*\*\*\*

In fact he made three. The first call was to his own family doctor, Sylvain Tessier, in Sudbury. I didn't listen in on that conversation, but according to my dad the gist of it was that the doses of Percocet that D-Ray's doctor was prescribing, especially given the frequency of the prescriptions, definitely sounded suspect. Certainly if D-Ray had been taking the pills himself there should have been some indication in his urine. Dad was careful not to name names and insisted that his inquiry was purely academic, although you have to wonder what his doctor might have thought if he hadn't been my dad's physician since Dad was a teenager. Still Dr. Tessier was sure to mention that no doctor he knew would ever over-prescribe a controlled narcotic like that; rather, he offered his opinion—should my dad's question go beyond idle curiosity— that it sounded to him like somebody had got hold of a doctor's prescription pad, and was writing 'scripts illicitly. If that were the case, one could assume that these prescriptions were subsequently filled unwittingly by a number of pharmacists all over the region. Dad thanked him and left it at that.

The second call was needed to set up the third, and this one I did listen in on, or at least my dad's side of it. It was another call to Sudbury, this time to my uncle Carl. Dad was unsure about the legal ramifications of everything and Carl, the lawyer, was the best resource he had. From what I could hear, Dad told his brother everything, starting this time with where the critical information had come from—namely me—which was followed by an extended quiet period. I could easily imagine Carl reading my dad the riot act, giving him the lecture I had expected a few days earlier. My uncle was going to take some convincing before he came on board, and in the end, they seemed to agree that if they could get some third party to connect the dots for them, it didn't matter where the evidence came from. After a lot of back and forth, the name that emerged was Ferguston Regional Health Centre's chief of medicine, Dr. Doug Campbell. He was Mom's boss and a trusted friend of both my parents since I was a baby. If Mom had told anyone what she suspected, it would have been Doug.

They set up a get-together with Doug for that Friday afternoon at our place, over beer and burgers. Dad regarded Doug as a friend, even if they didn't see much of each other anymore. He knew that his insight as chief of medicine could be extremely valuable, but suspected Doug might not be forthcoming if we came right out and accused a colleague—even a former one—of dealing in prescription drugs, even if it was a long time ago. It was therefore vital that the meeting stay relaxed and friendly and not come across as an ambush, so Dad asked Carl to show up a bit later and—at my suggestion—to bring along his fiddle.

At the same time, Dad didn't want to tip his hand as to where he got his info on D-Ray; if it came out that I was the one who uncovered it during my volunteer work at the records office, Doug might just end the discussion before it had even begun. Of course he might figure it out for himself eventually, but Dad preferred not to make it easy for him. That's when I suggested that Doug should come alone and not with his wife Irene. It had been Irene after all who'd gotten me the volunteer position at the hospital, and if she were part of the discussion, she might make the connection a lot sooner than her husband would by himself.

Knowing that Doug didn't work on Fridays as a rule—but that Irene did—Dad called him over for a midday BBQ at 3:00 p.m. Carl arrived almost a half hour later, and brought along his banjo—a more light-hearted instrument than his fiddle—and a selection of craft beers. By the time I got home it was past 5:00. As I turned onto Tremblay, I could see the unmistakable gleaming white hulk of Doug Campbell's giant Ford Navigator SUV from up the street. It was about the size of a Galaxy Class starship and took up most of the driveway. I stepped into the house and crept to the kitchen, where Dad had thoughtfully left a full plate for me: a burger, a hot dog, and a lump of potato salad. The three grown-ups were sitting out on the patio having already eaten, and after god knew how many beers they were sounding pretty relaxed. I silently took my plate to my room, where the soundtrack of hearty men's laughter and Carl's banjo wafted through my open window.

*****

After a while Dad expertly manoeuvred the conversation toward all things medical, then to the hospital, then, more specifically, to hospital personnel. Carl was uncharacteristically quiet through most of it.

"Do you remember a Dr. Coleman?"

"Coleman . . . Coleman . . . Geoffrey Coleman? Right, I remember him. He had a private practice at the hospital clinic. GP."

"Did you know him very well?"

"No, not really. We were colleagues, but I wouldn't call us friends."

"I hear he was David Raymond's personal physician."

"Was he?"

"Yep."

"Yes . . . now that I think of it, I guess he was. How did you know that?"

"It's a small town." A pause as Dad took a swig of beer, and then the clink of the bottle against the patio stone. "Apparently Geoffrey Coleman was over-prescribing painkillers to David Raymond back in '96."

*Wow! That didn't take long.*

"'96?"

"The year Élise disappeared."

"Really? What makes you think so?"

"Élise knew about it."

"She told you this?"

"No. I found out through another source. I can't go into more detail."

There was a pause as Campbell mulled this over, no doubt wondering where my dad was going with it.

"Well . . . 'over-prescribing,' you say? It's not usually that simple. That's a medical determination, Martin. It's up to the physician to decide what's appropriate for his patient. David Raymond, as I recall, would have had legitimate need for Percocet, especially in those days."

"Yeah, but it looks like Coleman was writing prescriptions for one hundred tablets every week, and this for several months." Another pause.

"Well, that does seem a bit high, but it depends on the dosage."

"Ten milligrams, Doug. That's the heavy-duty stuff. He should have been getting maybe forty-two tablets per week at the most, and that over a short period. I asked around. Plus, I have reason to think he wasn't taking them. It looks like Raymond was pocketing the pills and selling them, either directly to customers or, more likely, to another distributor. Around here, I'm thinking biker gangs. God knows there's a market. You know how rampant prescription drug abuse is. The street value for Percocet is . . . how much, Carl?"

Carl spoke up for the first time. "In the States it can go upwards of twenty dollars per pill."

"Twenty bucks per pill. Minimum. C'mon, Doug. Would it be so surprising?"

"Not for Raymond, but it would surprise me if Geoff was involved, is all I'm saying. He was a good doctor. Conscientious. It doesn't make sense that he would take a risk like that: he could lose his license. Maybe Raymond was getting them from another physician. Or maybe he swiped Geoff's prescription pad. That happens all the time."

"Sorry. It was Coleman, and he was an active participant."

Quiet. A swig from a bottle, the snap and hiss of a match being lit, the smell of Carl's pipe.

Doug spoke up again. "Martin, where are you getting your information, may I ask?"

"I'm not saying, Doug. Don't ask again. If Coleman was supplying Raymond with high-end Percocet and Élise found out, it puts their whole altercation in the ER in a different light, don't you think? Suddenly Raymond is no longer a simple addict begging for a quick fix."

"Well, you've obviously been thinking about this for a while. What's your theory, exactly?" There was the slightest trace of amused skepticism in Campbell's voice.

"According to those who witnessed the exchange in the ER, D-Ray seemed scared. Panicked even. Élise told him, quote, that his line was being cut off. Interesting choice of words, wouldn't you say? What I'm thinking is that she'd already found out about Coleman's dealings with D-Ray and had either confronted Coleman or was about to."

"And you think Raymond got rid of Élise so she wouldn't interfere with his dealings with Geoffrey?"

"She never mentioned anything to you?" Dad replied in a softer tone.

"No. But it is an interesting thought. It would explain a few things."

"Such as?"

"Geoff was . . . never comfortable with Raymond as a patient. Not surprising. A lot of people were afraid of Raymond, even in those days. He was extremely volatile. God knows what grief he must have put Geoff through. If Raymond had anything to do with Élise's disappearance, regardless of what their dealings may have been, I think Geoff would have been happy to see him apprehended. But he never was, and Coleman ended up leaving Ferguston shortly afterward."

"He just left?"

"Closed up his practice and didn't look back."

"How long after?"

"Not long. A month, maybe less. It was a huge blow to the community, losing a doctor like him."

"What about all his patients?" asked Carl.

"They all had to be referred to other practitioners."

"Any idea where he went?"

Doug blew out a sigh. "That was a long time ago. I never bothered to follow up on him, to tell you the truth. As I said, we weren't close. By now he could be anywhere. Not that he would have to go far: there's a huge demand for physicians up north, especially for someone with his specialization."

"What was his specialization?"

"Oh, you didn't know? He worked on staff at the hospital. He was an anesthesiologist."

# 30

The conversation eventually drifted into less useful territory. I suppose Dad might have felt that he'd already pushed Doug harder than he meant to and was hesitant to go further, especially considering how Doug had always felt partially responsible for Mom's disappearance in the first place. In any event, Dad didn't bring up D-Ray again, and the last words on the subject were Doug's as he was leaving.

"I'm hardly one to give you advice, Martin . . . but you're a rational person. You know about pattern recognition, how we construct things based on limited, biased perception that simply aren't there. Most of the time we just let them go, but when they relate to something that's important to us, we give them meaning. That's how conspiracy theories are born." Dad began to speak up then, but Doug pushed on. "All I'm saying, Martin, is I know this is important to you but you have to be careful with what you find, or think you find. It may seem compelling, but you have to maintain a rational perspective in all this. I don't know anything about your sources, but even if what you say is true, to call what you have flimsy is being generous. I'm sure Carl would agree with me: it barely qualifies as evidence of any misconduct, let alone"—Doug paused, looking for an appropriate term— "a major crime."

Dad murmured something at that point that I couldn't make out, and after a bit of a pause Doug continued.

"Look Martin, I know you never got the resolution you hoped for from that whole awful business. I can't imagine how you've dealt with it all these years. And I can't say I blame you for wanting to turn over every stone, especially in regards to David Raymond. It's just . . ." He trailed off for a bit, seemingly losing his momentum, then resumed. "Are you sure this is what you want? I mean, is finding a final answer really going to be satisfactory in the end?"

There was a clap of a hand on an arm or shoulder as they said goodnight and something that might have been "Good luck," and Doug stepped out into the warm summer evening. Dad waited a few moments before closing the door, then he and Carl returned to the kitchen, where sombre picking from Carl's banjo sang of weariness and painful loss, long passed but never fully healed.

*****

I made my way back downstairs in time to catch the post mortem. Dad was sitting on the kitchen counter, fresh beer in hand, while Carl sat at the table, his banjo now silent. Their voices were subdued to the point where I wouldn't have caught anything they said had I stayed upstairs. As I pulled a soft drink out of the fridge, Carl was saying something to the effect that, from a legal perspective at least, Doug was right: there was really nothing we could move on and, from what he could tell, Doug hadn't contributed anything of significance.

"Although," Carl said, "I did find it interesting that Doug didn't remember that Coleman was Raymond's GP at first, but once it came out, he seemed to have a lot to say on the matter."

"Yeah, I noticed too," my dad said.

Dad meanwhile was grinning. I knew that grin, as no doubt did Carl. It was the grin that said he knew something that you didn't know, and he was going to relish that fact for a few seconds before he shared it. I bet he was all the more pleased because he was one up on his big brother, which mustn't have happened very often.

"OK, I can see that Cheshire Cat shit-eating grin of yours, Marty. Spill it."

Dad gave Carl a wide-eyed *Who? Moi??* look, took another a swig of beer for dramatic effect and said, "Did you notice something else? Doug said that D-Ray would have had a legitimate need for Percocet at the time."

"Yeah. But that's true, he would have. He was a mess."

"But I never mentioned Percocet. I just said 'painkillers.'"

Carl's face was blank, but his blue eyes were sparkling.

"Do you know how many prescription painkillers there are on the market? Even if Percocet was the most popular one out there, which it isn't, he wouldn't have mentioned it by name. He would have just said 'painkillers' like I did. He knew about it, Carl."

Carl mulled that one over for a moment, his fingers curling little loops in his ample beard, his eyes fixed on his brother. After a while he said, "Interesting," as much to himself as anyone else.

"I have a question." My dad and my uncle turned to me, as if noticing me for the first time. "How come no one, like the police for instance, ever found out about the whole drug thing between D-Ray and Dr. Coleman? I mean, shouldn't that have come out a long time ago?"

Dad jumped at this. "Good question, Juss." Then to Carl, "Why didn't the police look into this? Shouldn't it have come out during the original investigation into Élise's disappearance?"

"The police would have had no way of knowing, Martin. First of all, they would have had no cause to look at D-Ray's medical file. They were investigating a missing persons case. They had no reason to suspect wrongdoing at the time, and one public outburst in the ER wouldn't have been enough to get a warrant for D-Ray's file." Carl narrowed his eyes the tiniest bit at us. "It's important that you both understand this. Even if and when D-Ray showed up on their radar as a possible person of interest, the police would have required not only a warrant from a judge to get access to those records, but permission from the hospital administration, and even then, the file would have been vetted to decide what information was relevant and what wasn't. And as Chief of Medicine, the last word on that would likely have been Campbell's. Like I told you over the phone, what Justin did in reading, and especially keeping, the contents of those files was a major breach of privacy. If you plan to do anything with that information, I'd advise you get legal counsel."

"But isn't it a bit like a shrink or a priest hearing a confessor's admission of a crime? He or she would be obligated to report it."

"No, it's not . . . unless the evidence of a serious crime was really compelling, which it isn't in this case. Even then . . ." Carl let the sentence drop. He'd made his point.

"There's something else," I said. "I found out a couple of things today. I was doing my rounds this afternoon, picking up files from the different departments, and I asked around if anyone knew or remembered a Dr. Coleman. I was told to ask at the surgery department, which was on my rounds anyway. There was somebody there who knew him. I think she's a nurse . . . Gail or something. Anyway, she knew who I was right away, and she remembers Mom. She told me that Dr. Coleman was asked to leave the hospital, not exactly fired but . . . something to do with not getting another contract?"

I looked up at my dad to see if he knew what I was talking about.

"His contract wasn't picked up again by the hospital. Meaning he didn't resign," he said, glancing at his brother as he spoke. "Did this person say why?"

"Well, actually, yeah. She said that there were stories about some serious incidents in the operating room involving Dr. Coleman, that he made some really major mistakes, and that he had to go. Apparently, it all happened suddenly, and like overnight he was gone."

This time it was Carl who spoke up. "Now that's not at all the impression Doug gave, was it? He said Coleman left about a month later. What was it she said, Juss?"

"'Overnight he was gone.'"

Carl continued. "An anesthesiologist making mistakes in surgery could be catastrophic."

"This Gail person said things like in one case a patient woke up in the middle of an operation . . ."

Dad's eyes got huge. "Ho-ly shit!"

". . . and that another time a patient didn't wake up after surgery . . . for like a few days or something." I paused for a second. "Funny Doug would say that Coleman was a good doctor, and that losing him was a huge"—I paused again, trying to remember Doug's exact words—"'blow to the community.'"

By this time Dad had come off the counter and was sitting next to me. "Who was this person you spoke to?"

"Gail something . . . I didn't get her last name. She was an older lady, really nice. But she didn't seem to like Dr. Coleman very much. She also said a few things about Mom, like she said Mom could be really tough at times. I'm guessing she meant that as a good thing?"

A wry raised eyebrow from Dad. "Sometimes."

"Did she say anything else about Coleman?" asked Carl.

"Yeah," I continued. "She said a few things to me kind of under her breath, like she was worried someone would overhear. She mentioned that Coleman was getting a bad reputation among the female staff at the hospital, saying and doing inappropriate things. She didn't give any details."

"Odd she would tell that to a twelve-year-old volunteer," said Carl. There was no missing the tone of disapproval. "Why do you think she'd tell you that?"

"Well, maybe she'd been keeping it to herself for a long time and she wanted to get it off her chest. Maybe I was just the first person to ask her the right questions."

Dad was grinning as he turned to his brother and, giving a slight sideways nod in my direction, said: "And the kid's only twelve!"

Carl looked at Dad who was beaming, then back at me, and I watched the smile slowly bloom under his whiskers. He looked down, nodded a bit then spoke up again.

"OK kids, let's just look at what we've got, or as Doug said, what we think we've got. First, there's David Raymond, celebrated community nuisance and notorious drug seeker. Throughout 1996 he may or may not have been getting large amounts of prescription painkillers from his family doc on a regular basis. Let's just say he did. His pharmacology records during this period show no evidence that he was using them. In early November he shows up at the hospital ER and in front of a room full of witnesses he loses his shit, demanding his meds, and confronts the physician on duty, one Dr. Élise François-Lambert. Élise tells him, in her words, that "his line has been cut," and to get the fuck out of her ER—sorry, Juss. Witnesses report that D-Ray is highly agitated, frantic, scared even, and he proceeds to issue threats toward Élise. He may or may not be accompanied by a friend; it would be nice to know who this character was. Anyway, D-Ray storms out."

Carl took a swig of beer and continued. "We have Dr. Geoffrey Coleman, hospital anesthesiologist and David Raymond's personal physician. Records suggest that he was overprescribing Percocet to his patient: massive amounts for short periods, and this repeated over the course of many months. Rumour has it that, right around this time, Dr. Coleman was responsible for an undisclosed number of incidents in the OR that may have endangered the lives of patients during or following surgery. We have no details or confirmation of this, just hearsay. There may also have been incidents of inappropriate behaviour toward female staff. Again, this is just hearsay. A few weeks to a month after the incident in Emergency, the decision is made not to renew Dr. Coleman's contract at the hospital—a decision that would very likely have involved the hospital's chief of medicine—and Coleman closes his practice, leaving Ferguston permanently. His current whereabouts are unknown.

"We have Dr. Élise François-Lambert, emergency physician at FRHC. We know she became suspicious of Dr. Coleman's prescriptions for David Raymond as early as 1995, maybe earlier. She apparently came across D-Ray's file and noted the frequency and dosage of Percocet that Coleman was prescribing. There is no evidence that she discussed her suspicions with anyone else, but when confronted by D-Ray at the ER she told him that his 'line has been cut off,' suggesting she may have already taken some kind of action; what action that is, we have no idea. She disappeared a few days later.

"Finally, we have Dr. Doug Campbell, chief of medicine at FRHC and immediate supervisor of both Drs. François-Lambert and Coleman, not to mention a Lambert family friend for over a decade. Dr. Campbell claims to have no knowledge of Coleman's Percocet prescriptions for D-Ray, which is odd becomes he mentioned Percocet by name without being prompted. He also claims that Coleman left unexpectedly of his own volition, suggesting that he was afraid of David Raymond, when in fact his contract wasn't renewed—possibly because of incidents in the OR, but this isn't confirmed. He praises Coleman's ability; maybe he's just being kind, maybe it's professional courtesy, doesn't want to bad-mouth a colleague and former staff member. Claims no knowledge of Coleman's whereabouts." Another gulp of beer. "Have I left out anything?"

Dad and I looked at each other for a moment, then each of us shrugged, Dad doing so as much with his face as with his shoulders. I couldn't help smiling at Carl; he hadn't, as far as I could tell, uttered more than one sentence during the whole discussion with Doug, and yet he recalled everything in detail, not missing a thing. I was in the presence of world-class listeners.

"So what do you want to do, Marty? All that still doesn't amount to much, certainly not enough to merit the attention of law enforcement. I suppose you could snoop around the periphery a bit, talk to hospital staff, people who know or knew all the major players who were around at the time. You might get a bit more out of them. There are downsides to this, though. These events happened ten years ago: people forget stuff, and even if they don't, their memories aren't perfect; stories might conflict, then who do you believe? Also, some people just move on. It wouldn't be easy to track everyone down. Second, it's not a big hospital, and people would talk: 'Oh, have you heard? Élise Lambert's husband has been poking around the hospital, asking questions,' that kind of thing. Ultimately word would likely reach Doug, and he might not like what you're doing. And finally, you have to remember that the police questioned everyone already, during their initial investigation, at a time when everyone's memories were still fresh. You'd be rehashing old info."

"Well, we've just learned that there are new things to be found. Obviously, the police didn't have the complete picture. But I agree with you: I'm not keen on snooping around the hospital, asking questions about my missing wife. I'd look like a ghoul."

"And I don't recommend going back to Doug about this. You got everything out of him that you're likely to get. Which leaves you with one option."

Dad nodded as he rose from his chair, clearing empty beer bottles from the table.

"We've got to find Geoffrey Coleman."

# 31

The next Monday was the day that Sandra was coming back from her Boston vacation and I was looking forward to seeing her. So when Dad got a call Sunday evening from Irene Campbell telling him to "let Justin know that he won't need to come in to the records office anymore, thank him very much for all the hard work, and to have a great summer," I was peeved. Doug had no doubt determined, with Irene's help, that Dad had gotten his D-Ray info from me via the records office, but in the absence of direct evidence and in the interest of good relations didn't want to come right out and accuse me of something unethical. Dad apologized to me, saying it was his fault, that he'd given Doug some pretty specific information about D-Ray and that it was inevitable that Doug and Irene would figure out where it had come from. Dad said he'd get in front of everything should the "crap ever hit the fan," saying it had all been his idea. As a still-grieving husband of a much-beloved community member, few people would blame him; and as an innocent twelve-year-old child, not much would stick to me either.

In any event, my dad reassured me that my release from the hospital records office was for the best, that I now had the better part of a month to enjoy the summer, and that there was still a lot to do. I should have seen the warning signs then, that what Dad had in mind was namely poring through the D-Ray file for more evidence, and trying to locate Dr. Coleman. He didn't mention time together travelling to see our relatives, possible camping excursions, movies, bike rides, hanging out on the beach, visits to Science North in Sudbury, or the big one, our trip to the American Southwest. I was confident at the time that had I mentioned any of those he would have replied "Yes, of course, absolutely!" but as the days and weeks wore on and July melted into August it became obvious that the only thing that had any immediate interest for him was, in his words, "furthering the investigation."

The immediate impact wasn't huge: Dad still spent most of his days in front of his computer, while I was free to go about my business. But I noticed a few things, namely that he seemed to almost hum with a nervous energy that I'd never seen before. When we did find ourselves together, usually at meal time, he would regale me about what he'd found out: "D-Ray did this," or "D-Ray was admitted for this," or "This happened to D-Ray." He was becoming an expert on the arcane subject of David Raymond's medical history, as if it were a new course he was going to have to give in September. Within a week, I would have happily sacrificed any number of our usual summer activities if only to talk about something else.

Dad's other pet project, finding Dr. Coleman, was something he entrusted to me. Dad found a few on-line services to help people find a physician, the most promising of which was on the College of Physicians and Surgeons of Ontario website. It had fields where you could enter the doctor's name, gender, language, type of practice, including family doctors and specialists; registration status, meaning whether the doctor was active or inactive; location of practice, which had every conceivable city, town, and village in the province; hospitals where they work or have privileges, and a few other things. I started by putting in all the info I had on Coleman, entering his full name, his specialization, Ferguston as location of his practice, and FRHC as the hospital where he worked. I got nothing. Strike one. Hardly surprising seeing as he'd been gone almost ten years. I decided then to go the opposite route and cast a wider net: last name only and specialization. The results came back instantaneously. There were three anesthesiologists in the province named Coleman: George, Brandon R., and Janice. Strike two. At that point my dad suggested that I cast an even wider net; he reminded me that Geoffrey Coleman was also a family doctor, and that there was even the possibility that he had since retrained in another area of specialization in addition to anesthesiology. Plus, he might be retired, and there was a setting for that as well. I set the "Type of practice" field to "All," chose "All physicians" under "Registration status," remembered to set "Gender" to "Male" this time, and tried again. The finder spit out forty-one male doctors named Coleman in Ontario. I didn't find the Dr. Coleman I was looking for, although there was a Dr. Jeffrey—with a J—Coleman in some town I'd never heard of. I dismissed him knowing the spelling was wrong. Strike three, at least in Ontario. I figured that other provinces probably had similar organizations with similar websites that allowed similar searches, but I left it up to Dad if he wanted to chase Coleman around the country.

*****

Oh, and this happened. On Wednesday morning, August 9th, almost three weeks after my encounter with D-Ray in the hospital parking lot, I stepped out to pick up the mid-week edition of the *Clarion*. On that morning I was greeted by something altogether different: a dead rat.

We used to have a pretty grey tabby named Damsel who routinely dropped her prey offerings on our front porch—birds, rodents, the occasional frog—something Dad found mildly revolting but that I found cool in a nature-show kind of way. There was nothing cool about the rat I found that morning. It was big and grey-brown and bloodied, and even though it had been left there that morning it was far from a fresh kill. Worse yet, the creature's face had been mutilated. Upon closer inspection—which was really gross and I very nearly barfed—I could see that its mouth had been torn open and its tongue ripped out: D-Ray's idea of a message, and a decidedly unsubtle one.

I should have been more frightened. Clearly, I should have told my dad about it, rather than simply gathering up the poor creature's mangled remains and dropping them into a garbage bag. Instead, all I could think of was how pathetically redundant D-Ray was: tearing the tongue out of a rat's mouth. Yeah, we get it.

*****

I've often wondered about how my brain managed to deal with the whole idea of Billie during this time. Maybe it's just the way I remember things now. Time has a funny way of softening memories, rounding out the edges, making them easier to live with. I don't recall being freaked out. I was sitting on the biggest secret in the history of humankind, and maybe it was because I was only twelve and had no way of getting anything near proper perspective that I was able to go about my life as a pre-teen and not turn into a total spaz. Plus, I'm not sure I was ever completely convinced that Billie, or what she claimed to be, was entirely real. Somewhere in my mind, despite the miraculous transformations and apparitions and the simple innocent desire to believe, there was a firewall of skepticism that held off full acceptance. Somewhere there was a voice I wasn't even fully aware of that kept ensuring me that I'd eventually catch a glimpse of the man behind the curtain.

I was already a bit pissed when I caught up with Billie at Lakeview Cemetery on Friday. I was mostly annoyed at my dad for becoming so obsessed with the D-Ray file, and ultimately angry with myself for letting the genie out of the bottle in the first place. It got so that he was ignoring phone calls, forgetting to make dinner, and leaving other things around the house undone. I didn't mind doing chores—I could mow the lawn, keep the kitchen tidy, stuff like that—but at twelve years old I wasn't about to take on things like doing the shopping and cooking the meals. Not that we ever lived in squalor, but as I looked upon the piled-up pizza boxes and takeout food containers and a near-overflowing wastebasket in the kitchen that morning, I was given yet another reason to get to the end of whatever adventure I'd snared my dad into joining me on.

I rested my bike against the trunk of one of Lakeview's giant white pines, and then collapsed in a heap in the shade. It was nearing the hottest part of the day on one of the hottest days of what was becoming the hottest summer in living memory, and although I hadn't exactly sprinted to the cemetery, I was thoroughly drenched and parched. I could see Billie a short way off, examining the grave markers, tracing the etched names and dates with one hand, while in the other she daintily held something between thumb and forefinger that I couldn't make out. I was in no hurry to call her over: dealing with Billie required above-average levels of patience and energy at the best of times, and I was hot and tired and cranky and needed a few minutes to shore up my reserves. I closed my eyes, breathed in the thick warm air, and willed the knot of stress that had formed at the base of my skull to dissolve.

*****

*Warm sun on my face. My eyes are closed, my face is pointed skyward. I'm breathing deeply, slowly. I could sleep here. There are some faraway noises, a truck grinding past, a small engine whirring, nothing of consequence. A gull crying out. My limbs, so tired and sore from the exertion of cycling uphill to the cemetery moments ago, are still, light. I'm floating. An odd sensation to be having here, but I'll go with it. I'm relaxed for the first time in what seems like days . . . weeks even. Everything is far away for now: Dad is no doubt at home on his computer, looking at . . . what exactly? I can't remember, but it seemed so important only a little while ago. It doesn't matter now. I'm happy here. I'm floating. My eyes open, just a crack against the sun. It's hard, fierce even, but I don't protest. Funny, I thought I'd been sitting in the shade. I look for Billie . . . across a field, the cemetery . . . It's so vast and far away, I can barely make out the gravestones, even the big ones. I can't see Billie; she would be a small but colourful dot in her purple hoodie. There's no way I can be this far from the cemetery, but the sun is too bright for me to get a good picture. I close my eyes; I want to open them again, but I'm so tired and I feel so light, floating here . . . I could sleep. A gull crying again, soon joined by another, then another. I should open my eyes again; I need to find Billie. I open them, but I see nothing but sky. Looking around, I see the cemetery again, but it's farther than before: there's a road and a meadow and a wooded area between me and the closest gravestone. I've drifted farther away . . . then I notice the water. I really am floating. The water is up to my neck, my feet aren't touching the bottom. The water is dark, murky, and warm like blood, but there are no waves and I can see I'm far from the shore, much too far. I must be one hundred, two hundred metres, maybe more. Maybe a lot more. Am I drifting away from shore, or am I staying still and the shore is moving away from me? There's a tiny purple dot moving against the green of the cemetery grounds. I open my mouth to call out to her, but I realize she's too far to hear me just as my mouth fills with water. My legs are exhausted, they think they're cycling again, but now they're treading water. My strength is failing, my mouth is full of water, and the last thing I see is a dragonfly that lights on my face before I slide beneath the surface.*

# 32

Something, either a change in the direction of the light, or the whine of an insect next to my ear, or a drifting particle of fluff brushing my face, dragged me out of a deep and troubled sleep. It was a disconcerting slumber, too deep for that time of day. I snapped awake, momentarily baffled about where I was and how I got there. I had no idea how long I'd been asleep, but sufficient time had passed for the sun to swing far enough to the south to move my patch of shade to my right, leaving me completely exposed. The inside of my mouth had a cottony feel, and my eyes were crusty which, along with the strength of the naked sun, made it hard to look around. Mostly I was warm, hot even, propped up directly under the sun. Heat seemed to come from all directions, and as I turned to move back to the shade, I noticed Billie sitting next to me, her back against the trunk of the pine.

"How long was I out?" I asked.

Billie gave a quick dismissive shrug. She was focused on the object she was keeping in her cupped hands. There was movement inside, visible between her fingers.

"Look what I found," she said, never taking her focus away from her prize. She opened her hands as slowly as possible, like they were the halves of a jewellery box and she was presenting me with an engagement ring. Splayed in the middle of her palm was a dragonfly, brilliant green and motionless. Billie was delighted. "It's not afraid of me! Pretty, isn't it? Did you see its wings?"

"Yeah . . . I've seen dragonflies before. What about its wings?"

"Just look at them. They're beautiful! They look like they were made where I come from."

A typical, obscurely provocative Billie statement. I didn't bite, nor did I want to look too closely; I was still a bit stressed from the dream and it seemed I had gotten an all-too close look at a dragonfly just moments ago, but I gave the insect a quick glance to see what she was talking about. The insect's two pairs of wings stuck straight out from the body, forming a narrow X. They were intricately veined, with hundreds of tiny irregular facets, no two identical. The wings were perfectly translucent, except for a very faint blue sheen. I'd never looked at a dragonfly that closely before: it was beautiful, its body an iridescent green and its wings almost impossibly complex in their detail. It made me feel all the more exhausted, and rather than show my appreciation, I pushed out a sigh and leaned back against the tree. I was hot and grumpy and felt like picking a fight.

"You know, you don't sound like a nine-year-old." It came out sounding like an accusation, which was precisely the idea. Billie either didn't notice or didn't care.

"Well, I've been talking and listening to a lot of other people, you know."

"Where? Ferguston?"

"No, not so much here. A lot of other places. Like I told you, you might know me as Billie but I'm not always a little girl. I've met many people, and I've learned a lot from them, so maybe I sound more grown-up."

I felt a momentary pang of jealousy at the idea that Billie, or her in some other human form, was interacting with other people. Older, more mature, probably more interesting people. We were quiet for a while. Billie returned her attention to her dragonfly, which to my amazement remained motionless in her upturned palms. It probably liked the warmth. In time, she turned to me.

"You're not happy today," she resumed.

I hadn't spoken to Billie since before I found the D-Ray file in the hospital records office. Consequently, I had no idea of how much she knew about anything, but I was in no mood to explain. She'd stop me if she had any questions.

"Ever since I found that file on David Raymond my summer has turned into total crap. I told my dad about it and he got all excited, which is what I wanted at first. I thought he might find something."

"Like what?"

"I dunno, maybe some answers about what happened to my mom, so he could finally know for sure and be satisfied, and maybe the police would then take over and arrest D-Ray, and be done with the whole thing, you know? So that he . . . so that we could, I dunno, move on."

"And that didn't happen."

"No. Not yet, anyway, or at least not completely. He found out that D-Ray and his doctor were maybe involved in some crime, and that my mom found out about it. But he can't really prove it for sure and he can't tell the police because the way we found out isn't exactly legal, or something. The worst is now my dad has become totally obsessed. He spends his days in front of the computer, looking for more evidence on D-Ray, and he wants me to help him find this doctor who he thinks might know everything."

"And you haven't found this doctor yet?"

"Nope. He's not in Ontario, that much I can say. I've kind of given up looking for him; my dad will be only too happy to pick up where I left off, and that's what worries me. Already we've cut back on some of the stuff we normally do in the summer, and it's looking more and more like we might not even go on our big trip to the US."

Billie sat in silence, looking down, soberly nibbling on her lower lip in thought. The dragonfly fluttered its wings for a moment and was still again.

"If you find this doctor, what would you do?"

"Talk to him. Ask him if he knew about D-Ray and what he did to my mom."

"Do you think he'd answer? Do you think he'd even know?"

"I dunno . . . but it's all we've got." I paused for a second, then turned to Billie. "Why? Do you know something? Do you have any inside information?"

She just stared at me.

"But you can go back in time, right? You can go back to any time you want, just as easily as you can walk to those shrubs over there."

"Justin—"

"If you wanted, you could go to the exact time and place my mom disappeared. You could find out exactly what happened!"

"Please, don't."

"You could help her!!!"

"I'm sorry, Justin, it doesn't work that way. Really. I mean, what are you expecting? You think I'm going to go back in time, change . . . whatever, and all of a sudden your mom is just going to show up?"

"How the hell should I know??? You're the one popping in and out of reality, telling me you're from outside the universe, that you can move through time backward and forward and, what, sideways, too? You tell me what I can expect!"

She paused, gathering her thoughts.

"Yes, I can move back in time. Yes, I could go back to the moment when your mom disappeared. But Justin you have to understand: even if I did, you'd never know the difference. Nothing would change for you. The past in your timeline, the one you live in right now, is already set: in your timeline, your mom disappeared. That's it. I'm sorry, but I can't do anything about that."

"My 'timeline'?"

"Think of time as a tree or a bush. It has branches, billions of trillions of branches, all growing outward, forward in time. Each branch is a timeline. You, everything you know, the whole universe, exist on a timeline. Sometimes a timeline will split, and time will go forward in two different directions: so basically, you'll suddenly have two versions of history moving forward from some moment in time, each one unfolding in their own way from that point forward."

"OK . . ."

"So say a timeline split in two, I dunno, ten billion years ago; those two versions of the universe have been each unfolding in their own way for a very long time. They'd look very, very different by now. You follow?"

"Yeah."

"OK, and if it split more recently, the two versions would look a lot more alike, at least in the early going." She looked at me to make sure I was still with her, and continued. "This has been going on since the beginning. Timelines split, sometimes in two or three or a whole bunch more, and then each of those will, at some point, split again, and again, and again. And it's still going on, all the time. But most importantly for you, when it does happen you would never know the difference. From your timeline, nothing has changed."

"Are you talking about parallel universes?"

"In a way, I suppose, except that it's all different versions of the same universe."

Billie paused again. She closed her eyes and lifted her head to the sun, enjoying the warmth. She was in no hurry. After a while she turned back to me and continued.

"There have been many, many timelines that have split off since you were born. There are timelines where things have played themselves out very differently, others are more similar to what you're living now. And no I can't take you there."

"But . . . Can you go back and stop . . . whatever happened from happening?"

"I can't go back and change things. All I can do is go back to before that happened and start a new timeline, but, even then, I can't control how it plays out. For all anyone knows it could be worse. Besides, I don't need to: as I said, it's already happened, many, many times."

I stared at her for a moment. "Wait. Hold on. You mean *you* can start a new timeline?"

"Well, yeah . . ."

"So all these . . . versions of the universe . . . You're the one that creates them?"

"Only some of them. And I wouldn't put it that way. I've told you before: I don't *create* anything. I just . . . help things move in different directions."

"On purpose?"

"Sure."

"Why???"

"To see what happens. It's kind of an experiment. Have you ever played in a stream, and dug channels in the sand to see what the water does when you divert it? It's like that. The stream goes on no matter what you do. It's the same with time: I'm just giving it different possible directions."

"An experiment? We're just an experiment???"

"*We?*" She laughed. "Well, first of all if by 'we' you mean the entire universe, then yes. Justin, it's not like I'm focused on just your planet, or even your galaxy. The universe is a big place. And second, the universe isn't an experiment in itself. That's not why it's there. But since it *is* there—"

"But . . . you make it sound like a game."

"I wouldn't call it that. It's more like a research project. It's like going back to an earlier time, starting again from there, and then watching how things turn out. Sometimes things go more or less the same way, other times it's really different. Observation and experimentation: the scientific method. You know all about that."

"And you've been doing this for a long time?"

"Since the beginning."

"So then, are you responsible for us, humans I mean, being here?"

"Well, I . . . we . . . no one created you, if that's what you're asking. We're not directly responsible for you being here, any more than we're directly responsible for you being absent in other timelines. You're the product of your own evolution, plus a lot of lucky breaks."

"But are you responsible for the lucky breaks?"

"No, certainly not directly. Everything happens on its own. We just create the possibility for . . . new possibilities."

There was something Billie was missing, something vital, and I couldn't quite put my finger on it. It gnawed at the back of my mind.

"But . . . You said you can't change things. But you do. You . . ." It went off in my head, like a gunshot. "You *intervene!* You get involved, just by being here."

"I'm just here to observe. Sure I might interact with people and things, to learn, but I keep it to a minimum."

"Really? Tell that to Paul Worthington."

"Who?"

"He's the man whose wife was killed when their SUV was hit by the cement truck on Barrette Street."

She stopped completely, her momentum evaporated. She seemed totally confused, incapable of making any connection. Having gained the upper hand, I pressed.

"Their car was crushed because he had to swerve into the oncoming traffic so that he wouldn't run into you . . . you, who decided to just materialize in the middle of the street."

"Yes, but—"

"And what about the sinkhole? Remember? The big hole behind the McIntyre house back in May: that was you again, wasn't it? The McIntyres lost their home because of you, and it could have been a lot worse."

Billie was staring at me blankly.

"You just show up, all 'la-dee-dah, no big deal, I can come and go as I please,' except someone ends up getting killed because of it. Because of you! Mr. Worthington lost his wife and their children lost their mother *because of you*! Do you have any idea what that's like? What it means to lose someone close, to have someone torn out of your life like that? I mean, you spend enough time wandering around this cemetery, reading the grave stones . . . Are you getting any idea of what loss is?"

Billie was completely mystified. As I watched her, I was beginning to understand her limitations. Even if she was everything she claimed to be, she'd provided herself with a major handicap. Whatever she was, despite everything she'd learned, she had copied the emotional intelligence of a nine-year-old girl. It was all she had to filter out the moral implications of what had happened, of what she'd done, and she could comprehend little more than guilt and recrimination. For my part, I could do nothing but press on.

"You could actually help, you know? Bring some peace to people who are hurting. But you talk about just observing, learning, which is total bullshit because you end up hurting people in the worst way!"

I don't know if Billie knew how to cry and, if she did, if she even knew what was happening to her. At that moment I didn't care.

"If you're for real, you're totally useless. If not, you're just a pitiful liar. Either way, I'm an idiot for listening to you."

I walked around the tree and lifted my bike off the ground to leave, slinging my backpack over my shoulder in an extravagant show of disdain. Billie watched me silently, her eyes huge and bewildered, her body unable to move. I shoved my bike forward, and with a final backward glance, saw Billie standing motionless like yet another monument in the sunlight, and the fragile form of the dragonfly as it escaped her grasp and fled toward the lake.

*****

I was still fuming as I headed home, and the bike ride through the crushing midday heat didn't do much to lessen my anger. A longer ride might have. As I rode through my shitty little town, I only wished I could ride right through it and out the other end, take the highway and head south, or east, and keep pedalling. Nothing was ever going to change about Ferguston.

I glanced to my left toward Morin Hill and saw the water tower staring down at me. It was a relic from a mostly sad era, but its gleaming white surface was misleading, boasting of stability, of continuity: from a distance it was always pristine, it never rusted, it never showed any signs of the passing of years. It stood there smugly, towering some thirty-five metres above the rest of the town, quite satisfied with the way things have been for the past fifty or sixty years. I wouldn't be the first to bail on this town; many others had done it over the decades, and Ferguston never really missed them. Ferguston was going to do things its own way, the way it always had, even if that meant not doing much of anything at all, and all those whiny, discontent rabble-rousers looking for growth and newness and change didn't have to like it. It was almost like the town had some kind of invisible aura or shield covering it, or emitted some kind of power, or a disease, a virus, maybe something in the water. In any event, it was as if the longer you stayed, the more Ferguston got its hooks into you and lulled you into listless complacency and wouldn't let you leave. Dad wasn't even from Ferguston, and look at what it had done to him? He'd become just as stuck as anyone. Oh sure, now he'd found some crazy new obsession to keep him in town—the fact that it was all my doing hadn't escaped me either—but even in the best of times he, like all the adults here, was living in a perpetual now, with no vision over the long term. At least I sort of understood my Dad: he was looking for some kind of closure. What was Ferguston's excuse?

I approached downtown where the dark steeple of Ste. Anne's still dominated, like a declining monarch, an aging figurehead who was only wakened to preside over the occasional ceremony, then allowed to sleep while others saw to the day-to-day affairs of the realm. I thought of Dad, at that moment no doubt busying himself over some illegible notes left by Dr. Coleman, and I cursed myself for the umpteenth time. I'd given him all that D-Ray material thinking he'd actually find something real, something he could act on, that in the end would provide him with answers and finally some *closure*, that fabled and elusive creature that haunted the deepest parts his soul. It made me wonder about closure, the idea of closure, and why was some ritual act needed before a person could move on after a loss. In the end, was there even such a thing? Didn't it just come to a point when you decide once and for all to get on with your life, ritual or no? Ste. Anne's wasn't going to provide any answers: it owed its very existence to the need for ritual, and like the water tower, was supremely secure in its indispensability.

I dumped my bike unceremoniously on the floor of the garage; it made a loud clatter as it landed on my dad's toolbox, which he'd left open during some random unfinished repair job. I watched idly as the contents spilled out over the cement floor. I didn't apologize about the noise as I stepped into the house, I didn't announce my arrival, I didn't even poke my head through my dad's office door to say "hi." He'd be hunched over his computer, scrolling, searching, totally absorbed in some bit of D-Ray trivia. I poured a huge glass of water, downed it in a few seconds, poured another, and went upstairs to my room. It would be a while before he'd come see me, ask me what he'd like me to order for dinner and, as an afterthought, what I'd been up to. My bed creaked in protest as I stretched out, and I gradually dozed off as my stare tried to bore its way through the ceiling.

*****

*I'm standing at the bottom of a dark pit. It's not too scary at first: the pit is dark partly because it's getting into evening and the sky is overcast. Also, although the pit is deep it's also pretty wide: I don't feel trapped or panicky. Not yet anyway. But it's getting dark and I can't see too well. The floor of the pit is uneven and I'm up to my ankles in mud; there are dirty puddles all over. At first, I think I'm standing at the bottom of a construction site, the foundation of a big city building, but there's shattered concrete and twisted steel beams and huge piles of rubble everywhere. There had been a building here, but this isn't a construction site: it's a crater, made either by an explosion or an impact. But where I am isn't important, nor is the fact that I'm utterly alone. What is important is that I have to dig and keep digging. The shovel I'm holding was intended for a much bigger person, that or I've shrunk to the size of a small child. My hands are blistered and my arms and back are killing me, but I'm compelled to continue. The hole I've made is full of brown water; it's up to my knees now, my hands are bleeding, and still I keep digging. My shovel splashes into the muddy hole, and I heave the contents out, again, and again. It's getting darker, I'm soaking wet and despite my efforts, I'm so, so cold. There's an urgency I don't understand, and I barely pause to catch my breath. When I do there's a silence in the pit like death, which I can't stand, so I continue digging, filling the world with the sound of splashing, the heavy squelch of mud, and my own breathing. My breath fogs before me, but I can see little else. Finally the darkness and cold become overwhelming and I stop. There's not a breath of wind but there is something else on the air, which is felt at first rather than heard. A faint humming, like a stiff breeze through power lines, and under that . . . something else. I strain to hear. It's just there, beneath the surface, a soft cadence . . . a voice. It's coming from directly below my feet, and suddenly I hear it plainly, like it was always there. It's a woman's voice, and it's calling to me. Suddenly frantic, I begin digging again, faster, deeper, the water now reaching my waist, and still the voice implores me, louder and more urgent than ever, until I can go no farther without going under. And then suddenly, breaking through the inky darkness, a faint light appears beneath the surface at a distance that must be far, far below my feet. It makes no sense, and yet there it is: a faint milky light, dozens, maybe hundreds, of feet down. The voice calls me again, and I realize that's where I need to go. The icy water is now up to my chest. I can see nothing else but the light below me. There is no sky, no pit, only the dim glow and, for just an instant, an immense shape that passes in front of it before vanishing into the depths. I cannot stay where I am, because there is nothing there. All that is left, for better or for worse, is down below. The voice speaks again, softer now, knowing I'm coming. I take a final breath, close my eyes, and plunge . . .*

*You people could learn an awful lot from termites.*

—Billie

# PART 2

# 33

Our trip to the American Southwest was almost everything I hoped it would be. The first six days of it, at least, were amazing. It was shaping up to be the stuff of family lore, right up until the night when *it* happened, when I stepped into the Big Weird and everything changed.

You see, despite the disappearances, transformations and other Billie-related weirdness of that summer, I've always believed that I could have had a more or less normal life had I made a different decision in that critical split second on the night of August 19th, 2006.

A normal life, but not necessarily a better one.

My memories of the trip are strange, patchy in places. It's like this amazing movie that I'm told I saw but all I can remember is the trailer; certainly nothing like the memories that Debbie Williams claimed I would cherish forever.

Maybe that has to do with what happened. Or maybe it has to do with the weeks of hype and build-up around the trip, only to have it go so disastrously wrong at the end.

I'm grateful for what little I have. Hell, I'm grateful I got home in one piece.

I'm left with impressions for the most part: the overwhelming spectacle that was Las Vegas, all light and colour and people; sequoias like sky scrapers; the sweeping emptiness of the Mojave Desert; baffling roadside attractions; absurd restaurant portions that would feed the AFC East; dust and rock and cactus in the Canyon; and, everywhere, the insane heat.

The trip was planned as a big eight-and-a-half-day loop. Vegas to Sequoia National Park via Death Valley and the Sierra Nevada on Day One. Then south through the Mojave and east along famed Route 66 through Arizona to the Grand Canyon. On Day Three we began crossing the Canyon from the South Rim to the North, a trek that would take three days and two nights. We got two thirds of the way across when it happened, and whatever we'd planned for after that was quickly scrapped.

Of course not everything was blotted from my memory. I remember a few things with surprising clarity, a handful of events preserved intact like a fossil insect in amber. In one case, a random episode of weirdness that should have raised a red flag, the foreshadowing of something bigger and stranger. But by that point in the summer, my definition of what was extraordinary was already set at a pretty high bar.

It was about to get a serious readjustment.

*****

The landscape of Death Valley was like nothing I'd ever seen. Parts are mountainous, like jagged, rocky teeth; others are very flat, just cactus and scrub stretching out endlessly in all directions. The most unforgiving part is a salt pan south of a place called Furnace Creek, which is as lifeless as the moon; and with temperatures hovering in the mid-forties Celsius, it was easy to imagine yourself on another planet.

Aside from a smattering of other vehicles that passed us and the clumps of shrubs that dotted the terrain, we saw no signs of life . . . except for one instance that my dad eventually wrote off as an optical illusion. We'd been riding along in silence when Dad suddenly hit the brakes, pulled over and got out with a pair of binoculars, scanning the desert for a few moments before the crushing heat prompted him to get back behind the wheel. Dad remained quiet for a bit, absently shaking his head, until he sensed me looking at him.

"Sorry about that, Juss. I dunno, it was weird. Just for a moment I could have sworn I saw somebody out there, at least a mile off. There was movement and a blur of colour. But when I looked again, it . . . he, she . . . was gone."

"A person? Out here??"

"I know. It's unthinkable. They wouldn't last long in this. That's why I stopped."

We sped off again, and I settled back into my seat as we resumed our quiet ride, satisfied with watching this alien world as it zipped by. I didn't bring it up again, and would have forgotten about the incident completely except for my dad's comment about the blur of colour, and I found myself wondering if that colour was, perchance, purple.

*****

I remember more driving, the road rising out of the desert; snow-dusted mountains that had seen the great mammoths and mastodons come and go; and a forest like a cathedral, tourists in Tilley hats gape-mouthed, their sugar-addled kids awed into silence.

And my stoic dad, a Lambert if ever there was one, a man who greets his own father with a handshake, with his arm around my shoulder. An alien gesture, a foreign language, and yet the most natural thing in the world. I barely breathed as I leaned into him, and though we hardly spoke ten words between us before we returned to the car, I don't think I'd ever been closer to my dad than at that moment.

\*\*\*\*\*

Still more driving, now along fabled Route 66, Dad singing one of Mom's songs about getting his kicks, and roadside diners promising—threatening?—to serve grilled roadkill or alien jerky. Every so often the drive would be punctuated by sudden snorts and spit-takes and gushes of laughter at the genuine absurdity of the attractions along the route. Ferguston, Ontario, had never seemed so far away.

Our conversations were economical, with sometimes many kilometres between utterances, but something was happening that I didn't expect. I didn't know if it was the extreme environment, the isolation, the mental and physical distance we'd placed between ourselves and Ferguston, or the simple camaraderie of sharing a new adventure, but there was a sudden ease in one another's company that was unlike anything we lived back home. The scope was at once both vast and intimate. Dad talked about his job, about how teaching kids *how* to think was so much more vital than *what* to think, and how he knew he'd never have to worry about me in that regard. Then, perhaps feeling that some threshold had been crossed, he explored new uncharted areas with me, talking about fatherhood, how if there'd ever been a guide or textbook to parenting he'd chucked it long ago, and how painfully aware he was of the huge cultural gaps in my life resulting from his own ignorance, gaps that would have been filled seamlessly if Mom were still around.

Later on we'd reflect on those moments, determining that they had made the entire trip, the whole summer in fact, worth everything we'd been through until then.

Leave it to me to fuck everything up only three days later.

*****

Almost exactly forty-eight hours and some 1670 kilometres after we landed in Las Vegas, Dad and I stood at the edge of the parking lot at the Grand Canyon Visitor Centre on the South Rim. The earth opened up before us, a drop of a thousand metres, in layers of blue and purple and green and orange. I can't remember how long we stood there, gaping; I might have stayed there for hours had not Dad said, in a near whisper, "Kind of makes you appreciate what's under the ground you walk on every day," and led us back to the car.

My recollections seem to become a bit clearer at this point, but I can't be sure. I don't trust these memories any more than I can trust the memories of my mom. Dad took a lot of photos.

The descent into the Canyon began the next morning. In addition to us and our guide, an energetic graduate student in palaeoclimatology named Gabriella, the group consisted of a retired firefighter and veteran wilderness hiker from Seattle; a playful and horny young couple from San Antonio; and the Hilgenbergers, a God-fearing family of three from some Indiana suburb, who didn't know from or care much about geology or palaeontology or anything else that suggested the earth was more than six-thousand years old. Dad got a kick out of them, figuring they'd be right at home in Ferguston.

We completed the first leg of the trek, eleven kilometres of bone-jarring zigzagging trails to our campsite on the canyon floor, in five hours. We were, to a person, dusty, scorched, dehydrated, and utterly famished. After devouring our lunch, we were assigned to our respective cabins and were then free to have a shower and a well-deserved nap; others browsed through overpriced T-shirts and trinkets at the souvenir shop or generally snooped around.

I lay stretched out on my bunk, enjoying the tingly relief in my feet after shedding my hiking boots, eavesdropping on a hilarious conversation between Gabriella and Mr. Indiana. Apparently, he'd been out scouting the general vicinity of the lodge, wandering through the cottonwoods, camera in hand, hoping to catch a glimpse of the local wildlife. He wasn't disappointed. He managed to snap a few shots of what he claimed was a white-tailed deer, and, his mission accomplished, quickly sought out our guide to show her the fruits of his labour. To his credit, I think he was genuinely trying to make amends for his otherwise standoffishness during the trek down and this was his olive branch. It didn't last long.

"It's a bit of a blur, but you can see it here through the trees," he offered sheepishly. "I got a better view of it earlier, but by the time I got my camera it had moved off a bit."

Gabriella was obviously happy to see Hilgenberger so pleasant and forthcoming and didn't want to burst his bubble. "Yes, I see it. Hard to make it out, but it's lovely that you saw it, Donald." Then the scientist in her took over, if only for a second. "Of course, it would be a mule deer, not a white-tailed deer. There are no white-tailed deer in the Grand Canyon."

That was all it took. From there the old Donald Hilgenberger returned to full form, going on about how he knew white-tailed deer when he saw them, that he'd seen enough dead ones on the roadside when he lived in Pennsylvania, that he'd shot plenty when out hunting with his dad, and that he'd even "smacked into more'n a few" with his Benz. Dad, in the bunk beneath mine, let out a tired snort and muttered, "Donald Hilgenberger: animal lover."

*****

The second leg of the journey began soon after sunrise. It was to be a different kind of hike from the first one: a simple and direct route that ran twelve kilometres north/northwest with little or no change in elevation. This meant that while there was no strenuous climb to deal with, the heat in the bottom of the canyon would be like an oven. Gabriella said it was going to be like spending the day doing light exercise in a Las Vegas parking lot. In July.

After breakfast, we learned that the Hilgenbergers wouldn't be joining us on this part of the hike. Donald had grudgingly concluded that the trek was more than he or his family had bargained for and arranged for a mule to be sent to help them back up to the South Rim. As a result, they got to sleep in.

We hiked until noon, keeping to the shade of the canyon walls as much as possible, refilling our water bottles directly out of Bright Angel Creek. Dad and I plodded along, mostly in silence, Dad sometimes with his arm around my shoulder, reaching Cottonwood Campground just as the sun was cresting. We did little with the rest of the day—the soaring temperatures at midday saw to that—and contented ourselves with finding a comfortable place in the shade, staying hydrated, and watching the shadows slowly get longer.

Later, under a sky thick with stars, I listened as the grown-ups traded tales about their homes, their travels, and their experiences. In spite of the heat and the fatigue, I'd never been happier. My muscles were a bit sore but in a good way; I found that I was a lot tougher than I'd ever believed; and Dad and I had shown ourselves once again to be a pretty good team. Tomorrow was going to be the last leg of the journey; after a daylong climb we'd spend that night at the North Rim Lodge where—thanks to some ingenious planning on Dad's part—our rental car would be waiting for us. A day and a half after that we'd be back in Vegas, and then home. I couldn't even imagine what was waiting for me back in Ferguston. Everything associated with home seemed so distant and unimportant, just minor details I'd see to when I got back. What was important was what my dad and I had become since we left, and that there was nothing Ferguston could throw at us that we couldn't handle together.

*****

I wasn't sure right away what had woken me up, whether it was a dream, my dad snoring next to me, or some noise from outside the tent. It was a warm night, and I found myself lying on top of my sleeping bag, rather than in it. I held my breath and listened.

Nothing. I exhaled and flopped back down on my improvised pillow. Aside from my dad's breathing there was no sound, not so much as a lick of wind or even the sound of crickets. I was trying to decide if and how the sound fit into the dream when I heard it again, or something anyway. A snap, low but clear: a twig breaking by being stepped on. A moment later there was another one, not quite as loud, followed by a soft scuffing sound. It didn't sound like a person: some*thing* was just outside our tent. My imagination went immediately into overdrive: a bear, or maybe a mountain lion, snooping around our site, scrounging for remnants of our dinner. My heart began pounding, and I strained to hear more, like the animal's breathing or maybe grunting and sniffing, but there was only silence.

I glanced down at my dad again, thought about waking him up, and no doubt things would have been very different if I had. Instead I quietly pulled on my hiking shorts—there was always a chance of running into Gabriella, maybe going to use the washroom, and I didn't want her to see me looking like a total dork in my underwear—unzipped the netting of our tent, and lifted the outer flap.

Still nothing. My heart relaxed a bit and, giving a last quick glance at my dad, I crawled outside. I gazed skyward, and my breath caught for an instant. The night was clear, moonless and choked with stars. I'd seen the Milky Way before in the hills north of Ferguston far from the lights of town, but never with such clarity. For the second time I thought of waking my dad, to share this with him—he would never have faulted me for that—but a soft noise to my right caught my attention, reminding me of why I was out alone in the wilderness in the dead of night. I moved onward a few feet. "This is nuts," I thought. "What the hell am I doing out here? I should at least have a flashlight. Christ, I'm not even wearing shoes." I was grappling with the idea of going back to get them when I saw it.

It stood not ten feet away, directly in front of our tent: a female, about a year old or so I guessed. It had its back turned, but it lifted its delicate head and looked directly at me. I could tell the species instantly; some people might have a hard time telling them apart from their western cousins, but even to me that big white tail was a dead giveaway. It had no business in the Grand Canyon, and damned if Hilgenberger hadn't been right all along. Of course, there were extenuating circumstances that only I knew about, but they would have been hard to explain.

I followed the young deer—her—away from the tents, maintaining a comfortable distance if only because my bare feet weren't going to let me go any faster. She looked untroubled and in no particular hurry, stopping every now and then to turn around and make sure I was still there, eventually making her way to a small outlying building at the edge of the campsite. She disappeared momentarily from view amidst the shadows of the building and the surrounding trees; by the time I got there, Billie was sitting on the ground, her back to the shed, her arms wrapped around herself.

"It's so cold here," she said.

I tried not to be impressed. For a time it wasn't hard.

"Only you would say that." Billie didn't answer. Then I thought of what my dad had seen a few days ago and asked, "Was Death Valley more to your liking? You know, if you want to be inconspicuous you shouldn't be wearing a purple sweatshirt in a desert."

A shrug, intended to neither confirm nor deny. I took it as a confirmation.

"You screwed up, you know: wrong kind of deer. It caused a big scandal. Scientists are going to be arguing about it for years."

I paused to see if I'd made an impression. Apparently not.

"What are you even doing here?"

"You and . . . you both seem really happy. It's nice to see."

"You're not going to help us, are you? Because you can't interfere."

"Even if I did, even if I helped you and you found out whatever it is you want to find out, what makes you think it will do any good? How do you know you'll get anything like what you want in the end?"

I couldn't answer. Now it was Billie's turn. She pushed on.

"Don't you see? You two are closer than you've ever been. You've managed to do exactly what you wanted to do when you set out on your little project; you never needed that stupid file. You can build on what you've found here. You can go home now and move on, get past . . . the past."

She was right and it made me furious. I didn't want to leave it at that. I didn't want to be reasonable, or noble, or take the high road. I searched for the first thing I could think of and flung it at her. It wasn't much.

"I don't believe you're what you say you are. I think you're a big phony. I think you've figured out a few tricks to move around the way you do, or something to make me hallucinate, but it's something that science is going to discover sooner or later. There's nothing special about you. I can't believe I fell for your crap: your *continuum!*" I spat that last word out like it was something foul. "You must think I'm an idiot."

Billie didn't look hurt, just a little sad and resigned. "It's OK, Justin. It's better that way anyway." She stood up slowly, rubbing her hands up and down her arms in order to keep warm. "I'm going now. Goodbye, Justin. Turn away. Shield your eyes."

To this day, I still wonder what possessed me to do what I did then. It might have been the prospect of Billie leaving for what looked like the last time, and I just wasn't ready to let her go. Maybe it was because I was still angry with her. I'd become skeptical about what she claimed to be; I wanted to see for myself and I didn't figure she'd willingly take me along if I'd just asked. Either way, it wasn't something I thought about: I just acted impulsively and, as it turned out, at the last possible second, just as she had done in the cemetery, she put out her right hand and made an opening into reality like she was separating drapes or parting vertical blinds. And just like before, an incredibly intense light exploded out of this opening. It was much too bright to look at, especially at night, so I tried to focus on Billie instead. I had less than a second. I shut my eyes tight, lurched forward in Billie's direction, and grasped as best I could for her left arm. I found it and held on with both hands just as she stepped forward. She was warmer than ever. I felt myself being drawn forward as by a riptide, and in the last fraction of a second I felt her left arm tingling in my hands as she started to disintegrate, and then the world started to come apart beneath my feet and then HOLY SHIT—

# 34

I was told that I was found half-conscious just before sunrise the following morning, curled up under a birch tree at the North Kaibab trailhead, at the top of the North Rim. No telling how long I'd been there. It was a group of hikers who almost literally stumbled over me as they were beginning their own trek down the trail; they immediately notified the on-duty officer at the ranger station, who then brought me to an infirmary on-site. Apparently, I was delirious at first and they had trouble getting information out of me, like my name, what I was doing at the trailhead at 5:30 in the morning, and where my parents were. For my part I had trouble seeing or hearing anything: everything was dark, and sounds and voices were somehow fuzzy. Eventually the cobwebs cleared just enough for me to tell them that I'd been with my dad at Cottonwood Campground in the Canyon, that his name was Martin Lambert, and that he'd need to know where I was or he'd be really, really worried. After that I must have passed out.

I was in and out of consciousness a lot over the next twelve to eighteen hours, so details for that period are sketchy. I don't remember when or even how my dad reached me, but I'm told that we were eventually flown by helicopter to a clinic in Grand Canyon Village back on the South Rim. What I do remember is while I was awake, I was aware of a dull thudding headache, buzzing in both ears, persistent cold, and continual darkness. I could see around me but it seemed like it was always evening or night, even when there was clearly a lot of activity going on. The gloom reminded me of those cloudy November evenings back home, lights out, curtains drawn, driving rain hammering the windows. On the other hand, I could escape the darkness, the cold, and the pain in my head by drifting off to sleep and reliving my experience "over there": the warmth, the dazzling light, the heart-stopping speed, and the impossible scale and detail and texture of everything.

\*\*\*\*\*

*HOLY SHIT HOLY SHIT HOLY SHIT I'm being pulled forward, my eyes are closed tight because it's so, so bright, and my hands are still clutching Billie's left forearm, which is hot and has become tingly and it's because she's dissolving she's actually fucking dissolving as she crosses the threshold but I can still feel her in my hand, and the earth, the world, OH MY GOD frigging reality itself is coming apart beneath my feet, and I can feel it running between my toes like sand in a riptide being dragged away by the current and I'm not aware that I've taken a step, in fact I'm sure I haven't, but suddenly I've passed into something . . . and ewwwwwww!!!! . . . it's . . . it's like walking through a wall of cobwebs but waaaaaay worse! . . .*

\*\*\*\*\*

The doctor at the clinic told my dad that I was showing symptoms of heat exhaustion—elevated body temperature, clammy skin, sweating, headache, dizziness, nausea, dehydration, etc.—which was odd considering the time of day and temperature when I was found. I was made to drink a lot of sports drinks—which I liked—and to take a long, cold shower—which I hated—and my temperature was lowered to something more like normal, at least for a little while. Within a few hours the rest of my symptoms gradually lessened and for the most part went away entirely, but there were a few things that the doctor couldn't explain that caused her some concern. The first was that both my eardrums had somehow ruptured; there was dried blood in my ears when I was found. The second was that my pupils were oddly dilated and yet I found it hard to see no matter how bright it was. The doctor wanted to send me to a larger hospital in Flagstaff for further tests, but by then I was already coming around and Dad just wanted to get as far away from the Grand Canyon as possible. Apparently, he lucked out in that the person who was supposed to drive our rental car all the way around to the North Rim hadn't done so yet: one fewer problem to deal with.

During the time I'd been resting in the clinic, I picked up bits of conversation; with the damage to my eardrums it wasn't easy, but I got the gist of it. The park ranger and the doctor were giving my dad a gentle grilling over some issues that didn't add up.

"You have to admit, Mr. Lambert, it sounds . . . extraordinary. According to what you've told us, your twelve-year-old son, an inexperienced hiker completely unfamiliar with the trail and the environment, undertakes a ten-mile hike that is very hazardous— if not downright dangerous—under the best conditions, in the dead of night without so much as a flashlight, by himself, without food or—most importantly—water, and does it successfully in less than five and a half hours."

There was a pause, then my dad spoke up. He sounded exhausted, confused, and there was a trace of something else in his voice that I rarely ever heard: fear.

"I don't know what to tell you. In fact, I should be asking you the same questions. Did you speak to the others in our party? They were all there. We'd been talking all night. They all saw Justin go to bed; he was the first to turn in. I didn't go to bed until 12:30 a.m. He was fast asleep."

"You couldn't be off a bit on the time? He'd have to be an elite athlete to pull off what he did."

"*Justin?* He's in decent shape, but come on. He's a bookworm, not a jock."

"It's a treacherous uphill climb, Mr. Lambert. You've seen it. Experienced hikers rarely do it in less than seven hours in broad daylight."

"And there's something else, too," the doctor interjected. "When he was found, he was barefoot, but his feet showed no signs of a difficult walk. Not a scratch. Nothing. They weren't even dirty."

"Yeah," said my dad. "He left his boots and socks in the tent, along with everything else."

"Did he have an extra pair?"

"Yeah, but he left them in the car before we even set out. And no one else in our group reported anything missing." Dad paused again. "I can't explain any of this. Hell, I was hoping you'd be able to tell me."

"To be honest, Mr. Lambert, we're at a loss."

"A mule, maybe?"

Silence, except for a stifled snort. Someone must have found the mule comment funny. Dad didn't.

"I don't find any of this amusing," my dad hissed, his voice becoming increasingly loud and anguished. "Do you have *any* idea what I've just been through? To wake up and find my son missing, without a trace, like he'd vanished into thin air? I've already been through this: my wife vanished ten years ago, and was never found. To lose my son the same way, to go through that again . . . I thought I'd go insane. Don't you understand? *He's all I have left!*"

There were a few apologies and muttered condolences after that, and the conversation wrapped up. In the end the ranger was content to shrug it off as a mystery that would likely be explained

---

sooner or later. The doctor made a final plea for more tests on me but Dad was insistent: aside from a bit of fatigue I looked fine, and he promised to have me checked out as soon as we got home. Clearly, he just wanted to move on. A little while later Dad signed a few papers, uttered some vague thanks to the travel insurance gods, and we headed out.

\*\*\*\*\*

*. . . OMIGOD, what the hell have I done, it's so hot I hope I'm not going to burn up and my ears have popped, there must be a difference in pressure like I've suddenly changed altitude or something and all I can hear is a kind of fuzzy static and I can't see anything because my eyes are still clamped shut, but I know that Billie is still with me, I'm sure of that, I can feel the heat of her arm on the inside of my hands even though . . . didn't she disintegrate? . . . but I'm not really aware of my own body so I have no idea where my hands are and I can't tell if there is anything under my feet to support me, but I suspect there isn't, and it's hot, it so hot, like a sauna, and somehow I know I'm moving, fast, REALLY fast, like insanely fast, or at least it feels like I'm moving, with my eyes shut I have no point of reference but I'm somehow aware of movement even through closed eyes I can tell that I'm moving because there are now variations in the light: instead of a single overwhelming glare there are many different sources of light that appear from all around, but it's not like being on a road where the scenery flies by, nothing here gets left behind, so either I'm gaining altitude or I'm getting bigger, I'm expanding, or at least my awareness of what's around me is expanding, like an inflating soap bubble and I should be shitting-my-pants-terrified, right? Why am I not? . . .*

\*\*\*\*\*

When I wasn't sleeping, I spent most of the next hours and days in a tense, bowel-clenched cringe as I waited for the skies to open and for my dad's holy apocalyptic, end-of-times shit storm to come down on me. I couldn't blame him. This was so, so much worse than the whole D-Ray medical file episode. That was a transgression, true, and a deliberate one, but somehow, I felt he understood my motivation behind it; in my own naïve and deluded way I saw that as something I was sharing with him, as an attempt to connect with him. Plus there was the bonus of a potential pay-off in the end in finding out what happened to Mom or at least having D-Ray put away. My disappearing on him, in the middle of a strange wilderness at that, was—given our history—inexcusable. I couldn't begin to imagine what I'd put him through, and every minute he *didn't* talk about it made my guilt pick up mass and acceleration as it took my soul spiralling down into the abyss.

Of course by that age I knew full well that the quiet anticipation of the coming storm *was* the punishment, but that didn't make it easier. I knew that sooner or later he'd ask: he'd want to know what happened, why I put him through such anguish, and, as a bit of a sidebar, how the hell I pulled it off. There was no dodging this one, and worse still, I had no idea how I'd even begin to answer.

When we left Grand Canyon Village that morning the temperature was pretty brisk, so Dad didn't think too much of my initial request to turn up the heat in the car, or the fact that I was wearing a jacket over top of my hoodie. "It'll warm up pretty soon," he promised. "You'll see. We're heading downhill. There's almost five-thousand feet difference in elevation between here and Vegas. By the time we get into Nevada we'll be sweltering again." I just nodded, afraid that my teeth would chatter if I'd tried to say anything. Before long I was asleep.

\*\*\*\*\*

*. . . and I notice something for the first time it's a smell and it's nice it's wonderful and sweet and spicy like cinnamon and vanilla and brown sugar, it reminds me of warm kitchen smells, like a bakery . . .*

\*\*\*\*\*

The drive back to Las Vegas was a blur. We didn't talk much during the journey; in fact I slept through most of it. During brief waking spells I saw Dad throw occasional side-glances my way as he was driving; he seemed especially intrigued by my eyes. "We'll get your eyes checked as soon as we get home," he reassured me. "Don't worry." Then, in an effort to lighten the mood, he added, "On the upside, you smell really good. Like breakfast."

The climb in temperature did little more to warm me up than the added layers or the heated car or the sleeping bag Dad retrieved from the trunk. I must have looked like a freak when we stepped into our glacial, air-conditioned hotel lobby in Vegas. Dad really had no idea how bizarre the whole situation was until his hand accidentally brushed against mine as he handed me my suitcase from the trunk of the car. "Holy crap, Justin, you're hot!" He stopped to look at me for a moment, holding both my hands in his. "Are you sure you're feeling OK?" I nodded as matter-of-factly as I could, but the truth was that I was still exhausted, fuzzy-headed, and freezing cold. Once we got to our hotel room—some twenty floors up with a spectacular view that I barely glanced at—we agreed to have some lunch though I wasn't very hungry—and then a nap. There was no talk of visiting the strip: we'd both had more than our share of hiking by then.

Once we were in our hotel room, I checked myself out in the mirror of the washroom. The eyes were one thing—the pupils made me look a bit stoned or whatever—but for the first time that I could remember I had a sunburn. My skin does get darker in the sun but I don't ever burn. This was different. I looked scorched: the creases in the skin of my forehead and around my eyes were pale: tan lines. When I scrunched up my face they disappeared. It might just have been the result of trekking through the Grand Canyon for two days under a mid-August sun . . . or something else entirely.

*****

. . . *things are coming into focus, I'm seeing without my eyes, which is weird, so maybe it's time for some science, a quick experiment, nothing stupid, let's just test this, so I somehow get one hand to loosen its grip on Billie's arm, not by much, I go from a death grip to just a really firm one, and the light instantly fades a bit, becomes less intense, and the sense of movement, of expansion, of rising, whatever, slows down a little so I tighten it again and things brighten, grow, speed up, OK, so Billie is definitely my connection to all this, my feed, my conduit, so I slacken my grip again just a bit, and the light dims again, and I take a big chance, shit I hope this works, and I let go completely with my left hand, I'm still holding on with my right I'm not an idiot, and the light dims to a more tolerable level so at least I know I won't go blind with my eyes closed, and I don't know where I am or what it is that I'm seeing, it's like a bright golden sky, there's no up or down but it's not outer space it's too bright and there's no star field, not really, but there are globs of light I have no idea what they are or even how big they are they may be stars or galaxies or something else and there's something, there's definitely something, I want to say it's huge, it's vast and it's far away, like really far away, behind everything else but there's nothing I understand to provide scale but I know it's huge, it's beyond the sky, the universe, and there's structure to what I'm seeing, and there's texture and colour and shape, trying to decide is it natural or, like, artificial, it kind of looks like a grid, but it's not perfect, it's organic, it's more like, damn, what does it remind me of, it looks a bit like those slides of plant cells we looked at in science class, and I actually catch a few of them dividing, actually splitting into twos and threes making the whole thing that much bigger, and they're colourful, and the colour is constantly changing, coming and going in waves, flickering, like smaller waves on bigger waves on even bigger ones, I can't even tell what colours they are, but they're bright and intense and what's that word, there's a word for colours like that, oh shit what is it, it's a word they use for the colour of some insects and fish and birds, it's so beautiful and IRIDESCENT that's it, the colours are iridescent, and the cells, whatever they are, become more transparent as the wave of colour passes and for a moment I can see through them . . . no, into them . . .*

\*\*\*\*\*

Over a lunch of buffet Chinese food that I barely touched, Dad finally broke his silence about my disappearance. "You know, Juss," he began, "you're eventually going to have to tell me what happened. At least what you remember."

I was staring down at my plate. I couldn't look at him directly; there was still too much fear and shame to cope with without having to look into my dad's tired and worried eyes. "I know," I said. "I will." And then, to offer him some token of hope: "I want to. But you're right: I don't . . . remember everything." That wasn't a lie, but it wasn't the real point. Mostly, it was all the stuff I couldn't explain. My dad was always an open-minded guy, but what would he think of the tale I had to tell?

He seemed content with my promise of further details. Baby steps. Without more on the subject, we left our half-eaten food on the table and returned to our room. Dad stretched out on the bed opposite mine, fiddling with the remote for a few minutes, and I fell asleep to the sound of channels changing. I didn't dream, not quite. More like I remembered . . .

\*\*\*\*\*

*. . . it's what Billie described, yes it's her dragonfly wings, impossibly intricate, incredibly complex, endless facets no two exactly alike and*

*changing and in each there is depth each is a window onto something a world a galaxy a universe . . . or something else, and I feel like that astronaut, Dave, IT'S FULL OF STARS! but it's more it's different . . . and now I'm aware of other stuff it's all around now that I notice it, up close and far off in the distance, it's everywhere, like filaments or tendrils that are all interconnected, a web, endless networks of them, and they glow and shimmer where they intersect and where they're thickest, and if I focus on them, on it, they appear to be moving, changing shape like clouds or a school of fish or a flock of starlings, and one of these filaments leads directly to me and it's beyond huge and I'm right over the edge of it and it's made of tiny iridescent particles like smoke or dust and they sparkle, it's beautiful, I want to weep because it's so BEAUTIFUL!*

*\*\*\*\*\**

It all came pouring out after lunch on our second day home from vacation. I would have talked about it sooner but I wanted to sort out what I was going to say, plus I was asleep most of the time anyway. But I'd made up my mind to bring it up before my dad asked again. He was almost certainly going to mention Billie, and how my strange symptoms mirrored hers, and would no doubt suggest a connection. I wanted to be the first to bring it up: it would look less like I was piggybacking on his ideas, and would sound less like bullshit.

He was sitting opposite me at the kitchen table, but when I mentioned that I wanted to talk, he thoughtfully moved to the edge of the table so that he'd be at a right angle to me; it made it less like an interrogation. The less pressure the better.

I took my time, choosing my words carefully. Like Dad would do.

"We've often talked," I began, "about how people sometimes see things or . . . experience things they don't understand, right?"

I glanced up to look at him. I half expected a look to set on his face, an "oh-shit-here-it-comes" look, a hardening of his features that suggested that he knew—or at least strongly suspected—where this was going, and would be ready for a skeptical rebuttal. But there was no such look. He didn't stir, and his face remained attentive. So far, so good. I continued.

"People often can't make out what it is that they've seen and when it's all over they're left with a mystery they have to work out. And so, because they don't have enough information, or they haven't learned to think, like, scientifically, their imaginations take over and they just fill in the gaps with all the fantastic stories they've read or heard or seen on TV. And afterward they say it was something like flying saucers or ghosts or Bigfoot or something."

I looked at him as if I'd asked a question, even though I hadn't. He nodded.

"Back at the Canyon, I experienced something that I can't explain. I mean, I can tell you what happened, but it doesn't make sense."

Dad cleared his throat. "That's OK. You can just describe it to me, and maybe we can work out an explanation afterward."

He sounded so reasonable. I felt like I was going to betray him, and it made me ill.

"All right, but you have to understand it wasn't the first time. There've been a whole series of things in the past couple of months. Really weird things, fantastic things, things I haven't told you about yet. And they all involve Billie."

"Billie? Your friend Billie? I didn't think you were seeing her anymore."

"You make it sound like we're dating!" The blessed relief of laughter. I knew it was fleeting but it was nice while it lasted. "And yes, actually, I have seen her. Every week or so for most of the summer."

"You know the police were looking for her. How is she?"

"She's fine, the same as ever."

My narrative had slowed to a halt, but Dad nudged me onward. "You were saying about 'really weird things' involving Billie."

"Yeah. Well, first of all, there was the accident on Barrette Street. I was only able to put it all together later, but I more or less saw it all happen. It was just like Mr. Worthington told the police: there was a flash of light, and then Billie suddenly appeared in the middle of the street, and he had to swerve out of the way to avoid running her over. That's when the truck hit his car."

"Did you tell this to the police?"

"Not the part about Billie, but basically yeah. And there was nothing more to tell than what they'd already heard. That was pretty much it. Later on, in the hospital, when the doctor was going to give her an exam, she kind of freaked out. She told the doctor she had to go to the washroom and I went with her down the hall. She stepped in and closed the door, and then there was like a flash from inside the washroom. You couldn't see much except the light coming from around the door, and then it was gone. Just a flash. I knocked on the door and when she didn't answer I went in. She'd disappeared.

"Then, a few weeks later, I met her at Lakeview Cemetery. We talked for a while, and then she told me she had to leave. She . . . created a flash of light and then just vanished into thin air."

I waited for my dad to make a comment and when he didn't, I added: "She did the same thing three nights ago."

"When?"

I didn't answer.

It took a beat to register.

"Wait. Are you saying that Billie was in the Grand Canyon???"

I nodded. "She followed us the whole way. That was her you saw in Death Valley."

Direct hit. For a second Dad just stared at me without really seeing me, his mouth sort of hanging open. He managed a "How did . . ." before his words fizzled out.

"You thought it was her, didn't you?" I asked. "Or at least a little girl. But you couldn't even believe it yourself; you figured you must have been mistaken, so you didn't say anything."

A head shake. "Sorry. Hold on a bit. What was a nine-year-old girl from Northern Ontario doing all alone in the middle of Death Valley?"

"Billie's not from Northern Ontario." I tried to lighten the mood. "She probably liked the weather in Death Valley." Then I added, rubbing my arms to keep warm, "I know the feeling."

Dad's face then became very serious as he started to pull things together: the chills, the dilated pupils, the ruptured eardrums. "Did she do something to you? Tell me. What did she do?"

"She didn't really do anything. She just took me to . . . wherever it is she's from. Actually, I didn't give her the choice: I just decided to go with her, so I took her arm and kind of tagged along. It was my fault."

My story, my whole attempt at explaining what had happened was going off the rails. My dad was getting angry, but worse yet he was beginning to make up his own mind about what happened.

"She *is* part of a cult then, isn't she? They're using her to lure you in, making you believe it's something you want. Then they tried to abduct you, steal you away in the middle of the night! Did you see anyone else, Justin? Any grown-ups?"

It was going all wrong. I thought I was going to be able to ease into my story, set it up properly, explain everything in a way that sounded rational and intelligent. Now I was backpedalling, and I was more discouraged than anything. "No, Dad, it was nothing like that. Not at all."

"But she took you away somewhere, didn't she? Where did you go? Who else did you see?"

"There *was* no one else . . ." I began, and then ran out of steam. Dad, on the other hand, was just getting started.

"How did you end up on the top of the North Rim? Did they leave you there? Did you escape? Justin, something awful was done to you. You were abducted, you were hurt, and I want to know who's responsible!"

"Don't blame Billie."

"I don't know why you're defending this strange little girl. She's part of a dangerous cult, and *she's* not looking out for your best interest. I'm your father, Justin: *I am!*"

He was on the verge of tears now, and I was beginning to see for the first time what all this had done to him. I wanted to give him the answers he wanted, but making stuff up would only make things worse.

"Dad, you're not getting it. Billie isn't part of a cult. She's not a strange little girl. She's not even human."

\*\*\*\*\*

*The particles are approaching, they're much closer now, I can see them, individually, they're tiny, kind of oblong in shape, and they're sparkling and iridescent and constantly changing colour, each one with a unique and impossibly complex texture to it, it's like looking down at a huge city from orbit, zooming in, I could spend forever staring at the surface of just one and never see the whole thing, and they're all different and moving in numbers that defy comprehension, impossible in their numbers, this infinite cloud, these tendrils of smoke and dust that fill the . . . the world? . . . the universe? . . . they're made up of these gorgeous little . . . I don't know what to call them . . . these glittering seeds, grains, pods, each one a whole being onto itself, but also like a city, a civilization, impossibly ancient and complex, and they're swirling all around me now, I feel them over every part of my body which I can now feel for the first time since I came here . . . how long ago was that . . . a moment ago . . . days . . . centuries . . . it's a funny feeling, not unpleasant, it tickles a bit, it's like I'm swimming in the midst of an endless school of tiny fish, and each one is making . . . it's not a noise precisely, more like a vibration, as they pass over me, somehow it's familiar, it's so familiar, it's the same exact thing as the tingling in my hand where I'm holding on to Billie, and it finally dawns on me, it's so obvious I'm an idiot for not realizing it before, this cloud, this interminable stream of living jewels filling all of forever, all this, this is her, this is Billie, this is her continuum, her "I, It, We," this is what she is, a single, collective consciousness extending far beyond the reach of our known reality. It's not God and it's not the Universe, not how I recognize it anyway, not like you see in photos from the Hubble Telescope, it's something else, something outside of that, it's more, so much more than either of those, it isn't good or bad, it just is, but it is SO, SO MUCH.*

*****

I told him everything. I described my whole experience as best I could, and then went into my best interpretation of what Billie was, according to what she told me and to what I "saw." I didn't bother going into timelines or ant farms.

Dad didn't say anything the whole time, nor for a good while after I'd finished. He no longer looked afraid or angry, just exhausted, weary, and sad. Eventually he got up slowly from his chair, stretched a bit, and got himself a glass for water. He moved as if in pain, like he'd aged thirty years in the past few minutes.

"OK, Juss . . ." There was a long pause as he put his thoughts together. "I really don't know what to do or think about any of this, or of you for that matter. I mean, it's not even so much this . . . unbelievable story: it's you *telling* me this story. You must have known how I'd react to it."

I held my tongue. Of course he was right. There was no sense in arguing with him. I wanted to tell him how hard it was to bring myself to confide all this to him; that I was telling him the truth, as I always did; that I couldn't explain any of it, only describe what had happened; that I didn't blame him for doubting me and that I would no doubt react exactly the same way if I were him; and that if Billie came back she could prove everything. But she was gone.

I had no doubt of that. This whole bizarre story was over, and as frustrating as it would be to know I'd have no way of proving any of it to anyone, there was a kind of relief. Life could go on as it should, I'd get used to living with what I knew, and eventually the memory of it would dull in my mind to the point where I'd doubt any of it ever happened. And anyway I was tired of talking, my head still hurt, and I just wanted to go to bed.

Dad's cell started ringing. He turned and looked at me again for a moment like he was going to say something, then left the room to find his phone. The conversation was brief. The look on his face hadn't changed much when he returned but there was something a bit different in his voice.

"That was Carl," he said. "He's coming over. Apparently, he has news."

# 35

"You look like shit, Marty. You gonna need a holiday from your holiday?"

Carl arrived minutes after he'd finished talking with my dad, like he'd been waiting right around the corner the whole time. He showed up empty-handed: no food, no beer, no musical instrument. This wasn't a social call.

I was still in the kitchen when he came in, and he laughed a bit when he first saw me. "Dude! You look fried." His tone changed when he saw my eyes. "Jesus Christ, Justin. What the—"

Dad cut him off. "It's a long story. We're still kind of working it out."

Carl's eyes went back and forth between my dad and me, but he remained silent.

"You said you have news?"

"Yeah, right. I do. It looks like I may have identified our mystery man."

Blank stares from both Dad and me. We'd been away from Ferguston for what seemed like a thousand years. Everything having to do with the D-Ray case had become so distant by this time that Carl might as well have been talking about the identity of Sweden's new agriculture minister. He tried again.

"I'm talking about the guy who'd been hanging out with Raymond in the days around Élise's disappearance, who'd apparently been with him when he'd had his public row in the ER."

I clued in before Dad did. "You mean the maybe-accomplice?"

"Exactly. About a week ago one of my clients had a difference of opinion with a bouncer outside The Pit. It quickly turned nasty. I met up with him as he was getting his face patched up by none other than one Deborah Williams—she's heading up your fan club by the way, Justin. Anyway, we had a coffee afterward and got to talking about Élise's case, about David Raymond, and about all the different theories and angles that have come up since then. She talked a lot about the individual who was seen with Raymond at the hospital and whom she thought might have been the same person who was savagely beaten by Raymond a few days after Élise vanished. She had a theory that this person knew something about Raymond's activities and D-Ray wanted to make sure he didn't talk. It sounded like a bit of a reach to me, but it got me thinking. Debbie definitely feels that there was a lot more going on than what came out in the official story, and she doesn't even know what we know now."

Carl got up and went to the fridge, drew out a pitcher of water and poured a glass. It was another hot, sticky evening.

"So," he resumed as he sat down again, "while you guys were gone, I poked around a bit. I called up some friends in the police force, just to see what they recalled about those days, stuff that maybe I hadn't been made aware of. From what my police contacts could piece together from their old notes and fuzzy memories, it took the better part of a week after Élise disappeared before anyone heard about the altercation in the ER. That means that until then David Raymond wasn't on anyone's radar, not for Élise's disappearance anyway. Remember, there was no reason at the time to even suspect a crime had been committed: the cops were investigating a missing-person case, that's all."

"And they were pretty happy with me as their only suspect," my dad hissed.

"At first, as the husband of the missing woman, yes, naturally you'd be their first choice. At least until they could eliminate you, which didn't take long. Of course once the word got out that a known multiple offender had had a very public blow-up with the missing person in question—and I suspect Debbie Williams may have had some hand in getting that out—the police obviously had to look into it. They had a brief sit-down with Raymond, but he had an alibi that was corroborated."

"What was this alibi?" I asked.

"You'll love this. He was with his doctor: Geoffrey Coleman."

"What?" asked my dad.

"Yep. D-Ray had gone over to talk to his doctor about something or other. There was some disagreement as to the substance of the meeting, but it wasn't—"

"What do you mean?"

"It didn't seem major at the time, but apparently Coleman claimed that D-Ray was very agitated so he called him in for an emergency appointment, while D-Ray said it was Coleman who had called him in to talk about his meds."

"Funny time for a doctor's appointment," I piped in.

"Yes, it is. Convenient, too. D-Ray wasn't precise about the time, but Coleman was pretty emphatic that Raymond came in right around 10:30, and that he didn't leave much before 11:00. Of course, no one had any reason to question the good doctor's word at the time, so the police left it at that." Carl looked at Dad for a second and grinned. "What's wrong, Marty? You're thinking so hard it hurts to watch."

"Just something . . . Hold on." And with that Dad got up and left the room, and a moment later was thudding his way up the stairs. His departure was so quick and sudden that Carl and I just sat there gaping a few seconds, then burst out laughing.

"When you gotta go, you gotta go," said Carl.

I could tell that my uncle had a bunch of questions for me looking the way I did, so I tried to head him off at the pass with a question of my own.

"Sorry, but how long does it take to write a prescription?" Carl looked pensive for a second but before he could answer Dad had returned to the kitchen, nodding to himself.

"Sorry, guys, but something you said, Carl, jogged a memory and I needed to make sure. Something in D-Ray's medical file that seemed a bit out of place. Sure enough: on the day Élise disappeared Dr. Coleman wrote D-Ray a prescription for Diazepam." He looked at me and clarified. "Valium: a *very* potent anti-anxiety drug. It stood out because it's the only time it was ever prescribed for him. Odd, I know, but believe me I checked. It certainly seems to support their alibi that Coleman saw D-Ray on that day, but it kind of makes you wonder why D-Ray suddenly needed such a strong happy pill when he was never prescribed it before or after."

"It does make you wonder, doesn't it? And that jives with a detail the cops provided," Carl continued. "When Coleman spoke to the police, he described D-Ray as having been extremely distressed at the time. For his part D-Ray never mentioned being particularly agitated. All he said was that he went to The Pit right after and was there until 2:00 a.m. when they closed."

"And this was corroborated by staff at The Pit?"

"Yep, only they say he didn't arrive alone, that there was someone with him when they came in. D-Ray apparently referred to him as the designated driver."

"Holy shit. So D-Ray *wasn't* alone that evening. Any idea who the driver was?"

"No luck there: if the police ever took note of it no one remembers. It probably wasn't considered significant; Coleman could vouch for Raymond, as could the staff at the bar, and that was good enough. But I got to thinking: what are the odds that the person who drove D-Ray to Coleman's office and later to The Pit was the same as the one who accompanied him to the ER a few days earlier? Pretty good I'd say. D-Ray wasn't known for having a lot of close friends, but it's reasonable that he would keep someone around as a lackey to do his grunt work, especially given his physical limitations."

Carl had another sip of water and looked us over from the rim of his glass. There was sweat on his forehead, and his glass was coated with condensation.

"So what do we have? D-Ray and Unknown Associate confront Élise at the ER, looking for drugs. Élise tells them to fuck off— sorry Juss'—and that their supply of goodies has been cut. A couple of days later D-Ray, again accompanied by Unknown Associate, shows up late in the evening at the office of his doctor/supplier in a highly agitated state. His doctor prescribes him Valium to calm him down. Élise vanishes that same evening. Whoever this mystery person is, he was in the thick of it. But who was D-Ray hanging with during that time? It would have to be someone who had an awfully low profile if nobody remembers him. So I did some digging, asked around, and after a few days of following up on former Vipers band members and talking to cops, I got lucky."

"You got a name?"

"Not at first. Just initials: BD."

"BD? Shouldn't have been that hard to figure out."

"You'd think. But after all the digging not one person with those initials turned up. Apparently 'BD' was a nickname, not initials: widespread enough that most people only knew him from that and not his given name, and old enough that no one seemed to know what the letters stood for."

Carl was grinning now. He obviously had something up his sleeve that he thought was hilariously funny, but I wasn't amused. The idea of Carl chasing down friends of D-Ray and asking questions about the old days made me uncomfortable. I still had very vivid memories of the time D-Ray ambushed me in the hospital parking lot. I was certain that someone had overheard my conversation with Debbie at the Boneyard Diner and had relayed it to D-Ray.

"Do you think that's a good idea?" I asked. "I mean, if D-Ray finds out you've been asking questions about him . . . He could get pissed off and take it out on me or my dad." And though I didn't mention it, he might also do a lot more than just leave a dead rodent on our front porch.

"Yeah, I hear what you're saying. Not to worry. This isn't like a conversation being overheard in a bar. This is a public defender talking to cops and current and former associates. This has been going on for years and Raymond knows it. He might be annoyed if he got wind of it, but it isn't anything new. Anyway, after asking around a bit, I got the answer from a cop who used to be a classmate of BD back in high school. None other than police constable Dale Franklin." My eyes must have widened because Carl added: "It's a small town, Justin."

"What did Franklin have to say about him?" Dad asked.

"Not much, but once he provided the name, I was able to dig up a bit more. His actual name is Craig McLaughlin. He'd be in his mid-thirties by now. Never finished high school; in fact, I don't think he got beyond the tenth grade. No father in the picture, his mom died when he was nine, after which he was raised by his aunt. Lived in almost desperate poverty most of his life. A loner, had all kinds of developmental difficulties, a tough life all around, but despite that he's somehow managed to keep a clean record: not so much as a traffic ticket. Keeps a really low profile; in fact, he hasn't renewed his driver's licence in years. His current whereabouts are unknown, but that's not surprising: McLaughlin isn't the kind of guy people keep track of."

"Why the nickname?"

"Turns out he's been going by 'BD' since the eighth grade. It was a result of his IQ test: he scored a seventy-five, the highest mark he ever got in school. According to Franklin, the joke at the time was that when McLaughlin got the result, he went around for days boasting: 'I passed! I passed!' BD stands for 'Brain Dead.'"

"Nice," I said.

Dad had been pretty quiet this whole time. I couldn't help thinking that since the trip to the US he'd had quite enough of this whole business; he'd gotten it out of his system like a bad cold and was now ready to move on with life. Just two weeks ago he would have been all over this new information; now he just looked tired. "So you're saying no one knows where he is?" He sighed. "How do we find him?"

"Well, we know *who* he is; we have a photo from an expired driver's licence so we can ID him in a pinch. We probably can't count much on the address but I'm not too worried. He'll turn up. Members of the Vipers are pretty easy to spot with their rattlesnake tattoos."

"The Vipers have rattlesnake tattoos?" Dad asked and shook his head. "Jesus. Leave it to D-Ray."

Something clicked in the back of my mind. It was my turn to have a brain fart, a swamp bubble from earlier in the summer. I spent a couple of seconds furiously trying to dredge it up.

"Wait. What kind of tattoo?" I asked my uncle.

"Rattlesnake. You might have seen it on D-Ray that time, depending on what he was wearing."

Yeah, that made sense. Maybe that was all there was to it. But something else was nagging at me. I needed more detail.

"What does it look like?"

Carl could tell I might be on to something. "Well, it's just an image of a snake that begins at the back of the neck, just below collar level, its head pointing downward. It wraps over the shoulder like a sports bra, goes across the chest just below the throat, then over the other shoulder and ends in the middle of the back with—"

"—the rattle tail pointing upward," I finished.

He paused a moment. "Does that seem familiar?"

Dad leaned in at that point. "What is it, Juss?"

"What did you say BD's first name is again?"

"Craig," said Carl.

"I saw him. Back in July, at the Boneyard Diner. And there's a waitress there who might know how to find him."

\*\*\*\*\*

Carl left shortly after without saying a whole lot more. He had a peculiar look on his face, and whatever course of action he had in mind as he set out, he didn't look like he was going to wait on anyone's blessing. Neither my dad nor I knew for sure what he was going to do, but Dad could read his brother like a book and said he had a pretty good idea. Carl knew Ferguston, he knew its people, and he knew the system. He was no doubt going to expand his search, make a bunch of calls, talk to a lot of people on the street, send out feelers. People would talk:

- *Did anybody know Craig McLaughlin? You might remember him by his high school nickname: BD. Where could he be found?*
- *Who's asking?*
- *Some guy, might be a lawyer. I think his last name is Lambert.*
- *Why?*
- *Oh, just for some routine questions.*
- *Wait: "Lambert?" Wasn't that the name of the woman who disappeared?*
- *Right. Brother-in-law, I think. They always thought David Raymond was involved in that, didn't they?*

Word was going to spread through Ferguston like herpes. As he stepped out into the warm night and the front door clunked behind him, he left a scent of expectancy behind that lingered like his pipe smoke. We knew something was looming.

Dad was harder to read. You might have thought after almost ten years of wondering what had happened to Mom, and then finding out that an answer might finally be coming to light within the next few days or weeks, that he'd be bouncing off the walls or at least show some kind of excitement. Certainly after watching him pore over David Raymond's medical file a few weeks earlier, you would have thought by now he'd be smelling D-Ray's blood in the air. But he wasn't talking about it much. Not to me anyway. He wasn't talking to me much about anything since I'd told him about my trip with Billie into her netherverse . I could tell he was concerned about me. He'd begun keeping the doors to the house locked even in the afternoon, something nobody does in Ferguston and certainly something he never did before. He also ordered me not to stray too far from home by myself until everything had blown over. I didn't need much convincing. Raymond was probably going to be visited by the police, at the very least, and while I imagine that probably happened with a certain regularity, given how quickly he reacted following my conversation with Debbie Williams earlier that summer I wouldn't want to see how pissed he'd be when he learned why the cops were on his case again. He'd likely be leaving a horse's severed head on our doorstep next time.

Meanwhile, Dad was making an effort to keep himself busy, hurrying away on errands—taking me along if he thought he'd be more than a few minutes—or shutting himself up in his study. With him locked away and me under what amounted to house arrest, I looked around for something to keep me busy. I would have preferred to be outside where it was bright and still unusually warm for late August, rather than being indoors where Dad insisted on running the air conditioner. I spent most of my time in my room wearing my warmest hoodie, with the curtains wide open, and all the lights on. My recent Billie-like aversion to the cold and dark was the reason I still hadn't put our luggage away like my dad asked; since our return, the suitcases had been lying around the living room like forgotten cars in a parking lot, rather than their usual nesting place under the stairs in the basement.

I drifted into my dad's office the day after Carl's visit, idly pulling books from his shelves as he sat at his computer working on some teaching plan or other, trying to make chit-chat. He was busy and I knew that so I tried not to be obnoxious about it, but I wanted him to indulge me. Instead he blew out a sigh and, removing his glasses and tossing them onto his keyboard, gave me a restless glare.

"Bored?"

A shrug. "Kinda."

"Have you put the suitcases away? You know, the ones that I asked you to put away three days ago and that are currently sprouting roots in the living room?"

I gave up without protest, but I wasn't going to descend into the mines of Moria without a flashlight, a toque, and an extra sweater.

*****

The luggage was stowed away in moments, but despite the cold and dark I lingered a bit. The basement, especially the unfinished part, was weirdly compelling. It was where all the stuff from our past was kept, old things that nobody used anymore but that were somehow too precious to throw out or give away. Dad said it's where our history was kept and that gave the basement a mysterious allure.

As expected, the basement was much darker than I was used to. There weren't many lights in that part of the house, just two 60-Watt bulbs suspended from the ceiling, and with my new insensitivity to light they weren't much help, neither was the natural light that spilled in at this time of day from the window wells at ground level. I was glad to have brought the flashlight, but after a quick sweep of my usual targets—old books and *National*

*Geographic* magazines—I found it was going to be too dark to read anything.

I moved deeper into the basement, exploring its darkest recesses to the left of the furnace. I usually left that area alone. Dad never spent much time down here either: it was dusty, there were cobwebs, and the only things that were stored there were boxes and boxes of grown-up stuff. A lot of it was Dad's past lessons and teaching plans, plus other stuff labelled "taxes," "insurance," "hydro," "car," and so on. Mom had some boxes down there too. It was no mystery. Dad said they were mostly medical journals and correspondence from professional associations, stuff he just never got around to or—my guess— didn't have the heart to get rid of.

There were also boxes of inactive patient files, and those were off-limits; Dad said they were supposed to stay sealed until 2010. These were plainly marked with a stamp that read "FRHC," and "CONFIDENTIAL: Patient files" in red marker; you could tell it was my mom's handwriting by the characteristic way she dotted the letter *i* following the *f* and the *t*. Prior to the events of this summer, I wouldn't have given any of these boxes so much as a glance.

After a few minutes of random un-stacking I began to inspect the first few. A quick perusal confirmed that my dad was largely right: these boxes contained mostly correspondence, journals, and newsletters. Boring. I was about to give up and begin re-stacking when I noticed that some of the remaining boxes along the bottom, at least half a dozen that I could see, had small, rectangular labels along their sides. Each of these labels had a red bar along the top that said "Confidential," and something written by hand, apparently in pencil, just underneath. The labels were faded and hard to read in the dim light, so I pulled the first box out and pointed the beam of the flashlight onto it: in my mom's rapid scrawl was the single word COLEMAN.

# 36

"Dad, why does Mom have a bunch of confidential boxes in the basement marked Colem—"

He was still in his office, apparently on the phone. I could only hear half of the conversation through his closed office door and he didn't seem to be in a good mood. Probably Carl. There was a pause and rather than tap on the door I pressed my ear against it. There was nothing for a moment, and when I heard Dad's voice again it was much lower and much more intense.

"How the bloody hell do you know that? *Nobody* knows that!"

As I pushed the door open, I saw immediately that he wasn't on the phone. I followed his eyes as I stepped in, and there standing by the window in a beam of mid-afternoon sunshine was Billie.

After an uneasy pause, without turning his eyes away from Billie, Dad finally said "Just having a little chat with a friend of yours, Juss. So nice of her to drop by unexpectedly, don't you think? Personally, I'm still trying to figure out how she got into the house with all the doors locked. Did you let her in?"

No one seemed eager to follow that up. Dad glared expectantly at Billie, like he was disciplining a student, waiting for an explanation for some prank or an incomplete assignment. Billie for her part seemed unfazed, standing patiently next to the window, enjoying the sun, all of her attention focused on a row of small plants that lined the windowsill. When Dad's cellphone began to ring, an annoying ringtone from some '60s psychedelic band, no one so much as looked at it. It stopped after a few seconds as if reprimanded.

Dad was the first to break. "I'm trying to get some answers from her. So far, she's backed up your little sci-fi story down to the finest detail. You guys been staying in touch, keeping your stories straight?"

Billie looked completely satisfied to stand there and ignore the question, so I jumped in. "No," I said mostly to the floor. "We haven't. I haven't seen her since the Grand Canyon."

Dad snorted. "When she took you away into space or some other dimension or something, right? What are you, some kind of alien?"

"Well, you could say that I'm alien in a way, yes, but—"

"And you pop in and out of our dimension, is that it? Yeah. That must have been some trip." There was a mocking nastiness in his voice that I didn't like. "Sorry, I still need a bit of convincing on that one. Maybe you could take me along. What do you say, Billie? You and your friends?" His cellphone rang again. Again it was ignored.

"Actually, I don't have friends. It's just me. It's just that there's, well . . . a lot of me. Also, I didn't bring Justin along anywhere. He kind of hitched a ride."

Dad stared blankly at Billie for a moment, so I spoke up before he could say anything.

"That's true," I said. "That one was on me. I grabbed hold of her just as she was leaving," and then just for good measure: "Like I told you."

"He was lucky," Billie continued. "He could have been hurt."

Dad found his voice then. "He *could have been* hurt?? He *was* hurt! When he was found he was unconscious, he was burning up with fever, his skin was scorched, his ears were bleeding, he could barely see . . ." Poor Dad didn't know the half of it. "I mean, what did you people do to him?"

"Dad, there *aren't any others!* It's just Billie. It's always been just Billie."

Finally, she spoke up. Her voice was soft, but clear and absolutely firm. Confident. "You'll just have to accept that there are things beyond your understanding here. I'm not what I appear to be."

"Yeah, well, I'm sorry, Billie, but like I said I'm going to need some convincing."

"Well I'm not going to do any dumb tricks, so don't ask me."

Dad was trying to keep his cool, but there was confusion and something approaching outrage in his eyes. "How old are you?" he said in a near whisper. Clearly, he'd never heard a nine-year-old talk that way before.

I tried to wedge my way half-heartedly into the conversation, breaking another awkward and uncomfortable silence. "What is it you know that you shouldn't—" I began to ask Billie.

She shot me a quick glance, then responded to my question as if my dad had asked it.

"I know a lot of things. I could tell you what you had for breakfast yesterday, or last week, or a year ago today, or thirty years ago; or how you faked being sick one day in the second grade because you didn't want to do a math test only to end up with an actual ear infection and missing the whole week; or about the time you had a button stuck up your nose when you were three and sneezed it out at the dinner table and it landed in a lake of gravy you'd made in your mashed potatoes; or the time you accidentally broke your grandfather's neighbour's basement window with a Pepsi bottle when you were eleven and never told anyone; or the time you shot a frog from a canoe with your brother's pellet gun, then watched as another frog ate it; or about your secret crush on Natalie Brazeau that lasted all through high school . . . I mean, do you want me to go on?"

With Dad finally stunned into complete silence, Billie continued. "And I can do the same for anyone and everyone you've ever known, or anyone your neighbours have ever known, as far back as you'd like. How's this: the German soldier who shot your mother's great uncle in Belgium in 1916 was named Werner Koehler. He was from a small town northeast of Stuttgart. He died the same year. He was eighteen. He was crushed when the stable he was sleeping in was struck by a mortar shell and a wall fell on him. Too bad, because he was having a good day until then: he'd had a hot breakfast that morning for the first time in weeks—sausage, fresh eggs, bread and cheese. The French soldier who fired the shell that killed him, Francis Chevillard, survived the war and had two daughters, one of whom, Raymonde, later moved to Montreal. She married a man from Trois-Rivières named André Charbonneau and they had five children. The youngest, whose name is Jean-Robert Charbonneau, today lives a block away from your sister-in-law's apartment in Outremont. He didn't have breakfast this morning.

"You can check any one of these facts out for yourself, or test me however you want. I think you already know how that will go."

Dad was just trying to tread water by this point. "There must be some . . . logical explanation . . . I mean you must have spoken to my family . . ."

"None of them know any of that stuff," Billie continued. "Anyway, I don't expect you to understand or even accept any of this. Believe it or don't believe it, it doesn't matter. It won't change anything."

Billie and my dad were now engaged in a bit of an awkward standoff that would have lasted a while if not for the sudden rattle and thud of the front door opening and closing, followed by Carl's voice booming from the entrance. Good thing he had keys to the house, I thought, otherwise he would have been pounding on the door all afternoon. "Marty! For Christ's sake why don't you answer your damn phone?"

Dad sighed. "You two wait here," he said wearily and left the room. As the stairs creaked under his steps, I turned to Billie. "Why didn't you show him? You could have made him believe you so easily."

She was eyeing the open door. "Listen," she said.

We moved a bit closer. Dad's voice sounded tired. "Justin's friend Billie has made a sudden reappearance. She broke into the house somehow—"

Carl interrupted decisively: "David Raymond has been arrested."

*****

"When?"

"A couple of hours ago. The cops executed a search warrant early this morning for his property and began tossing the place. His place is huge and he's a notorious hoarder: they'll be at it for days. He was brought in on charges of possession of prohibited firearms and ammunition, and a separate charge related to narcotics possession."

"OK. But doesn't he get arrested about as often as he gets his oil changed? It's not exactly earth-shattering news, Carl."

"True, but there's more. While they were searching his house the police found something else: an old cellphone, a Nokia 2160 to be exact, prehistoric by today's standards. They brought it in and had their techs look at it. There's no doubt, Martin: it's Élise's phone."

There was a beat before anyone spoke again.

"If you remember, Martin, when Élise's Rav4 was found after her disappearance, all of her belongings were accounted for: her purse, her keys, everything except her phone. That detail was never made public by the police. Obviously, we know that she had it that night because she called you from it later that evening. Wherever she went that night, it was always believed she took it with her."

"Or it was disposed of when she was."

"Of course it's only circumstantial evidence, and it's still going to be difficult to charge D-Ray with murder without a body, but it's pretty compelling. He's got an awful lot of explaining to do."

I heard their voices move off in the direction of the kitchen, so I quickly left my dad's office and went into my room where I could hear everything. I even turned off the air conditioner in my dad's office to get rid of any white noise. I didn't pay any attention to Billie.

Carl was still talking: "—strictly in terms of means, motive and opportunity, the first two have never been in doubt. Opportunity has been the only sticking point: his doctor provided an alibi at the time. He'll need to be found and questioned again. But this new evidence suddenly throws a lot of doubt on everything."

I could hear Dad's breathing. "So . . . Where is he now?"

"He's being held at the OPP detachment right here in Ferguston. The police have twenty-four hours to hold him before his bail hearing."

"And then what?"

"Well, then it's up to a judge, but I'm guessing he'll be formally charged with possession of illegal firearms, plus there's the drug charge. It's not like he's a first-time offender so it's likely that he'll be held without bail. That will give the cops time to investigate the cellphone and re-open Élise's disappearance. I can certainly think of a couple of people they'll want to talk to."

The conversation continued in the kitchen for a while, Carl speculating about evidence, Dad about how close we all were to finally getting answers. Meanwhile upstairs, Billie had disappeared again. I should have known better than to turn my back on her. Whatever her reason for showing up in my dad's office in the first place, she probably didn't figure she was going to make much headway with him and that things weren't likely to improve with the arrival of Carl. There was no flash this time, but I'd come to understand that she only did that when she stepped back into her wherever world. But she didn't always do that, not if she wanted to stick around in the here and now and not draw attention to herself. She was perfectly capable of morphing into eighty or so pounds of air and dispersing silently through the house, only to recombine outside in the form of a shrub or a stray Labrador retriever or an immense flock of starlings or a nine-year-old girl.

Needless to say Dad was pretty pissed when he called us downstairs and only I showed up. For my part I was getting just as annoyed at him for refusing to accept reality.

"She's gone, Dad."

"What do you mean 'she's gone'? Did you let her climb out a window or something?"

"No, Dad. She's just gone. You know the way she came in? That's how she left. She just does that. Kinda like Batman."

"Well, she couldn't have gone far. I still have a lot of questions for that kid." He paused, then seeing the huge smirk growing under Carl's beard, asked: "What's so damn funny?"

"She's a slippery little thing, isn't she? C'mon guys. I suggest we go out and grab something to eat. My dime. The two of you have been cocooned in this place for two days now; it's about time you got some air and re-entered society. We'll try someplace new. And you can look out for your little escapee as we go."

"She could be anywhere," Dad said.

*That's putting in mildly.*

Carl laughed again and slapped Dad on the back as we stepped out the front door and piled into our car, and by then I had completely forgotten about what had brought me upstairs from the basement in the first place.

# 37

The next day Ferguston officially went ape-shit. It began a little after 9:00 in the morning with a phone call for my dad, followed by three others in less than ten minutes. All were from either newspapers or TV or radio stations asking for Dad's reaction to the arrest of David Raymond in connection with Mom's disappearance. The phone rang all day. Dad was caught flat-footed by the sudden attention from reporters over the phone and, in more than one case, on our doorstep, and to his credit he initially did a decent job in fending them off.

The reporters came from everywhere and from all types of media, but the questions were all pretty much the same:

"Mr. Lambert, how does it feel now that your wife's murderer has been identified?"

"Was there ever any doubt in your mind that this day would come?"

"Is there anything you would like to say to David Raymond now that he's been apprehended?"

"What do you think would be a satisfactory outcome to this process?"

"What do you plan to do now?"

Dad did his best to be vague, each time repeating patiently that he didn't have all the facts and that he couldn't comment until he did, all the stuff you're supposed to say for the most part, but you could tell he wasn't in his element. He had a hard time suppressing his emotions, and the reporters who had cameras did a good job in capturing that. I watched one report online later that afternoon and it made me cringe.

The next day we saw this on the front page of the *Clarion*, and variations of it all over the web:

### Suspect held in 10-year-old missing persons case

**Jason Bremmer**
**The Clarion**

[FERGUSTON] The mystery surrounding the disappearance of an area woman almost ten years ago may have been solved with the arrest yesterday on unrelated charges of the only person ever suspected in the case.

David Luc Raymond of Ferguston is currently in Ontario Provincial Police custody following a search of his property that resulted in his arrest on weapons and drug possession charges.

During the search, police uncovered evidence that Raymond may have been directly involved in the disappearance of Dr. Élise François-Lambert in November of 1996, although a police spokesperson would not reveal the nature of that evidence. A source close to the police, however, suggested that during the execution of a search warrant, one or more objects directly linked to Dr. François-Lambert were uncovered on Raymond's property.

"We'll certainly have to see what the police turn up," said husband Martin Lambert, who showed visible relief yesterday when interviewed, "but I have to say that I'm very happy that [David] Raymond is off the street. He's been a threatening presence in this community for a long time."

Dr. François-Lambert, a physician at the Ferguston Regional Health Centre—FRHC—failed to return home following a dinner with friends on the night of November 5ᵗʰ, 1996. Although regarded initially as a missing persons case, suspicion turned to Raymond, a known repeat offender, when allegations surfaced that he had had a public altercation with François-Lambert a few days before her disappearance. The altercation, which took place in the FRHC Emergency Department before a number of witnesses, pertained to the doctor's refusal to provide Raymond with prescription narcotics and allegedly resulted in Raymond uttering death threats.

Although he was thoroughly questioned and investigated by police, no evidence connecting Raymond to Dr. François-Lambert's disappearance was ever found, and the file remained open as a missing-persons case. That was until yesterday's discoveries and arrest.

While a decision on bail is still forthcoming, given today's events it seems unlikely that . . .

I stopped reading. Dad's remark surprised me. It surprised Dad, too; he didn't remember saying that, certainly not in those words. Jason Bremmer was well known to be a bit elastic when it came to quoting people, but if Dad had said anything like that it would be completely out of character. Over the phone Carl described his comments as "a bit ill considered," that it might have been better to wait until the judicial process had taken place, and that if Dad was going to be talking to the media, he would have been more careful. Dad's response was while that may well be, he wasn't going to apologize for his emotions either. Even though this moment had been a long time coming, he had never planned on what he was going to say when it finally came, let alone prepare a statement for reporters.

The calls continued for a couple of days, not just from the media but from friends and family as well. Some of the teachers from the school wanted to know how Dad and I were doing; Principal Lalonde asked if she could do anything and if either of us might need some extra time before coming in for the new school year; Debbie Williams called and spoke to both me and my dad—she sounded at once excited, relieved and a little bit smug; Granddad Lambert called in typical Lambert fashion to get specifics—who, what, where, when; and Dad's sisters inquired as to what was going to happen next.

But it was the calls from my mom's family that kept Dad on the phone the longest. As soon as I heard him speaking in his best French, I knew Grandpapa François was on the line from Montreal, and I immediately gave them some privacy. The look on my dad's face when he took the call was like he'd been kicked in the shin: I knew Dad would have preferred to make that call rather than have Grandpapa call us—worse yet, Mom's family learned the news from a reporter who tracked them down in Montreal— and I heard him stammer through an awkward apology about being swamped with calls and requests from the media, and how he would have called as soon as things settled down. Obviously, he would have liked to be better prepared and to have something more definitive to say: like him, they'd been waiting for this news for almost ten years. I knew that there had always been a faintly glowing ember of hope with my mom's family that someday she'd be found alive, so this call would be potentially devastating. The conversation lasted over an hour, and it was longer still before Dad said anything to me.

*****

As usual, Carl came by to provide us with the missing details, only this time he was accompanied by a police detective who did most of the talking. The search of D-Ray's estate—I saw photos of it: funny to think of his glorified landfill as an estate—was going to take a while yet. There were several buildings in addition to his house—a huge garage, two sheds and a barn—and each one was spilling over with all manner of crap. Raymond was a classic hoarder: he'd never throw anything away, or donate it, or even sell it. His property was cluttered with a staggering collection of broken, failed or abandoned hobbies. The grounds were a graveyard for anything that burned fuel, along with the endless equipment, parts and accessories that went with them, in addition to countless trash bags and boxes full of gear, clothing, and assorted junk that D-Ray couldn't be bothered to do away with.

As difficult, tedious, and unpleasant as this work was, there was an upside to D-Ray's hoarding habits, which became apparent with the chance discovery of an additional piece of evidence that was directly tied to Mom's disappearance. Just as the missing cellphone had been withheld from the media, so was the existence of a solitary work glove that was found under the driver's seat of Mom's Rav4 shortly after it had been discovered. In fact the only person outside of law enforcement who knew anything about it was my dad—investigators showed it to him to be sure it wasn't his—and he dutifully kept that info under wraps. The glove was a fairly run-of-the-mill deer-hide work glove with a removable wool liner; in itself not remarkable, but what identified it as unique were the small droplets of green paint on the fingertips and top part of the hand. As luck would have it, the glove's mate, complete with matching flecks of green paint, was uncovered in a bag of old clothes and recognized by a veteran police investigator for what it was. As for the cellphone, its provenance was less detailed, with the detective only saying that it was found in a box in D-Ray's basement.

Not all the news was good. Police were disappointed with the total haul of guns and drugs. D-Ray had a sizeable armoury but most of it was perfectly legal. Rumour had it that Raymond had the beginnings of a stockpile of illegal—meaning fully automatic—weapons and was likely to be acquiring more in the coming days. Unfortunately, either the tip was wrong or D-Ray was a step ahead of authorities, because all the police were able to dig up was a single converted fully automatic assault rifle, along with a handful of magazines that exceeded legal capacity. The drug haul was even more disappointing, with the detective describing it as little more than a couple of bags of weed. Until something else came up, the police were going to have to hold D-Ray on the strength of the glove and cellphone alone.

D-Ray for his part had been screaming bloody murder from the moment the police showed up on his property, denying any knowledge of the evidence found there, demanding access to his lawyer before he was even picked up, and threatening to sue everybody he could think of. He yelled about conspiracies and how the town of Ferguston had been out to get him and the whole Raymond family for years, and had been accusing him of things he'd never done. He even singled out my family as being at the forefront of these accusations.

*****

Later that afternoon, as a way of getting our minds off all things D-Ray, Carl took us out to dinner for the second day in a row, this time to a family restaurant on top of the hill near the town limits. I had never been to it before; it had just opened that spring, part of a Canadian chain that specialized in pizza and figured it would have more credibility with an American-sounding name. There were a couple of others like it in that part of town, restaurants that survived on summer people and locals shopping at the big box stores nearby. It was the middle of the afternoon and the dinner rush hadn't begun yet. The restaurant was dark and cool, with shitty elevator music playing in the background—I immediately thought of Las Vegas. Carl was happy to escape the heat, and his mood improved considerably when we stepped in. The same couldn't be said for our host/waiter—his name tag said "Hi My Name Is Kevin"—who greeted us at the door, looking positively shocked and more than a little irritated that he should have to wait on customers at this hour. We were met with a grunt that might have been "Good afternoon," and a confused garble and an absent toss of the head that indicated we were free to sit anywhere.

Within a few minutes Carl had managed to get my dad and me to lighten up. He was good at that. He had a limitless supply of funny stories, usually involving the criminally stupid who would eventually become his clients. That day's account had to do with a burglar who, having broken into someone's home and brazenly stolen a wallet and some jewellery from right under the noses of the sleeping occupants, stopped in the kitchen for a quick bite. Upon opening the freezer a seven-kilogram frozen turkey came sliding out like a boulder in an avalanche, landing squarely on his foot and breaking three bones. His screams of pain awoke the homeowner, who waited for the intruder to leave then followed him at a safe distance all the way to the Emergency Department of the local hospital. The icing on the cake came when the burglar mistakenly opened the wrong wallet and provided the victim's health card at the admissions desk instead of his own, all with the victim standing directly behind him.

"I've seen enough in my time not to believe in karma," Carl said as he finished his story, "but it is nice to see balance restored to the Force every once in a while."

Movement behind my uncle caught my eye. From where I was sitting, I could see over Carl's shoulder to the entrance of the restaurant, where bright light of day poured through the glass front doors. A figure silhouetted against the light had just come in and, content to ignore any attempt at a greeting from the establishment's lone waiter, began to move into the main dining area in our direction. From his position next to me in our booth, Dad couldn't see the approaching stranger, but I knew. I'd only seen him once before, over a month ago, fleetingly and from behind, but I just knew.

He was average height but would have been a lot taller if he didn't stoop so much. He was also really skinny, not quite sickly but he certainly qualified as gangly. Despite his long legs he walked with a choppy, shuffling gait, like he was afraid his shoes—beaten-up black Converse All Stars—would come off if his strides were too long. His jeans were old, patched and resewn in places, and clung precariously to his narrow hips. His dirty white T-shirt bore an aged, peeling graphic of some kind, and on his head was a battered baseball cap. Old Soggy-Shoes himself. Mr. Everyman, Ferguston edition.

He stopped next to our booth, and stared directly at my dad, standing silently as if waiting to be acknowledged before speaking. He stood right next to me, smelling of gasoline, tobacco and sweat and something spicy I couldn't put my finger on, looking over my head to my dad who sat to my right in the booth. My uncle sat opposite me looking almost comical, like a cat surprised by an intruder.

"Yes? Can I help you?" my dad inquired.

"You're Martin Lambert, right?"

"Yes I am. And you are . . . ?"

"My name is Craig."

"McLaughlin," I whispered. The man's face had an odd birdlike quality to it; with his prominent nose, sloping forehead, and receding chin, it looked like his face was made of rubber and someone had taken him by the nose and pulled it straight out. And he had that big hairy mole on the side of his neck that kept drawing my gaze. Poor guy sure missed the boat in the looks department. He glanced down at me, as if realizing for the first time that I was there, then returned his attention to my dad.

"A lot of people are looking for you, Craig," Carl said. McLaughlin ignored him completely.

"I gotta talk to you, man."

I'm sure Dad was about to ask him to sit with us, but Carl wouldn't give him the opening.

"What can we do for you, Craig?" my uncle asked. McLaughlin's attention didn't waver.

"I seen you on TV. I seen you talking about David. You said you were glad he was arrested and that he was in jail."

"Well, when reporters asked me how I felt I—"

"You talk like you *know* David made your wife disappear. You talk like you got it all figured out. But you don't know shit, and you gotta go back on TV and say so."

*David.* It was hard to think of D-Ray as anything but D-Ray. Hearing him referred to by his first name was uncomfortably humanizing.

Carl took over at this point. "Craig, these accusations haven't come out of the blue. The police have found very strong evidence tying David Raymond to Dr. Lambert's disappearance. And in fact he's been the only person ever suspected in the crime."

"Yeah, that's right. Seems like people made up their minds a long time ago."

"Well, as I said there is also new evidence that ties him to the disappearance, and his alibi has always been a bit shaky for the evening in question."

"That's crap. I don't care what they're saying 'cause I know he didn't do it. Don't you see? I *know!*"

Something in the way McLaughlin said those last words caused both Carl and my dad to look at each other for just a second. Then, just as Carl opened his mouth to speak again, Hi-My-Name-Is-Kevin showed up to take our order. Dad barked out a quick "Not now!" and the terrified Kevin scampered away like a scared rabbit. He didn't return.

"You mean you know, like, for a fact? How do you know, Craig?"

"I know exactly what he did and where he was that night, 'cause I was with him the whole time, man."

Carl kept his poker face. "Tell me about it."

"We'd been at his place all evening, watching TV and just hanging out. Then he gets this call from his doctor to come and see him, which was like weird 'cause it was late, like around 10:00, but whatever. So we go."

Dad: "What time did you get there?"

"I dunno. Must have been just a little after 10:00. We weren't very far."

Carl: "Then what?"

"I waited in the car while David went inside. He came out like almost half an hour later and then we left."

"What did you do after that?"

"Well, David was hungry so we went to The Boneyard because their kitchen is usually open until 11:00, but when we got there, they were all like, "Sorry, dudes, we're closed." It wasn't even 10:45 and they were closing their kitchen already. They didn't even say why. David was pissed, so we went to The Pit and hung out there until they closed."

Knowing what we all knew, I imagined Dad, Carl, and myself all doing the same mental math at that moment, and each one of us coming to the same conclusion. Based on Craig McLaughlin's version of the story—if he was telling the truth, but he was certainly leaving the possibility for corroboration by others—there was simply no time for D-Ray to get to my mom, either before or after his meeting with Dr. Coleman.

Carl picked up the conversation after a pause. "OK, but as I said the police have new evidence tying D-Ray—sorry, 'David'—directly to Dr. Lambert. It hasn't been made public yet, but—"

"What? You mean the cellphone?"

A breath. Dad looked paralyzed, Carl's poker face was cracking, and my mouth went dry.

"What do you know about a cellphone?"

"I saw it, two or three days later."

Dad: "D-Ray showed it to you?"

"No, David never knew anything about it."

"Then who?"

McLaughlin looked like he was talking to a child. "Coleman."

Another beat. This time we all looked at each other.

Dad: "You saw Dr. Coleman, Dr. Geoffrey Coleman, with Élise's cellphone two or three days after she disappeared?"

"Yeah."

Carl: "How do you know it was hers?"

"He told me."

Dad again, this time his voice sounded strangled. He was barely holding it together. "You mean you had this information all these years, and you never went to the police?"

McLaughlin voice was quieter now, humbled. "He'd already got me involved by then, like without my knowing."

"Involved how?"

"It was the morning after . . . after she . . . anyway, Coleman called me and asked me to help him do something. It was simple: just to go with him and move some car from one spot to another. Dump it in the woods someplace. I knew he had some sketchy friends, bikers, people in the drug business, so I figured it must be about that. I had no idea whose car it was, honest. So I did it, and I got paid, and that was it. I didn't make much of it at first. It was only a while later that I got the whole picture, and by then it was too late, I was involved, like, after the fact. That was when Coleman showed me the cellphone. He told me everything, then he said that if I told anybody I could go to jail as an accomplice . . . or I could be bumped off . . . or get bumped off while I was in jail.

Think anyone would give a shit if I disappeared? Think anyone would send out search parties? Or start an investigation?"

We were all quiet for a moment. I turned to my dad. He looked awful, like a cancer patient after a round of chemo. Carl finally spoke up.

"Coleman told you everything?"

"Mostly."

"Who decided where to dispose of the car?"

"Coleman."

"How did that go down?"

"Well, he picked me up in his car, like really early, it was still dark out, and we drove to where this Rav4 was sitting –"

"Where?"

"Somewhere on Baker. The sun wasn't out yet when we got there. Then, he had me follow him in the Rav, while he led the way in his Audi. It was way out of the way, middle of nowhere."

"Did you know the area at all?"

"No. Neither did he, by the looks of it. I think he got the idea from someone else. He didn't seem to know where he was going: he'd written all the directions down."

"Then what?"

"Nothing. We left the car on this private road. You could barely see it with all the trees and bushes. Then he drove me home and paid me."

"How much?"

"Three hundred bucks."

Dad intervened: "How did he know where to find Élise on the night? Or was that just luck?"

McLaughlin shook his head. "Sorry, man. He never told me that."

"Why did he keep the cellphone?" Everyone was surprised to hear my voice, including me. It seemed to come out of nowhere.

"To frame David, I guess."

Dad: "And he just showed it to you?"

"Yeah."

"Why would he do that?"

"He knew I was afraid of David. David has a temper, you know, and he was really scared and freaked out about the biker gangs and how he was going to get them their drugs because of what your mother said to him. I told Coleman about it and he said don't worry about it, then he showed me the phone. That's when he told me everything that happened and how we were going to set David up. He must have thought I'd be happy to see David go down. David was nuts."

Carl: "Any idea how Raymond ended up with it?"

"The phone? Not really, but it wouldn't have been hard. If Coleman wanted to hide it, or make it look like David had it all along, he just would have had to put it in a box of medical stuff. Coleman sent him all kinds of stuff all the time, and David didn't open half of it; and he never threw anything out."

"Tell me: why did Coleman get you involved in the first place, having you help him with the car and all?"

McLaughlin looked at Carl; his face was granite. "At first it was because he needed help, and he wasn't going to ask David; he had other plans for him. Coleman was my doctor, too, and he knew me, or at least he thought he did. He must have figured he could trust me not to say anything. He was just like everyone else: he thought I was too stupid to figure anything out, and so he didn't worry about it. When he saw that I knew what was going on he started threatening me, warning me to keep my mouth shut."

"So why, after all these years, are you coming forward to clear David? You changed your mind about him?"

"I was going to tell David all about it right then, what Coleman did, the frame-up, everything. But before I could he got drunk and crazier than usual and beat the shit out of me. He was brutal, man. So I thought 'fuck you, then, asshole' and split. Never came back."

"Until now," my dad said. "To clear D-Ray's name."

"I know who killed your wife, man, and it wasn't David."

"Did Dr. Coleman say where he . . . left my mom?" I asked after a pause.

McLaughlin's face softened. He looked miserable, ill. He shook his head wordlessly, avoiding my gaze.

We were all quiet for a while, then Carl finally stirred, sliding out of the booth.

"Craig, you know you're going to have to repeat all this to the proper authorities. You could be facing some very serious charges. If you go to the police right now, of your own volition, tell them everything you know, they might go easy. Especially if you can help them find Coleman." He paused for a beat. "I have to tell them that we spoke. If you like I can take you right now. It's better that way than if you wait for them to come for you. And they will."

McLaughlin simply nodded, his black muddy eyes fixed on the floor. He looked completely devastated; whatever bluster he'd come in with had evaporated in a matter of minutes as the importance of his tale finally hit home. This was no doubt the first time he told anyone in ten years. Carl walked him out of the restaurant, half a step behind him, a hand placed just behind his lower back. Dad and I watched them leave, and sat in silence for several minutes before leaving ourselves. We never ordered anything, and skipped dinner that evening.

# 38

**CLARION EXCLUSIVE**
Missing persons suspect released following
surprise witness testimony, new evidence
Police seek former Ferguston doctor for questioning

**Jason Bremmer**
**The Clarion**

[FERGUSTON] The investigation into the disappearance of Dr. Élise François-Lambert took an unexpected turn yesterday with the release of David Luc Raymond, long the only suspect in the unsolved case that has puzzled area residents and law enforcement for almost a decade.

Raymond, a resident of Ferguston and well known to police for numerous infractions over the years, was arrested last week by Ontario Provincial Police on charges of illegal weapons and narcotics possession. During a search of Raymond's property, police uncovered evidence that seemed to directly link him to the disappearance of Dr. François-Lambert in November of 1996. A cellphone belonging to the victim was found in Raymond's basement, along with a glove that was an exact match with one found in the victim's vehicle. These were considered extremely compelling in confirming that Raymond had had direct contact with François-Lambert just prior to her disappearance, as was the fact that Raymond was completely unable to explain them.

The case took an unusual twist last week with the sudden emergence of a surprise witness who not only corroborated Raymond's alibi for the evening in question, but identified an alternative suspect who had allegedly claimed responsibility for the crime.

Dr. Geoffrey Coleman, a former anesthesiologist at the Ferguston Regional Health Centre, was interviewed by police at the time of the disappearance but was never considered a suspect in the case. This changed when Mr. Craig McLaughlin of Ferguston, a long-time associate of Raymond's and, like Raymond, a former patient of Dr. Coleman, approached police last week with as-yet unheard testimony regarding the activities of both men on and around the time of the disappearance.

The case against Dr. Coleman was further strengthened a few days later with the unearthing of new evidence by Dr. François-Lambert's family. This evidence had apparently been compiled over an extended period by the victim herself and implicates Dr. Coleman in numerous illegal activities including prescription narcotics distribution, not to mention several cases of sexual harassment of patients and co-workers, and incidences of gross incompetence. In an exclusive statement to the *Clarion*, Mr. Martin Lambert, husband of the victim, stated that he knew his wife had boxes of documents stored in the basement, but had no idea that some of them contained documents gathered as evidence against Dr. Coleman.

"Actually, it was my son [...] who uncovered them entirely by accident," Lambert said yesterday. "Élise never indicated anything to me at the time that she had been keeping tabs on Coleman's activities. She vanished without ever breathing a word about it."

According to McLaughlin, Dr. Coleman learned that Dr. François-Lambert was planning to notify authorities of his activities and connections with drug traffickers and allegedly took actions to prevent this from happening.

Mr. McLaughlin admitted to police that he helped Dr. Coleman dispose of the victim's vehicle, although he claimed to not have known whose vehicle it was at the time. He also suggested that the cellphone and glove that allegedly tied David Raymond to the disappearance of François-Lambert were likely planted in an effort to frame Raymond, and that Dr. Coleman's statement to the police at the time was fraudulent. Following independent corroborations of these statements by police, David Raymond was released from custody yesterday, although he still faces narcotics and weapons charges.

According to an OPP spokesperson, a Canada-wide warrant has been issued for the arrest of Dr. Coleman on multiple narcotics trafficking and other charges. Coleman's current whereabouts are unknown, and it is believed he may have left the jurisdiction years ago and could be living under an assumed name ...

*****

There was a photo of Geoffrey Coleman next to the article. I don't know what I was expecting, but it wasn't this. An average, middle-aged white male with a slightly receding hairline, wearing glasses and a striped tie. A thin mouth, slightly jowly cheeks, widely spaced grey eyes, low-bridged nose. Not what I'd consider handsome, but by no means hideous. Remarkably unremarkable. Disappointing, even. I didn't know if he should have had horns sprouting from his head, or some ghastly scar slashing across his cheek, or even a mono-brow, but he looked completely and utterly average. He could have been anyone.

The media didn't seem to be bothered one bit with the sudden shift from David Raymond to Geoffrey Coleman as the principal villain in the case. In fact, they moved pretty seamlessly from one bad guy to the next, with one story emerging after another describing in lurid detail the catalogue of sins of FRHC's former anaesthesiologist.

It appeared at first that Mom had built up a pretty exhaustive file on the good doctor over a period of two or three years, documenting everything from shoddy record keeping to putting patients in short-term comas to the prescription of controlled narcotics, not to mention inappropriate behaviour toward colleagues, hospital staff, and his own patients. But Mom had only scratched the surface.

Ferguston, it turned out, was just Geoffrey Coleman's latest stop on what was emerging as an odyssey of addiction, incompetence and professional misconduct across small-town Ontario that spanned almost two decades. Police were able to trace Coleman's movements from his medical school days—Queen's University, class of '70—to his many professional postings around the province, right up until he left Ferguston and seemingly fell off the map. According to the cops, following his residency he'd gone from one under-serviced area to another, places where no one else wanted work, setting up a family practice and—wherever possible—taking on a job in the surgery unit at the nearest hospital. What no one suspected was that he'd gradually become a steady supplier of prescription narcotics across the north, and as an anesthesiologist he could get his hands on pretty much any drug he wanted—most notably Percocet, OxyContin, Morphine, Ativan, Valium, and Demerol—which he'd then funnel to biker gangs.

But he didn't stop there. In his family medicine practice he'd routinely place prescriptions for fake patients to different pharmacies, then get flunkeys like D-Ray or McLaughlin to pose as said patients and pick them up for him. Or he'd make up fictitious ailments or medical procedures for patients and order medications when they didn't need any. He even went so far as to ask his patients—especially his female ones—to bring their medications to their appointments with them; then, while the patients waited in the examination room, he'd go back to his office, root through their purses, and harvest whatever he liked.

The pattern was always the same. After establishing himself in a new region, Coleman would keep his nose clean at first and try to get his life back together following his latest debacle. Then, after a year to eighteen months, things would begin to get ugly: complaints from his patients and slip-ups in the ER. Professional complaints followed, as sure as the snow in December. Some communities managed to tolerate Coleman's antics longer than others, and he'd somehow always manage to get himself reassigned and resettled in a new locale before any real shit hit the fan. Many suspected someone higher up on the food chain was looking after him; that or the governing bodies that oversaw such things must have figured a physician like Coleman—with his enthusiasm to work in the most far-flung areas of the province—was just too rare and valuable a commodity to let a few unfortunate habits like malpractice, drug addiction, and sexual harassment get in the way. Dad said it reminded him of how the Catholic Church dealt with wayward priests.

I couldn't speak for other communities, but I knew I'd seen this pattern before. Ferguston had a history of attracting nastiness over the years. I'd always said that Ferguston was a hole that nastiness fell into, even if not everything stayed. Maybe it was more like a celestial body creating a depression in space-time, drawing predatory creatures like Geoffrey Coleman into its orbit; gravity would pull them down, they'd rain damage upon the residents for a little while like crumbling meteors, and then they'd be slingshot back out into space, never to be seen again.

*****

Police were able to confirm a lot of from Craig McLaughlin's testimony. For one thing, McLaughlin identified more or less precisely where Mom's car was left before Coleman had asked him for his help to move it: the spot was pretty much where expected on Baker Side Road, a stretch of road that meandered through a heavily forested area about six kilometres away from the Campbells' residence and about three kilometres from where it connected with Route 5. Finally, after ten years, police had a starting point in reconstructing the crime.

Counting from when Mom left the Campbells' house, it appeared that Coleman had intercepted her on Baker Side Road between 9:45 and 9:50 p.m. That he should be driving on Baker wasn't, on the surface, that unusual—after all, he lived nearby on Carlyle Road, another side road that zigzagged through the woods, roughly parallel to Baker and about five kilometres southeast—so the possibility of this being a random encounter wasn't unthinkable. The problem was, if he was driving home from the office as everyone suspected, he would have had to go out of his way to get to Baker; the turnoff from Route 5 to Baker was *after* the one to Carlyle and his house, not before. Maybe he'd just been distracted at the wheel and missed his turn. Maybe not.

Either way, after killing my mom, he would have had to hide her body—at least temporarily—then make his way to his office, no doubt contacting David Raymond en route to set up a bogus appointment, all within fifteen to twenty minutes. It would be tight but doable. After the meeting with D-Ray—during which he swiped one of his gloves—Coleman likely went back to Baker Side Road, made a static-filled call to my dad using Mom's cellphone to skew the timeline, and dropped D-Ray's glove under the driver's seat of her car. He then would have had the rest of the night to properly dispose of her body. The next morning he called an unsuspecting Craig McLaughlin to help him dispose of the Rav4. Again, how and why he chose the spot he did was another mystery.

Elsewhere, the police were satisfied that D-Ray's glove had probably been taken by Coleman during D-Ray's visit to the doctor's office that evening without him noticing. The cellphone, meanwhile, which was found in a box of medical supplies, could have easily found its way to D-Ray's home; in fact, Raymond probably brought the box in himself, and then left it aside and promptly forgot about it. The frame was virtually flawless.

For all their seeming readiness to jump from one villain to another, the media did get one thing right: even if neither turned out to be a killer, Coleman was, in the end, a worse offender than David Raymond. They had a lot in common: both badly damaged people, ultimately cut off from society, with no real regard for anyone but themselves. Nor did either of them ever seem aware of the wreckage they left behind in other people's lives. Collateral damage never factored into their actions. But for everything he did or was accused of, nobody in Ferguston actually trusted D-Ray; everyone in town knew exactly what he was and D-Ray made no effort to conceal it. Unlike Coleman, nobody had ever counted on D-Ray for anything, and certainly no one willingly placed their well-being into his hands.

\*\*\*\*\*

August had bled into September, but even though the Labour Day long weekend was right around the corner, September's arrival wasn't terribly convincing. It was still just as hot as it had been throughout August—which had already been a scorcher—and Dad was still toying with the idea of taking a bit of time off once the school year got started the following week, leaving the option open to me as well. The nervous rush that I usually felt in my stomach and that characterized this time of year was conspicuously absent. The fact that my Billie-like symptoms had mostly abated by then was no help either. By all evidence this long, hot summer was just going to linger on indefinitely, regardless of what the calendar said.

The media buzz surrounding the case had faded to almost nothing in the past few days, like grazing animals wandering off to better pastures. The police were continuing their search for Geoffrey Coleman, but according to Carl—who significantly called me rather than my dad to offer an update—there was no sense holding my breath for any results on that score.

Craig McLaughlin was eagerly doing everything he could to assist police in the investigation; he was looking at some pretty serious charges, having to do with moving Mom's car and withholding evidence, so cooperating with authorities was the smartest move available to him. D-Ray for his part came out swinging the moment he was released from custody, getting in front of the media and threatening to sue everybody he could think of including the police, the town of Ferguston, the hospital, even Dad and me. He then shuffled off, letting his attorney finish up with the reporters while he stewed behind the tinted glass of the lawyer's Beemer. He'd presumably spent his time since then celebrating his release at his compound, drinking himself stupid, and plotting elaborate schemes of revenge.

Meanwhile Dad was as about as gloomy and sullen as I'd ever seen him. The developments in Mom's case over the past week had had a devastating effect. Dad had spent the better part of a decade nursing his hurt, his hatred, his resentment, and his dread of David Raymond. His need to bring him to justice, to expose him for what he was convinced Raymond was, had defined my dad for ten years. It had hijacked any personal or professional ambition, any goals he might have set for me, and any ability he had to move on. I don't think he ever considered what might lie on the other side of a resolution to the case, either positive or negative. When it became clear that D-Ray, for all his sins, was not a murderer, Dad was blindsided. Making it worse was the fact that he'd been replaced by what amounted to a ghost: Dad had never met Coleman before, had never seen a photo of him until it appeared in the paper, and had never even heard, or certainly did not remember, his voice. Now, it turned out, he was in the wind, and the prospect of a resolution was more remote than ever.

It was hard to watch him now. Normally at this time of year he'd be scurrying around like a squirrel preparing for winter: buying the supplies he'd need for his classes, shopping for back-to-school stuff for me, getting groceries for the impending brown bag lunches, doing laundry. Instead, he spent most of his time in his office, usually with the door closed. Some of that time was on the phone: I could hear him chatting with Carl, with his dad, and with Mom's family as well, speaking in French with a hushed, craggy voice that sounded much too old. Dad had gone back to his pattern from before our trip, except without the urgency associated with the D-Ray file. He was a bit like a caged animal, but without the need or desire to escape. He didn't eat much, and rarely ever cooked. At night, when the rest of the world was asleep, I could hear him moving around downstairs, though he would never switch on a light or turn on the TV.

Looking forward to the coming days I felt torn. Heading back to school on Tuesday would be a chance to get out from the constant gloom my home life had become, to see different people, and redirect my thoughts. On the other hand, the idea of leaving Dad to spend his empty days alone at home with whatever dark thoughts he was entertaining felt like betrayal.

Of course what I didn't know was that before the end of the weekend all this would be moot anyway, as three things would happen that would pretty much settle everything . . . that is until just a few days ago, when I started writing this.

*****

The call came on Friday night, late enough to be out of place. The calls from the media had pretty much stopped a few days earlier, Dad had already done the family phone rounds that afternoon, and Carl always called Dad's cell. It felt weird, such a late call on the landline, and the first thing I thought was that it must be bad news from someone. Dad clearly wasn't concerned. He was in his office; he had a phone right next to him but he was focused on his computer monitor and was content to let it ring, guessing it was probably a 1-800 call urging us to upgrade our phone/TV/Internet package. None of our cordless phones in the house were in their cradles—typically—and for some reason the call wouldn't go to voicemail.

The ringing continued. To my ears, each ring was louder, longer and more desperate than the one before it. I ended up picking up the phone in my dad's office just to put an end to the tortured shrieking. The call display showed a number with an area code I didn't recognize.

"Lambert residence," I said.

Nothing at first, just static, strangely amplified.

"Hello?" I wasn't going to give this caller many chances. Answer now, buddy, or this convo is over.

Breathing. Heavy, and through the nose. Male? And something else . . .

*Clink*

Ice in a glass of water.

"Hel-*loh?*"

A gulp and a swallow. This was getting annoying.

"Hel—"

A male voice through the static: "Is this Justin?" Old enough, older than my dad anyway. Friendly but a fake, awkward kind of friendly, like a salesman or someone who is painfully inexperienced with kids.

"Yes," I squeaked. I immediately hated the way I sounded, like a pathetic second grader being called out in front of the class.

Another loud breath through the nose. I could hear a smile in it.

*Clink*

*Gulp*

"Nice to finally meet you," he responded, smacking his mouth as he swallowed. His voice was like tepid apple juice: cloying sweetness unable to mask an underlying acidity. "Do you know who this is?"

"N-no," I said. I was almost whispering.

"My name is Geoffrey Coleman."

I stopped breathing. My stomach was a clenched fist, and there was pain in my bowels. I wanted to scream for help, but Dad was a billion miles away and my mouth was filled with cotton balls.

"I guess you've been hearing a lot about me lately, haven't you, Justin? Bet you think you know everything about me, about what happened? To your mom?"

He paused as grown-ups always do when they're reprimanding a kid, stupidly waiting for a response to a question to which they already know the answer. When he realized that no answer was forthcoming, he clinked his glass again, gulped something, and continued.

"You don't understand, Justin. No one does. Your mom sure didn't. There was so much more going on than she knew. There were a lot of people involved. *Important* people. She was going to ruin everything, you understand?"

A wave of nausea broke over me in a rush. I had the devil himself on the phone, and he was pedantic and condescending, a self-righteous schoolmarm.

"Your mom thought she knew a lot of things but she didn't *understand* anything, Justin." I wanted to scream at him to stop using my name like he knew me, but my mouth was welded shut. "Nothing was going to happen. She should have just stayed out of the way, stayed out of what she didn't understand, what didn't concern her."

Another *clink* as Coleman paused again. I could hear his breathing; it was slow and a bit laboured.

"What happen' to her was a real sher . . . a shame. A tragedy. It's sssilly, really."

*Silly???*

His speech was slurred. The bastard was wasted.

"It never shoulda come to that. I didn't set out to hurt her; I just wanted to talk to her, reason with her. Really. You understand that, don't you Justin?"—it came out "Jussin"—"But she wouldn't listen to reason and things just . . . got out of hand. You'd be proud of her, though. She was brave, right 'til the end."

My fear was beginning to ebb, and anger, for now still mute, was filling in the empty spaces.

"I was very fond of your mother. We were good friends. We didn't always agree . . . but I like to think we had . . . a special bond." Pause. Gulp. Swallow. Sigh. "And she was such a *beautiful* woman . . . I mean really gorgeous. I don't know if you have any idea, Justin, but your mom . . . was . . . a real beauty. Your dad was one lucky fella . . ."

It wasn't so much the words he said as a noise, a kind of wet clicking he made with his mouth, that broke my paralysis. Even then, all I could manage was "Bastard." It was enough.

There was a loud metallic creak as Dad's office chair swung back and around my way. The look on his face morphed quickly to one of concern, to horror, to as close to rage as I've ever seen in him. He saw me as I was shaking with fear and hurt, tears streaming, standing with the phone held out to him, looking to him for help. He launched himself out of his chair in a blur, and before I knew it, he had the phone in one hand and was holding me behind him with the other, shielding me from it.

"Who the hell is this?" he snarled. Somehow, deep down, I think he already knew.

There was a pause as Coleman responded, probably some sick version of "Howdy, Martin! It's the Geoffster!"

What followed was a profanity-laced barrage from my dad that surprised even me with its fury, its vitriol, and its imagination. I never imagined my soft-spoken, kid-friendly dad even knew that kind of language. In any other context it would have been funny.

"Listen, you sick fuckwad," he raged, "the cops are on your ass right now and they're going to find you. It doesn't matter what slimy shithole you've crawled into. They'll find you, motherfucker. And when they do, when your sorry fucking ass is handed over to the cops down here, don't think for a second they're going to go by the book. They know my family, and they know what you did to Élise: you're going to be beaten so fucking bad you'll wish you were dead. I just hope they give me ten minutes with you alone, you pussy, before they turn you into hamburger and then leave you to rot in Millhaven to make a career of being someone's bitch. You better like taking it up the ass, you fuck—"

He suddenly stopped as a wave of bewilderment washed over his face.

"What? Who? Who's going to . . . ? Well, bring 'em on, dickface! You hear me? Yeah, that's right, you fucking coward. You think I'm afraid of—" He stopped again, this time for my benefit. He then looked at me, pointed to his cellphone next to his computer, and mouthed the words, "Call Carl."

I'd been in such a state of shock that my legs weren't fully thawed as I stumbled to my dad's desk. Nor did I realize how sweaty my hands were until I grasped his cellphone and saw it slip from my grip and bounce off the floor like a bar of soap. I seized it again, fumbled with it and dropped it a second time. "Shit," I hissed. I sat on the floor with it this time, and tried to coax my fingers to navigate through the phone's menu to find Dad's Favourites list. It was like picking my nose with a boxing glove. I managed to find Carl's number on the third try, and Carl's cell was ringing when I heard my Dad spit out a final curse.

"Shit! Shit, shit, *shit*! The bastard hung up. Dammit!" Dad's face was ashen, except around his eyes, which were swollen and red and still full of tears. He handed me the landline and took his cell as Carl's voice answered at the other end. His hands were trembling.

Dad gave his brother a complete rundown of Coleman's call, at one point putting Carl on speakerphone so that I could contribute to the conversation. Carl said he'd call the police right away, and that they'd send someone over to take a statement from us. It was going to be vital that we remembered every word that was said, as well as other details about the call that could prove useful. Carl himself was on his way over as he spoke to us, patiently allowing Dad to vent his anger and frustration. Dad was beating himself up about not behaving more rationally and less like a hysterical asshole. He reprimanded himself for not keeping Coleman on the phone longer while I called the police; maybe they could have done something, arranged to have the call traced. Carl reassured him that tracing a call was a lot more complicated than that, and that Dad had behaved in a way that was perfectly understandable. Dad took the phone off speaker mode and continued to talk with his brother, collapsing in exhaustion in his office chair. Then, acting on an almost subconscious impulse, I picked up the landline again—it was still warm and damp from Dad's grip—and pressed "Call History."

"Dad," I asked. "Why do you think Coleman didn't bother to hide his phone number?"

# 39

The Ontario Provincial Police began converging on Geoffrey Coleman within hours. The call he'd made had originated from a Southwestern Ontario town called Kettering; the mysterious fact that he didn't bother to conceal the number he was calling from was not a deliberate gesture to mislead—as many of us had feared—but rather a simple consequence of Coleman being completely loaded when he placed the call. The two detectives who came to our house to interview my dad and me were quick to caution us against getting overly optimistic, but said that it was looking good. The phone number was registered to a J. Smith: no surprise there, many of us had suspected Coleman would be using an assumed name, if perhaps a more imaginative one. There were a number of J. Smiths in the region, and the phone number was registered to a post office box in Kettering, but the police had his photo and a decent physical description. Police were expecting to have Coleman in custody "soon."

The cops asked us a lot questions about the call, including whether there were particular sounds in the background that might say something about where Coleman was calling from:

vehicle noises, passing trains, church bells, the lap of water, overhead voices like public address announcers, music, etc. Or perhaps he'd said something that might imply a location. We told them that the only noteworthy sound aside from Coleman's voice was the clink of ice in a glass and the noises related to his drinking. What Dad and I were more interested in talking about were the threats Coleman uttered: he'd said that "people" were likely to come after us now, as a result of all this criminal activity being brought to light. To both my dad and me, that sounded like pissed-off bikers. Both detectives dismissed this fear outright, saying this was all old news to the bikers and that police weren't looking at them for mom's disappearance anyway.

The police seemed a lot more interested in what Coleman had to say about other people being involved and what he might have meant when he described them as "important." Dad just shook his head: aside from the aforementioned bikers and David Raymond, who wasn't really part of the discussion anymore, he couldn't think of anybody.

By the time the police wrapped up it was past 1:00 in the morning, and I was nodding off. With what Coleman had told my dad, I was more than a little nervous about letting the cops leave, but they reassured us again that there was nothing to worry about. Carl had driven over from Sudbury right after he'd spoken with my dad, arriving just before midnight, and volunteered to stay over; he and Dad talked in the kitchen until sunrise over a late-night pot of coffee. Once again, we'd been supplied with new details about the case, and once again we were left waiting for answers to the most important questions, answers that could only be provided by Coleman himself. We were all exhausted and on edge, and all we could do was wait around.

*****

Saturday morning was bright, cloudless and already warm when I stepped out after 9:00. Here we were in early September and we had another scorcher in the making. It was unnatural. The humidity made the air so thick and hot it was like breathing soup. Ferguston had barely seen any rain in going on five weeks, and even that was just a tease. Everything and everyone had pretty much had enough already. Neighbourhood dogs panting on front porches or under trees, who'd normally get up to bark out their presence to passers-by, couldn't be bothered to even lift their heads. The squirrels and the birds were moving in slow motion. Even the trees looked tired. Nature was saying "Fuck it, I'm working to rule until conditions improve." By now my chills had run their course and I was beginning to feel the oppressive crush of the heat like everyone else. I wheeled my bike out of the garage, hoping to get in a quick ride by the lake before breakfast and before the heat of the day made the prospect of any outdoor activity a lot less appealing.

Our neighbour Mr. Lovato, he of the Lawn Fauna Rescue Centre, was out with a garden hose watering his flower boxes and what little lawn he had in his front yard, in flagrant violation of the municipal water restrictions implemented weeks earlier. He looked to have aged ten years since the early summer—and he didn't look young then—and he wore his wariness like a heavy wool cardigan. I was going to head off before he noticed me, but he lifted his head just enough to see me and waved me over.

"Another hot one," he said, squinting up at the sky from under his Tilley hat.

I approached, looking over his parched menagerie and suddenly remembering that I hadn't refilled my water bottle.

"Times like this I don't envy the McDonalds, with their big lawn," he continued. The McDonald family owned a big colonial-style house on the corner lot up the street. Even from our end you could see how their lawn had yellowed.

I offered a weak nod in response.

There was a pause, and I was about to shove off when Mr. Lovato said casually: "I've been reading about Geoff Coleman." My stomach tightened just a bit, but I didn't move.

"Did you know he was Alice's family doctor?" he asked. Alice was Lovato's wife; she passed away from ovarian cancer a few months before my mom disappeared, and over the next months and years Mr. Lovato and my dad became companions in mourning.

I tried feebly to change the subject. "Is that a new . . . what is that . . . a curlew?" I asked, pointing to a daintily carved bird standing in the shadow of a huge chrome elephant, Lovato's centrepiece made entirely of scrounged auto parts.

"You've got a good eye, Lambert." He almost grinned. Lovato puttered to the side of the house to turn off the water, and came back wiping his hands with a rag. "I don't think he'll live there," he resumed, referring to the latest addition to his lawn collection. "He's a handsome fella. I think I want to show him off a bit more." He paused again, surveying his kingdom like a benign monarch. "She suffered a lot, you know, especially near the end. She was in a lot of pain, all the time. It was awful."

I was quiet. He didn't need any feedback.

"She had so much trouble getting her pain medication at the time. There were always delays when we went to the pharmacy: they weren't ready, the prescription was never updated, nonsense like that. I was furious. We blamed the pharmacist. When Alice finally passed on, it was a blessing for her. Over the years I'd forgotten all about that, until I read about Coleman last week. It brought it all back." He shook his head grimly then turned to me. "He caused so much suffering. I wonder if he'll ever know how much."

I stared at Mr. Lovato helplessly. As with Dad, I wished I had something to share with him, to offer something that resembled hope or at least the possibility of some kind of restitution. To tell him that Coleman at that moment was in all likelihood running from police like a desperate rat, that he was going to be cornered and bagged and dragged in to face justice for all the senseless suffering that he caused, would be not only premature at this point but hopelessly inadequate. I knew that. I knew that for a fact.

*****

When I got home, I was starving. It was too early for lunch, but happily Carl was in the kitchen making breakfast: scrambled eggs and sausages. Apparently, he had gotten very little sleep and was just starting his day; Dad, meanwhile, hadn't slept at all and was still in his office with the door closed. I sighed, poured myself some coffee and sat down heavily as my uncle tended to breakfast.

We sat in silence for a bit. When I looked up at him, he was looking at me; his swimming-pool eyes looked tired, and his mouth was set in a grim smile behind his tangle of whiskers. I knew he was worried, for his brother as much as for me; each of us wanted the same thing, we all knew what it was and why it was so elusive and that it might be a long time before it came, so there was no sense in talking about it. Instead, he picked up his coffee mug and deliberately made a loud and obnoxious slurping sound to get me to laugh. It almost worked.

When Dad finally came down to join us, his footfalls on the steps were quicker than they'd been in a while, and when he came into the kitchen, he had a look on his face I hadn't seen since before Las Vegas. It was sharp, alert, thoughtful, like he was turning something around in his mind. Even his movements were brisk. He poured himself some coffee, and noticing the sausages cooking, began to pull dishes from the cupboard.

"Damn, bro," Carl said. "For a guy who hasn't slept you've got a lot of energy."

"I just had a *very* interesting phone call."

"Who with?"

Dad sat down, looking at us both. He had a bit of that "I know something you don't" look on his face, and he was setting up how he was going to tell us what it was. He wasn't quite smiling, but he wasn't displeased either. He sipped his coffee and began.

"So I was thinking. You remember when Craig McLaughlin told us about how he and Coleman disposed of Élise's Rav? Coleman called McLaughlin on the morning after his encounter with Élise and asked him to help him with something. Coleman picked him up, drove to the site, and then had McLaughlin follow him in the Rav while Coleman led the way in his car. Remember?"

Carl was wearing his poker face. His lawyer face. "Go on," he said.

"McLaughlin said that Coleman didn't really know where he was going, that he had the directions written down. It's a very remote area, not many people would know of it. So, on a whim, I figured I'd go straight to the horse's mouth and track down the owner of the property."

"Right. What was his name again?"

"Patrick Collins."

"And I take it you found him, little brother?"

"It wasn't hard: a quick search of land property records on the Government of Ontario website. Patrick Collins: lives in Forest Hill, Toronto. I called him up this morning, and we had a lovely chat."

"Learn anything useful?" Carl was still playing the skeptic, but I think it was mostly for show. Dad had him hooked.

"You could say that. So far, the only thing we ever knew about Collins was that he was a real estate investor. That doesn't say much. But guess what he does for a living?"

A glint in Carl's eye. "Medicine."

Dad smiled. "And guess where he went to medical school, kids?"

It was my turn. "Queen's University. Same as Coleman!"

"Class of '70. Turns out they were buds. In Collins' words, Geoff was 'a party animal, a real wild man, always knew where to score the best stuff.' I asked him if he'd heard from Coleman lately and he said no, not in over twenty-five years. In fact, he said he'd lost track of him shortly after Queen's, and asked me how Coleman was doing."

Carl chewed on that for a bit. "OK, it's a pretty striking coincidence, but legally it's still circumstantial. What's the thinking here? Coleman bumps into Élise, kills her, disposes of her body but panics about the car; so he calls his old buddy from med school who happens to own a remote property nearby. Maybe he tells him what he needs it for, probably not. Coleman enlists McLaughlin's help in disposing of the vehicle, and it's forgotten until hunters stumble upon it months later. Collins tells police at the time that he'd forgotten he even owned the place, and today he tells you he hasn't heard from Coleman since the late '70s."

"Obviously, Collins is lying about when he last heard from Coleman. I think he's covering for an old friend, who maybe has dirt on Collins."

Another pause. Carl looked annoyed by something. "But the property. I still don't . . . Do you know how long Collins has owned it?"

"According to Ontario land property records, since 1987."

"Wow. And you think that lot is remote now, imagine when he bought it. It would have felt like the moon. Must have bought it for a song. He's never done a thing with the property in all those years; I can believe that he'd forgotten about it. And if he's telling the truth and hasn't spoken to Coleman in decades . . ."

"He's lying, Carl. There are just too many coincidences."

Carl nodded. "OK, maybe. But in the end what does it all mean? Collins is an accomplice, after the fact. And again, you'd have a tough time proving it . . . unless Coleman himself speaks up."

Dad looked frustrated, and fatigue was starting to wear on him. He took off his glasses and pinched the bridge of his nose. "Look, I'm just trying to get the whole picture here. And until Coleman is in custody, I'll get my own answers . . . my way."

"*Tabarnak, Martin!*" Carl must have been pissed because he even pronounced Dad's name in French. "That's why we have police!" His phone began to buzz in his pocket, but he continued, not yet finished with his brother. "I can understand your frustration but for Chrissake stop playing amateur detective and let the cops do their job." He took a moment to let the message sink in and regain his composure, then withdrew his cell and flipped it open.

"Carl Lambert. Yes." A beat, and his face changed subtly. He then suddenly held out his palm in a "hold on" gesture. "When? . . . Where? . . . I see . . ." Carl's eyes were fixed straight ahead as he listened. There seemed to be a lot to take in. "Look, you wouldn't happen to know if they f—" Another beat as his hand went down. He nodded. "OK. No, of course, I understand. Can you keep me in the loop? Thanks, I appreciate that. Bye."

My uncle folded up his phone, shoved it back in his hip pocket, and blew out a huge sigh while Dad and I exchanged a "what now?" look.

"Well," he resumed, "the police have found Geoffrey Coleman."

Dad and I responded at the exact same moment, but with different questions.

"When?/Where?"

Carl's face didn't change. He looked like he was still processing. His voice was perfectly even. "Early this morning. Looks like he took a swan dive off the railway bridge in Heronford. I know the place. That bridge is over thirty metres high. Like a ten-storey building."

\*\*\*\*\*

Another pot of coffee was brewing. The three of us were sitting in our usual spots around the kitchen once again, with Carl leading the conversation, sharing what little he knew. Apparently, Geoffrey Coleman's crumpled body was found around 5:30 that morning on a stone-and-concrete pier beneath the Heronford railway trestle by some early-bird kayakers on the Heron River; the circumstances sounded eerily similar to when I was found on the North Rim of the Grand Canyon three weeks earlier, and I felt a faint shiver. The time of death wasn't yet pinpointed, but considering where he was when he called our house after 9:00 p.m., the time it took to get from there to Heronford, and the time his body was found, best guess had it somewhere between 4:00 and 5:30 in the morning. The height of the fall was precisely 30.4 metres. Death was instantaneous.

The initial shock seemed to be wearing off my dad, but it was still hard to guess what he was feeling. I doubt he even knew.

"Any mention of a note, by any chance?"

"Sorry, Martin, that's all I've got. The police are treating this as a suicide, but it's still an ongoing investigation so they're limited in what they can say, even to me." Then, after a moment, "But you never know."

Dad was quiet. He was still holding it together—'cause that's what Lamberts do, I guess—but I could tell he was struggling. There were still so many questions, and to have come this far only to be denied the answers was more than anyone, no matter how stoic, could be expected to endure.

"We were so close, you know?" Dad, feeling out loud.

More painful silence, until a random question bubbled up in my mind. "Where's Heronford?"

Carl picked up the cue. "About an hour and a half from here. You know, I've been thinking about that. We know for a fact that yesterday Coleman was in Kettering, in southwest Ontario. Apparently, he'd been living there for a while. Then we assume he learned that the police were looking for him so he goes AWOL.

Hops into his car and drives off in the middle of the night. And he ends up in Heronford? Kettering is a good six-hour drive from here; Heronford is less than two. What was Coleman thinking? I mean, if you're on the lam for murder would you flee in the direction of the place where you committed the crime? It doesn't make sense."

"Who knows what he was thinking," Dad muttered. "He was desperate, on the run. Who knows what a person does in that situation? It certainly isn't the most intuitive direction to take, I'll grant you, but maybe that was the point. Or maybe he was just keen on making a dramatic exit and the Heronford rail bridge seemed appropriate."

"See, and that's another thing. Does Coleman strike you as a brave person, I mean the type who could muster up the courage to hurl himself to his death from one hundred feet up onto jagged concrete and boulders? Hardly. I mean he was an anesthesiologist, for Chrissake. If anybody could come up with a quick and easy way to do himself in, it would be Coleman. A quiet OD from the comfort of his own living room or bathtub sounds more like his style. How did he sound on the phone? Did he sound at all scared or desperate?"

"No, drunk and obnoxious but not scared. But then I don't have any experience with suicidal people."

"Well, I do. I dunno, maybe it's my turn to overthink things, but this just doesn't feel right. Anyway, the police are going through his things now: his car in Heronford where they found it, and his place in Kettering. If they find anything we'll know soon enough."

# 40

In a welcome respite from what was fast becoming a very stressful weekend, that evening we were all invited to the Campbells for a swim and dinner. Dad figured that both Doug and Irene felt bad about having me fired from my volunteer position—especially since nothing ever came out of my indiscretion with D-Ray's files—and wanted to make sure there were no hard feelings. Dad countered that he'd bring wine and Carl would bring a musical instrument, and that it would be a truly festive way to ring out the summer.

Dad saw this as an unexpected opportunity to corner Doug about Coleman again; of course it wouldn't likely be a popular topic and he'd have to be a lot more discreet this time around. I'm not sure how Dad planned to manoeuvre the conversation in the direction he wanted, what kind of machinations he had in mind or even what new information he wanted to draw out of Doug, but ultimately, and sadly in a way, none of it was necessary.

As much as I was looking forward to our evening with the Campbells, the drive up there was another matter. I hadn't been to their house since I was a small child, and after all that I'd learned about my mom's disappearance I found the long ride to their mansion in the woods to be unnerving. I couldn't believe how isolated it was, especially after we turned off Highway 5, and I shuddered when I imagined how it would have been on that cold and rainy November evening all those years ago. That changed the moment we got to the house; from that point I felt a lot like Sam Gamgee arriving in Rivendell.

As we drove up the circular driveway, I gaped at the towering A-frame, the walls of glass, the stone chimneys—all three of them—the wrap-around balcony, the sweeping manicured lawns, and the drive of patterned interlocking stone. Campbell's Maserati and his monstrous Navigator were both on display outside of the three-car garage. Dad parked behind the USS Enterprise and we stepped out into wonderland.

Doug met us at the door and promptly gave us a comprehensive tour. I'd heard Dad use terms like "open concept," and "post-and-beam construction" to describe it, but when I entered the Campbells' home I finally saw what he was referring to. Doug was clearly amused by my "OOOOOs" and "AAAHHHHs," and while he didn't want to appear overtly boastful, you couldn't really blame him for showing off a bit either. The house was spectacular. The main floor was pretty much self-explanatory. It was vast. Everywhere was wood, cathedral ceilings with hammer trusses of solid BC fir, and breathtaking views to the south and west out of floor-to-ceiling windows. The kitchen area was all black granite and brushed stainless steel, with walls of cabinets and recessed lighting, and even a hidden wine cellar beneath the floor.

I watched Doug as he toured us around. He was every bit the lord of the manor, the undisputed master of all he surveyed. Even in his leather sandals, khaki shorts, and cornflower blue linen shirt, left untucked to cover his slight paunch, he was the picture of aristocracy: his perfect tan, his massive watch, the glint of gold jewellery on his fingers and around his neck, even the way he wore his Ray Ban aviators on his head to hold back his silver hair, all spoke of a casually worn wealth and confidence that are known only to the truly powerful. Carl seemed somehow unaffected by any of it beyond the natural inquisitiveness of a museum visitor but I didn't like what I saw in Dad's eyes: sadness, and something that resembled resignation.

The tour was followed by games of pool and foosball, which were followed by a swim, followed by a soak in the Jacuzzi, which in turn was followed by a glorious meal on the terrace: slow-cooked barbecued ribs and chicken and corn on the cob and baked potatoes and salads and roasted vegetables. Carl regaled us with his fiddle intermittently, and even Mother Nature contributed to the evening with a gorgeous sunset and a somehow complete absence of insects, save for the chirp of the crickets and a subtle spray of fireflies. By the time we were wrapping up dessert Dad's mood had mellowed, and he sat contentedly sipping coffee and trading travel stories with our hosts, who had apparently been everywhere. To my relief no one brought up the subjects of Mom or D-Ray or Geoffrey Coleman—Dad seemed to have had a change of heart—so I was pretty surprised toward the end of the evening when it was Carl who tested the waters.

"Doug," he said casually, "I don't know if you've heard but Geoffrey Coleman was found dead today in Heronford. They're calling it a suicide."

Doug hesitated just a moment upon hearing the news. I don't know if anyone else noticed, but from where I sat it was pretty conspicuous. His face didn't change, but his eyes seemed to flicker, as if he was trying to decide how he was going to react. It was just an instant, but it spoke volumes.

"Really," he said. "No, I hadn't heard. That's terrible. I know the police were looking for him; it was all over the news. They even gave me a call last week, asked if I'd heard from him. Obviously, I hadn't. Dreadful business he got himself into. Looks like you were right about him after all. Do you know how he died?"

It was dark and Carl's face was in the shade, impossible to read, illuminated only by the faint red glow of his pipe. There was a click as the tip of the pipe touched his teeth.

"Looks like he threw himself off the railway trestle there. You know it? It's a hundred-foot drop. Nasty way to go."

Doug was shaking his head solemnly, his lower lip drawn out in thought. Dad, for his part, hadn't said anything, hadn't even moved. He had his best poker face on, and there was no way to tell if he was drinking it all in and preparing to strike, or had had quite enough and was tuning out.

"How awful!" Irene gushed, then to her husband in a slightly more hushed tone, "Did Geoff have any family?"

*Geoff?*

"Oh, honey, I have no idea. I barely knew him. Heronford, eh?"

"That's where he was found this morning."

"Did he leave a suicide note?"

"Not that I've heard."

"Any chance it was an accident?"

A snorted chuckle from Carl: "Well, I guess anything is possible, but considering he was halfway across an over fourteen-hundred-foot railway bridge, almost one hundred feet above the river, in the wee hours of the morning some six hundred kilometres from home, I think it doubtful."

"Well, he was a troubled fellow, that's for sure." Then, for good measure: "From what I can make out."

Again I watched both my dad and Carl for their reactions, but no one rose to take the bait. There was a bit of a pause, but not an uneasy one. And that was the end of it. That conversation was done, maybe for good, and they were content to move on to other things.

By 10:00 p.m. the sun had long set, conversation was flagging, stomachs were full, and all the best jokes had been told. Dad was looking content but tired and while his brother was deflecting Irene's final offers for coffee, Dad discreetly gave me the "time

357

to go soon" look. I was in almost a dream-like state and, coaxing my body out of a ludicrously comfortable lawn chair with a groan befitting a much older person, I asked Irene where the washroom was. She offered me a choice of five, but in its relaxed state my brain barely registered the last two, and I wandered around for a while, going up staircases, opening random doors and peeking around corners before finally finding a lavatory.

I didn't use the first washroom I found: it was simply too luxurious, plus there were major apparatuses that baffled and intimidated me and I didn't want to risk misusing the equipment. The second one was simpler and more to my liking, but once I was done and stepped out, I found myself disoriented and no longer sure how to find my way back.

Turning a corner I saw a stairway heading down—a good sign—and a door left ajar at my right. Peeking in I saw a huge office, dimly lit yet somehow warm and inviting. The room was immaculate but also pristine in a way, like it was never used, like a museum display; you could almost hear the tour guide saying *"And this is where Dr. Campbell did his most important work in his latter years, on a desk that once belonged to Sir John A. McDonald blah blah blah . . ."* The space was dominated by a massive desk and upholstered office chair that occupied a place of power at the rear center of the room. There were big windows on either side of the desk and numerous bookcases and shelving units against the remaining walls, a fireplace, thick well-fed plants in exotic looking pots, elegant reading lamps, and a skylight above. In front of the desk and flanked by leather armchairs was a superb coffee table, handcrafted and featuring Asian motifs and what looked like inlaid ivory, and beneath that a fabulous fringed rug of some mysterious origin. Everywhere there were books, and art was hanging from every wall, along with countless framed photos and certificates. While a lot of guys might have a man cave to retreat into, stocked with an array of expensive electronic toys, Doug had his office. There was a maturity and a seriousness that

I loved about that. I could tell right away this was his sanctum, his holy-of-holies, a safe refuge where he could sit and work, read and think. No doubt there were other features I couldn't see, like hidden filing cabinets, a bar fridge and a wall safe, but I knew they were there, hiding amidst all the brass and green felt, the ferns and leather.

I heard my dad calling me from the stairs and was about to back out when I spotted the aquarium on the left side of the office. How I'd missed it until that moment was a mystery. The huge glass structure was easily two metres wide and built right into the wall, an oasis of light and colour on the edges of the gloom. "I'm here," I called back, moving deeper into the office instead of heading back out to join my dad. As I stared through the glass, the tank's primary occupant came into view: a lionfish, moving lazily from underneath an overhang of colourful rocks and coral. It was about ten inches long, with reddish brown vertical stripes that covered the fish's body from nose to tail. It bristled with spines, its ornate fins flowing in the faint artificial current like sails in a breeze.

"Pretty impressive, huh?"

I hadn't realized how quiet the aquarium was until my dad spoke up behind me, and I jumped a bit.

"Incredible," I said. My eyes wandered around the tank, searching for other movement. There were hardly any other fish, and the few that I saw were small and rather plain looking. "Especially compared to the little ones."

Dad's face got a bit closer to the glass, which fogged a bit under his breath. "Hmmm . . . I'm guessing those are his dinner. Lionfish are predatory." A beat. "We have to go."

He moved away to give me a few last moments to enjoy the spectacle before leaving. I continued to marvel at the fish, seemingly suspended and motionless above the gravel. I knew the spines were venomous and could cause horrific pain if touched, and thought how duplicitous it was that something so beautiful and graceful and majestic could be so dangerous.

The lionfish gave me a parting glance as I was turning away— *What? Leaving so soon?*—which left me with an uneasy feeling in my gut. I was going to make a joke about it to my dad when I noticed him staring at some of the photos and certificates on the wall beyond the desk. A few of them were framed diplomas which were completely illegible, written as they were in Latin with ornate gothic typefaces. But it was a photo that had seized Dad's attention, or more specifically many photos. It was a composite graduation photo, sixty or so smiling faces of young adults in neat black-and-white rectangular blocks. Many of the men wore longish hair and there were lots of thick sideburns and cheesy moustaches. Written in the center were the words: Faculty of Medicine, Queen's University, 1970. Dad's face was hovering inches away from the upper left side of the frame, his eyes zeroed in on the first three photos of the second row: all male, all bedecked in oversized glasses, all sporting the same baleful smirk.

Arranged alphabetically, the names under the mug shots read: Douglas A. Campbell, Geoffrey R. Coleman, and Patrick N. Collins.

\*\*\*\*\*

I would like to say that Dad, now armed with what looked like the final piece of the puzzle, stormed down to confront Doug Campbell in one final, no-holds-barred onslaught of righteous fury. In my imagination at least, during the months and years that followed, that ultimate confrontation did happen. After ten years of torment and uncertainty Dad could finally savour his glorious *"J'accuse!"* moment. In my mind, Dad returned to the patio, confronted Doug with all the facts, and succeeded in compelling him to confess to everything: he exposed Campbell's long-standing relationship with both Coleman and Collins, and his involvement with organized crime. He played out the whole scenario of the night of the murder: how Mom approached Campbell and confided her concerns and her evidence of Coleman's drug activities, activities that Campbell not only knew about but benefitted from; how Campbell called Coleman just after Mom left his house to tell him where to find her on the road; how Coleman murdered her in cold blood, then called him back asking for counsel on what to do with the body and the car, with Campbell suggesting the long-forgotten Collins' property; then, all these years later, with the mounting pressure of law enforcement on his back, how Coleman contacted his old med school buddy and headed back to Ferguston in desperation, while Campbell arranged—probably through his biker contacts—to have Coleman intercepted en route and tossed off the Heronford railway bridge, to simulate a suicide. Meanwhile Irene was shrieking in the background that none of this was true, it was all lies, all of it, wasn't it, Doug? Tell them that we can't come to their home and enjoy their hospitality and then accuse our hosts of such terrible things. Finally, Doug, overwhelmed with weight of guilt and the strength of the evidence Dad has assembled, crumbled into a wretched heap of sobs and *mea culpas*, admitting to everything, and wailing pleas for forgiveness. Ultimately Carl called the cops, who showed up a short time later and took Doug away, with Irene's anguished cries following them out the door.

But of course none of that happened. Dad wasn't a police detective, he was a schoolteacher; but he was smart enough to know he didn't have any evidence to support his theory, just a lot of conjecture, a few coincidences, and a burning need for resolution. He couldn't prove that Doug Campbell had been in touch with Coleman the night Mom disappeared, or at any other time for that matter. Nor could he prove that Campbell was involved in any kind of criminal activity or had connections with anybody outside the law, be they bikers, drug dealers or hired killers. All Dad had was a few connections around which he'd built a story that, appealing as it might seem, like the Kennedy assassination probably wouldn't stand up to the rigours of forensic scrutiny. Dad knew all this, and I'm sure the very thought of entertaining what amounted to a conspiracy theory must have turned his stomach. Plus he'd been wrong before, with D-Ray; he not only fell flat on his face that time, but succeeded in severely pissing off a potentially dangerous person. He wasn't going to make the same mistake again. Dad was a born skeptic, and while he might have had a glaring blind spot when it came to Mom, he was also well aware of it. So he said nothing.

*****

And in the end, he didn't have to. On Sunday afternoon, we learned that police had brought Doug Campbell in for questioning. Apparently, detectives had spent all of Saturday turning Geoffrey Coleman's Kettering home upside down, a task that was no doubt a whole lot simpler than it was at the estate of David Raymond. Coleman, for all his faults, was no hoarder and his house gave up its secrets quite readily. Most useful among them were scores of boxes found in his basement, containing hundreds of audiotapes dating back decades. It seems Coleman had made a habit of recording telephone conversations, thinking "Hey, you never know, they could come in handy someday, right?" although he might not have suspected that "someday" would be after his death. He secretly recorded conversations with other doctors, hospital staff, patients, medical suppliers, his accountant, the mechanic who serviced his Audi, drug dealers, prostitutes, loan sharks, everyone. It was a habit he'd begun shortly after his residency in the mid '70s— different technology, same results—and continued until the very day he died. He even recorded the drunken exchange he had with me.

Investigators had hit the jackpot. While only the starting point, the tapes would reveal that Geoffrey Coleman was implicated in a sprawling network of illegal activity, mostly related to the trafficking of prescription drugs, spanning over two decades and stretching across huge chunks of Ontario and Québec. Closer to home, they showed that Coleman's connection with Doug Campbell had been uninterrupted since med school, and that Campbell was up to his teeth in the drug trade, especially in the early years. Later on it looked like Doug was trying to distance himself from his old school chum, but when Coleman's career started to fall on hard times in the early '90s Campbell was actively involved in bringing Coleman to Ferguston. He got him a position on the surgical staff at FRHC as an anesthesiologist, a place at the clinic for a private practice, and a whole bunch of new connections, with the simple proviso that he keep his nose clean . . . and if not entirely clean, at least out of the spotlight.

Most important to Dad and me, of course, were the conversations that were recorded on and around the night Mom vanished. It was obvious from the tapes that Coleman and my mom had had a difficult history from the early going, and most upsetting for Dad were the handful of brief but really uncomfortable conversations between the two: the first few calls with Coleman sounding overly friendly and awkwardly flirtatious, Mom clearly annoyed but trying to remain professional and keep her cool; and the later ones with Mom calling Coleman on his shit and threatening to go higher up the food chain, Coleman desperate and pleading. More calls to Campbell who continues to put him off, telling Coleman to "just deal with it," until the night before the dinner when Campbell says he'll try to "talk some sense into her." Of course it didn't work out that way, as Campbell reported to Coleman the moment after Mom left his house. He doesn't specifically suggest what action to take, but what he did say was chilling: "If you leave now you can still catch her on Baker [Side Road]; there won't be anybody else out there at this time of night."

There were two more calls that night. In the first, Coleman tells Campbell that he'd "met Lambert on the road" and that "she won't talk anymore." He doesn't sound panicked at all, just a bit tired. Campbell's response is to "leave her there for now and head back into town and make sure you're seen," that he'd "look after Lambert" but that Coleman would have to deal with her car as soon as possible. The second call went something like this:

Coleman: "OK, I think I'm good. I called Raymond into the office for an emergency appointment. He obliged, can you believe it? At this hour? Anyway, I got what I need. If anyone ever finds her car, they won't be looking for me, I promise you. Plus I called her husband from her cellphone: as far as he's concerned, she's still on the road. So what about the car?"

Campbell: "You'll need to get someone up here before first light and move it. You can't do it alone. I've got a spot you can hide it; it's Patty Collins' property, some twenty-five miles northwest of town. It's in the middle of nowhere; nobody ever goes there. Write this down—"

Coleman: "Hold on, hold on, I gotta find a fucking pen, hold on, Jesus . . ."

Campbell: "Fuck, Geoffrey, the shit you get me into."

Coleman: "Hey, I'm sorry Doug. You know we had to do something."

Campbell: "You can't do anything right, can you?"

Coleman: "Hey I'm dealing with it. Don't worry."

Campbell: "Don't worry?? She was still breathing, you idiot!"

[silence]

Coleman: "Shit! Really?"

Campbell: "Yes, really."

[silence]

Campbell: "It's OK. I took care of it."

Coleman: "Where . . . did you . . . put her?"

Campbell: "Don't worry about that. Better you don't know. You just worry about ditching the car. Find someone you trust, and pay them whatever you have to. And for fuck sake don't say anything."

Coleman: "'kay. I know just the person. And Doug?
Campbell: "What?"
Coleman: "I'm sorry about this."
Campbell: "Fuck, Geoff. Once this has died down, assuming we're not both serving life sentences, you're getting the fuck out of Ferguston. You hear me? I don't care if you end up working the cash at a Shoppers Drug Mart in Flin Flon. I'm done with you. Got a pen? Here are the directions . . ."

\*\*\*\*\*

There were two final conversations at the end of Coleman's life that were worth noting; they, along with a number of other earlier ones, were recorded on a pocket-sized digital device that was found in his car in Heronford. The first one was recorded not long after he'd spoken to me. It was short. He'd called Doug again, telling him that the police were on his tail and that he needed help. After a few moments marked by angry sighs and muttered "What the fuck, Geoff?'s, Doug told him to pack his things, prepare to get out of town, and to call him back in twenty minutes. He'd tell him where to go. The second call was even shorter:
Coleman: "Doug. I'm ready to go. What do I do? I'm scared, man."
Campbell: "Don't worry about it. You sober enough to drive?"
Coleman: "Yeah, I think so. Where should I go?"
Campbell: "Look I'll help you out, but you've got to do what I say. Can you do that? Can you be rational for a minute?"
Coleman: "Sure, Doug. I'll be OK. Just tell me what to do."
Campbell: "That's my boy. OK. I want you to get in your car and drive north. You and I are going to have to meet up at some point and—"
Coleman: "What, you mean Ferguston?? Are you nuts?"
Campbell: "Shut up, Geoff. No, of course not Ferguston. You're going to drive to Heronford. You know where that is? If

not, use your GPS. It's a long drive and it's late, I know, but if you don't do anything stupid and draw attention to yourself, you'll be fine. You sure you're good to drive?"

Coleman: "Yeah. I'm good. I'll get a coffee on the way out. So I go to Heronford. What then?"

Campbell: "I can't get there myself tonight, but I have a friend who lives nearby. He owes me a favour. There's a coffee shop and gas station just as you enter town from the south. Wait in the parking lot. What are you driving?"

Coleman: "A blue Ford Focus."

Campbell: "How the mighty have fallen. OK. If you leave now, you'll be there by 3:30, 4:00. I'll get down there as soon as I can. Meanwhile my friend will find you, and he'll take care of you."

Coleman: "Thanks, Doug. What then?"

Campbell: "One thing at a time, Geoff. Just stay calm, and drive safely. Wouldn't want to have an accident."

Coleman: "Thanks again, man. You're a life saver."

# 41

Monday morning I left the house early, leaving Dad alone to face the inevitable onslaught of reporters that were bound to start calling or showing up at our door, now that Doug Campbell's role in the whole story had been revealed. One of the perks of being twelve is that you got to bail on stuff like that.

Labour Day broke warm and sunny, but breezy; in fact, it was the unsettling rattle of the wind shaking my bedroom window in its frame that got me out of bed. Shredded low-lying clouds hurried across the sky, causing the dappled shadows of leaves and branches on my floor, like grasping hands, to fade in and out.

I was thinking that this might be my last day of summer holidays—the option of going to school the next day was still on the table—so I was determined to make the most of it. Soon enough I was going to be spending the lion's share of my time indoors, and I didn't want to be kicking myself for not having taking advantage of the opportunities when they came. I did that a lot.

Plus I wanted to see Billie again. I was still feeling terrible about the last time we'd spoken at length, that night in the Grand

Canyon. I'd said some awful things, things that weren't true but I'd said them anyway in an effort to injure. Whatever she was, Billie had the feelings of a kid and I knew I'd hurt them. I'd been surprised and relieved that she'd come back since then, but she left before we could talk. I had more questions than ever, and knowing that each time I saw her could be the last, I decided that morning to head to the cemetery and hope I'd find her there.

She was easy to find, a bright purple blot on the rolling green lawn of the cemetery, but I felt an instant twinge of unease to see she wasn't alone. Billie appeared to be in conversation with an adult, a woman, wearing—I determined as I approached—a military dress uniform. They were next to a fresh gravesite. It was hard to tell the woman's age. Her back was turned to me and her hair was tied up under a hat or beret of some kind, and while there was a restrictiveness and severity to the uniform, her body language suggested a softness in her manner. She was looking upward as she spoke, her head tilted a bit, reflective, and her hands were expressive. Next to her, Billie looked as relaxed as I've ever seen her with an adult. She was nodding a lot, sometimes glancing over at the gravestone or playing idly with small clumps of soil, other times looking up and saying something, perhaps asking a question. If she saw me, she gave no indication.

I lay my bike down as gently and quietly as I could and plunked myself down next to another grave marker, enjoying the sun and content to wait out Billie's chat with the lady soldier. After a few minutes the woman held out her hand and helped Billie up, and once she was up, held on to her hand for a moment. I couldn't hear from where I sat but I could tell what was going on: the woman had clearly noticed Billie's elevated temperature and was no doubt asking her if she was OK. Happened all the time. Billie smiled and gave a half shrug and pumped her hand again, to show she was fine, and the woman then cupped Billie's cheek, and touched her shoulder. There was an affection in the gesture that Billie seemed to appreciate and she was still smiling sweetly as the woman, with a few more words and a friendly wave, turned away and walked toward the parking lot.

*****

"Someone you know?"

"Her name is Corporal Audrey. She's really nice."

"What were you talking about?"

"A friend of hers was just buried here. Another soldier."

It took a second or two, but the story came back to me. It had been the big news item in town during the week Dad and I were in the US, and was eventually overwhelmed by all the D-Ray/Coleman/Campbell hoopla afterward. Private Gregory Robert Johnson was killed by a roadside bomb in Kandahar on August 15th, making him the first soldier from Ferguston to die in combat since World War II. He was twenty-one. Rather than be buried at the National Military Cemetery in Ottawa, Johnson's family decided he should be buried at Lakeview Cemetery in Ferguston, like his maternal great-grandfather, Sgt. Arthur Smithson, who died during the Battle of Passchendaele in 1917.

"She talked about a lot of things. I didn't understand it all, but she was really nice about it."

"Like what, for instance?"

"Well, for one thing she explained about leaving coins on graves. She said people have been doing it for a long time. For army people, she said that a coin left on a grave is a way of telling the dead soldier's family that you came by to pay your respects. If you leave a penny it means you just visited; if you leave a nickel it means you trained with them, a dime says you served with them, and a quarter means that you were with them when they died."

"Interesting. I didn't know that. What else?"

"Oh, stuff about why countries go to war with other countries, and how the old men who are in charge of those countries send their young people to fight, and why those young people choose to join armies knowing that they could be killed and their families will never see them again. And how many are killed and if they're on your side they're called 'heroes'; and how many more come back badly hurt, and when they get home they aren't the same any more, and some even try to hurt themselves; and how after they come home people don't think of them as much, especially not the old men who sent them off to fight in the first place."

What in the world does a twelve-year-old small-town kid say to that? I said nothing at first, then tried a different tack.

"I'm sorry I got so mad at you that time. I shouldn't have."

Billie glanced at me for a second, trying to parse what I was talking about, then gave a quick dismissive head shake. The wind was picking up, and she daintily pulled out a strand of hair that had been blown across her eyes. Then, without a word she stood and extended her hand, and when I didn't respond right away, she wiggled her fingers a bit.

"Come," she said.

I took her warm hand and allowed her to pull me up to my feet. We began to walk westward toward the path that would take us downhill and to the old part of Lakeview. She held on to my hand the entire way.

She was quiet for a bit, looking over the burial markers, running her fingertips over the engraved letters of the stones as she walked past them. Her face was solemn, and something else . . .

"You're not happy today," I ventured after a moment. "I didn't know you could be happy or sad."

"I feel what Billie feels." She looked around again. "I've learned a lot since I've been here," she continued, "through Billie and others. There's a lot I can pick up from just watching people, but what I've been able to learn by walking in your shoes for a bit, feeling what you feel—"

"By pretending to be a person?"

"Well, it's more than pretending. It's like if you were to dress up like a cat and suddenly have great night vision and an appetite for mice." She paused, looking for words. "It's part of the reason I do this: to experience the world in ways I wouldn't normally." A beat. "In the same way that what I am is outside of your experience, what Billie feels, what all of you feel, is outside of mine. It's really complicated: you have no idea."

This Billie wasn't a little girl. Despite the convincing façade, I could see that now more than ever. Her voice, her words, even her level gaze, all came from a much, much older being. An ancient one, even.

"You mean you don't have emotions, like we do?"

"Oh, sure I do. Lots. Most you couldn't come close to understanding."

Now it was my turn to pause. In all the depictions of aliens, I'd never seen one that portrayed them as having emotions: they were always cold, calculating, dispassionate. Billie continued.

"Our emotions are just different. For one thing, because I don't have to worry about time there's no panic, no anxiety, no boredom, but there's also no urgency. It affects the way you react to things. And because I've never known another entity but myself, I've never been lonely, and there's never been anything to be afraid of."

Billie stopped and took in her surroundings, the perfect green lawn sloping downward to the west, the scattered trees and the slabs of grey and pink granite.

"I'm still getting used to the things you have to deal with all the time: sadness, guilt, shame, hate, anger, fear. Interesting, but wow, I don't envy you. But I've also learned how you hold on to things that you know won't be around for long. It's nice, but it's sad too."

She looked directly at me, her eyes at once full of wonder and confusion.

"You're so alone and you're so . . . I don't know . . . limited . . . temporary . . ."

I thought for a moment. "You mean 'finite'?" Good word. I was pleased with myself: Billie wasn't the only one speaking like a grown-up.

"Finite," she said as if trying on the word for first time. "Yes. Finite. Everything and everyone you know is gone so quickly. You get attached, to people especially, and then they're just . . . gone. On another level, you just barely start to understand things, you just begin to learn, to see and to appreciate and . . . and suddenly it's over. How do you *stand* it?"

By "you" Billie was referring to the entirety of humanity, for as long as there'd been humanity. This was so beyond anything I'd ever contemplated that I just stared at her; my mouth hung open for a bit, as if I were going to offer something resembling an answer, but I just snapped it shut and gave a weak half shrug. Billie looked down and away, a bit embarrassed as if realizing her question was more than I could process, and continued walking. We were quiet again, Billie scrutinizing the grass and me looking up at the clouds as they began to pile up, crowding out the blue.

I let an appropriate amount of time pass before I clumsily attempted to re-engage. And I had some questions of my own.

"Soooo . . . You're just kind of here to watch and learn, right?"

"Yeah."

"You take the shape of people . . . and other things too, I guess . . . and interact with others to understand us?"

"You and your world. That's right."

"Not just as Billie."

"Right."

"So, I'm not the only one you speak with."

"No, no. I speak with a lot of people: men, women, children, old people, from here and . . . elsewhere."

"Plus me? All at the same time?"

Billie laughed, the prettiest, most genuine, and totally unexpected sound given the surroundings.

"Yes, Justin, all at the same time." She paused for a bit. "I've learned a lot."

That much was pretty obvious. I wanted to tell her that she was fast outgrowing her Billie persona, but dreaded the thought of her adapting a new one.

I was quiet for a bit. So many questions.

"About when I hitched a ride with you, back in the Grand Canyon: can you tell me what I saw?"

"Ah, yes," she said grinning. "Did you like it?"

"It was . . . big. Overwhelming."

"Yeah, I guess it must have seemed that way."

"What was it?"

"Which part?"

"Ummm . . ." How does one even begin to describe the indescribable?

"Well, you were right on part of it: the cloud you saw was me . . . us."

"And all those flashes of light? They were like stars going on and off. Millions of them."

Billie's smile got a bit bigger. "I bet you can guess that."

Shrug.

"Entry points."

"You mean, like when I see you . . . ?"

She nodded.

"Wow. I guess you're busy."

"Well, like I said: there's a lot of me."

"And that endless . . . I don't know what to call it. It was like a wall at the back of everything, a wall that was made like . . ."

"Cells. Or a dragonfly wing," she completed the thought. "Not sure what you'd call that. Kind of like an archive, or a big library, but one that divides and grows with changing timelines. Each one is full of time and stories." She paused for a second. "You know, Justin, you're very lucky. You're the only human being in history who will ever see that. It's never happened before. It'll be interesting to see what, if anything, it does to you."

I paused for a moment, trying to keep together thoughts that were in danger of blowing away in a thousand different directions, like November leaves.

"So . . . where do you come from, like, originally? How did you become what you are, or do you even know?"

"My origin, you mean?" Billie asked, still smiling. "I guess bits and pieces gradually came together, squeezed out or scraped off from other places, universes, dimensions. We weren't all the same at the beginning, but we learned to share everything we were, everything we knew and loved. Eventually we became a single consciousness, one mind that continues to grow, always searching, always discovering, always learning."

"But . . . you use words like 'gradually' and 'eventually' and 'in the beginning.' So you must experience time in a way."

"Yeah, in a way. But remember, where I am there is only me . . . us. Sure, I have a beginning but it's not a subject I spend any time on. I don't have much of a history; I haven't done much, and nothing ever really happens to me. All I do, all I've ever done, is grow and learn. The future doesn't mean much to me either. For me, it's kind of always now."

"I know the feeling." I pushed out a sigh and changed direction. "And Billie is . . ."

"Like I told you, the Billie you know is a copy of a real person," she responded. Then, sensing I needed more info, offered: "Not someone you'd ever meet. She exists in other timelines; she's just never existed here. It's a lot safer that way: I wouldn't want to run into myself, right? And there are a lot of people to choose from. You can't imagine just how many people there are who are never born in any given timeline."

In later years I would do the math. A woman produces roughly one hundred thousand eggs in her lifetime, while a man creates about four trillion sperm. That makes

four-hundred    quadrillion—400,000,000,000,000,000—
potential combinations—or, to put it another way, potential
siblings—for every single person ever born in the history of
humanity.

"Plus," Billie continued, "she has a lot in common with you. I
thought she'd be a good person for you to get close to."

"And you've never shown anyone else . . . what you really are?
Where you're from?"

"No, not precisely."

"Then why me?"

"Well, it was reaching the point where the simplest thing was
just to show you, and hope you didn't freak out completely. I was
never really worried, to be honest: you were a pretty safe choice.
And it's not such a big deal, as far as I'm concerned. As long as it
doesn't happen too often, or on a huge scale, your knowing doesn't
affect things much over the long run."

"How can you say that?" I asked. "Doesn't just your talking
with me or the other people you interact with have an effect on
what happens? Just by being here you're probably changing how
my whole life will play itself out. Like I mentioned before, you
cause stuff to happen that wouldn't have happened otherwise. And
not to guilt you out or anything, but Mrs. Worthington probably
wouldn't have died if you hadn't shown up on Barrette Street when
you did. How can you just let that happen?"

Billie gave me a gentle, level stare, breathed in deeply through
her nose, and paused a bit before speaking again. By then we'd
arrived at the middle of the old section of the cemetery, and had
stopped next to the mausoleum in the center.

"First of all, you don't know that, Justin. You can't know all
the different outcomes that are possible at any given moment. Sure,
some are more likely than others, but the possibilities are endless.
*Literally* endless. What if I told you that in another timeline Mr.
Worthington had a heart attack at the wheel, or that in another a
wasp flew into the car while he was driving and made him swerve

into the oncoming truck and *both* he and his wife were killed, or in others they survive that intersection only to be killed a few minutes later, or that they died in a house fire hours before, or—much more likely still—that neither was even born at all? Second, from where I sit, these are just tiny details. Less than insignificant."

"Easy for you to say—"

"Justin, you have to understand something: as interesting as you people are, you only occupy the tiniest space in the universe, and for just the shortest sliver of time. Galaxies collide, stars are born and burn out along with the planets that orbit them, species become extinct while new ones appear. It happens *all the time*, everywhere, and it's been happening since the beginning. I hate to be the one to tell you this, but in the grand scheme of things the daily events in people's lives don't change anything."

The wind was picking up and she wrapped her arms around herself to keep warm. Her hair was beginning to fly in all directions.

"That's cold, Billie."

"Really? What, you think that I'm supposed to be somehow all knowing and all good? I'm not. First, if I were all knowing I wouldn't be here, but it's a big universe and there are still a lot of rocks to turn over. And second, I'm not good or bad. Those are human inventions. I don't have some great, noble, divine purpose. I just am: I learn and I grow. That's it. I do have emotions and I even get excited about things, but aside from that I don't have much of a personality. What you like about me is all Billie. She's sweet and kind and caring of others. And you're right: she wouldn't want to hurt anybody. But as for me, as I actually am, well . . . I'm more interested in the bigger picture. And the big picture is really, really big, Justin."

"Then what's to stop you from wiping us out completely? You could do like the aliens in a book I read and blow us up to put in an interstellar freeway."

"Justin—"

"Or you could copy an asteroid and point yourself at the Earth, or a supermassive black hole and put it right next to our sun."

"No. I'd never do that."

"Why not? If we're so insignificant, what would you care?"

Billie looked at me flatly.

"First of all, even *I* don't mess with black holes: those things are weird. Second, do you have any idea just how incredibly rare you are?"

"Really?" I asked.

"I may be just starting to understand people on a personal level—like I said, you're complicated—but I've been able to get the big picture of your species in general and others like it. Civilizations like yours don't happen very often. When they do, I notice. Yours are the rarest. Some are, in a funny way, a lot more like me: billions of separate organisms that come together as a single mind, kind of like the biggest termite colony you could imagine. They usually survive the longest and progress the furthest. You guys are like the other extreme: billions of individuals fighting to be different from one another, and yet you're all the same deep down. You're all the same species, made of the same stuff, you all need and want the exact same things, and yet you're so . . . I dunno . . . tribal. You fight and destroy each other over it. It's like you'd rather protect whatever little group you belong to than protect your own species. It's crazy and it's sad. Civilizations like yours, as interesting and colourful as they are, don't hang around for long. I know: I've watched it happen over and over and over again, in endless timelines, right here. Cities, countries, empires are born, they rise and they fall and get replaced all the time. They don't always look exactly the same, but even you would recognize the patterns: *they* never change."

She looked out again, over the town, the lake, the hills beyond.

"Do you know what an opportunity has been given to you?" she continued. "You're poised to do great things, you know, in spite of everything. You're right there on the edge. There are so many other species out there—and some right here on this planet—that are blessed with intelligence, with culture, with a sense of history, but can do so little with it in a practical sense, or through no fault of their own they get wiped out before they can go any further. You, on the other hand, can do so, so much. You're just reaching the point where you're not only asking the really big important questions, but you're starting to be able to answer them. That's huge. You're a rare precious moment of your universe actually becoming self-aware. And you weren't that even a couple of hundred years ago.

"And yet you spoil it. You make huge advances and then spend so much effort trying to undo them. You're so afraid of things, of what you don't understand and even of each other because you think of yourselves as all so different, and rather than learn about what you're afraid of you stay afraid and then insist, even fight, to be wrong. Why do you insist on being wrong about so much?"

For a brief moment, by the way she was staring at me, I thought she was expecting a legitimate answer, a real explanation, that I was going to have to justify the actions of the entire human species. Instead she just smiled at me, shook the hair from her face and turned toward the prevailing wind. "Anyway . . ." she said, putting a gentle end to the conversation.

The sky had darkened and the wind had picked up. A lot. I wanted to stay and talk, make up for lost time, but the weather was changing.

# 42

B y the time we reached the spot where I'd left my bike, I could
see right away that the weather situation was worse than I'd
thought. This wasn't just the heralding of a quick summer storm
that would be over in ten minutes; this was a major system coming
in, and it looked angry. The sky to the southeast was almost black,
and although the wind seemed to be blowing from every direction
at once, that dark sky was definitely coming our way, in a hurry.
And the wind was cold, as cold as anything I'd felt in Ferguston
since the spring. It was time to go. Normally it took about twenty
minutes to get home from the cemetery, and I wasn't sure I'd get
there before the skies opened up.

"Can I ride with you?"

I wasted valuable seconds in utter, if useless, befuddlement.
*"What??"*

"I could ride with you on your bike. I'll sit, you pedal."

"You're kidding, right?"

"I've never ridden on a bike before. It'll be fun."

"Why do we have to ride double? You could just pop a bike
out of thin air."

She looked a bit hurt, sulky. "I want to ride with you."

Shaking my head, I straddled the front of the bike and turned to Billie. "OK, climb aboard."

Billie stood there for a moment, smiling awkwardly, like a little kid who's been asked to ride a pony having never seen one before. She looked at me, then at the bike, then back at me and might have stood there all day had not the first plump raindrop splashed my face.

*"Get on!!!"*

I'd never ridden double on a bike before, not even as a passenger with my dad, and the crazy wind combined with the added weight of Billie made it nearly impossible to get going. I wobbled a lot, over-compensated, and nearly fell over a few times. Billie, meanwhile, thought it was the funniest thing ever, and despite the cold wind she laughed maniacally the whole time.

*Glad someone is having fun.*

By the time I got to the main entrance to the cemetery on George Street, the rain had started for real. The wind was picking up as well, and beyond the hills ahead of me the black wall of the storm was closing in. I was going to ask Billie if there was a way she could intervene in some other-dimensional fashion, and only the prospect of reappearing a day or two in the future and miles away from home kept me from doing so . . . that, and the fact that my cellphone had begun to ring.

"Justin, there's a big storm coming. Where are you?"

Dad. Serious enough, but not panicked. That was good.

"I'm on George near the cemetery. The storm is already here." I was hunched over, shielding the phone from the rain.

"You OK?"

"I'm fine. Just wet."

"You want me to come and get you?"

"I don't think it would be worth it, I'll be soaked by the time you get here . . . Besides there's no shelter until I get down the hill."

*Not that I'm going to get much wetter.*

"Should I meet you someplace?"

"How about downtown? I might be able to get there before the worst hits."

"All right. Find a place to wait indoors and call me when you get there."

"OK."

"And be careful going down the hill."

I slapped the phone closed. The rain was really driving now, the gullies on the side of George Street had become churning muddy canals racing downhill, carrying wrecked branches and other refuse. I stood on the pedals, driving forward, head down and eyes ahead. It was a short ride to the intersection with Highway 5, and we had to stop again at a red light. The traffic on the highway was slow in the blinding rain; vehicles rumbled through, headlights on, sending up a cold spray in all directions. There was a sudden crackle and boom of a nearby lightning strike and as we waited for the light to change, I wished not for the last time that I'd paid better attention to the sky and left sooner. I was looking at the grim reality of heading down the steep incline of Morin Hill in the driving rain, with lousy visibility and a passenger behind me; and as much as I was convinced deep down that Billie would never allow me to be harmed, I was more than a bit unnerved.

The light finally changed, and with a half-turn backward I told Billie to hold on. Until that moment she'd been hanging on to the bike's saddle with both hands, but as soon as I spoke, I felt her arms reach around my midsection as she clasped her hands together. Her warmth, unaffected by the wind and rain, was a blessing and it gave me the courage to plunge forward down Morin Hill.

The ride to downtown was only about a kilometre, but most of it was downhill and I spent it largely with my hands squeezing the handle brakes. If anything, the rain had worsened and the overloaded gullies along George were spilling their banks, brown water racing downhill in a torrent. At one point a huge truck—a cement mixer, appropriately enough—suddenly blared its horn at me as it roared past, startling me enough to cause me to wobble a bit. For just a fraction of a second I thought I'd topple over, spilling both of us onto the road and into the path of oncoming traffic. I even had an ironic flash as I realized that we'd just about reached the entrance to the FRHC driveway:

*If I got smooshed, at least the ambulance ride would be a short one. Ha, ha.*

By the time we got to the bottom of the hill, where George Street intersects with Morin in the west and Centre in the east, the wind had dropped almost to nothing. The rain, on the other hand, was as strong as ever. In fact, in the relative shelter of the basin, the rain came straight down in a grey curtain that obscured everything. Visibility as we rode east along Centre Street into downtown was almost nil. I was also struck by how deserted the streets were, which is when it dawned on me that it was Labour Day and that almost nothing was going to be open. So much for finding refuge in a shop or a café. An awning would have to do.

"That was fun," Billie chirped behind me. Despite the cold, the wet and the relative dark, she was having the time of her life.

"Glad you liked it," I said evenly. "We're not doing it again." As if on cue, a clap of thunder boomed overhead to add emphasis.

Arriving at McDonald Street, which more or less marked the beginning of downtown Ferguston, was like rolling into a ghost town. There was not a soul to be seen, and only a handful of cars parked along the streets, although with the sporadic gusts driving needles of rain into my face and forcing me to keep my eyes down most of the time, I wasn't getting the full picture. Still, I was doing my best to keep at least one eye open for my dad, and as I turned right on McDonald, I caught a brief glimpse of a lonely vehicle a couple of blocks away coming up Centre than veering left onto Victoria. With any luck it wouldn't be a long wait. We continued south one more block, then turned left onto McEwan.

At the intersection of McDonald and McEwan, occupying the southeast corner, was the Baxter Hotel. It was as much of a historical landmark as we had in Ferguston. It was the largest and the oldest hotel in town, and sat facing the Ferguston Museum—formerly the Ferguston train station—directly across McDonald Street. The Baxter took up the whole southeast corner of the intersection, and had a great big burgundy awning that wrapped around the building's west and north faces, covering almost the entire width of the sidewalk. I dismounted my bike—after explaining to a disappointed Billie that the ride was over—leaned it against the north wall of the hotel, pulled out my phone and called my dad to tell him where to find us. He was already on his way. I considered stepping into the hotel lobby to dry off a bit, but the prospect of missing my dad when he drove past and the fear of having my bike stolen—in Ferguston that wasn't out of the question, even during a monsoon—were enough to keep me outside. Standing only a few feet from the curb, under the dark shelter of the awning and the steady scolding of the rain pounding above, I kept my eyes fixed eastward down McEwan for the first sight of Dad's car.

"Justin—"

Billie's voice was cut off by a sudden screech of a heavy vehicle braking in the rain and the abrupt thud of a tire striking the curb. The right front tire and neon green fender had climbed onto the sidewalk from behind, only a few feet away from where I was standing. I never saw it coming. I was so startled by the appearance of the truck that I froze, and was abstractly aware of the almost violent opening and slamming of the truck's door. It was only Billie's voice and her firm, hot grip around my arm that snapped me out of it.

"*Justin!!!*"

"Yeah, Juth-tin!"

David Raymond splashed around the front of his truck in an awkward lurch, then tried to regain his composure by leaning against a parking meter less than two metres from me. He stood like that for a moment, his grey-green eyes fixed on me, seemingly impervious to the downpour. He'd left his truck idling, which I didn't take as a good sign, and he was toying with something metallic in his hands which I'd thought at first were his keys, except no, you idiot, his keys were obviously still in the ignition. He gave no indication that he'd noticed Billie; for that moment at least I was his whole world.

"You didn't think I'd forget about you, did you?"

I stared at him. I'm not sure I was breathing.

"Huh? Your ol' buddy?"

I looked beyond him down McEwan Street. The rain was still pelting down, and there was no movement except the water rushing into the storm drains and the swaying of the street lights over the next intersection. Another violent crack of thunder reverberated across town. Raymond didn't seem to hear it.

"You didn't think just because the cops figured out I didn't kill your ma that everything would be okey-dokey, that we'd be chill . . . off the hizzle?" Despite my fear, or maybe because of it, the smart-ass voice spoke up in my head.

*God, is there anything more painfully awkward than hearing such a hopelessly white guy trying to sound street?*

"See, I'm still pissed. You and your dad have been trying to fuck me over for years. I heard what he said on the news. Think that doesn't stay with a person? Cops drop the charges and people still think I'm a killer. So, I figure fine, maybe I should give 'em something to talk about. Whaddaya think . . . Juth-tin?

"My dad is going to be here any minute. He's picking us up." It was all the bravado I could muster. Again the voice:

*Oh well, the good news is that you're already so wet that if you piss yourself now no one will notice.*

"D'at so? You know, I kinda doubt that. I think you guys are all alone. Ain't nobody out here gonna help you."

"You don't scare us!" Billie shrieked. Her voice sounded like an outraged gull fighting for scraps in a McDonald's parking lot: sincere but not exactly threatening. Obviously, the thing that inhabited Billie's body had no reason to be frightened of anything; her human-shaped shell was reacting instinctively, but it ended there. This was theatre, method acting at its best.

"I don't? Hmm . . . Maybe I'm not trying hard enough." Raymond seized the door handle on the passenger side of his truck and swung it open. He then lifted his hands to reveal what he'd be holding, prying open the shining edge of a switchblade. "Get in the fucking truck. Now."

I looked around, trying to keep panic at bay long enough to weigh my options. McEwan Street had become a river. Behind me was Billie, and beyond her, leaning against the wall of the Baxter Hotel, was my bike. Raymond was only a few feet from me: even with his many injuries reducing his mobility, he'd be able to grab me before I ever got close to it. Billie was my only way out.

"I said, get in the fucking truck, you little shit. Both of you."

I almost said it. The words *"Billie, get us out of this"* were on my lips, and to this day I wonder what she would have done if I'd said them. But I never did. I didn't have to. Looking over Raymond's shoulder I could see the unmistakable shape of Dad's car, ploughing through the torrent that was now McEwan, about a block away. He was moving toward us, his progress painfully slow through the deluge, but in a moment, he'd recognize Raymond's truck and he'd accelerate. I was saved . . .

. . . or at least I thought so for a moment, until I saw the red turn signal of his car begin to flash. He was turning south down Bank Street. He hadn't seen me. *SHIT!!!*

"BILLIE! IT'S MY DAD! *RUN!!!!*"

She bolted, as if launched from a cannon. Raymond was distracted by Billie's movement for just an instant, but it was enough to distance myself from him by maybe a couple of steps. Raymond's agility despite his handicap astonished me; I never would have believed he could move so quickly. He reminded me of a crocodile: not difficult to outdistance over the long haul, but deadly within short range. He made a grasp for me with his free hand and I would have been caught if not for the rain. His hand slid down over the wet skin of my forearm and I gave a violent shake when he reached my wrist to set myself free.

Raymond was now fully in the middle of the sidewalk, spreading his arms wide, trying to corral me. He was trying to close the distance, and corner me against the wall of the hotel. He seemed to have lost interest in Billie, who incomprehensibly had come to a full stop a few metres ahead. Why wasn't she running? Why wasn't she coming to help me? Instead she just stood there, pointing to the opening of the Art Alley only a few metres away.

"Go!" I yelled. But instead of running down the alley, Billie came back, grabbed my hand and pulled me toward her, at the same moment that Raymond's blade came down. There was no sound, no pain, only the patter of raindrops on my bare skin telling me he'd successfully slit open the back of my shirt. I could hear Raymond hiss *"Fuck!"* as I turned right and followed Billie down the alley. He was following, splashing through puddles behind us, but we were gaining distance on him. As we raced between the murals of the alley Billie's pace slowed by a half step, allowing me to catch up. "Straight," I said, "then turn left, then right, and we're out." For just an instant I glanced at her face, and was momentarily stunned: Billie was smiling, beaming from ear to ear.

The Art Alley is a familiar enough feature in small-town Ontario. It's a gap between buildings about a metre and a half wide whose walls are adorned with commissioned pieces by local artists, many depicting snapshots of local history. Ferguston's opens at its north end onto McEwan Street; its left wall is the west side of Margo's Restaurant, while the right wall is the eastern side of the Baxter Hotel along with the backs of a number of other buildings next to the Baxter whose fronts face McDonald Street. There's a bit of a zigzag about three quarters of the way down, as the buildings toward the south end are quite a bit deeper than the other ones before and jut out farther. As a result you have to make a ninety-degree left turn, and then another one to the right, before you can get out. The alley culminates in a parking lot that is accessed from Lalonde Street at the south end. I figured if Billie and I were quick enough, we'd be able to reach Lalonde just in time to flag down my dad who would be driving by.

We slowed as we reached the turn, stepping around puddles and assorted refuse. I could hear Raymond cursing at me as he struggled to keep up. As I turned to shoot a quick backward glance, a flash of lightning illuminated the alley. I could see him hobbling along after us in vain pursuit, using the walls for support. I kept thinking of little Danny Torrance racing through the hedge maze to evade his crazed father at the end of *The Shining*, and just as Danny had, I knew we'd outsmarted our pursuer.

That was until I ran headlong into Billie who had come to a full stop after the final turn. "Billie, what the . . ." I began, but she stared straight ahead at the immense obstacle that had sealed off our exit.

"What's that?" Her question was matter-of-fact, posed in idle curiosity.

It was a huge, battered industrial dumpster, no doubt placed there by the owners of Margo's Restaurant. I'd never noticed a dumpster there before, but then I hadn't been this way in a long time. The colossal steel container was placed with its back to the alley. It also stood almost two metres tall and was wide enough to completely cut off any way around it. The only option was to go over.

"Quick, we've got to climb it," I said and without waiting for a response I launched myself as high as I could, gripping the heavy corrugated plastic lid with my slippery hands and trying to shimmy my way to the top. Either by momentum or sheer adrenalin, I instantly found myself on the slanted top of the dumpster, and was turning around in triumph to urge Billie to join me. "Come on Billie, it's eas—"

"Get down, kid."

Raymond was standing behind Billie, a muscular forearm wrapped around her shoulders, just under her throat. In his other hand he brandished his switchblade. Billie's face was marble, her black eyes showed nothing and her arms, like her hair, hung dripping limply at her sides. Steam was rising from her sodden sweatshirt.

There was another flash of lightning, and a cavernous boom a few moments later that shook the alley. It didn't seem possible, but the sky had darkened even more and the downpour had intensified. The rain was now at a dull roar.

"There's something wrong with your little friend here," Raymond shouted in mock sympathy. "She's burning up. I think she's sick. You sick, kid?"

Billie's expression didn't change. She did absolutely nothing, but her eyes were locked on mine.

"I don't really want to hurt her, you know. But I will if I have to. Don't think I won't. Now get down from there."

"You let her go, and I'll come down." To my surprise, Raymond agreed.

"Sure. Why not? I can be reasoned with. Like I said, I don't want to hurt her. See, I'm letting her go. You just come down."

He began to loosen his grip around her, holding out the switchblade in front of him with his other hand. He allowed Billie to step away, but maintained a grip on her upper arm. Still, Billie's expression didn't change.

"See, she's fine. As soon as you climb down from there, I'll let her go."

I sat down on the dumpster, and let my feet dangle for a moment. I knew that Billie was in no real danger, but I was also aware that I'd only convinced myself that Billie would never allow anything to happen to me. Now, sitting on that dumpster, trapped like a scared animal in that alley, I wondered for the first time why I was so certain. After all, despite all appearances, she wasn't human. She was a very accurate replica, and to some extent her disguise was so complete, so perfect, that she was sometimes under its control and not vice-versa. I was about to gamble everything on the likelihood that she'd copied human emotions and ideas like compassion and loyalty so flawlessly that she'd be powerless to act in any other way. But then she had allowed, in fact had caused, the terrible accident on Barrette Street earlier that summer that cost the life of Mrs. Worthington and severely injured her husband. Billie was an entity for whom the affairs of humans might have been of some interest, but they could be shuffled and manipulated any number of ways. If what she said about timelines was true, if there were in fact billions of billions of them, what was the big deal if a couple of people died in a given scenario? In the grand scheme of things, what difference would it make to her? It was just another possible eventuality in an uncountable multitude of potential outcomes.

Another flash of lightning and ear-splitting crack of thunder; it seemed to come from just over my head. I watched the two of them standing in the downpour as they stared back at me, their forms flickering in the lightning, then falling back into darkness. There was another option. I could do the last thing that D-Ray expected, which would be to let myself slide down the lid of the dumpster into the parking lot on the other side, and leave Billie to fend for herself. Maybe that's what she wanted. What would D-Ray do, after all?

But for some reason I couldn't.

"OK, I'm coming down," I said, and hopped off the dumpster in front of them.

"Good boy," said David Raymond and, true to his word, he released his grip on Billie. But it was what Billie did then that surprised everyone. As soon as she was free of D-Ray's hold she instantly grabbed on to his forearm, digging in hard enough to get a look of pain and surprise from Raymond. And then she smiled at him. I still see that smile in my nightmares: any stray thoughts I may have had until that moment that Billie was in any way human vanished with that smile.

"Justin!" It was Dad's voice, coming from the far end of the alley, a million miles away.

The rest was over in less than a second. With a parting wink to me, she used her free hand to open a seam of light in mid-air, brighter than the brightest bolt of lightning. In one motion she spread the seam open a bit and stepped through, pulling on D-Ray's arm and exploiting the weakness in his hip to topple him over. He stumbled through the seam behind her, a look of unknowable terror etched on this face. There was a faint clatter as the switchblade fell harmlessly to the pavement, and they were gone.

*****

I was in my dad's arms moments later. He'd swung around the corner of the alley to find me standing alone in the driving rain. All that remained of the other two was D-Ray's switchblade lying open on the ground.

"The others . . ." he began. "You were with Billie, and I saw David Raymond chase you down here. Where are they? Did he take her?"

"No," I said. "She took him."

# 43

David Raymond was right about one thing: there had been no one around to witness our confrontation in front of the Baxter Hotel. Sometime after Dad and I left the alley, an employee from the Baxter reported D-Ray's abandoned truck idling halfway up the sidewalk on McEwan Avenue. As his truck was well known to authorities, police investigated the area and a short time later found his switchblade just where he dropped it at the end of the Art Alley. Nothing else was found, and no one had either seen him or spoken to him for several hours before he vanished. The idling car and the open knife, coupled with D-Ray's violent past, suggested to police that it had been some kind of set-up, a well-organized hit by someone with a score to settle. The fact that there was no blood nor any sign of violence was not considered significant, as the rain would have taken care of that pretty quickly. Whispered talk around law enforcement was that he would be found eventually, just not necessarily in one piece.

I told my dad that I was just glad we thought of retrieving my bike before going home. Dad responded that maybe we should have called Craig McLaughlin to dispose of D-Ray's truck.

"Too soon?" he asked.

It was weird to hear him make a joke like that, but I'm sure he felt perfectly vindicated about what happened to D-Ray. Dad felt it was justice, and reminded me how Raymond had publicly threatened to take revenge on our family on more than one occasion. And if that wasn't enough, the slashed opening in the back of my T-shirt from D-Ray's switchblade provided a clear reminder of just how dangerous he was. That he hadn't drawn blood was just dumb luck. I just felt sad. Of course I told him exactly what happened in the alley, that Billie had pulled D-Ray into another dimension in a brilliant flash of light, the same as she had done with me in the Grand Canyon. Dad didn't respond much, except to say that the flash was visible from all the way up the alley, and he speculated that any witnesses would probably conclude it was a lightning strike. He also pondered half seriously if Billie would do with D-Ray as she'd done with me, and whether we should worry about him re-materializing somewhere across town in the next few hours. I admitted that I hadn't considered that before, but I guessed we wouldn't ever see D-Ray again. The reason I thought that—the terrifying smile I saw on Billie's face—I kept to myself. She had something else in store for him.

Unsurprisingly, the headlines the next day didn't mention D-Ray. They were all about the record-breaking downpour that put a decisive end to summer, and the police investigation of Dr. Doug Campbell. There hadn't been any newspapers in the past two days because of the holiday weekend, so Ferguston only really heard about Campbell on Tuesday. To everyone's astonishment, Doug Campbell pleaded guilty to my mom's murder. And like Craig McLaughlin before him, he did his best to cooperate with police following his arrest, but despite his best efforts was unable to remember where he'd hidden my mom's body. He insisted that it had to be somewhere on the Collins property, but weeks and weeks of scouring the area would turn up nothing. It was sadly reminiscent of the initial search for Mom all those years ago, and it left a sourly familiar imprint on all of us that fall.

As far as the whole Billie situation was concerned, I could tell Dad was really conflicted and so, in typical Lambert fashion, he hesitated to talk about it. The one and only time he opened up about my mysterious friend's origin, he maintained his stance that Billie was as human as he or I was, and when I pressed him about her ability to appear and disappear at will and how she knew the things she knew, he shrugged and gave the same answer the park ranger at the Grand Canyon had given back in August: it was a mystery that would be explained, rationally, sooner or later. Yet even as he said this, I could tell he wasn't completely satisfied, that there was something specific that didn't sit right with him. I'd have to wait a while yet before finding out what that was.

Dad gave me the option of staying home from school the day after Labour Day while he took calls from friends, family and reporters, but I figured there would be a lot more good than bad in going. I needed to get away from the house and, frankly, away from Dad. I wasn't too worried about people asking me a lot of questions during class, and whatever time I'd spend between classes would be with Tommy Chartrand who'd been away since early July and had no clue about anything. He was like that most of the time anyway.

*****

And so, after fifteen weeks—counting from the Victoria Day weekend in May—the long hot summer of 2006, a time when everything I thought I knew was completely turned upside down, finally returned to some sense of normalcy. The daily grind of school took over my life again, and the case of my mom's disappearance and who was responsible for it soon took a back seat to other concerns. The injuries that Ferguston had sustained over the summer, the death of Mrs. Worthington, the wrongful indictment and ultimate disappearance of a local troublemaker, and the arrest of an esteemed member of the medical community to name a few, soon scabbed over. Hell, by Ferguston standards it had been a relatively uneventful summer. Dad was back at work after only two days off, and by the end of the following week he and I had largely forgotten what had completely consumed our lives only a few weeks earlier.

We did, however, get two surprise visits before the end of the month. The first one was from Grandpapa François. He called early Thursday morning to say he was flying in from Montreal that same day; Dad told me as soon as he heard, but seeing the way he went into a sudden housekeeping frenzy, I could have guessed. There was something about my mom's family, especially Grandpapa, that made everyone, Dad, me, even Carl, stand a bit straighter, enunciate a bit more clearly, and even dress a bit better. Grandpapa had a natural elegance about him; it was in the way he wore his clothes, the slow, deliberate way he used his hands when he spoke, the studied incline of his head when he listened. His posture was always perfect, his manners and diction always exquisite, his demeanour always gentle, and every time we visited with him there was an effort amongst us small-town barbarians to rise somewhat to his level.

Grandpapa was already there when I got home from school. He'd come alone; Grandmaman wasn't up to the trip. He laughingly said that seeing as we hadn't travelled to Montreal that summer to visit him, this time the mountain would have to come to Mohammed. He embraced me warmly, asked me how my summer was—I restricted my answer to the Las Vegas/Grand Canyon trip—what I thought of my classes after three days, and if I was reading any of the French books he'd sent me. With Grandmaman in Montreal, I was spared the questions of who I was hanging out with and whether I'd made any new friends: as a fellow introvert, Grandpapa understood that regular social interaction wasn't an essential need for some people.

As much as I adored my grandparents and looked forward to their visits, there was always an element of unease that came with them. Dad felt it, too. On one hand, even though we never talked about it, I'm sure we both felt a certain degree of responsibility for what happened to their daughter. Of course we understood that the guilt wasn't rational, that we didn't do anything to cause her disappearance, and that none of her family ever held us in any way culpable for it and would be sad to know we did. But there was the inescapable fact that what happened to Mom happened on our watch. I couldn't speak for Dad, but even at the age of twelve I was already resigned to the prospect of living with that for the rest of my life.

The other thing that made me uncomfortable was how my mom's parents brought their religion with them everywhere they went. You could understand it at home. It was like antique living room furniture: beautiful, ornate, massive, and very old. It was a cherished heirloom that was kept in the family for generations; you didn't actually use it much, but you kept it in the most privileged place in the house and admired it when you walked past. And the few times when they didn't have home field advantage, they always packed the travel version. Knowing that Dad was a long-lost cause, my grandparents would talk to me in private about God and Jesus and how They were watching over Mom, wherever she was. I'd always smile and say thank you, and try to change the subject— or not talk at all—but sometimes they'd persist and even read passages from the Bible that they thought I'd appreciate. I couldn't blame them: it was their thing, they'd grown up with it, it was part of them, and they valued it enough to want to pass it on to me. But it wasn't my thing. Never was. So you can imagine how grateful I was when Grandpapa seemed to tacitly acknowledge it for the first time on that visit. He didn't once mention God or Jesus or the Virgin Mary or the Holy Ghost, or Heaven or Hell or Purgatory; rather he kept the discussion to the here and now, content to talk instead about the legal, medical, and forensic details of the case. I was being allowed to grow up; as a rite of passage it was the next best thing to getting a driver's licence.

On Friday evening there was a candlelight vigil for my mom in Garrison Park. It had come together soon after the news of Campbell's arrest, as a kind of public acknowledgement of what had happened to Mom. It was to be a very loose and informal affair. With his disdain for ritual, Dad would never have gone for any kind of formal ceremony, especially one that would have involved public officials and—even worse—clergy getting in front of people and saying how sorry everyone was. At some time in the future he'd probably have to think about a proper memorial service, but in the meantime a vigil was something he could get behind. There had been vigils during the initial days of Mom's disappearance, and they sort of just happened spontaneously. Whoever wanted to speak could do so; people were allowed to move freely, express their grief, their memories. There were no podiums, no microphones, no agenda or timetable. It was totally freeform, improvised, a bit like jazz. Mom would have loved it.

It was a gorgeous late summer evening when people began to gather at Garrison Park. All the expected faces were there, and a few that weren't expected. Mom's friends and colleagues from the hospital made up a sizeable contingent, including people like Sandra from the records office and other people like Gail who I recognized from my rounds. Of course Debbie Williams was there. She gave me a big hug when she saw me, and after brushing away a few tears and asking me how I was she moved off to talk to Grandpapa. Her friend Iris from the Boneyard Diner was there as well, as were Mr. Nguyen from the Mekong Restaurant and our neighbour Mr. Lovato who were both chatting with Carl. There were a few people I'd never seen before, including one particularly enormous man with greying hair who I could only assume was the elusive Jason Bremmer of the Ferguston *Clarion*. He tried to remain as inconspicuous as possible for a person of his size, keeping to the periphery of the group, but I was touched that he emerged from his basement for the occasion. My breath caught a bit when I saw Mr. Worthington, now moving around fairly comfortably with a cane, talking with my dad. Worthington had a hand on Dad's shoulder and their conversation looked warm and cordial—why wouldn't it?—but I was still left with a heavy place in my stomach.

Someone—I suspect Debbie Williams—brought a framed photo of Mom and placed it near a semicircular clump of bushes, and within minutes an impromptu shrine had come into being. There were flowers of all kinds, a plush toy or two, and lots and lots of candles; I guess folks had come prepared. People left notes and cards, many approached me and Dad and Carl with their best wishes and thoughts and prayers, and Dad introduced Grandpapa around, and people smiled and said how much Mom had looked like him, and how that likeness was carried on to me. It could have become really soppy, but it didn't. The past decade had done wonders to take the worst of the edge off everyone's bitterness, and most people felt good to speak their hearts without breaking down. There were some tears, of course, and that was fine. Debbie took it upon herself to call everyone's attention for a moment of silence; more candles were lit, and more tears fell, and as the sun began to set over the west end of the lake a few people took turns speaking. Dad thanked everyone for coming and for their continued support over the years. Some of Mom's friends spoke as well, expressing hope for our family and for the town. But the best speech was Grandpapa's. He delivered most of it in French, of course; almost a third of the people in attendance understood everything perfectly, and the rest could say they caught the gist of it. There was only one moment when someone in the back yelled out "English!" and I turned around in time to see Tweedle Dumb from the Worthington funeral getting firmly slapped upside the head by an off-duty Constable Dale Franklin. No more trouble came from that end.

As modest as Grandpapa always was, he couldn't help but stand out in the crowd. While others clustered in the chilly evening in their fleece sweaters and hoodies, Charles François, father of Élise François, stood in the center of the gathering in a dark suit and open collar. He stood a half head taller than his son-in-law who stood next to him, and simply towered over his grandson around whose shoulders his arm rested. He spoke of his gratitude to the community, of his memories of his daughter, and of the peace he wished for everyone who was hurting by her loss. But what left the greatest impression on the crowd was his appeal for forgiveness, that those responsible had already paid for what they'd done, or were paying for it now, and that no healing could begin in earnest until the bitterness we all harboured was let go. As a person who'd dedicated her life to the process of healing, it's what Mom would want us to do, and after ten years it was time for us all to mend.

\*\*\*\*\*

Dusk was quickly turning into night by the time the gathering began to disperse. There weren't any lampposts in this part of the park, and the remaining candles were a faint and quickly diminishing source of light for the stragglers still milling about. I'd been talking to Tommy Chartrand in the encroaching dark, and when his mom came to tell him they were leaving, I reluctantly went off to find my own crew.

I was drifting from one cluster of people to the next, knowing I had to leave soon but only half looking for Dad. There was a comfort being amongst these people, even though a lot of them were strangers who wouldn't normally associate with my introverted, French-speaking, atheist, bi-racial family. But here they were, to a person sharing warm words or a friendly wave with me as I walked past.

"Have you seen my family anywhere?" I asked Iris as she swung by to say hello.

"Not sure where your dad is, but your grandfather is chatting with your friend over there," she answered.

"My friend left a while ago."

"Isn't that her right there?"

*Her?*

I cautiously approached my grandfather who seemed to be engrossed in conversation with Billie. My anxiety suddenly flared up. No good could be coming from this. What was she doing here, and what in the world could those two be talking about? Plus, who knew she could speak French?

"*Elle est charmante, ta petite amie,*" he said when he saw me.

Billie looked at me and positively beamed at the compliment.

"*Et son français est impeccable.*"

Grandpapa told me he was heading back to the house with Carl and my dad, and even though it was less than a kilometre walk, that I shouldn't stay out much later. Tomorrow was another school day.

"Making friends, I see," I said after my grandfather had left.

"Well . . ." Billie began. She was still gazing at his tall, stately form as he moved away. There was a lot of affection in that gaze.

I cut her off. "Has my dad seen you this evening?" She shook her head.

"He talked about you recently. He's still not sure what to make of you. And of course he's wondering what happened to D-Ray."

"What did you tell him?"

"That you took him."

She nodded. Apparently, that was the right answer.

"Where?" I inquired.

"Someplace he couldn't hurt anyone."

"So . . . you mean he's not dead?"

"No, no. He had a bit of a bumpy ride, but he'll be fine . . . mostly."

"Mostly?"

1e0

"Well, he didn't do as well as you did. I'm not sure his eyesight will ever come back. Maybe it's for the best: he'd have a tough time dealing with everything if he could see."

"Dammit, Billie, where is he? Did you leave him on some alien planet halfway across the universe?"

She laughed. "No. He's on Earth. He's safe. He's just out of his time: five, maybe six hundred years in the future. In a huge city someplace where no one can understand him. Even if anyone speaks English, he'll just be some poor crazy blind person babbling a lot of nonsense. He'll be a bit scared at first, but someone will look after him . . . eventually. But he won't be able to hurt anyone again, I promise."

"Wow . . ." was all I could manage for a while.

We began an unhurried stroll toward my house. My thoughts were a scrambled mess, imagining D-Ray stumbling blindly through some sprawling ghetto in the distant future, yammering in incomprehensible gibberish to passers-by. I had Billie's assurance that he wasn't dead, which I guess was a comfort of sorts: D-Ray, despite his faults, wasn't a murderer. It was a unique brand of justice, and over the years since then I've wondered about other people who may have also deserved that kind of forced relocation.

The evening was peaceful and we didn't speak for a while, neither of us wanting to break the silence. As we approached Tremblay Street, I could hear Carl's violin from our yard, and the occasional bits of conversation and bursts of laughter.

"If I understand what you told me, D-Ray is in the same timeline as I am now, right? Just far in the future?"

"That's right. A person in one timeline is stuck in that timeline, and can only move forward. I just placed D-Ray *waaaaaaay* forward on this timeline."

"Isn't that like a major disruption?"

"Not really. His existence there, for the time it lasts, won't change a lot."

"And what about you?"

"What about me?"

"This person you've . . . copied, I guess. Billie. Is she from this timeline?"

"No, no. You see *I'm* not restricted to any timeline, so I can pop in and out of any timeline I want. Billie is someone I copied who has never existed in this timeline, one of the countless billions and billions of people who were never born here but who exist elsewhere. It's safer. You think I'd copy a person who is already alive here? What if I bumped into that person? Awkward! Even worse if I copied a dead person, and then met a loved one by accident."

"They'd be literally seeing a ghost."

"Yeah, kinda."

We reached the driveway. More music from Carl's violin, and my grandfather's singing.

"One last thing," I said. "There's something about you that's been troubling my dad for a while. I'm not a hundred per cent sure what it is, but I can guess. A while back, on the day D-Ray was arrested, you dropped in on my dad and you had a talk. You told him something that got him really upset. I was standing just outside his door at the time, but I didn't hear what it was. He said: 'How do you know that? Nobody knows that.' What was he talking about?"

"Oh, that. I was trying to think of something that would convince him about what I am. So I told him something that no one else could know, something important."

"What was that?"

She looked at me and paused, as if appraising how I'd react.

"Your mom was six weeks pregnant when she died. Besides her, the only person in the world who knew that was your dad. She hadn't even told her doctor yet, and your dad never mentioned it to anyone after she was gone."

I felt a shudder, a chill, but also a big warm place began to grow in my stomach. I wanted to laugh and to cry.

"Was it a . . ." I couldn't finish my question, so Billie did it for me.

"Yeah," she said. "A girl."

I didn't fall on my ass. I didn't scream, or yell for Dad and everyone to rush over. It was funny. It all made sense. It was so obvious, anyone could see it, and I think in some ways a few people did. I thought of that line by Princess Leia from *The Return of the Jedi*. I knew. Somehow, I'd always known.

"You're . . . you're . . ." I began, but couldn't finish.

Billie just nodded.

"Your mom loves you, Justin. In millions of timelines, your mom loves you so much."

I squeezed my eyes shut in a fruitless effort to hold back the tears, and was overwhelmed by a wave of emotion. The floodgates fell open and I wept and wept like I had never done before, or since. Billie put her arms around me, her surreal warmth easing my sobs, and her soft voice breathed in my ear.

"And so does your sister."

She left the lightest kiss on my cheek, and after another moment released me. When I opened my eyes she was gone, leaving me in her warm afterglow and a smell like cinnamon. I paused for a minute or two, breathing the still evening air filled with the sounds of night creatures, of music, and the lively voices of my family, and strode up the driveway.

# 44

They found her body four days ago.

Doug Campbell's best efforts back in '06 had yielded nothing but frustration, and for a while everyone thought he was just having the police for a ride, looking for an excuse for a leisurely walk in the woods. Others, myself included, were convinced that he was genuinely confused, that ten years after the fact his memories had become tainted, the error compounded by the inevitable changes in the landscape. He'd insisted that he'd disposed of the body on the Collins property, sometime before Coleman and McLaughlin had left her Rav4 there. With Campbell clad in a bright orange prison jumper pointing hither and yon in the deep green forest, police with sniffer dogs probed the densely wooded area with a fine-toothed comb, turning over every rock, peering under every bush, even climbing a tree or two to investigate suspicious-looking clumps of vegetation. Aside from an assortment of deer, moose and bear bones, they came up with nothing.

Anyway, something must have recently jogged Campbell's memory as he stewed in his cell at Millhaven, because all of a sudden there was a renewed flurry of activity, not on the Collins property but deep on another private lot off Mountain Road, a lonely secondary artery that stretched parallel to Highway 5, ten kilometres north of town as the crow flies and almost three times that if you're driving anything but an ATV. To date no link has been found between Campbell and the owners of this property, and Campbell has maintained that he chose the place at random. Once he was on the site, having taken a few minutes to get his bearings, Campbell was able to identify the spot fairly precisely, and within half a day Mom's remains were found in a canvas bag at the bottom of a shallow stony grave. An autopsy is being performed for what it's worth, despite what Campbell told the police ten years ago: the shattered hyoid bone would reveal the cause of death to be asphyxiation—his doing—and not the attempted overdose of morphine delivered by Geoffrey Coleman.

Dad and I have been talking about an informal memorial service, but we haven't decided what form it will take; we'll probably just get some family members together along with a few close friends, once we've agreed on what to do with her remains. It's odd to think of it now, but for twenty years Mom has been defined by her absence. Now that we have her, we're not sure what to do with her. I like the idea of having her cremated, and then maybe pouring her ashes in a meadow or forest clearing someplace, and planting a tree over the spot: the whole Circle of Life thing. I don't think either of us are even considering bringing her back to Ferguston; not that the good people of Ferguston didn't show us kindness, but it wasn't her home for very long, and while Ferguston may have taken her, Dad and I both agree it can't keep her.

\*\*\*\*\*

In apparent defiance of the laws of physics, a few people managed to escape the black hole that was Ferguston, starting with my dad and me. The following summer, as soon as I'd finished eighth grade at St. Marc, Dad accepted a job as vice-principal at a new French language high school in Cumberland, Ontario, a suburb of Ottawa. It's where I went too, but only for a couple of years—more on that later. Debbie Williams ended up moving back to her hometown of Sudbury, and for a while she and my uncle Carl were quite an item. They lived together very happily for a few years, but then Carl was diagnosed with stage III pancreatic cancer. He died four years ago, in his home, surrounded by his loved ones. His death hit my dad really hard, and he continues to struggle with it to this day. Debbie still lives in the home they shared, and we see her a few times a year. I heard recently that Irene Campbell left Ferguston as well; in 2010 she divorced Doug, sold their palatial house, and is now living in Alberta someplace under her maiden name.

One person who sadly never made it out of Ferguston was my long-time school chum Tommy Chartrand. He ended up quitting high school in the eleventh grade, and tried finding work here and there, at restaurants and gas stations and department stores. He quit or was fired from each one within days or weeks, started getting into minor trouble with the law, and after eventually landing with a local gang, began to pad his arrest record. The last I heard he'd done time for stealing a car, drug trafficking, and fraud.

As for me, I started to notice something had changed by mid first semester of Grade Eight, in early November of '06. I was already having a very good year, but when classes resumed after the Christmas break it was as if someone had hit a switch, a super high-voltage one. I didn't think I was paying particularly more attention in class than usual, or that I was studying any harder at home, but I hit a string of perfect or near-perfect exam scores—especially in science and math—that went unbroken through June. Dad wondered if it was something the teachers were doing differently, but no one else's marks had improved so dramatically in my class so we chalked it up to a renewed sense of purpose following the events of the summer. When we moved to Ottawa and I entered high school I expected things to settle a bit—better teachers, increased competition, higher standards of performance—but by the end of October 2007, it was clear something had to be done. I was flying through my readings, completing all my assignments within hours of getting them, and acing my quizzes and exams without breaking a sweat. I was moved into the Grade Eleven classes in January for everything except gym, and even that changed by the following fall. I was taking a full load of senior classes before I turned fifteen and, in subjects like calculus, algebra, physics, chemistry, and biology, I was challenging the limits of my best teachers. They allowed me to graduate from high school that spring, and I entered the first year physics program at the University of Waterloo a month and a half before my sixteenth birthday. Two years later I was fielding scholarship offers from across the continent and Europe for my doctorate in theoretical physics. My dad pushed for MIT, but I decided to stay at Waterloo—Carl was on his last legs by that point and I wanted to be close. I'm still at Waterloo, doing postdoctoral work related to Hugh Everett's Theory of the Universal Wave Function, better known under its more popular title, the Many-Worlds Interpretation. I guess you saw that one coming.

There were physical changes too. I expected to hit a growth spurt sometime; I was only five foot two in the seventh grade and there's height on both sides of the family. It was only a matter of time. As it turned out, it hit at pretty much the same time as the sudden increase in brain function. I began eating like a starved bear in the late fall of 2006, and by the spring I figured I was consuming 3500 calories a day. A lot of it must have been going to my brain, but my body was also reaping the benefits. I grew another eleven inches in the next year and a half, and squeezed out another two inches before I stopped. Unsurprisingly I was a bit awkward to start, and I didn't stay in high school long enough to take advantage of the new height to play basketball. It was one of the few things I missed about not having a real adolescence.

*****

I've never seen Billie again since the night of the vigil in September 2006. I still think about her though, at least a few times every day. For a short while when I was still in Ferguston I'd keep my eyes open for signs of her, either around me in town or scanning the Internet for reports of inexplicable phenomena or of people in the wrong place at the wrong time. I quickly abandoned that course of action: at times it seems that the Internet was created for the sole purpose of disseminating all brands of paranoia, conspiracy theories, and pseudoscience, and even at thirteen I had a pretty finely tuned bullshit detector. Was it possible that someone else out there might have experienced the same thing that I had and decided to write about it? I suppose, but finding that needle in the boundless haystack of the Web wasn't proving to be a smart use of my time. In any event, I figure if Billie ever decides to swing by and say hello, she won't be shy about it. I can wait.

A couple of years ago I started hearing anecdotal stuff from Ferguston about the summer of '06 that piqued my curiosity. It was all unrelated, and I was pretty sure that I was the first one to put these bits together. It was just a hunch to start, but knowing what I knew I thought I'd make inquiries to see if a genuine pattern came to light. The data were all there for anyone to see; it just required somebody who knew what to look for to connect the dots. The first place I called was the FRHC, and when I told them who I was they were more than happy to provide me with access to their data. I also spoke with people from the four major schools in Ferguston—again using family connections—the Ontario Provincial Police, different departments at City Hall, and the Ferguston Chamber of Commerce. Within minutes of crunching numbers a pattern did emerge, and it was startling. To the best that I could determine, during the time that Billie was present in Ferguston and the weeks and months after she disappeared—between May 10th and roughly late November—total arrests, incidents of violence, break-ins, thefts, drug-related offences, suicides, public disturbances, and even driving infractions were down dramatically, as were incidents at the hospital's Emergency Department. The change was no less remarkable in schools but didn't become noticed until the fall. Nevertheless, it was still noticeable enough for teachers to remember it ten years later: truancy was down, and there was a bump in grades across the board, in all schools, at all levels, during the final weeks before the summer holidays of '06. For the few kids who had to repeat in September it certainly wasn't because of their performance in May and June. The pattern then picked up again that autumn for close to two months. Elsewhere, summer unemployment was down while the number of new businesses in town spiked in August, as did enrolment in summer courses during the same period. Overall, the economy of Ferguston saw an odd swell over the summer months, tourism was up, attendance at the only live theatre venue in town hit an all-time high, and even the Ferguston Public Library saw more users than at any point since they began keeping records. When I pointed out all these trends, people would joke that there must have been something in the air. They weren't far off.

\*\*\*\*\*

I don't know if Billie's gift to me was intentional or accidental, whether it was the inevitable outcome of physical and chemical changes to my brain when I crossed over the threshold between our reality and hers, or if it was just a fluke. Either way, I was given a fleeting glimpse of something beyond humanity's experience, and maybe—just maybe—the beginning of an ability to understand it. I can't help thinking about the one other person who might benefit from its effects, and hopefully use them to some constructive end in a faraway place and time. As for myself, I know with each day that I've barely scratched the surface. It's like I've been in a dark room all this time, unaware that I was surrounded by unimaginable treasures. Ten years ago a strange little girl hit a light switch, and I've spent the last decade getting used to the glare.

# Epilogue

There's a final loose end that has come up recently, one that is likely to remain loose for a very, very long time.

A couple of years after my uncle Carl died, I received an envelope from the law firm that was handling his estate. On the front was my name and a stamp that said CONFIDENTIAL. On the back was a seal that said the envelope was to be opened only by myself and not before 2014. The seal was intact. Inside was a brief note from Carl and another, longer document.

"Justin," wrote Carl with typical Lambert succinctness. "The story contained in the attached document came from a former client. It's disturbing to me because I know the source: he was always nothing but reliable. I'm not sure I completely believe the story, but I believe that *he* believed it. Anyway, I doubt it will go anywhere. Even if there were more to act on than just a good yarn, I'm in no shape to do any investigating, and nobody in the system will waste their time on it. If nothing else, I thought it would interest you."

The brief chill I got reading Carl's words two years after his death was soon replaced by a chill of a different kind. The longer document was a transcript of a conversation recorded in 2010 between a pair of detectives and a former biker named Morgan

Hartling. Back in the '90s, Hartling had been a member of the same motorcycle gang that controlled most of the drug trade in the territory that included Ferguston. He left the gang before the decade was out for a more honest and less violent way of life, mostly thanks to my uncle. He'd been working at a car dealership in Sudbury ever since, until he was diagnosed with advanced small cell lung cancer in 2010.

Later that same year, Hartling was invited to the Ferguston detachment of the OPP to help some detectives who were doing background work on the drug trade during the 1990s. Hartling was not under subpoena, and the statement he was to give was completely voluntary; the cops just wanted to "pick his brain," so they said. Hartling, with the end of the line in sight and no fucks left to give, happily complied. He didn't even ask for legal counsel to be present, which would have been my uncle Carl at the time.

It's hard to say whether Hartling's big reveal was intended as a bombshell for the local cops, or a final opportunity to fuck with them, or just the confused ramblings of a dying ex-biker, but it was summarily dismissed as fantasy: no tangible evidence to support it, and all the reasons in the world to toss it down the crapper. When the interview was over, the cops thanked Hartling for his time, wished him Godspeed, and sent him on his way. He died five weeks later.

Carl, whose own clock was ticking, got hold of a transcript of the interview and entrusted it to his lawyer, with instructions to forward it to me after his death. What, if anything, I chose to do with the information was up to me. It was a bizarre and startling loose end, but it was also—in Carl's opinion—a dead one.

Of course I—and only I—know the full significance of Hartling's revelation, but try explaining that to anybody above the age of twelve. As for its implications . . . well, I'm still working on that.

\*\*\*\*\*

EXCERPT FROM TRANSCRIPT    no. T0015720100822003F
Subj: Morgan Hartling
Date: August 22, 2010
Time: 13:10
Testimony provided by Mr. Morgan Hartling, to Detective Sergeant [redacted]—Det. 1—and Detective Constable [redacted]—Det. 2.
Recorded by [redacted]
Ontario Provincial Police, Ferguston detachment

00:00:00

DET. 1:    Today is August 22, 2010, the time is 1:10 PM. My name is Detective Sergeant [redacted], with the Investigations and Organized Crime command of the Ferguston Regional detachment of the Ontario Provincial Police. With me today is Detective Constable [redacted], along with Ms. [redacted] who will be recording this interview with Mr. Morgan Hartling of Sudbury. Mr. Hartling has declined to be represented by legal counsel.

Mr. Hartling can you please state and spell your full name, and give your date of birth, for the record?

HARTLING:    Morgan Hartling. M-O-R-G-A-N, H-A-R-T-L-I-N-G. Date of birth January 3rd, 1972. [cough]

\*\*\*\*\*\*\*\*\*\*

00:01:48

DET. 1:    Mr. Hartling, can you tell us what your primary occupation was in the years between 1993 and 2001?

HARTLING:    My occupation? I was a member of the [redacted] motorcycle club, based in [redacted].

DET. 1:    And what was your primary responsibility with this organization?

HARTLING:    That depends. It changed over the years.

| DET. 1: | During the period up to and including November 1996. |
|---|---|
| HARTLING: | I was pretty low-level. Started off as a glorified delivery boy. I was also a bit of an enforcer; kept people in line. [INDISCERNIBLE: 00:02:40 – 00:02:48] Hard as that is to believe now. |
| DET. 1: | Why do you say that? |
| HARTLING: | Well, I don't exactly look the part now, do I? I'm just a wisp of the man I once was. [laugh/cough]. Cancer does that, I guess. [INDISCERNIBLE: 00:03:10] |
| DET. 1: | What kind of cancer are you suffering from? |
| HARTLING: | Lung. |
| DET. 1: | Sorry to hear that, Morgan. What's your prognosis? |
| HARTLING: | I'll be lucky to see another 6 months. [INDISCERNIBLE: 00:03:24 – 00:03:26] |
| DET. 1: | Shit. So, is your . . . um . . . terminal prognosis the reason you're so willing to come forward? |
| HARTLING: | What do you think? [cough] |

**********

00:04:37

| HARTLING: | [cough] I'm OK. Thanks. |
|---|---|
| DET. 1: | Take your time, Morgan. |

**********

00:6:24

| DET. 2: | All right, let's get back to the Ferguston supply line, Morgan. What did you know about Dr. Geoffrey Coleman? |
|---|---|
| HARTLING: | He was a mid-level supplier of prescription drugs, well known in the region. |
| DET. 2: | And David Raymond? |

| | |
|---|---|
| HARTLING: | D-Ray was his mule. He had his uses, but he wasn't what you'd call irreplaceable. He was a wannabe. Had a lot of cash in those days, which was useful, and he was really eager to please. But he tried too hard, you know? We never got him involved in anything. Kept him on the periphery. |
| DET. 2: | Just because he was a keener? |
| HARTLING: | No, mostly because he wasn't too bright. Plus, he had physical limitations. |
| DET. 2: | Did you know he suddenly went missing in 2006? |
| HARTLING: | No, I didn't know that. |
| DET. 1: | Yep. Vanished without a trace, right around the time that the whole Coleman/Campbell thing was exposed. You think that was a coincidence? |
| HARTLING: | Well, like I said, I don't know anything about that. But unless things changed pretty radically after I left, I can't imagine it was the [redacted]. There would have been no need. He was kept out of the loop, didn't know anything. He wasn't a threat. |
| DET. 2: | Getting back to Coleman: how would you describe his role in the drug trade at that time? Meaning the mid-'90s. |
| HARTLING: | It was important enough. No one wanted to see it terminated. |
| DET. 2: | And was that ever a danger? |
| HARTLING: | Yeah. There were rumblings about a certain doctor at the [INDISCERNIBLE: 00:8:11 – 00:08:13] who was sniffing around Coleman a little too close. She could have complicated things. |
| DET. 2: | And what, if anything, did you—and by "you" I mean the club—do about it? |
| HARTLING: | Nothing. It was Coleman's problem. We might have urged him to take care of it. And he did, to the club's satisfaction. |

| | |
|---|---|
| DET. 2: | Meaning what, Morgan? |
| HARTLING: | Meaning Coleman took her out of the picture. Old news, man. |
| DET. 2: | And what about David Raymond? |
| HARTLING: | What about him? |
| DET. 2: | You—sorry, they, the club I mean, the [redacted]—didn't find it necessary to "take care" of him? At the time? |
| HARTLING: | No. What would be the point? I told you, he was useful to us, he didn't know anything, he had cash, and Coleman did a great job in framing him. Besides, you don't want to leave a trail of bodies if you can afford not to. |
| DET. 1: | Why? Were there others? |
| HARTLING: | Well, there was one loose end the club didn't like: the semi-retarded guy they called BD. |
| DET. 2: | Yes, McLaughlin. Craig McLaughlin. I remember him. |
| HARTLING: | You do, huh? |
| DET. 2: | Sure. Spoke with him back in '06. |
| HARTLING: | Yeah, well, I'll get to that in a second. He might have been a bit slow, but he was slippery, you know? He'd spent his whole life living under the radar, even totally off the grid at times. Some people thought the whole retard shtick was just that: an act. So late in '96, when the club found out that Coleman had gotten sloppy and involved him in the whole mess, they became . . . concerned. |
| DET. 2: | So what did they do? Relocate him? Scare him into hiding for ten years? |
| HARTLING: | The club doesn't work that way. They don't take chances. If they think that someone is a problem or a threat, the club deals with them. In no uncertain terms. |
| DET. 1: | Wait. What? |

DET. 2:      That doesn't make sense. Sorry Morgan, but I'm afraid you're mistaken there. I personally saw McLaughlin in 2006, on a couple of occasions. So did a lot of people. He was ID'd from a driver's license. He helped out in the Coleman investigation. Hell, he gave sworn testimony, for crying out loud.

HARTLING:     Yeah, yeah, I heard all that. It was in the papers: BD suddenly showed up, came out of nowhere to clear D-Ray, avoided jail time by cooperating with the cops, was the model repentant patsy, blah blah blah. [cough] What can I tell you? The club took him out ten years earlier. I know. I was there. Whoever you saw in '06, whoever it was who claimed to be Craig McLaughlin, it was someone else.

DET. 2:      Well, who do you think it was, Morgan? It's not like he had a twin brother or—

DET. 1:      Hold on. Hold on. His identity was confirmed. There isn't any question.

HARTLING:     Oh, yeah? Bet you can't account for any of his movements after 1996, can you? Where did he go? What did he do? Who did he talk to? And where is this person who miraculously showed up in '06? I'm sorry. I don't know what else to tell you: it wasn't McLaughlin. He'd been pushing up daisies for ten years.

DET. 1:      Well, obviously the club screwed up, Morgan. They got the wrong guy.

HARTLING:     [laugh/cough] They weren't stupid. They knew who he was. Hard to mistake him for someone else: tall gangly dude, all bent over, he looked like a shrivelled-up chili pepper with legs. Had that dumb-ass upside down rattlesnake tattoo, big old hairy mole on his neck, face like a chicken. It was him. We picked him up one night, shuffling along the road. It was November, cold, and he'd just had the shit kicked out of him by David Raymond, so he was happy for the lift.

DET. 1:      You were there?

HARTLING:    I was driving. We took him out to some remote
             location, I forget where exactly, put a bullet in
             the back of his head, buried him on the spot.
             Easy-peasy. It'd be a miracle if anyone found
             him now. Amazing how easy it is to dump a
             body up there.

[End of excerpt]